"What do you know about the hijack!" he asked. "Do you know when or where it will take place, who will do it, who will be the victims?"

"No," conceded Khaled, "I don't."

Almost there, thought Abu Nabil, they were almost there.

"In that case, I don't see it's immoral to agree to be a negotiator."

Saeed Khaled nodded his appreciation. "In that case—" he repeated the first words of Kenshaw-Taylor's last answer "—I wonder if you would mind if I asked you something else."

The Foreign Minister felt his excitement rise again.

Is he satiated? Abu Nabil had asked. No, Khaled had told him, he has tasted power, he is insatiable.

"Of course not," Kenshaw-Taylor said.

Khaled looked hard at him. "If there was a hijacking, and if there was a need for a major European negotiator, I wonder if it would be in order to suggest the British Foreign Minister, John Kenshaw-Taylor?"

John Kenshaw-Taylor sat back. "I think it would be most in order," he said.

At the backgammon table, Abu Nabil knew it was done.

"Who else knows?" asked John Kenshaw-Taylor.

"No one else."

"In that case—" Kenshaw-Taylor took the initiative "—I suggest we keep it that way."

GORDON STEVENS

DO NOT GO GENTLE

WORLDWIDE®

TORONTO · NEW YORK · LONDON · PARIS
AMSTERDAM · STOCKHOLM · HAMBURG
ATHENS · MILAN · TOKYO · SYDNEY

DO NOT GO GENTLE

A Worldwide Library Book/May 1989

ISBN 0-373-97101-X

First published by St. Martin's Press Incorporated.

ACKNOWLEDGMENTS

Dylan Thomas, *The Poems of Dylan Thomas*. Copyright © 1952 by
Dylan Thomas. Reprinted by permission of New Directions Publishing
Corporation.

I Believe in Father Christmas by Greg Lake and Peter Sinfield. Copyright ©
Manticore Music Ltd. Reproduced by permission.

For Emily and Joe, who do not know.
And Souraya and Dyala, who do.

And in memory of the family in the
Dachau photograph, exhibit 400, and the
millions of others whom no one should
ever forget.

Prologue

THE BOYS WERE NINE, almost ten.

They sat on the rock, the man beside them, watching the sun rise over the valley of the Jordan, the sweep of light spreading from the East, the shadows of the night disappearing.

"When will you tell us the story?" they asked.

"What story?" replied the man.

He remembered the morning he had sat on the rock and waited, the morning he had sat on the rock and wished he had never been born, the morning he had sat on the rock and wished they had never set him free.

"The story that began with a verse from a poem."

"The story that began with a dream."

"The story that began with the family from the far-off land."

They knew that he was playing the game with them, that he always played the game with them, wondered why he would not tell them. The sun was growing warmer.

"When will you tell us the story?" they asked again.

"What story?"

One day, he knew, he would no longer be able to hide the truth from them. One day he would tell them.

"The story about the little boy."

"The story about the little boy who was born in Bethlehem."

He knew what they were going to say.

"The story about the little boy who died to save us all."

He thought about the boy, about what the boy had done when he had grown to manhood, what the boy had done when he had been their age. The shadows had gone from the land. He knew that they were old enough to know, that they were too old *not* to know.

"Today," he said at last. "I will tell you the story."

BOOK
ONE

The verse from the poem

"And you, my father, there on the sad height,
Curse, bless, me now with your fierce tears, I pray.
Do not go gentle into that good night.
Rage, rage against the dying of the light."

from Dylan Thomas
"Do not go gentle into that good night."

The dream

THE TUNNEL WAS LONG, filled with smoke, the flames coming at him. He was moving down it, eyes sweeping from left to right. Not his eyes, she dreamt, it was as if he was behind his eyes, as if he could see the destruction around him through the sockets of his eyes. His breathing was deep and rasping, as if it was not his breathing. She heard the voice, guiding him, telling him where to go, what to do. Protecting him, committing him. She tried to wake from the dream, to take him from the tunnel, saw the death around him, unsure whether it was his death or the death of another. The hold-all, she knew, the death from the hold-all in the wardrobe at the foot of the bed. He was moving on, the smoke and flames coming at him, engulfing him, as if he was descending into Hell. She heard the voice again, saw the death again. His death or someone else's, she was still not sure. He was moving on, deeper into the tunnel, till he had almost gone. The hold-all, she was dreaming, the hold-all which he brought home each evening, the hold-all in the wardrobe at the foot of the bed. She could no longer see him.

The family from the far-off land

1

THE WEATHER THAT MORNING was cold, even for Moscow.

Yakov Zubko knew what it meant—that the winter would be long and hard. He rose, moving quietly and carefully so that he did not disturb his wife and children, and left the flat. The streets were still empty. By the time he reached the metro station at Sviblovo it was twenty minutes past five, he paid his fare and hurried down the stairs. There was only one other man on the platform. Yakov Zubko tried not to look at him and wondered if the man was waiting for him. Somewhere, he knew, they were waiting for him; somewhere the men from Petrovka would always be waiting for him. Him and the likes of him.

He remembered the other man, the man in the house on Dmitrov, and stepped onto the train. There were three passengers already in the compartment, Yakov Zubko heard the doors shut behind him and chose a seat close to them. Never sit in a corner, never sit where they would look for you, where the men from Petrovka would think you were hiding. He looked to see what the man on the platform was doing and counted the kopeks in his pocket.

Alexandra waited till he had left the flat then crossed the room and watched him making his way along the street. He was a good man, a good husband and father; she thought of the way he played with the children, took them to feed the swans in Gorky Park, the way he left the flat each morning without waking them, not knowing that she was awake, listening to him, telling him to be careful. Even the way he did not tell her about the man in the house on Dmitrov, or the faceless men from the building on Petrovka.

There were twelve stops to Marx Prospekt, Yakov Zubko watched at each to see what the man who had been on the platform would do, and counted again the kopeks in his pocket. Each day he counted them, telling himself how the kopeks became roubles, reminding himself how precious was every single rouble. Precious enough now, while he still had work, while the tourists were still in Moscow and he could trade with the man in the house on Dmitrov. Even more precious later when the winter froze the streets, when the hotel found out about him and threw him out, when he and Alexandra could barely afford the *kasha* and the vegetable soup which scarcely kept them and the children warm. Precious, too, as he and Alexandra sat together each evening and estimated how many roubles they would need, how many roubles they had managed to save since they had applied again to the office on Kolpachny Lane.

He remembered how much was in the tin they kept under the bed, remembered how much to the last rouble, and thought again of the man in the house on Dmitrov. He did not give the best prices, Yakov Zubko could have got more in the streets behind Begovaya, but the man on Dmitrov was reliable, and no matter how much he and Alexandra needed the extra roubles it was a risk even he could not afford to take.

The train arrived at Marx Prospekt. He left the station and crossed to the hotel.

Alexandra waited till she could no longer see him then turned back into the room, feeling the cold, knowing it would soon bring the winter, wondering what else it would visit upon them. He was a good man, she thought again, remembering what he did for them, how he sought to protect them from what he did, from the inevitable day when he would be betrayed and caught, how he tried to hide from her the secret of the house on Dmitrov. She knew the secret anyway, had heard him talk about it in his sleep, even knew the name of the man, had heard her husband work out in his sleep how much Pasha Simenov would pay him.

She felt the cold again. Not today, Yakov Zubko, she asked him, please not today.

THE UNMARKED ZHIGULI left the building overlooking Petrovka at six and was in position by six fifteen. Iamskoy let the engine run, keeping the car warm, and instructed the militiaman at his side to make the first entry in the day's log. The operation was routine, he had already decided, routine but important, the sort of assignment that had been gathering momentum since those with political connections at Petrovka had begun to prepare for the tide of change that would sweep from the Kremlin now the new guard had taken control there. Big enough to make the statistics look good, especially if they netted someone deemed undesirable by the state, even more so if they managed to ensnare a foreigner upon whom they, or someone else, could exert the usual pressure, but small enough not to interfere with the private lives and arrangements of the big boys, the *bolshaya shiska*, for whom the statistics were intended.

The street in front of him was beginning to get busier, not busy, just busier, there was still no movement from the house under observation. He looked at his watch. There were two shifts on the operation, six to two and two to ten; he had organised it that way, using his authority to get the early shift, not so that he would be off-duty by mid-afternoon, but because that way he could exercise more control over who made the arrest. Not today, he had thought as they left militia headquarters that morning, not enough contacts noted in the log book for the arrest to be made today, probably tomorrow, certainly the day after. Routine, he had seen it from the moment the surveillance had been first planned, routine but important. Which was why his superiors had chosen it, why it would look good in their statistics. Why he, in turn, would make sure it was a success, why he had arranged it so that it would be he who made the arrest.

In an upstairs room he saw a curtain move and wondered who would be coming to buy, who, more importantly for the statistics, would be coming to sell. He checked again the name of the black marketeer in the house on Dmitrov.

Simenov, Pasha Simenov.

THE AMERICAN FAMILY breakfasted at nine. Yakov Zubko watched them from the side of the foyer, the mother and father, the two children. They had been at the hotel eight days and he had seen them on the third. Each day after that he had made a point of meeting them, of helping them with their bags, each day after that he had smiled at them. On the fifth day one of them had smiled back. Then and only then had he risked checking their names on the hotel registrar, noting both their nationality, which he had already guessed, and their date of departure.

By the time they finished breakfast and returned to their rooms it was twenty five minutes to ten.

THE LETTER ARRIVED at eleven.

Each morning Alexandra waited for it to come. Each morning after she had taken their son to school and settled their daughter in the flat she waited for the sound of the postman on the landing outside. Each morning she heard him as he put his bag down, knowing that he was only regaining his breath, that he would pick up the bag and walk on.

She heard the noise on the stairs, the silence as the man paused outside and searched in his bag for the letter that was bound to come, then heard the next noise, the sound of the man lifting his load and continuing his climb to the floors above. The child was looking at her; she sat back at the table, trying to concentrate, disappointed that the letter summoning them to Kolpachny Lane had not come, relieved that they had not yet been rejected again.

The footsteps came down the stairs and past the flat, quicker, lighter, fading till she could no longer hear them. Alexandra smiled at her daughter and thought of her husband and son, heard the footsteps again, slower, more laboured, the sound of the postman climbing back up the stairs. The man stopping on the landing outside, the first corner of the envelope beneath the door. Thin, she thought, crossing the room, suddenly not knowing what she was doing, it was so thin, just as before. She knew what it meant, opening it, ignoring the time and date of the summons, realising that they had lost again, that they had lost for ever.

The words were a blur. She put the letter on the table and looked at her daughter, wishing suddenly that she and Yakov had not tried again, had never tried. Not for their sakes, but for their children's. The girl was still playing. Alexandra picked up the summons again and saw the date and time of the appointment, realising it was for today, knowing that they had delayed the letter so that she and Yakov would miss the appointment, so that she and her husband would give them even more reason to refuse them again. No time to contact him, she was thinking, no way she could contact him at the hotel in any case. Time, she was thinking, looking at the clock, there was just enough time. If she hurried, if the trams weren't delayed.

Five minutes later Alexandra left the flat, her daughter wrapped against the cold, and began the journey to Kolpachny Lane.

In the hotel on Marx Prospekt Yakov Zubko saw the American family waiting for the official bus and remembered where all the tourists went on their last day in Moscow.

In the unmarked car at the top of Dmitrov Iamskoy told the militiaman to log the first visitor to the house of the suspect Pasha Simenov.

THE TRAMS seemed even slower than usual.

Alexandra reached the building in Kolpachny Lane five minutes before the appointed time and was told to wait till after lunch. She sat in the waiting room and tried to stop her daughter crying, thinking of Yakov Zubko; after seventy minutes she was ushered in and instructed to sit in the chair she had sat in last time and the time before, facing the official who had spoken to her the last time and the time before.

There were two stacks of files on the desk in front of him. He confirmed her name and selected a folder from those on his left, reading through it then checking the details against the information on the summons she had received that morning.

"Why is your husband not with you?" she knew he was going to ask, knew that it would be a trick, that they had already found out where her husband was, that the faceless men from Petrovka had been waiting for him as he had feared in his dreams.

"I don't know," she would lie, holding her child tight to her, "the summons arrived only this morning, he left before it came."

"And you don't know where your husband went?" There would be the first note of an interrogation in his voice.

Be brave, Alexandra Zubko, she would tell herself, do not let them frighten you. Remember, Alexandra Zubko, she would also tell herself, that they have refused you twice, that they have already decided to refuse you a third time.

"It doesn't matter where my husband is," she would wish already that she had not answered the official in such a manner, would know it was too late, "the invitation is to me. I am the one you must tell, not my husband."

The man began reading from the file, not bothering to look at her, reading the words he would forget the moment she left, the words she would remember for ever.

Fifteen minutes later Alexandra left the office on Kolpachny Lane and turned for home.

Not today, Yakov Zubko, she knew now why she had pleaded with her husband that morning, why she had been afraid of the sudden cold, of the winter it would bring, of what else it might visit upon them. For God's sake not today.

It was twenty three minutes past one.

AT TWENTY MINUTES TO TWO Yakov Zubko began to plan his afternoon so that he could make his approach to the American family. At fifteen minutes to two the unmarked Zhiguli left its position overlooking Dmitrov and returned to the militia headquarters on Petrovka. By two fifteen the next shift had taken over. Although there had been two visits to the black marketeer that morning, Iamskoy had instructed the militia-man to log only one: a further visit that afternoon was almost certain, two probably, three remote but possible, and a total of five visits on the second day of the surveillance was the point at which the team on duty could close their snare. Routine, Iamskoy had decided, routine but important. The following morning, he had also decided, he would arrest the suspect Simenov the following morning.

THE FLAT WAS QUIET. Alexandra looked around it, knowing what she was about to do, sensing that Yakov Zubko would understand. The furniture was sparse and functional; three of the chairs round the table had been bought over the years, but the fourth was a family heirloom, a wedding present from a beloved grandfather, now dead. Carefully, taking care not to damage it, she carried the antique down the stairs, perched it on top of her daughter's push-chair, and tied it in place with a piece of string. Then she gathered the girl in her arms, and went to collect her son from school.

He was ten minutes late. When he came out she kissed him then set off, still carrying her daughter, along the route her husband had taken that morning. The walk took twenty minutes, Alexandra managed the child for the first ten before she became too heavy.

The men outside the shop saw her coming, nudging each other to look at her, scarcely bothering to hide their amusement. They were all young, dressed in fur coats, lounging against the estate cars parked outside the shop. One of them was helping another man, someone she took from his clothing to be a foreigner, to load a desk onto one of the cars. She had heard about the shop, that it was where the foreigners came to buy the equipment for their offices and the furniture for their homes, one of the places to which the authorities turned one of their many blind eyes. The foreigner turned to watch her, slightly fascinated, slightly embarrassed by the image of the woman pushing the chair on top of the pram, the two children walking bravely on either side of her. He had been a correspondent in Moscow for six months, and had learnt sufficient Russian in the time to understand what the young men in the fur coats were saying, enough to understand the sexual innuendo of their remarks. The driver he had hired to take the desk to his office was becoming impatient. He told the man to wait, watching the woman as she struggled to push the pram and its load through the door, no one moving to help her, and followed her inside, calculating how much the man in the shop would charge him for such a chair, was not surprised when the man gave the woman less than a thirtieth of what he estimated it was worth. Outside it was getting dark. He watched the way the woman folded the notes into her purse and tucked the purse carefully into the pocket of her coat, the way she lifted the girl at her side into the pram and pulled the boy close to her, the way she disappeared down the road, wanted to know what she was doing, why she was doing it, wanted to wish her luck, tell her that one day all would be well for her. Behind him he heard his driver start the engine of the estate car; he turned away from the woman and went back to his office.

The American family returned to their hotel at five, their arms laden with parcels wrapped in the colours of the *Beryozka* shops. Yakov Zubko watched them from the side of the foyer. The official guide was laughing and joking with them, for one moment he feared that she had already arranged the same thing he had been planning since he had first seen them, then she turned away to talk to another group. He crossed the foyer, arriving at the lift as they did, holding the doors open for them and helping the children with their parcels, then followed them in, pressing the button to close the doors before anyone could join them. One chance, he thought, he had only one chance.

"Good afternoon," his English was formal, almost mechanical, from the books he had studied since he had lost his job as an engineer. "I hope you enjoyed your stay in Moscow."

The husband was looking at him with suspicion. "Yes, thank you," he replied carefully.

The doors were shutting.

"Everyone goes to the Beryozka shops on their last afternoon," Yakov Zubko explained, trying to relax them. One chance, he thought again, he had only one chance. The doors were almost shut. "How old are the children?"

An elderly couple pushed forward and tried to step into the lift. The husband saw them and jerked the doors open for them. Yakov Zubko understood why he had done it, that the man knew why he had joined them, what he was going to ask them. One chance, he told himself, already slipping away.

The elderly man thanked the American and asked for the fourth floor. Rooms 607 and 609, Yakov Zubko remembered, the Americans were in rooms 607 and 609, two floors above the others. The chance not gone, not quite gone. The lift stopped at the fourth floor and the other couple stepped out, the doors closing, the lift gathering speed again.

"How old are the children?" he asked again, looking at the denims they were wearing, not disguising the fact, letting the parents know there was a reason.

"Twelve and ten," said the mother, not looking at him.

He nodded, looking back at the denims, hoping he was right but fearing he was wrong. "Mine are the same age." They all knew he was lying. "May I buy the children's denims from you before you leave?" he asked.

The lift passed the fifth floor.

"No," said the husband. It was the third time he had rejected such a request that day. Be careful, his company had advised him when he informed them where he was taking a holiday, the Russians were always looking for people like him, especially in a profession like his, always seeking ways of entrapping them. "No," he said again emphatically, turning away.

Yakov Zubko sensed that the man would not change his mind and told himself there would be other families, other people who were not afraid, admitted to himself that it was already the beginning of winter, that there would be few other tourists before the weather set hard and the hotel found out about him.

The wife was still looking at him. "I understand," he was saying to her, the lift stopping and the husband and children getting out, "thank you anyway." His finger was drawing the pattern on the wall, the woman still looking at him, at the pattern. One chance, Yakov Zubko knew, he had one last chance, knew it would not work, that he should not do it, should not risk so much, the words coming anyway, telling her who he was, what he was. Telling her everything. *"Beshanah Habaah b'Yerushalaim,"* he spoke slowly, quietly, committing himself.

She was looking at him, knowing what he was saying, what he was telling her, knowing who he was, what he was, what he was trying to do, her finger repeating the pattern on the wall, the six lines, two triangles, one inverted upon the other. The star of David. *"Beshanah Habaah b'Yerushalaim,"* she replied, "Next year in Jerusalem."

"Next year in Jerusalem," confirmed Yakov Zubko.

In the corridor the husband was waiting for his wife to join him and the children. "We leave tomorrow," said the woman, "could you collect our cases at ten forty five?"

"Tomorrow at ten forty five," said Yakov Zubko.

ALEXANDRA FINISHED the *matzah* at six and placed it in the oven, then she laid the table and bathed the children. When they were dry she took their best clothes from the wardrobe they all shared and dressed them, then she went to the bathroom along the landing and washed herself. It was six thirty. From the same cupboard she took her one good dress, the dress she had worn when she had married Yakov Zubko eleven years before, and put it on. The night outside was dark, the cold penetrating the glass of the windows; she pulled the curtains tighter, wondering what she would say, how she would tell her husband. At nine his brother Stanislav, Stanislav's wife Mishka and their two children would join them, would share the food for which she had sold the chair that afternoon; before that,

Alexandra had asked, before that, they had insisted, she would have one hour alone with Yakov Zubko and their family.

It was almost time. From her handbag she took the forms she had been given that afternoon by the man in the office on Kolpachny Lane and placed them on the table, laying the food around them. The *matzah*, there had been no time on that dread night for the women to prepare anything other than unleavened bread; the single roast egg for new life; the salted water for the tears of the slaves and the horse-radish for their bitterness; the extra plate and wine glass for the stranger who might come alone. The last thing she placed, in a position where Yakov Zubko must see them first, were the *haroseth* sweets, then she called her son and daughter to her and stood facing the door, a child on each side, an arm round each.

The children were frightened, unsure what was happening; Alexandra herself had no tears left to cry.

She waited another ten minutes when she heard him on the stairs outside, the same pace, the same slight delay as he searched in his pocket, the same scratching noise as he turned the key in the lock. She leant forward and lit the candle. He was a good man, she thought, a good husband and father; she did not yet know how she would tell him.

Yakov Zubko pushed the door open, carrying the small plastic bag of food he had brought from the hotel, and entered the room. He felt tired and cold, glad Alexandra would be there to welcome him, hoping that the children would not be asleep so that he could kiss them goodnight.

He saw the shadow on the wall, the flame of the candle on the table, the dishes around it, his family waiting for him, his wife in her wedding dress, the children in their best clothes. He did not understand, did not know what to think, looked again at his wife, at the table. Saw the *matzah*, the roasted egg, the bowl of salted water beside it, the place for the stranger. Saw one thing above all, the *haroseth* sweets.

The beginning of the festival, he was thinking, the commemoration of the night the Angel of Death passed over the land of Egypt, the beginning of the Feast of the Passover, the celebration of the delivery of his people.

The *haroseth* sweets, he could not help think, the symbol of the sweetness of freedom.

Alexandra reached to the table and handed him the papers she had been given in the office on Kolpachny Lane. *"Be-*

shanah Hazu b'Yerushalaim," she said the words, did not know
she had said them.

The same words he had said to the American woman in the
lift in the hotel, the words she had understood and said back to
him.

Not the same words, not quite the same words. One word of
difference for which they had been prepared to sacrifice everything. Not "Next year in Jerusalem", not the saying which kept
Yakov Zubko and the likes of Yakov Zubko in hope through
the long Russian winters, the other saying, the saying for which
so many longed but which so few now heard.

"Beshanah Hazu b'Yerushalaim."

"*This* year in Jerusalem."

"We are going home, Yakov Zubko," Alexandra said, closing the door behind him and shutting the family Zubko off
from the rest of the world, "we are going home to Israel."

2

YAKOV ZUBKO had been born in the Ukraine in 1951; despite
the poverty of his parents he had shone at school, both as an
athlete and as a mathematician. His record, whether at the
University of Kiev where he graduated as an engineer or during his compulsory military service, had been impeccable. He
had twice been promoted in the precision tool factory where he
had first worked. In 1973 he had married Alexandra, then a
teacher, the following year they had moved to Moscow, where
he had secured a job in the ZIL car works; within six months
of his new appointment he had again been promoted.

Yakov Zubko was a model of the Soviet system. He was also
a Jew.

In 1977, after considerable soul-searching, he and Alexandra had applied to leave Russia for Israel. The request was rejected, partly on grounds of state security, Yakov Zubko having
served in the Red Army, partly on grounds which were not
specified, and they had joined what would shortly become the
swelling ranks of the *refusniks*. Within three months Yakov
Zubko had first been demoted then lost his job totally; since
then they had survived on Alexandra's salary during the period she worked as a teacher, and whatever he himself could

earn whenever he found casual work. Each month since then they had sold a possession in order to eat, each month since then they had also tried to place a few more roubles in the tin they kept under the mattress for the day they would be called to Kolpachny Lane and told they could leave. Increasingly, not through design, simply to help his family survive, and to save the money for their journey home, Yakov Zubko had been drawn into the fringes of the black market.

The following year Alexandra had borne him their first child, a son whom they called Nicholas. The boy was delivered late at night in the maternity wing of the local hospital; partly as a joke, partly as an act of defiance, they referred to the place where he had been born by the name of the place they thought they would never see, the town called Bethlehem. In the winter of 1978, as they carried their son home, in the later years when they told him, there was no way they could know the awesome inheritance of that family secret.

Their second child, a daughter, had been born in the same hospital three years later.

In 1979 his brother Stanislav Zubko had applied to leave Russia with his wife Mishka and their son Anatol; like Yakov and Alexandra they were refused. Later that year Mishka bore Stanislav's second child, a girl whom they named Natasha after her great-grandmother. Like her great-grandmother, who only saw her once, Natasha was small and pretty, with large eyes and like her great-grandmother, to whom she was the most precious creature in the world, she was cursed with asthma. Even on the hot summer days when the two families walked in Gorky Park or went in the car which Stanislav was sometimes able to borrow to the fields outside Moscow they could hear her suffering.

Just as there was no way of knowing the consequences of the secret of the birthplace of the boy called Nicholas Zubko, so there was no way of knowing the devastating legacy of the illness of the girl called Natasha.

In 1980 Yakov and Alexandra Zubko applied again to leave Russia and were again refused. The next year the distant uncle who had met the formal requirement of inviting them to Israel had passed away and they had spent the next two years finding another relative to meet the requirement. In 1984 Alexandra had been officially invited by a third cousin to join him: when she left the office in Kolpachny Lane that afternoon she and

Yakov Zubko had waited three months, two weeks and six days over seven years.

3

THE NIGHT was darker, colder.

Yakov Zubko kissed the children goodnight and returned to the kitchen; Alexandra had made coffee, they sat together at the table and read again the authorisation from the OVIR office on Kolpachny Lane.

"They can't change their minds," she asked, "they can't stop us now?"

"No," he lied, "they can't stop us now."

"How much do we need?" They had already worked it out, worked it out every week as they counted the roubles they had saved in the tin beneath the mattress: the rail fare to Vienna—it was quicker and safer by air, but cheaper by train—the cost of the exit visas, the money they would have to pay to renounce their Soviet citizenship.

Yakov Zubko took a single sheet of paper and began writing down the figures, carefully and neatly, not looking up, not able to look at his wife, both knowing they did not have enough, both knowing they would never have enough, even with the money in the tin under the mattress. He glanced around the room, aware of what Alexandra was thinking.

"Twenty for the chairs," he began, "twenty five for the table. Forty, perhaps forty five, for my watch."

"My ring," said Alexandra, sipping her coffee, "don't forget my ring."

"Your ring," he said, writing it down, "we should get thirty for your wedding ring."

IN THE HOTEL overlooking Marx Prospekt the American family finished their dinner and went to bed, the wife lying awake, thinking of what her husband had said, knowing that he was right, remembering that she had known from the first day who the man in the lift was, what he was. Thinking of her loyalty to her husband, thinking of the man with whom they shared a faith.

"THERE IS AN American family at the hotel," Yakov Zubko was unsure whether he should tell his wife, sensing she had known for a long time what he did, "they are due to leave tomorrow morning, they said for me to collect their bags." He realised that she had known from the beginning. "The children always wear denims, the wife has perfume, nice perfume, the husband always carries a camera." Alexandra waited, afraid to hear. "I think," he said cautiously, "that they are Jews, I think they will give me something."

He turned the paper over and began another list, guessing what the American family might give, calculating what he might get from Pasha Simenov, adding it to the money in the tin under the mattress. "We might do it," he said at last, not looking at his wife, wondering how much he was lying for her, how much he was lying for himself, "we might just do it."

He looked at Alexandra, seeing the way she was smiling at him, recognising, not for the first time how strong she was. "We *will* do it, Yakov Zubko," she said, "we *will* go home."

In the hotel the American woman thought again about her husband, thought about the Russian Jew who wanted only to take his family to Israel.

In his apartment on the other side of the city Iamskoy switched off the television and telephoned Militia headquarters. The afternoon shift, he was told, had been back an hour, they had logged one firm suspect, one possible. He thanked the desk man and went to bed. Tomorrow morning, he thought, definitely tomorrow morning.

4

YAKOV ZUBKO ROSE at four thirty, not needing to be quiet, he and Alexandra having lain awake all night. She pulled a coat over her shoulders and sat with him at the table. At five o'clock he kissed her goodbye, left the flat, and made his way to the metro station at Sviblovo; at a quarter to six Alexandra dressed the children and prepared them for their last days in Russia; at six precisely Major Valerov Iamskoy left the Militia building on Petrovka. The morning was cold, even colder than the day before. At six thirty Yakov Zubko began work, at eight thirty the American family took breakfast. He made sure he was in the foyer as they went to the restaurant, made sure the woman saw him as they left, hoping for a sign, any sign, of confirmation, seeing none. At twelve minutes past ten the militiaman accompanying Iamskoy noted that the suspect Pasha Simenov had appeared at his door.

At fifteen minutes to eleven, as the woman had told him the previous afternoon, Yakov Zubko made his way to the rooms of the American family; there were four large suitcases, he took two, remembering that the entire possessions which he and Alexandra would take with them when they left Russia would fit into one. Please, he prayed, may he have understood the woman correctly the previous afternoon, please may Pasha Simenov be at home.

The husband was at the reception desk, the wife talking to the guide. Yakov Zubko waited for her to turn and say something to him, the first doubts creeping up on him. He went back to the bedroom and collected the remaining cases. The family was almost ready to leave; he loaded the cases onto the coach and saw that the woman was still talking to the guide, he knew then that she had not been able to disobey her husband, that he and Alexandra would not go home.

"There's one more bag by the children's beds in 607," the woman turned to him briefly, not smiling. Watching him turn away from her, feeling the sense of betrayal. Seeing him for the last time, knowing that one day she would see him again. He cursed her under his breath and returned to the sixth floor. A maid was already cleaning the parents' room; he went past, hearing the sound of the vacuum, into 607. The room was empty. He knew why the woman had told him to go back, knew it was because she could not face him, but began to check the wardrobes anyway, looking between the beds. Beneath one was a Beryozka bag; inside were three pairs of denims, new, unused, the manufacturer's label still on them, two bottles of French perfume, and a Konica camera. "We are going home, Alexandra Zubko," he said, the relief coming upon him, "we are going home to Israel."

When he returned to the foyer the American woman had gone.

It was almost eleven o'clock.

On the corner overlooking the street called Dmitrov the militiaman logged the first visitor to the house of Pasha Simenov. "The next one," Iamskoy told him, "we'll pick up the next one."

It was less than three hours till the end of their shift. "What happens if there isn't one while we're on?" asked his subordinate.

For someone from the building on Petrovka, Iamskoy thought, the militiaman was remarkably naive at times. "There will be another one," he said simply.

Stick close to Iamskoy, the militiaman remembered they had told him at Petrovka, and you'll learn a lot. "The next one," he agreed.

YAKOV ZUBKO TURNED into Dmitrov, planning the conversation he would have with Pasha Simenov, working out how he would make sure that the man paid him enough. Be careful, Alexandra had told him as he left the flat that morning, be very careful. In front of him he saw Pasha Simenov leave the house and begin walking up the road towards him. One thing more important than Israel, Alexandra had told him, one thing more important than Jerusalem. Suppose Pasha Simenov did not recognize him, he thought, suppose he had just done a deal, had no money left, suppose Pasha Simenov did not want to talk to him in the street. One thing more important than anything else, Alexandra had said as she kissed him goodbye.

At the top of the road Iamskoy cursed his luck and instructed the militia to log the fact that the suspect Simenov had left his house and turned east.

"Good morning." Yakov Zubko knew Pasha Simenov was not going to speak to him, was going to walk straight past him. Five hundred roubles, he thought, they still needed five hundred roubles. He saw the look in the other man's eyes, saw Pasha Simenov was not looking at him, nor at the bag he was carrying. Iamskoy saw the Beryozka bag and knew what was in it, reached for the ignition. "Across the road and left at the corner," Pasha Simenov ignored the greeting, pointed with his arm as if he was giving directions, as if that was what he had been asked. Yakov Zubko saw the car, realised why Pasha Simenov was afraid, turned to follow his instructions.

For one moment Iamskoy thought he was wrong, then knew he was not.

Yakov Zubko was reacting instinctively, following Pasha Simenov's arm, as if he was in no hurry, as if he was clarifying the street directions he had been given. "Up the road fifty metres, through the block of flats," Pasha Simenov was talking quietly, quickly, "carpark on the other side, steps in the far corner to a tram stop. Good luck." It was almost, Yakov Zubko would think in the months and years he would have to remember the moment, as if Pasha Simenov knew what he was doing, as if he was sacrificing himself so that the Jew and his family could go home. "Thank you," he made himself pause, made himself move slowly, crossing the road in the direction Pasha Simenov had indicated. In the Zhiguli Iamskoy hesitated for the second time. "Screw him anyway," he thought aloud, half to himself, half to the militiaman, "we can always plant something on him."

Yakov Zubko was half way across the road when he saw the car begin to move. "No tricks," he remembered how he had lied to Alexandra the night before, "no way they can stop us now." Every trick, he knew, every way they could stop him. He turned the corner, out of sight of the car and began to run. Up the road fifty metres, Pasha Simenov had told him, through the block of flats. Which block, he suddenly thought, panicking, there were two blocks of flats, one on either side of the road. He reached them and turned left into the alleyway beneath the building, side-stepping to avoid the children and crashing into the dustbins stacked against the wall. In the Zhiguli Iamskoy saw Pasha Simenov walking up the road, the man with the Beryozka bag turning almost casually round the corner. "Simenov," he decided, "we go for Simenov." They were almost at the junction; in the street in front of them Pasha Simenov disappeared down a side turning, in the passageway beneath the flats Yakov Zubko regained his balance, feared he had chosen the wrong block. "The other man," Iamskoy changed his mind, "the other man and his suppliers."

Yakov Zubko broke into the sunlight and saw the carpark; wondered for the first time if Pasha Simenov knew who he was, what he was, felt his legs seizing up, felt himself slowing down. "Run," he heard the voice, "run for Alexandra, run for the children." His lungs were hot, the bag was heavy, impeding him. "Run," he heard the voice again, shouting at him, screaming at him, "run so that you can all go home." In the far corner he saw the exit; down the steps, he remembered, down the steps to the tram stop.

Iamskoy turned the corner and accelerated up the road. Nobody with a Beryozka bag, nobody running as if his life depended on it. In the carpark behind the flats Yakov Zubko was half-way to the corner. "You take the right block," Iamskoy slammed on the hand-brake, "I'll cover the left." He was out of the car, running, the door swinging open. He saw the dustbins rolling on the ground, the children staring. "This one," he shouted, "he's gone through this one." He sprinted into the dark, seeing the carpark ahead. "Run," the voice was screaming at the Jew for the last time, "run as you've never run before." Yakov Zubko reached the corner, saw the tram in the street below, saw it beginning to move. "Wait for me," he prayed, "please wait for me." He cleared the steps two at a time and hauled himself on as the rear doors clanged shut and the tram pulled away.

THE KITCHEN WAS QUIET, peaceful: Alexandra finished lunch, put the suitcase on the table and began to pack the children's clothes; at her side her son and daughter watched her closely. "Tonight," she told them, "your father will be home early, tomorrow we will have a treat, tomorrow your father will take us all for a train ride. I will make sandwiches for us to eat."

THE PASSENGERS on the tram were looking at him, at the Beryozka bag he was carrying. Someone was bound to question why he had it, someone was bound to report it. He knew what he had always avoided in the past, what he had to do now, remembered what Alexandra had told him. One thing more important than Jerusalem, one thing more important than anything else. He left the tram and took the metro to the black market behind the station at Begovaya.

At the observation point overlooking Dmitrov Iamskoy watched as the militiaman checked the house of Pasha Simenov and confirmed the door was locked. "We say nothing," he ordered the man when he returned to the car, "we simply log the fact that Simenov left the house and turned east."

"What about the man with the Beryozka bag," asked the militiaman, "if he *is* selling is there any chance he'll go to Begovaya?"

The possibility had already occurred to Iamskoy. "No chance," he said "if he does have anything to sell he'll lie low for a while." There was no way they could leave the observation point, he meant, no way they could concede that they had made a mistake. "Unless," he added as an afterthought, "he has a reason for off-loading the stuff today." No way that anyone would have that strong a reason, he was sure, no way anyone would risk the black market at Begovaya knowing the men from the building on Petrovka were waiting for him.

"But if the others pick Simenov up this afternoon, they won't know what to ask him."

"No," said Iamskoy, "but we will tomorrow."

IT WAS ALMOST THREE, the sun already pale, when Yakov Zubko entered the maze of streets behind the metro station at Begovaya; he walked slowly and carefully, checking the buyers and sellers, eavesdropping on the conversations and negotiations, till he had worked out who was paying the best prices for what he had to sell. The man he approached was overweight, already wearing a winter coat, a cigarette in his mouth. Yakov Zubko struck up a conversation, after ten minutes he asked whether the man was interested in American denims.

"Buying or selling?"

"Selling," said Yakov Zubko.

"What size?"

He realised he did not know. "New," he said, "the manufacturer's labels still on them."

"How much?"

"How much are you offering?"

The man gestured that he should follow him to a car parked on a side street. In the front passenger seat was a young woman, attractive, less than twenty years old. Money, thought Yakov Zubko, could buy anything, even in Russia. She saw them coming and moved to the back, allowing them to sit in the front.

"How much did you say?" the man asked again, fingering the flesh round his jaw.

"Two hundred each," Yakov Zubko double the price he had calculated, "a hundred and eighty each if you take all three." He pulled them from the bag and showed them to the dealer.

The man snorted. "Eighty each."

"A hundred and sixty."

"Ninety, that's as high as I can go."

He knew he had made a mistake, that he should not have allowed the dealer to trick him into being the first to suggest a price, then began to see the way he could retrieve the advantage. "A hundred and fifty," he said. "That's my lowest. After I've paid my man, that leaves me almost nothing."

"Your man?"

"The man I get them from." He used the present tense, as if he had a regular supply.

"You can get more?" The dealer took the first bait. Yakov Zubko thought of Alexandra and the children standing behind the table when he had returned home the previous evening. "Not this week, probably next, definitely the week after."

"New like these?"

"With the manufacturer's labels. Any size you want."

"A hundred."

"A hundred and forty."

"A hundred and ten."

We are going home, Yakov Zubko, Alexandra had said, giving him the papers from Kolpachny Lane, we are going home to Israel. "A hundred and thirty and they're yours."

"How many others can you get?" The dealer had always been greedy, now he showed it.

"Three, four pairs a fortnight." He was watching the man's eyes. "To start with," he added, "more if I can guarantee my man a good price." He could see the dealer trying to work out his source. An American, the man would be thinking, an American businessman with regular trips to Moscow, the denims only the start of things. Yakov Zubko reinforced the image: "What about perfume?"

"French?" The tone in the man's voice gave him away.

"Of course."

"I'd like to meet your man."

"You must think I'm mad." Believe what you're saying, Yakov Zubko, he told himself, make *him* believe what you're saying.

"A hundred and twenty five each."

"A hundred and twenty five each," he agreed. Enough for the visa and the renunciation, he thought, but not enough for the tickets, not nearly enough for the tickets.

The man pulled a roll of notes from beneath his winter coat. It was more money than Yakov Zubko had seen in all the seven years since he and Alexandra had applied to leave Russia. "About the perfume," he said, taking the bottles from the bag, watching the way the dealer's eyes flicked from the money to the contraband, seeing again the greed. The man reached forward to take them. Yakov Zubko moved them back.

"Genuine?" asked the dealer.

"Seals and tops unbroken," confirmed Yakov Zubko.

"Fifty each." It was the dealer who made the first offer.

"A hundred."

"Seventy-five."

"Seventy-five." He had the tickets for the children, plus something towards the fare for Alexandra. "And a good price for this." He took the camera from the bag. "Only a sample," he lied, "one a fortnight, make and model specified three weeks in advance, for as long as you like. Guaranteed delivery."

"Anything else?"

"You say, I'll ask."

"A hundred."

"Plus films."

"A hundred and ten."

"A hundred and thirty."

"A hundred and twenty."

He had their tickets to Vienna, plus something for his brother and his brother's family when Stanislav and Mishka were allowed to leave. "A hundred and twenty," he agreed.

5

THE FLAT WAS EMPTY, the single suitcase in the middle of the kitchen floor where the table had stood. The children were frightened, he had not told them what was happening or where they were going in case they did not get there, in case the men from Petrovka came for him.

"Mummy says that today you will take us all for a train ride," said his son. Yakov Zubko put his hand on the boy's head. "Your mother is right," he smiled, "today I will take us all for a train ride."

"But why have they taken the chairs and tables?" the boy asked, "Why have they taken my bed?"

"Because today," his father told him, "we are going for a train ride."

At three o'clock the friend from whom Stanislav sometimes borrowed the car for the family trips to the countryside came to take them to the station. Stanislav and Mishka, and their two children, would accompany them. They arrived at three forty-five, an hour and fifty minutes before the train was due to depart. In the square opposite was a Zhiguli similar to the one outside the house of Pasha Simenov. Yakov Zubko thought about the man and wondered where he was, if he had been caught, if he knew enough about him to betray him. He had not told Alexandra and did not tell her now; he had already decided not to tell her until they were in Israel, did not understand that she suspected.

The station was crowded. It took the officials twenty minutes to check the documents and tickets, twenty minutes for the people behind him to worry about their trains, and for Yakov Zubko to worry about Pasha Simenov. By the time he had been cleared, there was still an hour remaining. The two families sat together for the last time, not speaking. After thirty minutes they went to the square outside and asked the friend who had brought them to take a photograph of them together.

The photograph that was taken that day showed the men staring straight ahead, trying to hide their emotions, the women having the strength not to conceal theirs, the children holding hands, confused. Even in the noise of the square Yakov Zubko could hear the girl called Natasha fighting for her breath. At five minutes to five they said their farewell: the words they would remember later, the only words they would remember when they had reason to remember, were the last words Yakov Zubko spoke to his brother. *"Beshanah Habaah b'Yerushalaim."*

His brother could no longer hold back his tears. *"Beshanah Habaah b'Yerushalaim,"* he said, "next year in Jerusalem."

ON THE DAY that Yakov Zubko and his family left Moscow and began their journey to the West there occurred a number of events which seemed in no way to be linked, some of which were reported, some not. The first, published in the *New York Times* and reproduced in the *International Herald Tribune*, was an opinion poll predicting a landslide victory for the incumbent president, Ronald Reagan, in the forthcoming presidential election. The second, in *The Times* of London as well as the *Guardian* and *Daily Telegraph*, reported the promotion from the Department of Energy to the position of Minister of State at the Foreign Office of the Conservative John Kenshaw-Taylor. The move, suggested *The Times*, was one more step to the country's highest office.

That day the financial and industrial sections of a number of papers carried three items of information which again seemed of little importance. The first was the beginning of an industrial dispute among the staff of the Israeli national airline, El Al. The second was a drop of a little under a dollar a barrel in the international price of oil. The third was a fall of just over a cent in the value of the British pound. Although the last two were seen to be marginally connected, the pound being considered a petro-currency since the discovery of North Sea oil, little significance was read into either.

The same day there occurred two events which went unreported, the first because it had no reason to be, the second because it had every reason not to be. The first took place in the Palestinian refugee camp of Ain Helweh, in the southern area of the Lebanon. In a small room in a house off a side alley of the camp that afternoon a doctor diagnosed cancer in the body of a man forty years his senior; he did not tell the man, but he gave him less than six months to live. The second took place three hours later, in the heart of the so-called bandit country of South Armagh, in Northern Ireland, close on the border with the republic. At five thirty that afternoon a member of the Special Branch of the Royal Ulster Constabulary received a telephone call from an unidentified man claiming to be a ranking member of the Provisional IRA, saying he wished to liaise with the security forces. The call was treated with initial scepticism, but arrangements were made to act on the information which the caller, partly as an indication of his access to confidential IRA planning and partly, he said, as a sign of his good faith, passed to them.

That day also the first strands were woven in a pattern linking the old world to the new. At ten that morning the anti-terrorist division of the New York office of the American Federal Bureau of Investigation, the FBI, began an investigation into an approach to an undercover agent posing as an arms dealer by a man claiming to be the head of the Provisional IRA, in North America, stating that he wished to buy surface to air missiles for use against the British army in Northern Ireland. Two hours later, at lunch-time, a twenty-three-year-old single woman who, six months before, had decided that, in the short term at least, it was easier and more profitable to sell her body than her undoubted intellect, was introduced to the highly lucrative world of the United Nations circuit. The same afternoon, a sergeant in the United States Delta Force returned to America after six months, secondment with the British Special Air Service, the SAS. That evening an American living in London received word from his family in San Francisco that his grandmother was close to death. The old lady was ninety seven years old and he had met her only twice, but the second of those meetings had changed his life.

7

AT SEVENTEEN MINUTES past twelve the following day, a mere seven minutes late, the Moscow-Vienna express carrying Yakov Zubko and his family passed from the Eastern Bloc into Austria. The final check was remarkably brief, their papers were inspected, their single suitcase given the most perfunctory of inspections, and they were waved through. At three minutes to one that afternoon Yakov Zubko and his wife and children stepped into the West. Twenty metres away stood a woman from the Jewish Agency.

"*Shalom,*" she said, stepping forward to greet them. "Welcome."

"*Shalom,*" he said, putting down the suitcase. "We are the family Zubko. We are coming home."

BOOK
TWO

CHAPTER ONE

1

THE OPINION POLL predicting a landslide victory for Ronald Reagan was on the second page of the *International Herald Tribune*. The man reading it sat in the chair in the corner of the room farthest from the window, between the sofa and the desk. The paper, one day old, had arrived that morning; he had not stopped reading the article, not stopped thinking about it, all day. The only person he had spoken to during that time, the only person he allowed to be in his presence, was the young man seated on the sofa.

The room, on the third floor of the complex, was neat and sparsely furnished, the walls a bare white. The only ornaments on the desk on the left side of the window were a chess set and a framed photograph of a young family, the children in the arms of their parents. Abu Nabil had aged almost thirty years since it was taken, though he could still be recognised in it; he kept and treasured it because it was the only photograph he had of his wife and sons; others kept and valued it because it was the only photograph of Abu Nabil known to exist.

At the side of the young man on the sofa lay a sub-machine gun.

It was two hours to midnight.

"The car in ten minutes," Abu Nabil told him. "Saad at eight, Sharaf at nine." The bodyguard went to the telephone and dialled two numbers, passing on his master's instructions. The young men who took the calls, to be passed in turn to their masters, were surprised neither at the contents of the order nor at the time it had been issued.

At fifteen minutes past ten Abu Nabil left the safety of the complex in a black Mercedes, accompanied by three escorts, two to stay with him wherever he went and one to remain with the car. Even in Damascus, which he had made his home and base for the past six years, it was as unthinkable that his car should be left unattended as it was that he himself should not be protected. Not because of what might be missing from the car when he returned; rather for what might be added to it, as the Israelis had demonstrated during the maelstrom which had swept Europe after the massacre at the 1972 Munich Olympics, as the IRA, and, he suspected, the British army itself, had proved in Northern Ireland.

The café to which he led his shadows was in a maze of alleyways and passages in a quarter of the city they did not normally frequent, the entrance almost hidden behind a street hoarding. They left the car and completed the last fifteen minutes on foot, not knowing where he was going or why he was going there.

The room in which they finally settled seemed smaller than it was, the air filled with smoke, the floor packed with tables surrounded by men, mainly old, drinking arak and playing *tawli*. Abu Nabil settled himself against a side wall, almost lost in the semi-gloom of the room, as if it was the place he always sat, while a waiter in a dirty white shirt and floppy grey trousers brought them their drinks. They took them, no one seeming to notice the newcomer or the two men who sat on either shoulder, no one seeming to notice the weapons which hung beneath their loose-fitting coats.

Abu Nabil sat for half an hour before he chose his man, then he ordered more drinks, rose from his seat, leaving his escorts against the wall, and made his way to the table he had selected, ignoring both the game in the middle of the room, where the shouts seemed the loudest, and the one in the corner which attracted the most spectators, easing his way through to the inner circle of men so quietly and inconspicuously that they did not even register his presence.

The two men at the table had skin like parchment; they sat facing each other, rolling the dice from a worn leather cup, counting their moves, checking each other's moves. The game lasted another fifteen minutes, then the players began stacking the pieces in the wooden boxes at the side of the board, one of them finishing his drink, the other looking up at Abu Nabil.

"You would like a game, I think."

Abu Nabil knew he had chosen wisely. "I would like a game," he confirmed.

It was the beginning of the new day.

They played for thirteen minutes under the hour; when they finished it was not clear whether the old man had won or been allowed to win. The crowd began melting away till they were alone at the table.

"One question, old man," Abu Nabil asked politely, respectfully.

The old man knew it was why the stranger had come, why he had played him. "One answer," he agreed.

From the wall at his back of the café, the shadows watched intently.

"We have just played," said Abu Nabil, "and you have just won." His voice was quiet, yet the old man did not have to lean forward to hear the words. "If someone told you that you have just won and I have just lost, what would you say?"

The old man's eyes shone with a sudden pleasure. In the night outside, he knew, something was stirring, beginning, did not know what, had no way of knowing, knew that most people would say he would never know. Knew, in his wisdom and his years, that one day he would.

"My father," he began, "was a good man, a wise man. He was also an Arab. If a man took him outside at night and showed him the moon, then took him outside the next morning and showed him the sun, he would wonder why the man was telling him that the moon rose at night and the sun shone during the day." He saw that the stranger was nodding his understanding and reached for his drink. The glass was empty; Abu Nabil slid his own across the table. The old man took it and sipped from it, then placed it between them.

"Compared with your question," he went on, his voice faint with age, "such matters are simple." He looked down at the *tawli* board. "If you ask me whether I have just beaten you, I would answer no. I would answer that *you* have just beaten *me*."

"Even though everyone would tell you that you have just won?"

The old man's eyes shone again. "Especially if everyone tells me I have just won."

"Why?" asked Abu Nabil. He was close, he thought, so close, to the truth that only he would understand, that only he could know.

The old man fingered the *tawli* pieces.

"With you," he said, "nothing is as it seems. If the world tells a man he has won and you have lost, then he has lost and you have won."

"Why?" Abu Nabil asked again.

"Because you are more than an Arab," replied the old man, "you are a Palestinian."

"Thank you," said the stranger, rising to leave. At the wall at the back, the old man saw the two men with the loose-fitting coats rise to follow.

"I only told you what you already knew," he said.

Abu Nabil thought of the article in the newspaper, the plan that had been born of it, the single factor that would decide whether or not the plan would succeed. "That is why I thank you," he smiled.

2

ABU NABIL was fifty-three years old; his father had been a merchant, his two brothers were still prosperous businessmen on the West Bank, he himself had qualified as a doctor. For the past thirty years, however, his profession had been the exercise of whatever means he considered necessary to secure the return of his people to the land called Palestine. Others referred to the craft he practised as terrorism.

He had played a role, at first political, later military, both in the main body of the PLO and, increasingly, in the factions which splintered from it, till he himself headed one of the so-called extremist groups which opposed what it saw as Yasser Arafat's increasing and self-imposed impotence. He had been involved in most of the acts of terrorism from the late sixties through to the mid eighties, from Dawsons Field and Black September, to the Vienna OPEC hijack, to Mogadishu. More recently he had been at the centre of the power struggle within the ranks of the Palestinian movement itself, his organisation being held responsible for at least some of the assassinations which had spread from the Middle East across Europe. He had operated his forces in the Lebanon during the various stages of that country's civil war, and had played a key role in forcing the exodus of Yasser Arafat and his mainstream PLO grouping from their headquarters in the Northern Lebanese port of Tripoli in 1983.

The available information on him, however, was less than skeletal, the merest details of his birth and education, of his marriage and of the death of his family though this was rarely mentioned, especially by his enemies, who feared how even the barest details of the massacre of such innocents would feed the legend which had grown around him.

His name, Abu Nabil, was itself a *nom de guerre*. There were even those who questioned whether he, in fact, existed, whether he was the person his enemies, and his friends, thought him to be, or whether it was a committee who used his name, his reputation, to further their various causes. Others accepted that he had existed, but maintained that he had died some years previously, probably in an Israeli rocket attack on a house in which he had reputedly been staying. In the past eight years there had been four reports, all reliable, that he had died of cancer, two of them stating that he had died despite treatment in Moscow, and three more reports, equally reliable, that he had died of a heart attack.

3

By eight that morning Abu Nabil had slept for a little over three hours, showered and taken a light breakfast, then had gone again through the elements of the plan that was now taking firmer shape in his mind. Precisely on the hour, the first of his appointments arrived.

Malik Saad looked the accountant that he was, small, a sharp nose, heavy rimmed spectacles. He had headed the organisation's finances, welcoming its income and quarrelling over its expenditure, for the past five years; during that time he had also invested its money wisely, ensuring a fruitful return both in terms of finance and obligations, spreading its resources not only through the multitude of Palestinian companies which played a major role in the engineering and construction industries of the Middle East, but also into Europe and North America, both the United States and Canada. For the four years before that he had been imprisoned for his part in a bomb attack on an Israeli patrol on the West Bank.

Abu Nabil watched him arrive, then welcomed him to the flat on the third floor, and offered him coffee. For ten minutes they discussed areas of future investments, Malik Saad outlining what he saw as potential returns for the future; when what they both recognised as the formalities were completed, Abu Nabil turned the conversation to the reason for the summons.

"I need to know how our finances stand at the moment," he said to the accountant. "I am considering a medium-term strategy which will require, at certain points over the next few months, the transfer of substantial amounts of money to various organisations, probably within Europe. I will need you to ensure that the monies are available when needed, and that the transfers are completed with a minimum of complications."

Malik Saad had only one question. "You are anticipating a budget request. When will you approve it?"

"I have just approved it," said Abu Nabil.

Twenty minutes after the accountant had left, the soldier arrived. Issam Sharaf was thirty-nine years old and had been with Abu Nabil since the bloody days of Black September fourteen years before; his body bore the scars of a lifetime of fighting, there were the traces of shrapnel near his spine and his left arm had been rebuilt round a metal rod.

The conversation was even shorter, even more to the point, than that with the accountant; it was how both men had grown together, how they preferred to operate. It was also, Issam Sharaf thought, as if Abu Nabil had already decided what was to be done, how it was to be done, as if he had also decided there was little time in which to do it.

"I was wondering," Abu Nabil began, "how Europe was."

Issam Sharaf knew the man well, knew how he approached a subject, even when time was short; he settled back onto the sofa and accepted the coffee.

"Quiet," he said, the inflection in his voice suggesting that Europe had been too quiet for too long. "People have been regrouping, we have been training them, giving them a little finance. As you know." He was already wondering where Abu Nabil had decided the conversation would end.

For the next few minutes he listed the activities of the various European groups with which they had contact, giving updates on changes in personnel and philosophies, as well as a breakdown of the strengths and weaknesses of each. In West Germany the Red Army Faction, the descendants of the Baader-Meinhoff group of the seventies, and the lesser-known Revolutionary Cells, the RZs; in Italy the Red Brigades and, again, the less known Prima Linca; in France, Action Directe; in Belgium the CCC, the Cellules Communistes Combattants;

in Portugal The Popular Forces of April 25; in Spain the Basque separatist movement, ETA, plus the anarchist group GRAPO and the Catalan separatist movement, TL.

"Four things," said Abu Nabil when Issam Sharaf had finished. The soldier waited, knowing that the first would be the easiest, that the first was always the easiest.

"Firstly," asked Abu Nabil, "how would we persuade the various groups with whom we have contact to launch a coordinated campaign throughout Europe?"

"Easy," said Issam Sharaf. "We agree to finance them." He knew the other questions would increase in complexity.

"Secondly, how easy would it be to demonstrate that the campaign was, in fact, carefully coordinated rather than a series of isolated incidents?"

The soldier sensed again that Abu Nabil had already worked it out, "Equally easy." His mind was already anticipating the next question. "Exchange of weapons between groups to link assassinations, use of explosives from the same source for attacks in different countries, same targets or types of targets, joint communiqués between various groups, tied in with the exchange of weapons and sharing of explosives, claiming responsibility for actions. It would be simple to leave a trail all over Europe." He could see why Abu Nabil would want it, could see the type of fear a coordinated campaign would create, wondered what Abu Nabil had conceived for the next stage of the escalation of that fear.

"Thirdly," said Abu Nabil, "a hunger strike."

It was, thought Issam Sharaf, as if Abu Nabil was establishing a background against which a specific event could take place, but it was also as if, when that event took place, it would appear to be merely a consequence of what had gone before rather than the reason for it.

With you, the old man had told Abu Nabil less than five hours before, nothing is as it seems.

Why, Abu Nabil had asked him.

Because you are more than an Arab, the old man had told him, you are a Palestinian.

"West Germany would be the obvious place," he suggested. "The groups there have the right history, the right commitment."

"In that case," said Abu Nabil, "I will need a set of demands."

Connected to the hunger strike, Issam Sharaf knew. He thought for the last time that Abu Nabil had already planned both where it would start and how it would end. It was not yet ten in the morning. "Why?" he asked.

Abu Nabil told him. When he had finished he had only one question. "When can you leave?"

He should have known, the soldier thought, he should have known from the beginning. "This afternoon," he said. "I'll need a budget."

"I have already approved it."

Something else, Issam Sharaf thought, Abu Nabil was planning something else, something connected with what he himself would set in motion, something, however, which did not concern him. Like the pieces on the chess board which Abu Nabil kept on the desk, he thought, each piece playing its part, each piece allowed to know its part, but no more; he wondered who and what else would be involved.

"About the hunger strike," said Abu Nabil. "There is one more thing."

4

SIX HOURS AFTER HIS MEETING with Abu Nabil, Issam Sharaf left Damascus to begin his arrangements, four hours after that Abu Nabil himself departed. He took with him only one bodyguard whom he would in turn leave during the most delicate moments of the weeks ahead, his driver and other shadows remaining behind so that they could be seen in the city during his absence, another figure behind the smoked windows of the Mercedes confirming that Abu Nabil was still in Damascus.

As if this was not enough, he also left behind the one personal item he was known never to travel without, the photograph of the young family which he kept on the desk by the window.

THE DAY AFTER Abu Nabil and Issam Sharaf made their separate departures from Damascus, Yakov Zubko and his family left Vienna for Israel. Their stay in the city had been kept as short as possible, for reasons of finance: the Jewish Agency did not enjoy a limitless budget. And the address at which they stayed had been kept a secret, for reasons of security: Jews such as themselves were still considered targets for the Palestinian groups which lay waiting in Europe.

The El Al flight was crowded, they remembered little of it, each of them too excited to accept any of the food or drink they were offered. At fifteen minutes past seven in the evening the Boeing landed at Ben Gurion, at twenty-five minutes past seven they stood for the first time in the land for which they had sacrificed so much. The representative of the Jewish Agency in Tel Aviv was waiting for them; Yakov Zubko shook the woman's hand then asked to be left alone. The representative understood, remembering the day she had arrived, knowing she would never forget it.

Quietly, ignoring the sound of the engines and the bustle of the airport, Yakov Zubko and his family looked across the concrete of the runway to the purple of the hills beyond, the smell of the orange blossom drifting to them, filling the night air. *Beshanah Hazu b'Yerushalaim,* he thought, this year in Jerusalem. No more lying, he also thought, no more thieving, no more risks on the black market, no more people always waiting for him and the likes of him.

"We are home, Alexandra Zubko," he said at last, the first tears filling his eyes.

"We are home, Yakov Zubko," she said.

CHAPTER TWO

1

THE HOLE WAS WET AND COLD, the rain cutting in sheets across the corner of the field in front of them, the water from the branches which concealed their hiding place dripping down on them. They had been there three days, at two the next morning it would be four, one of them sleeping, wrapped in the waterproof bag they had smuggled in, the other watching, waiting.

The path through the trees into the edge of the field was almost lost in the dusk. Somewhere he heard a car, knew it was too far away, knew how sound travelled at this time of day.

They had come in at night, skirting the village, knowing the dogs were there, taking care not to disturb them, taking care not to leave even the slightest indication that they had come; by the morning they had dug the hole, concealed it and begun their wait. Fifty yards behind them lay the back-up, their hole similarly covered, running wet and freezing cold.

Between two and six days, the Special Branch had told them the informant had said, between two and six days and the men would come for the arms and explosives hidden in the cache in the corner of the field, between two and six days and the centre of Belfast would be hit. He lay still, the M16 dry by his side, looking across the field to the single track where they had worked out the men would appear. Three men, the Special Branch had said, all of them active Provos, one of them on the run since the break-out from the H-Blocks the year before. A small job, the Special Branch had also said, an indication by their man of the amount and quality of information he possessed, an indication of his standing in the Provisional IRA, a promise by the informant of things to come.

The informant who had placed his first call on the day Yakov Zubko and his family had left Moscow and begun their journey to the West.

In an hour, Graham Enderson thought, it would be dark, then it would be his turn to crawl into the sleeping bag and sleep; he had once spent fifteen days in such a hole, he reminded himself, fifteen days in a winter even colder than this one. He checked his watch again and wondered when the men would show.

His son's birthday, he had remembered that morning, today was his son's birthday; he had intended to telephone, could not send a card, knew his wife would have taken care of it as she always did. The light was fading. He thought again of the three men who would come to the cache, how many people they intended to kill, whether they had ever thought about the moment they themselves would die. He would be careful, as he always was, as his teams always were; he distrusted informants, wondered why they informed, wondered why the men he was about to kill were being set up, wondered who was being set up, them or him. So many tricks, he knew, so many times to be careful, never a time when he could not afford to be careful. It was almost dark.

He had been with the SAS nine years; the thought helped pass the time away, most of that time on active service, except for the training months in Hereford, except for the language courses, except, he knew others would find it ironic, for the six months he had spent in the emergency ward of the hospital learning how to save life instead of taking it away. On his belt Enderson carried not only his spare ammunition, but also a sophisticated medical pack.

His son's birthday, he thought again, wished he was not missing it.

In the grey at the top of the path into the field he saw the three men, knew immediately they did not suspect, did not know they had been betrayed. He slid his hand across the hole, not taking his eyes from them and shook the shoulder of the man in the sleeping bag. The man woke noiselessly and rolled over. There was a new silence in the air. As soon as they picked up the first gun, as soon as they uncovered the cache and picked up the first gun. The men were careful, Enderson thought, very careful, had checked the area, for cars, for traces of people like himself. They were edging forward, out of the trees, three of them, as the informer had said. He recognised the second man, the one who had escaped from the H-Blocks, remembered his reputation, the charges on which the man had been convicted, the other things he had done. No challenge, he thought, no formal procedure. As soon as the first man picked up the first gun. He was looking down the sights, knowing the system, watching the three men skirting the barn, heading toward the corner of the field, closing on the cache.

A trap, Enderson was still thinking, he and his men could still be caught in a trap. He had always distrusted people like the informer, had never trusted anyone except his own. As soon as the first man picked up the first gun. They had come to the cache, were looking around, looking for the last time, bending down. So many tricks, so many traps to walk into; he had not even inspected the cache in case it was boobytrapped, in case there was a sniper in the hills above waiting for him to show himself. The men in front were bending down, uncovering the cache.

Graham Enderson remembered again it was his son's birthday.

The first man picked up the first gun.

2

ABU NABIL began his entry into Europe three days later, having spent that time further concealing his departure from Syria. In his fifty-three years he had learned that it was as necessary to protect himself from those who called themselves his friends as from those he knew to be his enemies. He spent time in Amman, a seemingly unlikely choice given his role in Black September but which could only be viewed accurately in the light of what was to come, as well as Cairo and Rome, crossing and re-crossing his tracks, making the telephone calls to arrange the appointments he was seeking in the capitals of the West, before his flight to Paris.

Five days after he had left the flat in Damascus, he flew into Charles de Gaulle using a false name and passport issued in Kuwait, both of which, had the authorities checked, would have been found to be correct. Abu Nabil was a careful man.

His first appointment was the following morning. He took a cab to the Georges Cinq, which had been booked from Rome, and spent the rest of the afternoon and evening walking the streets. He knew the city well, though he had not visited it for many years, not since he had taken his lonely road after 1970. The places he visited in those hours, therefore, were places which

he, though not necessarily others, considered shrines to the
fallen, the streets and backstreets where the Israelis had executed their storm of revenge following the Munich massacre in
1972. By the time he returned to the George Cinq, he had made
his penance; subconsciously, he was wondering how many more
he was about to ask to take the same long road to martyrdom.

The meeting the next day was St Germaine-en-Laye. Abu
Nabil's movements for the two hours prior to it were a micro-
cosm of his movements the five days before: the false trails, the
checks and crosschecks to make sure that he was not being followed.

He arrived at the *quai* half an hour early, spending the next
twenty minutes examining the area in the quiet but efficient
manner his shadows would have employed if the politics in
which he was about to engage had not required him to travel
alone. Ten minutes before the meeting was due he completed his
inspection and returned to the side of the restaurant overlooking the river, from where he could observe both the jetty and
the road leading to it.

The Citroën appeared at eleven thirty precisely. He watched
as the car stopped in the parking area and the single occupant
got out, locked the driver's door, and made his way to the
wooden gangplank overlooking the Seine. Only when he was as
satisfied as he could be that the contact was not being followed did Abu Nabil leave the security of his position and walk
to the water's edge. The other man heard him coming and
turned to greet him.

"Ahlan wa Sahlan." They embraced, kissing each other on
the cheeks. It was ten years since they had last met and both
showed the passing of time. "I have missed you." The greeting was traditional, between old and dear friends. "I have
missed you more."

They turned away from the path and walked along the
wooden jetty to the line of boats moored at the end.

"So, Khalidi, I see you are still making a reputation for
yourself." The second man addressed Nabil by the name by
which he had known him when they were children together
forty years before. Abu Nabil smiled. "I do my best," he said,
"though sometimes it is not appreciated." He leaned against
the wooden railings. "And you, Ahmad Hussein, you are also
doing well. I read about your companies in the *Wall Street*

Journal, I even have shares in you." Ahmad Hussein laughed. *"Insh' Allah,"* he said. "God willing."

Abu Nabil looked across the water, turning, scanning the parking area, confirming Hussein had not been followed. "And your wife and little ones, they are still well?"

"Rima is as beautiful as ever, just as beautiful as when you suggested she choose you not me." They both laughed, both remembered. They had been friends, close friends, since birth. "The children are also well," Ahmad Hussein went on, knowing why Abu Nabil was scouring the area behind them, knowing he had to. "Leila is playing the piano, Jamil prefers American football."

He did not talk of the family of the man who had requested the meeting.

"Life has been good to you," said Abu Nabil. There was no malice in his voice.

"Yes," said Ahmad Hussein, "life has been good to me." He wondered where it was leading, why Abu Nabil had asked for the meeting.

"And yet," Abu Nabil drew the other man back to the single thread which linked them, "you have not forgotten, you still send money, still do what you can to help."

"No," said Ahmad Hussein, "I have not forgotten."

There was a sadness in his voice. They looked out over the river, watching the barge plough its way against the current. For the next ten minutes they stood almost motionless, talking of the old days, Abu Nabil talking of the monies that Ahmad Hussein had donated, the food and clothing he had sent unsolicited and unrecognised to the thousands who had poured into the refugee camps, the jobs he had created for the sons and daughters of the Diaspora, Ahmad Hussein shrugging his shoulders, saying it was nothing, saying it was the least he could do. Meaning it.

After ten minutes they turned back, away from the river, and went to the restaurant overlooking the jetty, taking a table in the corner, away from the window.

To the waitress who served them they seemed like two businessmen discussing their affairs. In one way, at least, she was correct. Ahmad Hussein was the president of the company he had created twenty-five years before. Although its head office was in New York, where he had moved as the eldest son of a refugee family in the years after the United Nations had recommended the division of Palestine and the creation of the state of Israel in 1947 its activities had spawned over Western Europe and the United States, as well as the Middle East, to the point where Ahmad Hussein held as much power in his chosen domain as Abu Nabil commanded in his.

Hussein poured them each a glass of wine, and broke the bread the waitress had given them. "There is something you want from me," he said.

"Yes," said Abu Nabil, "there is something I want from you."

On the river outside it had begun to rain.

For the next fifteen minutes he went through the single, sincere request, pausing only when the waitress served them or cleared the table between them. The two people, he said, the two people he wished Ahmad Hussein to find for him. Telling him why he wanted them, the objective he wished to achieve through them, not telling him the means he had already set in motion to achieve that objective.

Like the pieces in a chess game, the soldier Issam Sharaf had thought in Damascus, each required to play his part, each allowed to know his part, and no more. Himself, the accountant Malik Saad. Now, Abu Nabil would have added, the man he was now seeing in Paris, the two men Ahmad Hussein would identify for him, the politician he would meet tomorrow in London. Plus the man he himself would send out, as well as the man the others would send to stop him. And the innocents, always the innocents, who would come between them. Like a chess game, each move, each piece, a part of the game, each move a game in itself.

On the river outside it had stopped raining.

The two men left separately. By four that afternoon Abu Nabil had checked out of the Georges Cinq and taken a cab to Charles de Gaulle; at five thirty he took British Airways flight number BA313 to London Heathrow.

The flight was comfortable, and the service friendly; he asked for a soft drink and spent the hour going through the English newspapers on board, checking both the political and financial sections. The pound, he noted, had slipped another half-cent against the dollar, partly due to higher interest rates in the United States, partly due to industrial trouble at home, increasingly due to its position as a petro-currency. For several months the world's oil surplus had led to a gradual reduction in the price of oil, for those months the world's leading producers, both inside and outside OPEC, had been talking about a new price and quota structure. So far they had failed to agree.

He saw the lights of the city below and thought again of the man he would meet the following afternoon, what he would ask him to do.

3

THE SPECIAL BRANCH BRIEFING was brief, the Special Branch briefings were always brief: Graham Enderson was not sure whether the need to protect sources was as strict as the men concerned insisted, or because it was a game they played, not only with their contacts but also with him.

The informant who had passed them the details of the arms cache, said the sergeant, had approached them again. He would not say who the man was or where the meeting had taken place, would not even confirm that such a meeting had taken place. There was to be a high-level conference in Belfast, the man had said, some of the big boys were coming for it, from Dublin, from Derry, he had given them the time and the location.

"Who's involved?" asked Enderson. The meeting was taking place in the army centre in Lisburn.

The Special Branch sergeant gave him the names. Enderson knew all of them. "Where?" he asked. He remembered the night at the arms cache, how he had managed to phone home that evening after all, managed to wish his son happy birthday.

The Special Branch man gave him the address.

"The bar," said Enderson, "just along from McDonald's place." He knew the addresses, knew the IRA man who lived along the road.

"That's right," confirmed the sergeant, giving nothing away. "Just along from McDonald's place."

"Will McDonald be going to the meeting?" No problems, he was thinking; he already knew where they could keep watch on the house, where they had already kept watch on the house, the secret place from where they had logged McDonald's movements, his wife's movements, his son's movements, till they knew them all as if they were family: McDonald himself, the hard man, the planner behind the deaths and mutilations, the wife Eileen, even the son Liam. The son the same age, thought Enderson, as his own son.

"Yes, McDonald will be going to the meeting."

Typical Special Branch briefing, Enderson thought again, the sergeant had omitted McDonald from the original list; he knew, nevertheless, that McDonald was not the informant, knew that McDonald would never be an informant.

One problem, he was already thinking. He did not know the interior of the bar in which the meeting would take place, which rooms were above it, which doors led to it, away from it.

"When?" he asked.

The Special Branch man told him.

Not much time, he thought, only a matter of days, almost the end of term for the kids, he thought, knew he would not be home for Christmas, almost the beginning of their Christmas holidays.

"OK," he said.

The Special Branch briefing lasted a mere fifteen minutes, the briefing which Enderson gave to his teams lasted almost three hours; at the end of it they had worked out the covers, the approach routes, what they would do inside. The only things they did not know, the only things they still needed to know, were the movements of McDonald and the interior lay-out of the bar where the meeting would take place.

By five thirty the IRA planner called McDonald had been given the code-name Michael, by five forty-five Enderson had solved the problem of the lay-out of the bar. At seven thirty that evening a house in the Falls Road opposite the home of the IRA planner called McDonald was broken into whilst the family who lived there were out. Nothing was stolen and the entry was not even noticed. When they returned at nine that evening there was no way the family could have known that concealed in the roofspace of their house was a man, lying in a hammock strung beneath the beams of the roof, looking through a hole where he had removed a tile, his radio on whisper.

THE MEETING which Abu Nabil had arranged in London was at two forty-five.

Security in the West End that day was strict, the extra police vans on the street corners, the number of uniformed men in the area, the outlines of the marksmen on the roofs above them, the urgency with which the maroon patrol cars of the Diplomatic Protection Group and the white transits of the Special Patrol Group seemed to be moving.

Abu Nabil did not allow it to concern him, knowing it was to do neither with himself nor any of his plans, assuming, correctly, that it was connected with the meeting of international oil ministers which was taking place in London that day.

At ten minutes past two he took a cab to the Hilton Hotel in Park Lane, allowing himself extra time for what he knew would be the inevitable traffic delays and the equally inevitable security blanket round the hotel, arriving at twenty-five minutes to three, ten minutes before his appointment.

There were three police cars outside, uniformed officers at the entrance to the foyer and, again he correctly assumed, armed plain-clothes men inside. The receptionist did not appear to be affected by the intrusion. He introduced himself by the name in the Kuwaiti passport which he carried and asked her to inform Mr Yussef of his arrival. The receptionist had been efficient and polite, now she was even more so. Adnan Yussef was a regular guest, known by the staff to treat them well when he left; he was also the head of the political staff of Sheikh Saeed Khaled and it was the presence of those among whom Sheikh Saeed Khaled held such influence, the oil ministers in London for the OPEC talks, which was the prime reason for the massive security screens both inside and outside the Hilton and other hotels where the delegates were secluded with their staffs.

Five minutes later the appointment had been checked and Abu Nabil had been escorted to the eighth floor, past the discreet security line, to the suite occupied not by Adnan Yussef but by the sheikh himself. He was shown in, offered coffee, which he declined, and left alone. There was no way, he knew, that he could check the room for the multitude of eavesdropping equipment which it could have concealed, and no point;

such was his host's position that no one but Khaled would have even considered installing such devices, partly because of the technical difficulties involved, mainly because of the political repercussions were such devices to be discovered in the regular electronics sweeps which the sheikh's personal security advisors were known to conduct. And if the sheikh had introduced his own devices, which Abu Nabil considered more probable, then he would also have arranged for them to be switched off during the meeting that was to follow.

Three minutes later, exactly on time, Sheikh Saeed Khaled entered the room.

He was older than the occasional photograph which appeared in the international press suggested, only the slight yellowing in the whites of his eyes betraying the toll of the lifestyle he had chosen to inflict upon himself.

Saeed Al-Haitham Bin Khaled had been born the fourth son of one of the extended families which comprised the oil cartel of the Middle East. Partly because of the changing nature of international politics following the Second World War, partly because of the interpretation of a dream which his father had had whilst he himself was still in his mother's womb, he had been educated in France, Britain and the United States. He had also, because of both his father's influence and his own inclinations, turned aside from the limitations of national politics and the opulence and privilege which his birthright afforded him, and begun to steer his path through the web of manipulation and intrigue which emanated from the Middle East oil wealth, spreading his power base through the financial and political worlds which became increasingly linked to it, to the extent that his sway and influence, though little known to the general public, matched that of the Saudi oil minister Sheikh Yamani in the conference halls where the formal decisions were taken.

"Khalidi," he said, using his visitor's correct name, embracing him. "It is good to see you again." He ignored the coffee and opened the cocktail cabinet fitted along one wall of the lounge. "What would you like?" Though their religion barred alcohol and Abu Nabil drank little, he knew what his host expected. "Black Label," he said. Khaled poured two generous glasses, gave one to Nabil, then crossed the room and looked down from the window to the street below, shaking his head and smiling slightly. It amused him that the security net which surrounded the building, the visible elements of which he could observe from his suite, was designed to protect those he influenced from the likes of the very organisation whose founder he was now entertaining.

"The talks are going well?" enquired Nabil. The sheikh gestured with his hand. "Not well, not badly. OPEC has a problem which many do not wish to see solved." He settled into the chair by the window. "So, Abu Nabil," he changed the name by which he addressed his guest, "what brings you to London? Not the oil meeting, I hope, not another OPEC." In December 1975 the Venezuelan terrorist known internationally as "Carlos" or "The Jackal" had taken over a meeting of OPEC ministers in Vienna and held them hostage before flying them to North Africa. What was known publicly was that the drama had ended on the tarmac of the airport in Algiers when he had released the last of his hostages in front of the television cameras. What was not known was that Abu Nabil had contributed in a major way to the planning which preceded the operation, and Sheikh Saeed Khaled to the negotiations which ended it. It had been during those negotiations, initially conducted through intermediaries, that the two men had come into contact with each other, though it was not until ten months later that they had first met.

"No," said Abu Nabil, sharing the joke, "not another OPEC."

The sheikh rose and poured them each another drink. Saeed Khaled was too politically experienced to ask why Abu Nabil had requested a meeting with him, Abu Nabil too well-practised to speak of the matter immediately: when it was time to raise the subject, they both knew, it would raise itself. For the next thirty minutes they discussed the situation in the Middle East, the power game in the Lebanon, the role of Jordan and the divisions within the ranks of the Palestinian movement itself, including Nabil's own opposition to the PLO leader Yasser Arafat.

"The trouble with Arafat," he suggested, "is not that he gave up the armed struggle, but that he gave it up for the wrong reason and in the wrong way."

Khaled was aware the conversation was turning, as if of its own accord. "The trouble with you," he invited his guest to continue, "is that you cannot give it up."

"But by giving up violence, Arafat has nothing left with which to negotiate, nothing to offer in return for what he demands." Abu Nabil knew the conversation was at the stage where there was no point in delaying.

"And what can you offer in return for what your people want, when all you have to offer is your violence?"

Abu Nabil looked at him, turning his words back on him. "Perhaps all I have to offer," he said deliberately, "*is* my violence."

Saeed Khaled's instinct told him why Abu Nabil had sought the meeting, his experience reminding him that he had to be sure. He crossed back to the window, looking out, considering his response, thinking of the two interpretations of Nabil's statement, sensing that Nabil meant the second, testing him on the first.

"But your violence is the only thing that gives your people hope, the only way they see of getting what they want."

Abu Nabil ignored the response, as Saeed Khaled knew he would, and passed to the second interpretation. "But if they achieved what they wanted, then there would no longer be a need for that violence."

One day, Khaled knew, one day, they both knew, they would remember the conversation, what was said, where it was said.

"And how would you achieve that?"

With you, the old man had told Abu Nabil, nothing is as it seems. "By violence," he replied.

The telephone rang. Khaled picked it up and listened for fifteen seconds. "I am engaged," he said, "tell them tomorrow."

"The art of negotiation," Abu Nabil began afresh, "is the ability to know in advance what the other person will accept. The greatest form of the art, as you yourself counselled me long ago, is agreeing with the other person what you will decide before you even begin."

Khaled smiled.

"In the past," continued Nabil, "there has never been success in discussions about the Palestinian issue because there has never been agreement beforehand."

"There has been suggestion of agreement," Saeed Khaled corrected him, "the problem was that those with the power to insist upon the agreement, the Americans, could never be certain that the Palestinians would stand by their word."

"But if they could be convinced?"

For the second time, Khaled was aware that he would remember the afternoon. "You could not approach them direct," he cautioned. "It would have to be through a friend." They both understood he was not talking about himself. "And even then, the friend would need proof that you could and would deliver."

"What if I had already delivered to that friend?" asked Nabil.

"It would have to be important," said Khaled.

It was the reason Abu Nabil had sent the soldier Sharaf into Europe. "It will be," he confirmed.

Khaled noted the change in tense. "So what do you want of me?" he asked.

Abu Nabil had learned too much in his fifty-three years to give a direct answer to such a direct question. "I am thinking," he said, "about how I would find such a friend." It was the reason he had gone to Paris.

"That," said Khaled, knowing it was not what his guest was asking of him, "is up to you."

"But if I found him, would you help me?" It was the reason Abu Nabil had come to London.

"Yes," said one of the most powerful men behind the world's oil discussions. "I would help you."

5

THE HOTEL MAJESTIC overlooks the Paseo de Gracia, in the heart of Barcelona; one hour's drive to the South, off the highway to Tarragona, is the village of Comarruga. On the outskirts of the village is a complex of holiday villas known as Las Piñas. At three in the afternoon on the fifth Sunday before Christmas, Issam Sharaf, military advisor to Abu Nabil, checked into the Hotel Majestic. The passport he was using, like that which Abu Nabil was himself using, had been issued in Kuwait. He informed the receptionist that he would be staying three or four days, depending on business, and that he would probably wish to conduct a meeting in the hotel on the afternoon of the third day, confirming that the hotel would be able to provide a buffet lunch for his guests, with both wine and beer.

Issam Sharaf appeared to spend the remainder of the day sightseeing, despite the edges of winter that were touching the city, beginning the second day in the same manner, walking to Gaudi's Church of the Holy Family and taking coffee in a café off the Ramblas. At nine forty-five precisely he left the café, took a cab to el Corte Ingles, walking through the ground floor of the department store to the street on the other side, and taking a second cab to a restaurant near the Plaza de Cataluna which he had visited the previous afternoon. He walked through, left by the back door, and was driven away in the Seat that had been waiting in the narrow alley behind the building. At eleven fifteen he arrived at the villa in the centre of the holiday complex of Las Piñas near the village of Comarruga; he had stopped only once in the drive from Barcelona, to shake hands with the man and woman who had been waiting for him in the parking lot on the outskirts of the city.

The meeting, round the reproduction mahogany table in the lounge of the villa, began on schedule at eleven thirty. Those present represented the groups already discussed by Abu Nabil and Issam Sharaf in Damascus, the terrorist organisations whose actions would dominate Europe in the following months, plus, from Northern Ireland, the Provisional IRA and the INLA. Sharaf himself opened the meeting, thanking those present for attending and outlining the range of topics it had been agreed they would discuss. The first exchange was dominated by the representatives of the Red Army Faction and the Red Brigades; given their background, the move was both expected and accepted by the other delegates. In turn, however, both groups were influenced by the presence of the two people who accompanied Sharaf—the man and woman he had met in the parking lot outside Barcelona, both of whom had been involved in the campaigns of killings and kidnappings of the late seventies and early eighties, both of whom were still sought by the various security organisations of a number of countries.

The agenda was straightforward. Item One: the launching of a campaign of terror in Europe. Item Two: the coordination of targets during that campaign. Item Three: cooperation between groups including the issuing of joint communiqués and the inter-exchange of weapons and materials.

With minor exceptions the discussion which followed was free of political rhetoric, the delegates welcoming the opening of a new front, and accepting Issam Sharaf's offer of a range of facilities, both logistical and financial. The only conditions, suggested by the West Germans and seconded by the Italians, were that such support would not impinge on the autonomy of each group in its own country, and that it should be the Palestinians themselves who would carry out the first action of the campaign. Both conditions had been anticipated and were agreed to immediately.

The meeting lasted six hours and ten minutes. It ended seventeen hours and ten minutes before it was due to begin, if the security forces had shadowed the Palestinian to Barcelona and taken his request for a room and refreshments at the Hotel Majestic to indicate the time and location of the meeting.

In fact, they had not.

Twelve hours later Issam Sharaf left Spain for West Germany.

CHAPTER THREE

1

AT TWELVE FIFTEEN that day Graham Enderson confirmed the arrangements he had set in motion to examine the internal layout of the bar, close to the house of the IRA planner called McDonald, where the Special Branch informant had said the meeting between the men from Dublin, Belfast and Londonderry would take place. Eighty-five minutes later Jimmy Roberts flew into Aldergrove Airport.

If he had asked them, he knew, they would have said no; instead he left the flat he shared in Earls Court, took the tube to Heathrow and caught the twelve thirty shuttle to Belfast. There was no trouble with security or Special Branch at either airport. Jimmy Roberts was, after all, an American citizen.

It was almost six weeks since the first message from California that his grandmother was ill, three days since she had died, two days since he had known of it.

He arrived at Milltown Cemetery fifteen minutes before they arrived to lay her to rest, the rain sheeting across the headstones, the mud churned around the hole they had dug for her. He had met her only twice in his life, on the two occasions she had visited the branch of her family on the West Coast of America, yet even there, he remembered, even in America, she had been fêted, even there they had known of her republicanism.

Jimmy stayed at the gate till he saw the procession winding its way up from the city, the outline of Belfast almost lost in the clouds, and turn into the cemetery. Not many for such a fine woman, he thought, knowing again he should not have come, was glad he had. They passed by him, staring ahead; he watched the faces through the car windows, white, colourless, the men and women not looking at him, seeing him nevertheless, wondering who he was, what he was doing. Only when they had slid the wooden coffin from the hearse and the Holy Father was praying over his grandmother for the last time, did

Jimmy leave the gate and join the handful of mourners. They nodded at him and looked back at the priest.

He looked on as the box was lowered into the ground, remembering how he had listened to her, remembering the stories she had told him, the heady days of the Easter Rising, the mystery of the death of Michael Collins, the dread of the despised Black and Tans. Only when the coffin was still, and the earth had been sprinkled on it, did they turn to him.

"I'm Sean." He had already worked out what he would say, knew there was no way they could check, no way any of them would know. They recognised his accent, knew he was who he said he was.

"You're Sean," one of them was saying, "all the way from America, you're her Seamus's boy."

It was amazing, he thought, how the family ties still spread across the world, how they were still remembered. "Yes," he thought of his cousin, "I'm Sean."

The rain was harder: not a fitting day, they all agreed, asked him how he was getting back to the city, offering him a lift, someone suggesting he might like a drink. He thanked them, meaning it, was only sorry that he could not tell them the truth, that he never had the chance to tell his grandmother the truth.

Jimmy Roberts was twenty-six years old, his father had emigrated to America with his wife three years before Jimmy had been born. His uncle, the father of the man called Sean, had joined them two years later. They had settled on the West Coast, in the Bay area of San Francisco, where the old lady had visited them, once when Jimmy was four, the last time when he was eighteen. Jimmy Roberts was both intelligent and industrious, he also shared his grandmother's zeal for a united Ireland. In late 1982, after four years in the United States army, he had volunteered, through a complicated series of checks and cut-off points, for active service in the cause of the land he considered his own. His last meeting, in a bar in New York, was with a man introduced to him as the head of the movement in North America, whom he knew only by the nick-name or code-name, he was not sure which, of Chopper. The following summer he had been sent to the republic, where he met the men with whom he would live and fight until the movement tired of him, or he of it. Or, he always knew, until the day they buried him with the black beret and the tricolour on his coffin. Three months later Jimmy Roberts and three others had been posted to London as a sleeper unit of the Provisional IRA. The job of the unit was simple, to lie low, build up a supply of arms and explosives and to wait for the moment the men who gave the orders decided it was time to bomb both the body and the soul out of the mainland. It was for this reason, he knew, that they would have said no if he had asked them permission to attend the funeral of his grandmother, for this reason he had not asked them.

The Falls Road was already dark when the car stopped outside the drinking club three doors from the house of the IRA planner called McDonald. He followed the men inside, the car continuing, taking the women home. The room was small and warm, the condensation running from the windows. He reminded himself who he had said he was and knew that he should not have come. One drink, he told himself, one drink with the family and then he would leave, before anyone saw him, before anyone who might recognise him from the training in the Republic entered the bar. Not one drink, he knew, the family would not let him get away with just one drink. He knew again why he had not asked permission, knew he should not have come.

The door flew open and the troops came in. The Green Jackets, he knew, the goddam Green Jackets, smashing through the tables, forcing the drinkers to get up, pushing them against the wall. He felt the panic rising in him and forced himself to stay calm, to act like the others, tried to persuade himself it was routine, looking at them hurrying through the bar, through the door at the end, up the stairs to the flat above.

The man on the end, he suddenly thought, the bastard on the end, same uniform as the others, same badges, same weapons hanging from his arm, same beret. He wondered why he had noticed the man, why he had singled him out, told himself to remember the face.

They were gone as quickly as they had come, crashing out through the door, the last man covering the others. He heard them moving along the street, the engines starting, pulling away, then he finished his drink and left.

By ten thirty that evening Jimmy Roberts was back in the flat in Earls Court which the active service unit used as a base and a bomb factory. He did not tell anyone where he had been or what had happened. It was almost Christmas; he remembered feeling the sadness that his grandmother would not see it, was glad, at least, that he had said goodbye.

By eleven Graham Enderson had drawn out the plans of the bar from the details he had memorised on the raid that afternoon and briefed his teams. It was almost Christmas, he remembered; perhaps, thought, he could phone his wife on Christmas Day, perhaps he could speak to the children.

2

TWELVE DAYS AFTER the meeting in the villa outside Comarruga Issam Sharaf reported back to Abu Nabil. Except for the tight circle of advisors who had need to know, there was no indication to anyone that either he or Nabil had been away; even within that circle no one knew where they had been or why they had gone.

It was almost lunchtime. Only after the bodyguard who sat behind Abu Nabil had left the room did the soldier begin his briefing on the Barcelona conference and his meetings in West Germany; at no stage did Abu Nabil inform Sharaf of his own discussions in Paris and London and at no stage did Sharaf ask.

The sky outside had the thinness of winter, cold and watery.

Sharaf listed those present in the villa at Las Piñas, describing the general atmosphere and detailing the consensus on the three-point agenda, his summary brief and businesslike.

"Under the general policy that all actions must be seen as part of a coordinated campaign, it has been accepted that assassinations and kidnappings, if any, will be directed against figures connected to the military-industrial complex, and that bombings, which are more likely, will be restricted to companies and institutions linked directly to NATO." His voice was level, matter-of-fact.

Nabil nodded his agreement. "Weapons and explosives?" he asked.

"Arrangements have already been made for the groups involved to share weapons and explosives. There were some objections: some groups feared that it would suggest they were short of such items. It took time to persuade them that the effect would be the opposite."

Nabil nodded again. "And communiqués?"

"Also agreed. Communiqués will carry joint responsibility. There will also be a link-up between joint communiqués and the exchange of weapons." Nabil waited for an illustration. "If Action Directe, for example, carries out an assassination in France using a weapon previously used by the Red Brigades in Italy, then the communiqué claiming responsibility will be signed by those two groups. If the Belgians use explosives of a type already used in Germany, then the communiqué will carry the names of the CCC and the RAF."

Nabil looked up from his drink. "It should set them thinking," he mused. "I wonder how long it will be before anyone picks it up?"

"Not long," said Sharaf, "not long at all."

Nabil tapped the rim of his cup. "Anything specific?" he asked.

"Yes. Action Directe are already planning the execution of the man in charge of French arms sales, General René Audran. They will postpone that action until ordered to carry it out. The weapon they will use will be a machine pistol already used by the Red Brigades in Italy."

"What was it used for in Italy?"

"The killing of a magistrate in Turin in August." His voice was still matter-of-fact.

"Any other specifics?"

"The Germans and Belgians have agreed on a list of firms they will both attack, using explosives from the same source. They have also said that they are prepared to hold off."

Abu Nabil interpreted the nuance of his words. "They will hold off until what?" he asked.

"Until one condition has been met, the same with the French."

"The condition we assumed they would impose?"

"Yes," replied Sharaf, "the condition we assumed they would impose."

They stopped for lunch: Abu Nabil did not consider they should eat while discussing the next subject. The meal, in any case, was light and they completed it in fifteen minutes. When the plates had been cleared and they were again alone in the room, Issam Sharaf raised the subject of the second stage of his European itinerary.

"The hunger-strike," he began. It was the part of the plans Abu Nabil had requested him to set in motion which he had anticipated would be the most difficult, but the part which, to the contrary, had proved the easiest.

"The West Germans have agreed," he said. "Contact has been made with those in prison for what the state calls acts of terrorism or who have connections, at whatever levels, with the Red Army Faction; all these are prepared to join a hunger strike." One other requirement, Abu Nabil thought, one other prerequisite he had emphasised to Issam Sharaf. "Contact has also been made," continued the soldier, "with those in prison in West Germany for political offences not connected with acts of violence; of these, a number are also prepared to join a hunger-strike."

"How far are they all prepared to go?" asked Abu Nabil.

Sharaf looked at him. "As far as necessary," he replied simply.

"What about the authorities? Will they try to stop the hunger-strike in any way?" He did not ask how the man had communicated with those in prison.

"No," said Issam Sharaf.

"What about forced feeding?"

"The authorities will view the hunger strike as an extension of the campaign against them. Any attempt at force feeding would be considered a victory for the hunger-strikers."

"And how will the German public react?"

Sharaf was realistic. "At first," he said, "they will not care a damn, they will not even notice. As the first death draws near, however, they will begin to think about it, about what it means."

They would begin, Abu Nabil knew, to sense the fear. "How long will it take?" he asked, partly out of consideration of those he was about to sacrifice, partly out of necessity for his timetable.

"The key," Sharaf began to explain, "is water. On average, the human body can only survive ten to fifteen days without water, so a hunger-strike with no food or water would be over very quickly." Too quickly for them, he was thinking, though he did not say so.

"And if the person took water but no food?"

"A lower limit of thirty to forty days, an upper limit of approximately seventy to seventy-five."

"Is there any way of calculating the probable length of a hunger strike given the individual's personal characteristics, his weight and body type for example?"

Sharaf guessed the reason for the question. "Only within broad outlines," he said. "It depends on more factors than just body size and shape. The amount of fat on the body is important. Women therefore tend to survive longer then men, but it also depends on how much exercise the person takes, even the temperature of the room. In the IRA hunger-strike of 1981, Bobby Sands was expected to die after about fifty days but survived sixty-five. Joe McDonnell lasted sixty-one, but Kieran Doherty took seventy-three days to die."

Abu Nabil was staring across the room. "So what do you suggest?"

Sharaf's recommendation was brutal and straightforward. "We start one a week, as the IRA did in Belfast. That way the public are made aware of the campaign as each person joins in, that way they are more exposed to the pressure as the deaths become imminent or the people start dying." He realised Abu Nabil was looking at the photograph on the desk at the side of the window. "In a way," he said, "the pressure only comes after the first death."

Abu Nabil took a long time to reply. "So the really important person is the second one to die?" he said at last.

"Yes. The first death is a necessary sacrifice; it is the second death which is important."

Nabil was nodding slowly, thinking of it, thinking of the fear it would bring, of the full awesomeness of the pressure he had asked Issam Sharaf to set in motion. "You have arranged the second group as I requested?" he asked.

"Yes."

"And they have all agreed?"

"They have all agreed."

Abu Nabil knew how important they would be, how important they would all be. "Who goes first?" he asked.

"Klars Christin Mannheim."

Abu Nabil knew it would be Klars Christian Mannheim. "He knows he will die?"

"Yes, he knows he will die." For the second time, Nabil did not ask how Sharaf had communicated with those in prison.

"How long will it take?"

The soldier had already made the calculation. "He weighs sixty-eight kilos. Within the limits we discussed, about seventy days."

"When will he start?"

"He will announce his intention to go on hunger strike on Christmas Eve. He will start in the New Year."

Nabil knew that Klars Christian Mannheim had worked it out, that he had set himself a timetable, that there was a reason for it.

"How will it be for him, for all of them?" he asked quietly.

"Hell," said Sharaf simply, "absolute hell."

Neither of them spoke for thirty seconds.

"You said the campaign in Europe was dependent upon one condition?" It was Nabil who broke the silence.

Sharaf nodded. "They ask that we start the campaign."

"As we expected."

"Yes, as we expected." He knew Nabil had already worked it out, selected both the target and the place.

"Hassan Nabulsi," Nabil said, his voice without emotion. "The PLO man in London."

The choice neither surprised nor displeased Issam Sharaf: the target would satisfy those who had made the request at the Spanish conference, and assassinations within the various factions of the Palestinian movement were not uncommon.

"Nabulsi is in Tunisia with Arafat at the moment," he said. "He returns next week."

Sharaf did not need to know how the other man knew. "When?" he asked.

"Before Christmas. Before Klars Christian Mannheim announces his hunger strike. That way he will know we are serious."

"Who will do it?" Sharaf asked at last.

If Walid Haddad was going to end it all, Abu Nabil had already thought, then it was only fitting that Walid Haddad should begin it.

"Walid Haddad," he said.

THE MOOD in the centre of the city, even a city continuously under siege like Belfast, was festive; the mood in the operations room was tense. Today, the Special Branch had confirmed, their informant had said the big men were coming today, coming up from Dublin, down from Derry.

At two in the afternoon Graham Enderson left Lisburn and drove into the city; although he was wearing civilian clothes, he carried his personal Browning inside his coat and was accompanied by two members of his team. In Belfast, they had long learned, in the civil war in Ireland, they never went anywhere unaccompanied.

The streets were busy, the shop fronts lit and decorated; he realised how close it was to Christmas, how he had forgotten it was almost Christmas. Tomorrow, he thought, and the kids would be breaking up from school, tomorrow and they would be asking if their father would be home for the holiday. The driver stopped the car outside a hamburger bar and they went in, not because they were hungry, simply to pass away the waiting. It was crowded. Even at the table they did not relax, one always looking at the car, another at the door, looking at who might be looking at them, leaving, setting them up as they left. Outside the afternoon was already getting dark. He looked across the road at the shoppers, hearing the music in the background, the words of the carol.

"They said there'd be snow at Christmas,
They said there'd be peace on earth."

Today, he thought, the Special Branch had said it was today, this evening. Definitely, they said their informant had told them, without fail. They rose and left the café.

THE MAN whom Abu Nabil had personally chosen to both begin and end his campaign of terror arrived at Heathrow fifteen minutes late at ten forty-five in the morning on Scandinavian Airlines SK501 from Copenhagen. Neither the timing nor the flight was a coincidence. SK501 was one of seven flights to arrive from Europe in a half-hour period; the immigration halls would therefore be crowded and congested. And passengers from Copenhagen attracted less attention from immigration and Special Branch than those from other European cities, such as Rome and Athens, with reputations for terrorist connections.

Walid Haddad was twenty-eight years old, neatly though not expensively dressed in a dark blue business suit. The briefcase he carried contained, among a number of other items all related to his supposed profession of petroleum analyst, a diary with a list of business appointments in London over the next two days which had been easy to arrange but which, if they had been checked, would have provided him with justification for visiting Britain.

He followed the line of passengers off the plane, through the walkways and connecting doors, and into the large impersonal hall lined, at the far end, by the immigration desks. Four queues, he saw immediately, knowing he would have no problem, looking anyway for his insurance. The queues were longer than he had anticipated, with three officials on duty at each desk. Normally two, he thought, wondering why the security was tighter than he had expected, glancing again at the desks. One official checking passports, a second looking over his shoulder at the person at the desk, looking for the tell-tale signs, the third concentrating on the queue itself. He moved forward, wondering again about the increase in security, looking again for the insurance he needed.

A flood of passengers from another flight began spilling into the hall. There was a moment of confusion as the new group mingled with those already in the hall, deciding which queue to join. He looked round, ignoring the mêlée and saw the woman. She was young, in her mid twenties, of Arab appearance, with olive skin and dark piercing eyes, taller than average with long black hair. She also had the one quality above all, the single characteristic he was looking for: that of arrogance. In the way her eyes flashed, the way she held herself. He knew the men at the desks were already looking at her.

The woman was moving towards the third queue from the far side of the hall. He hurried after her, waited till she had almost joined the queue, then stepped in front of her, almost bumping into her. He turned and apologised, politely, not friendly. The queue moved forward. He knew again they had already seen her, already singled her out. The queue to his right was moving faster, already growing shorter. Stay behind me, he spoke silently to the woman, stay where you are, give me cover. The queue shuffled forward, he reached the desk, gave the official his passport, entry visa on page five.

"Name?" The voice was harsh. He knew the other two men at the desk were looking at the woman and gave the name in his false passport.

"What are you doing in London?"

"Business. I'm a petroleum analyst." He thought about the appointments he had arranged in case they questioned him, knew it was a formality, felt himself relax, did not let it show, controlling the degree of eye contact that would give the woman away even though she was entirely innocent. Abruptly the official stamped his passport, snapped it shut and handed it back to him. Forty-five minutes later he had retrieved his one suitcase, cleared customs, collected his hire car, and was driving down the M4 motorway into London. Behind him, he knew, the first tentacles of the security net were beginning to tighten round the woman, the first arrangements for a Special Branch surveillance, the first requests, formal or informal, for a telephone intercept wherever she was staying.

By two thirty he had checked in at the Holiday Inn in Swiss Cottage, unpacked his suitcase and showered. The telephone in the room was direct dial. He checked the number he had been given in Damascus, and phoned the London office of the Palestine Liberation Organisation in Green Street.

"Good afternoon," he spoke politely. "This is Mohsen Masri from *An-Nahar*." He named a prominent Middle East publication. "Is it possible to speak with Mr Nabulsi?"

The receptionist was equally polite. "I'm sorry, Mr Nabulsi is away at the moment, can anyone else help?"

He thanked her, but said he needed to speak to the PLO representative personally and asked when she suggested he should phone again.

"He flies in tomorrow and will be back in the office on Friday. Can I get him to contact you then?"

"Don't worry," Walid Haddad told her, keeping his voice friendly and informal, "I'll try him then."

"Make it early," she answered. "He's busy after eleven."

He thanked her and put the phone down. Abu Nabil was right, he thought, Abu Nabil was always right.

The traffic in London's West End, where the offices of the PLO were situated, was congested, made worse by Christmas. It took Walid Haddad twenty minutes to drive from the hotel to the office and another ten to find a parking space, even though it was on a yellow line. If a traffic warden came, he knew he would only have to move.

The black Ford Granada was parked outside the building which housed, amongst other offices, that of the London office of Yasser Arafat's faction of the Palestinian movement. It was interesting, he thought, that the chauffeur came to work even when the representative himself was away, even more interesting that he came in the Granada. On a car radio he heard the sound of a Christmas carol. He waited, lost in the crowd of shoppers, the afternoon losing its light, the Christmas lights already on, shining in the dusk.

At five o'clock a man he supposed was the chauffeur left the building and unlocked the car. The man, he noted, checked neither around nor underneath the vehicle. Either, he imagined, because the car was visible from the front windows of the PLO office, or because the man assumed that because the representative was away, there was no security risk.

It was interesting, thought Walid Haddad, how often people made the wrong assumption.

The traffic was heavy. He followed the car across Oxford Street, skirting behind Marylebone station and through the side streets to the west of Regents Park. At the intersection on the corner dominated by the cricket ground at Lord's, he had checked on the street map, the chauffeur should drive straight on, towards the representative's house in St Johns Wood and the security of the garage, electronically protected, at the side of the house. He knew what the man would do, that when the end came it would be so sudden and unexpected that the chauffeur would have no time to question when he had made his mistake. In front of him, the man turned right, away from St. Johns Wood, towards Camden Town.

Ten minutes later Walid Haddad watched the chauffeur reverse the Granada into the garage below the mews flat where the man lived with his wife. In front of the entrance to the flat was a Ford Escort which he assumed was their own vehicle. He parked the hire car and walked down the mews, the air cold, his hands pushed into his pockets, taking his time, as if he had every right to be there. The chauffeur was concentrating on his driving, taking care not to scratch the Granada as he backed it into the narrow space, giving Walid Haddad plenty of time to see what he needed to know. No security, no tell-tale wires, not even a burglar alarm, or the pretence of one. Just the wooden door with the Yale lock.

He returned to the hotel, had another coffee, and waited till it was time to make the telephone call. The same number, Abu Nabil had instructed him, the same time each evening.

At seven o'clock exactly he dialled the number. To his surprise, the voice which answered was American. West Coast, he thought. "Hello, John," he began, using the names of the code. "Is that you?"

"Yes," replied the American in the public telephone kiosk. "Is that you, Peter?" The same public telephone kiosk, his masters in Belfast had told Jimmy Roberts, the same time each evening.

"Yes, it's Peter." Walid Haddad wondered why it surprised him that the IRA contact was an American. Definitely West Coast, he was thinking, the accent too soft to be anywhere else.

Jimmy Roberts thought about Belfast, the cold in the cemetery as they lowered his grandmother into the ground, the man at the end of the army patrol in the drinking club the same evening, waiting for the next part of the code, wondering why the IRA should give a bomb to the Arabs, why the Arabs needed it, had asked for it specifically, even the type, when he knew they had plenty of their own.

The same thoughts had occurred to Walid Haddad when he had been briefed by Abu Nabil in Damascus. He had not queried it, assuming there was a reason; with Abu Nabil there was always a reason. "Look, John," he continued the coded conversation, "I've got a couple of girls and I need someone to help me out with them."

"When?" asked Jimmy Roberts.

"Tonight," Walid Haddad told him.

The Arab was in a hurry, Jimmy Roberts thought. "Do I get the blonde or brunette?" he asked. Blonde for a straightforward meeting, brunette if he needed to bring the explosive device and detonator.

"They're both brunettes."

Christ, Jimmy Roberts thought, the Arab was in a hurry. "OK," he said. "I'll see you in the saloon bar at eight thirty."

5

THE FIRST REPORT came in at four. The car carrying the men from Dublin had crossed the border and was heading north. Three hours, thought Enderson, standing by. The second report came in half an hour later. The car carrying the men from Londonderry had left the city and was heading south. Two and a half hours thought Enderson, standing by. He went through the plan again, how the man in the roofspace would tell them what was happening, who was arriving, how they were protected, the signal for the moment the unmarked cars would close in, which of his team would cover the back, the ways out, who would go in front, what they would do when they were inside.

"Michael leaving his house with his wife and son, getting in cars." Enderson heard the voice of the man in the roofspace overlooking the street. McDonald, he thought, the IRA planner, the man whose house was less than thirty yards from the drinking club where the informant had said the meeting was to take place. He wondered why he was leaving, what he was doing, why he was taking his wife and son, thought for a moment that the informant was wrong then knew that he was not, realised what McDonald was doing. Putting on a front, acting normally, covering himself for what lay ahead. Two hours to go, he thought. Stand-by, the voice in his head told him, stand-by, stand-by.

The second report from the south came in at five, the men from Dublin were en route, closing on the city; he checked with the tail on the car from the north and heard the confirmation. An hour, less than an hour, he thought, then he and his men would move into position, any later and they would be too late, any earlier and they would be noticed. Stand-by, he thought again, stand-by, stand-by.

The car from the south entered the city, the car from the north closing fast. They seemed to have been waiting for ever, Enderson thought. It had been dark two hours. Time to move in. McDonald, he thought, where the hell was McDonald?

"Vehicle check, urgent." It was the voice of the man in the roofspace. Enderson took the make and registration number of the car and passed it to Lisburn; knew they would only take seconds to run the computer check. "What's up?" he asked.

"Probably nothing, but the car's been up and down the road twice now, first day I've seen it."

The computer check came through.

"Stolen three hours ago from the city centre," Enderson told the man in the roofspace. Not kids, he thought, not the sort of car the teenagers stole for their joy-rides.

"Passing by again." He heard the voice. "Slowing in front of Michael's house."

The other reports were coming in, the men from Dublin driving through the city, the men from Derry just entering Belfast. He wondered what the car was doing, who it was. Not the Provos, definitely not the Provos.

"Three men," said the man in the roofspace. "Windows wound down."

He knew what it was, began to radio the information back to Lisburn.

"Michael's car in street, slowing down. Stopping outside house. Michael and wife getting out."

He saw what was going to happen.

"Car coming again. Opening fire, front and rear seats." The voice of the man in the roofspace was cold, clinical, factual.

He knew the operation was off, that the men from Dublin and Derry would already have been warned.

"Michael and wife OK, sheltering behind car. Other car still firing."

He knew they could not move, could not betray their positions, disclose the fact that they had been waiting for the men from the north and south. "Alert RUC and army," he was informing Lisburn. "Probably ambulance as well."

"Bomb going in," said the man in the roofspace. "Car catching fire."

The kid, Enderson was suddenly thinking, the IRA man's bloody kid: he wasn't there, the man in the roofspace hadn't seen him. He knew that McDonald had expected trouble, had left the boy somewhere.

"Boy in car," he heard the voice, still dispassionate. "Mother trying to get door open, door seems stuck. Car on fire. Attackers' car moving off."

"Move it," Enderson was saying, the driver already accelerating, tyres screeching as they turned off the street. The women were already on the street, the crowd already gathering. "Fire spreading in car," the man in the roofspace was saying. "Can see boy inside."

He knew what they would say when he returned to base, how they would tell him he should not have blown the operation, knew the Special Branch people would accuse him of endangering their informant. They were in the Falls, the driver cutting between the crowd, he could see the car, the flames beneath it. "Cover me," he was saying, the driver braking hard, the men moving fast.

Eileen McDonald heard the sound and knew it was the car again, knew they had come back for her and her husband, ignored it, pulled at the door, trying to get her Liam out. On the other side she could see her husband, picking himself off the ground, coming round, trying to help her. The car behind her was stopping, she half-turned, waiting for the bullets, the next bomb, saw the men, faces blackened, British army uniforms. No insignia, she saw, no markings, knew who they were, did not have to think what they were doing there. The flames were spreading, the door handle jammed. The man was coming forward, the others protecting him, not looking at the car, looking out, guarding him. She saw the weapons on his body, the sawn-off shot gun in his hand. He was pushing her out of the way, pushing her husband out of the way, blasting the door open, pulling her Liam out, the fire licking at the petrol tank.

The door was only half open, Enderson reached in, trying to open it, felt the tearing and burning in his arm as he pulled at the door, the flames on his jacket.

She saw the man pulling the boy out, saw he had been injured, one of the other men coming forward, putting out the fire. She saw the injury to his arm, tried to move to help him, watched as he pulled her son away from the car, the men round him moving with him, everyone moving back, away from the car, away from the explosion. She was looking at her son, at the way the man was laying him on the ground, seeing the red, so much red she was suddenly thinking, the blood pouring from her son's body, knew he was not breathing, knew he was dying, his insides pouring out, his tiny lungs giving up the fight for breath. Somewhere, she did not know where, she heard the ambulance, knew they would not know what to do, would not know how to save her son, knew they would be too late.

The man with the blacked-out face was reaching to his gun belt, pulling out a pack, inserting the tube into her son's mouth, clearing the airway, enabling him to breathe, pulling his body together, ramming the padding and bandages on his wounds, stopping the red pouring from him. Just like the accident unit at Birmingham Hospital, Enderson was thinking, just like when he had done his six months on the emergency unit, just like the night they had brought in the first victims of the motorway pile-up.

The photographer was parking his car by the drinking club on the corner, his camera on the seat beside him. He had been on the nightly tour, hoping for a picture, knowing there would be nothing so close to Christmas, when he had heard the shooting, known where it had come from. He heard the sound as the car blew up, knew he had missed it and ran anyway. The crowd were parting, he saw the woman kneeling over the boy, knew who the man treating the boy was, not who he was, not his name, what he was. The ambulance was pulling up, the ambulancemen pushing through the crowd. One chance, he thought, he had one chance, was reacting automatically.

By the time he had reached his car and started the engine the ambulancemen had taken over and the men with the black-ened faces had disappeared. Seven thirty, he checked the time, worrying about the deadlines, if he would make them, if the photograph was as good as he thought.

Within twenty-five minutes he had developed the film and alerted the picture desks in London.

The image began to appear, he tilted the tray, letting the liquid run evenly over the print, and watched the details emerging, growing stronger, saw that the photograph was even better than he had remembered, knew without thinking what he would call it, what they would all call it. Christmas, he thought, it was so close to Christmas. He knew the impact the photograph would have, the impact the three words of the title would have.

He would call it *Peace on Earth*.

6

THE SALOON BAR of the public house in Charlotte Street was busy, it would get even busier later. The walls were draped with decorations and a sprig of mistletoe had been pinned on the ceiling by the fireplace. Walid Haddad arrived five minutes early, bought himself an orange juice and stood against the bar, sipping it. Behind him a group of men he could not help overhearing were talking to two attractive young women he assumed were their secretaries. At eight thirty he made his way across the room, through the door at the side of the bar, and followed the signs to the gents toilet. A man in a business suit was leaning against the urinal singing to himself; he looked up, his eyes red and blurred, then turned back to the wall. The cubicle was empty, Walid Haddad closed and locked the door and felt behind the cistern. The envelope was taped in place, he pulled it off, flushed the toilet and left.

Fifteen minutes later he collected the briefcase from the left luggage locker at Euston station and returned to the Holiday Inn, stopping at a chemist shop in Camden Town to purchase a pair of surgical gloves and a torch. Only when he was in his hotel room did he open the case, pull on the gloves, and examine the contents. The four ounces of plastic explosive were in a soap container, the transmitter, receiver unit, detonator and battery wrapped separately. He connected the receiver unit and battery to the bulb from the torch, and activated the transmitter seeing the bulb light up, confirming the system was working, then he disconnected the bulb, replaced it with the detonator and began to assemble the bomb. At twenty minutes to ten he locked his bedroom door and left the hotel.

The mews in Camden Town was quiet and dark, the only light was through the curtains of the windows of the flats on the first floors and the street lamp thirty yards away at one end. It took Walid Haddad less than a minute to open the garage door and another eight to attach the bomb to the petrol tank of the Granada. By eleven thirty he was back in his room. He helped himself to a drink and turned on the television, searching the channels for the in-house feature film. As he passed BBC 2, a late-night news flash caught his attention; he flicked past, then back again.

"We are receiving more details," the announcer was saying, "of the terrorist incident in Belfast earlier this evening."

He turned up the sound.

7

THE RAIN OUTSIDE was heavy, the windows were running with condensation. In the corridor outside she could hear the clamour of the children as they began their morning break. In the corner someone was smoking, they had tried to ban smoking in the staff-room, but some people had objected. She joined the queue for tea, enjoying the atmosphere, and sat down. The morning newspapers were on the table in the center of the room, the men amongst the staff were talking about them. "Amazing," she heard one of them saying, "absolutely amazing." She hadn't seen the papers, been too busy to look at them. End of term, carol service that evening, the reports for her English class to finish. And the Christmas shopping, all of it, for her and the kids. One day, she sometimes thought, she ought to sit down and work out how she managed it all by herself, except there wasn't any time. In the far corner the men were still talking about the newspapers. "Incredible," one of them was still saying, "absolutely bloody incredible." She took a cup of tea and sat down.

"What are they on about?" she asked.

"Haven't you seen the photo in the papers today?"

She said she hadn't had the time; a colleague reached across, pulled one from the pile and gave it to her.

The picture filled the entire front page; it had been taken at night, she knew, the image grainy, almost unreal.

In the centre, lying, screaming, on the ground, was a small boy. He was burned, she could see, horribly burned and shot, the insides of his body seemed to be pouring from him, the remnants of his clothes hanging from his limbs. He was looking up, white-eyed with fear, at the two people bending over him, at the woman—she knew instinctively it was his mother—

kneeling beside him, holding his hand, looking at the other
figure, the man in the camouflaged clothing of the British army.
She looked at the man, not aware she was sipping her tea; not
aware of the noise in the staff-room. His hair was long and his
face was streaked with black. He was bending over the child, his
hands pulling the remnants of the shattered body together,
stemming the blood that was flowing from the boy's arteries,
soothing the terrible burns. Even in the photograph she could
see he was treating the child as if he was a doctor, as if he himself was a father. From his left shoulder hung a short squat
weapon, she did not know what it was, a belt of cartridges
across his chest, the pistol and grenades hanging from his belt.
His left arm appeared to be injured, she could see by the way
he was holding himself, see the way his own clothing had been
burned away. The woman beside him was looking at him, ap-
pealing to him. She stared at the picture then read the handful
of words below.

Late the previous evening, the single paragraph stated, a
British army unit had gone to the help of a Catholic family who
had been bombed and shot in their car. Both the father, a
leading member of the Republican movement who was high on
the Protestants' wanted list, and the mother had escaped un-
harmed.

She read the words a second time, still not hearing the conversations around her, then looked at the three words of the
headline across the top of the page, "Peace On Earth".

Christmas, she remembered, it was almost Christmas.

"Anyone noticed this chap here?" The deputy head was
looking out the window. "He's been standing there since half
past nine." She put down the newspaper and went to the window, wiping away the condensation. On the pavement opposite the school entrance was a man, his hair was long and he was
wearing a mackintosh, the collar turned up against the weather.
The rain had flattened his hair and soaked through the shoulders of the coat.

The left sleeve of the mackintosh seemed empty.

The school bell went, she finished the tea and returned to the
classroom, not concentrating, thinking of the photograph in the
newspaper, thinking of the man on the pavement. When the
bell went for lunch she hurried back to the staff-room, left her
books on the table, and pulled on her coat. At the last moment she remembered that those staff not on duty were going

for a Christmas drink and that she had said she would go with
them. They were waiting for her. She apologised to them,
waited till they had gone, then went to the car park and started
the car. It was still raining. She drove out the gate. The man was
still there. She pulled across the road, stopped and opened the
door for him.

"Hello, Grah," she said.

"Hello, love," said Enderson.

8

WALID HADDAD knew the route from Heathrow, every inch of
the route from Heathrow. He had driven it that morning, again
and again, till he was sure.

He looked at his watch and decided to check it again, make
sure there were no last-minute obstructions, no hold-ups.

He started the car, left the short-stay carpark, and followed
the road through the tunnel from the airport towards the M4.
At the precise moment he pulled onto the motorway he pushed
the indicator to record the mileage, remembering that he was
accustomed to thinking in kilometres and forcing himself to
think in miles. The traffic was light and moving quickly, he
moved into the centre lane and headed towards London, noting again the marks he had identified earlier. One mile, first
bridge over motorway; two miles, A312 exit and second bridge;
three miles, service station. He ignored the time it took and
concentrated on the distances. Four miles, fourth bridge; five
miles, fifth bridge. Not much time anyway, even at the speed
limit of seventy miles an hour, and the PLO driver wouldn't
stick to the limit. Six miles, three-lane carriageway into two
lanes. And the cameras, the bloody cameras. Two of them, two
hundred yards apart, the first facing west, the second east, towards London. He assumed they were for traffic control, that
at the time of day he would follow the PLO car along the
motorway the police would be paying little attention to them,
knew nevertheless that they might be recording the pictures on
tape, that it was a risk he could not afford to take. Seven miles,
onto the flyover. Plenty of distance, he thought, as long as
nothing went wrong; not much time though, he also thought,
wondered what would go wrong. Eight miles, off flyover, al-

most into the suburbs. Nine miles, traffic lights at Hogarth roundabout. If it wasn't over by now, he thought, there would be problems, major problems. He circled the roundabout and turned back for Heathrow.

The black Granada arrived thirty minutes before Tunis Air flight TU 790 was due. Walid Haddad followed it into the airport complex, overtaking it as it parked outside the terminal then drove back to the short-term carpark. The driver of the Granada parked outside the main entrance of the building, in front of a policeman, got out of the car, showed the man his credentials and disappeared inside. Walid Haddad confirmed it was the man he had followed to the mews in Kentish Town the evening before and watched as the uniformed policeman spoke into the radio he carried on his left shoulder. Two minutes later an unmarked white transit van pulled up thirty yards behind the Granada. Ten minutes later the chauffeur came out, spoke to the policeman, and pulled away, the unmarked transit remaining in position.

The chauffeur, thought Walid Haddad, had stepped up the security level, was acting as he should do. Except that it was already too late. He sank back into his seat and looked again at the newspaper he had bought in the hotel foyer that morning, the picture covering the entire front page, the image of the man stemming the boy's life as it flowed away from him. After fifteen minutes the black Granada returned and parked in front of the unmarked transit. The chauffeur got out and went again into the terminal building. Walid Haddad laid the newspaper on the front passenger's seat of the hire car, pulled the transmitter from beneath the seat, placed it on the newspaper, and folded the paper over it. The picture of the man in Belfast, he could not help notice, was staring at him.

He had waited another ten minutes when the chauffeur reappeared, carrying a suitcase; with him was a middle-aged man, slightly balding, whom Walid Haddad recognised from photographs as the PLO representative in London. The driver put the case in the boot and opened the door for the delegate, thanked the policeman, put up his hand to the unmarked transit then pulled away.

No second man, thought Walid Haddad, no bodyguard. Only the driver. Careless, very careless. Not, he reflected, that it would have done any of them any good.

He moved after the Granada, not wanting to be either too close or too far back, remembering the points before the motorway at which he could become separated from his target. The traffic lights at the roundabout before the tunnel were green, the driver of the car in front of him was lost, the man's wife telling him what to do. The Granada was almost at the lights. Still green. He was getting too far back, tried to pull round the car in front, was cut off by an airport coach crowded with schoolchildren. The lights turned to red. He looked for the Granada, saw that it had also stopped, and breathed a sigh of relief.

The lights changed, he followed the cars down the slope and into the tunnel. The Granada was in the left-hand lane, not travelling as quickly as he had imagined it would; the airport coach was in the right-hand lane, pulling away. He drove out of the tunnel, turned right at the roundabout, and headed towards the M4. Nine miles, he began to think, nine miles in which he had to kill the PLO man and his chauffeur. It did not occur to him that they were Palestinians like himself. He passed the Trust House Forte Hotel on the left, drove round the roundabout beneath the motorway and turned back onto the M4 towards London. At the precise moment he did so he leaned forward and pressed the mileage counter. One mile, first bridge. The Granada picking up speed, the driver talking to his passenger. Not much traffic, even less traffic than before. The Granada pulled into the central lane and began accelerating. Two miles, A312 exit and second bridge. Never much time, he thought, almost a quarter the distance already gone.

In front he could see the airport bus, the one filled with children. Three miles, service station. The PLO driver was sticking to the speed limit, he suddenly thought, knowing he could not do it from behind, could not be caught in the traffic jam that would pile up behind the blast, knowing also that if he was too far in front he would not be able to check that the road round the Granada was clear. The airport bus moved into the inside lane, the Granada overtaking it. Slowly, he thought, too bloody slowly. *"Yallah,"* he urged the driver. "Move it, for the love of Allah, move it." Four miles, fourth bridge. How the distance was going down, he thought, the Granada pulling away from the coach. Half a mile, he thought, he would need half a mile between the coach and the car. Could do it with less, could overtake and do it now. Run the risk of killing the kids.

Kids had died before, would die again. He hung back, cursing the PLO driver. More cautious than he had assumed, how he wished the man would get a move on. Three hundred yards past the coach, the Granada accelerating. Four miles gone, another five to do it.

Plenty of time, he told himself, not believing it, beginning to accelerate, preparing to overtake the Granada. The coach six hundred yards behind. Two hundred yards. That was all he would need in front of the Granada. Closing fast.

The sirens blasted in his ear. Instinctively he slowed down, saw the white police BMW level with him, lights flashing. A setup, he thought, he had been set up. The detonator was only six inches from his left hand. Do it anyway, he thought, get the PLO man. The Granada driver had heard, was slowing down. Fool, Walid Haddad thought, he should be reacting, pulling his man out of trouble. Do it anyway, he thought again. Saw the coach. Alongside him. The children looking at him, waving at him. The Granada only twenty yards in front. Too close, he thought, not thinking about the police. Too close to the bloody kids.

Five miles, fifth bridge, only four miles to go. He told himself to calm down, looked across at the police car, ignoring him, ignoring the Granada, already pulling away. Six miles, three-lane motorway into two lanes. Late, he thought, almost too bloody late, the Granada beginning to accelerate again. Not quickly enough, he knew, the coach still too close. The cameras, one facing west, the other east. Never much time, he thought, almost no time at all.

The blind spot, the two hundred yards between the cameras. He pulled the wheel violently to the left, jerking the hire car across the inside lane, braking hard. Behind him the coach driver slammed on his brakes, the children tumbling forward. In his rear view mirror Walid Haddad saw the coach suddenly fill the entire frame. The Granada was pulling away, three hundred yards, almost four hundred. Bloody drivers, the coach driver was shouting at him, waving his fist. The Granada five hundred yards away, nearly six hundred. The children picking themselves up from the floor. Madman, the driver was gesticulating at him, bloody loony. He changed into third, accelerating, pulling away from the coach. Seven miles, onto the flyover, the office blocks on either side. The Granada was three hundred yards ahead, two hundred. The road in front and behind clear. Almost out of distance, he thought, almost out of everything. Eight miles, off the flyover and past the Granada. A hundred yards two hundred yards clear, closing on another group of cars. In his rear view mirror he could see the Granada clearly. There was no sign of the children's coach.

He reached across to the passenger's seat and unfolded the newspaper.

9

PAN AM FLIGHT NUMBER PA1 arrived at John F. Kennedy airport on time, taxied across the runway, and began disgorging its three hundred and fifty two passengers into the terminal building. Three hundred and fifty one of them were innocent citizens, the three hundred and fifty-second was Abu Nabil. By six thirty he had cleared immigration and customs, using the passport he had used in Paris and London, and taken a cab to the Plaza Hotel. He checked into his room, switched on the early evening news programme and made a single telephone call confirming his meeting for the following morning.

The third item on the news bulletin was the assassination in London of the PLO spokesman Hassan Nabulsi. The report showed video pictures of the remains of the man's Ford Granada motor car, on the M4 motorway near Heathrow Airport. He had just returned from a meeting with Yasser Arafat, the report continued, adding that unofficial sources had confirmed that the type of bomb used was believed to be identical to that used by the IRA in Northern Ireland. The reporter, standing at the side of the motorway, the wreckage of the car behind him, speculated that the assassination was the latest episode in the struggle for supremacy within the various factions of the Palestinian movement. More sinister, he suggested, his collar turned up against the biting wind and the first cutting flakes of sleet, was the possibility of a link-up between the IRA and one of the extremist Palestinian groups.

If Walid Haddad was to end it, Abu Nabil had thought to himself in Damascus, then Walid Haddad may as well start it. He flicked between the channels, catching the same report on CBS and NBC. Walid Haddad had now started it.

He showered, took a light supper of cold meats and salad, and went to bed.

He woke at four, a combination of the time difference between Damascus, London and New York, and the air conditioning, which he found oppressive, slept fitfully for another two hours and rose at six. He left the hotel and spent the next ninety minutes walking the streets. The weather was brisk and cold. On the corner of Times Square he bought copies of the *New York Times*, the *International Herald Tribune* and the *Wall Street Journal*.

He was getting hungry. In a delicatessen six blocks from the hotel he took lox and bagels, sitting in the seat farthest from the window. The service was friendly, he wondered for the briefest of moments what the *shabab*, the boys, would have thought, how the owners would have reacted, if they had known that he, Abu Nabil, planner of death, executioner of violence, survivor of at least three Israeli attempts on his life, was breakfasting in a Jewish deli in New York, served by a smiling Jewish waiter whom he called David and who, as he left, he would tip and who would tell him to have a good day. His battle, however, had never been personal. Besides, the lox was good and the second cup of coffee was free. And the place was warm and crowded. He thought, not for the first time that day, of the photograph he had again left in the emptiness of his flat in Damascus and turned to the newspapers.

The assassination in London featured on the front pages of both the *Times* and *Tribune* and the international page of the *Journal*. On the front page of the *Herald Tribune* there was also a photograph, taken two nights before, of the moment in Northern Ireland when a British soldier had saved the life of the son of a leading member of the IRA. The British government, the article said, had declined to comment on press speculation that the soldier concerned had been a member of the Special Air Service, the SAS.

The waiter refilled his cup. He drank it slowly then rose to leave, paying the bill and leaving a good tip. As he left the man he had called David told him to have a good day.

10

AT EIGHT THIRTY that morning, Paris time, the head of arms sales for the French government, General René Audran, was shot dead at his home outside Paris. An hour later, in a communiqué to the Paris and Rome offices of *Agence France Presse*, responsibility was claimed jointly by Action Directe and the Red Brigade. Forensic tests conducted within twenty four hours established that the weapon used appeared to match that used in the murder of a magistrate in Turin the preceding August.

Two hours later a West German industrialist, Hans Martin Schneider, was murdered when he answered the door to an attractive young woman claiming to be a friend of his daughter.

In the next forty-eight hours there were bombings in West Germany and Belgium; in West Germany the targets were the American companies of Litton, MAN and Honeywell in that order; in Belgium the targets were the American companies of Litton, MAN and Honeywell, also in that order. In all the attacks, it was suggested, the explosives came from the same source: 816 kilos of plastic explosives stolen at Ecoussines, in Belgium, six months before.

The campaign of violence which Abu Nabil and Issam Sharaf had planned in Damascus had begun.

11

ABU NABIL'S MEETING with the industrialist Ahmad Hussein was at ten; it was almost seven weeks since they had met on the *quai* at St Germaine-en-Laye, on the outskirts of Paris. He walked to Macy's, enjoying the Christmas decorations, and bought two gifts, one of them a chess set, asking for both to be wrapped, then took a cab to the block which housed the offices of the businessman. His host was waiting. He poured them coffee from a percolator in the corner and asked whether Nabil had breakfasted. Abu Nabil confirmed that he had without saying where.

The room was comfortable, well furnished, a Persian rug on the floor and three paintings of Jerusalem by Suleiman Mansour on the walls.

"A sad affair in London," Hussein suggested, handing Nabil a coffee.

"A sad affair indeed," confirmed Nabil.

For the next ten minutes they discussed the implications of the London assassination; when they had finished Ahmad Hussein unlocked the top right drawer of his desk and took a file from it.

"Business," he said.

"Business," Abu Nabil agreed.

"In January," the industrialist began, establishing the background, "Ronald Reagan will officially begin his second term as president of the United States. He will be seventy-four years old when he starts, seventy-eight at the end. For reasons of his age, and because he cannot, under the Constitution, hold office for a third term, many people believe the next four years will be what Americans like to call a lame-duck presidency." He paused. "In Paris, we agreed this would not be the case. In Paris, we agreed that, partly because of his own background, partly because it is what every president wants, Reagan will seek to do something that will allow him to go down in history. In Paris," he concluded, "we also agreed that the obvious area is foreign policy. Within this, we agreed, Central America was too controversial, too many comparisons with Vietnam. The obvious area, therefore, other than any agreement with the new Russian leadership, was the Middle East."

He moved the file to the centre of the desk.

"You wanted two names. Firstly, the name of the man who will be the president's foreign policy advisor in the foreseeable future, the man who would run his Middle East policy for him, who would do the negotiations. Secondly, you wanted the name of the person most likely to have influence with that man."

He opened the file. "As regards the first," he said, "there are three possibilities. The first, and luckily for us not the favourite, is pro-Israeli, strong connections with the Jewish Lobby here." Abu Nabil listened intently. "The second," continued Hussein, "would be a strong candidate, except that his wife is seriously ill. It may be that she recovers by the dates we are discussing, it may also be that she is no longer with us." His voice had dropped slightly. "In which case," he said, "the man in question might have both the time and motivation to do something."

"But?"

"But he would be preoccupied with his wife's illness during the lead-up to that period, during the time he would have to be convinced that he wanted the job and others persuaded that he was the man for it."

"And the third candidate?"

Ahmad Hussein pulled a photograph from the file and handed it to Abu Nabil. "Henry Armstrong is fifty-six years old. He was associated with Reagan, albeit at a distance, when the president was governor of California, he is also reported to have had links with George Bush when the vice president was head of the CIA."

"Does that go against us?"

Ahmad Hussein shook his head. "Henry Armstrong is a wealthy man, a prominent businessman, a success in his own right. Fortunately for us, he is also a very practical man. His companies have close connections with companies in the Middle East, Arab companies."

"How will you manage it?" asked Abu Nabil.

Ahmad Hussein looked up from his coffee. "I have already started," he smiled, knowing Nabil wanted to know more. "A little financial backing where necessary," he began to explain, "sometimes a long way from the target itself, even from the people who will have influence when it matters, but the people who will influence those people." He laughed. "Sometimes you don't even say he's a good man to have around, sometimes it's better to say he's a real bastard and the last man they should let anywhere near the Oval office." His eyes gleamed at the thought.

"So Henry Armstrong will be the next major foreign affairs negotiator for the United States of America?"

"Yes," said Ahmad Hussein.

Abu Nabil leaned forward and turned the photograph of Henry Armstrong face down on the desk. Not from disdain or disrespect, but from habit. "And who will be the catalyst?" he asked. "Who will be the man who will have his ear?"

Ahmad Hussein took a second sheet of paper from the file, attached to it was another photograph and a cutting from a newspaper.

"The Jacksonian Institute is a political think tank in Washington. It is highly respected, both nationally and internationally, with considerable justification. Henry Armstrong is a regular contributor to its foreign affairs seminars, he is also a major benefactor of the institute.'' He smiled again. ''Most things in America are, of course, tax deductible.''

''That aside,'' he was serious, ''the institute plays an important role in Armstrong's life. It is one of the reasons he must be considered in line for a top post in government.'' Abu Nabil heard the words and knew that Armstrong was the man he wanted, wondering whether Ahmad Hussein's second choice would be as good as his first. ''Each year,'' continued the industrialist, ''the institute hosts a number of international forums to which guest speakers from various parts of the world are invited. Several years ago Armstrong himself chaired a seminar on strategic politics at which one of the guest speakers was this man.'' He unclipped the photograph from the sheet of paper in front of him and passed it to Nabil. The man in it was in his late thirties, good looking, immaculately groomed. ''The speaker was a British Member of Parliament, one of the up and coming breed who seem set to control things in the future. Armstrong was so impressed that he invited him back. They are now close friends.''

''How important was he?''

''He wasn't important then, he is important now, he will be extremely important in the future.'' He passed Nabil the sheet of paper with the newspaper cutting fastened to it.

Nabil took it. ''What do you mean?'' he asked.

Ahmad Hussein looked at him. ''John Kenshaw-Taylor entered the British Parliament in a bye-election in 1978 after a successful career in the City. Like others of his kind, it was important to him that he was seen to make his first million by the time he was thirty. Politics, in any case, was always a strong possibility for him; his family has had its hands on British foreign affairs for most of the past half-century, probably well before that. Since 1978 his rise has been spectacular. Two years ago he was made Minister of Energy.''

Abu Nabil knew there was more.

''Eight weeks ago,'' said Ahmad Hussein, ''he was promoted to Number Two at the British Foreign Office. The day he moved, the London *Times* said it was merely one more step to his becoming prime minister.''

Abu Nabil looked at the dates on the newspaper cutting Ahmad Hussein had given him. The day, he thought, that he had seen the article which had planted the first seed of the plan in his mind, the day he had played *tawli* with the old man in the café. The day, he did not know, that Yakov Zubko and his family had left Moscow and begun their journey to the West. The day when an IRA leader had informed on his movement. The day a doctor in a Palestinian refugee camp in the Lebanon had diagnosed cancer in the throat and chest of an old man.

"How can we get at him?" he asked simply.

"He's ambitious," Ahmad Hussein replied, equally succinctly.

The meeting finished at twelve. At twelve thirty Mudrun drove them to a Lebanese restaurant where they ate a quiet and discreet lunch. When they parted, Abu Nabil gave him the gifts he had bought for his children; that night Ahmad Hussein gave them to his son and daughter; when they asked who they were from, he told them they were from an uncle who loved them very much but whom they had never met. His wife knew not to ask.

At four thirty that afternoon Abu Nabil made a single international telephone call, checked out of the Plaza Hotel, took a cab to John F. Kennedy, and caught the six forty-five TWA flight to Rome.

CHAPTER FOUR

1

THE SHERRY was manzanilla. He had a standing order for it from Green's in the City and kept it chilled in a walnut cabinet in the corner of his office.

"If this is how a bad day ends, Minister, how do we end a good one?" The civil servant's question was only half a joke. For the first time since he had taken office the Foreign Minister had sent back a briefing with a request that it should contain more information.

John Kenshaw-Taylor sat down on the edge of his desk. "Edward," the Under-Secretary was his senior by at least fifteen years, "you know I will always take your advice, as long as you make me think it was my idea in the first place."

The man called Edward smiled. "Precisely, Minister."

The exchange had cleared the air, they settled back into the chesterfields and relaxed.

It was the way John Kenshaw-Taylor had always anticipated ending each day at the Foreign Office, a quality he considered the other newer members of the government lacked, a style, in addition to his ability to digest a brief and reproduce it with maximum impact in the House or in Cabinet committee, that had already marked him out in the minds of the Whitehall mandarins as the man to watch, the one who would get to the top.

The lighting in the room on the third floor overlooking Horse Guards Parade was subdued, in the semi-gloom he could see the outlines of the mementoes he had brought with him from the sanitised corridors of the Department of Energy. None of them referred to himself, at least not directly. On the left of the antique clock on the wall facing his desk was a portrait of his grandfather, below it a letter signed personally by George V. On the wall to the left of the desk, an original newspaper report of the Balfour Declaration, to which the same grandfather had been an advisor, in the gloom to the right a black and white photograph of his father standing behind the seated figures of Churchill, Roosevelt and Stalin at Yalta in 1945.

John Kenshaw-Taylor had dreamt of the Foreign Office, had savoured its charisma and its power, ever since his father had brought him there when he was eight years old. He had taken it with him when he returned to his prep school that evening, held on to it through Eton and Oxford, even during his days in the City, when his natural instincts, as well as his undoubted connections, had amassed him a considerable personal wealth. He remembered the decision to enter politics, the bye-election, his first ministerial post, remembered above all the evening a few short weeks ago, the telephone call inviting him to see the Prime Minister at Number Ten, the suggestion that he should leave Energy and take over as Number Two at the Foreign Office. He sipped the manzanilla and looked at the winter sky gathering outside the window. What a way to start Christmas, he thought, recalling his first day in the building itself, the portraits, their oils glinting in the strange light which seemed to stalk the corridors, the images of the men who had directed the nation's course and its relationship with the rest of the world, the men who had led the nation itself.

"Thank you, Minister." The Under-Secretary rose to leave, placing his glass on the silver tray on the side. "Perhaps it has been a good day after all." He meant it. For forty years, the British Foreign Office had presided over the dissolution of an empire; after the Falklands Campaign, it had been said by some, even the Prime Minister had seen fit to question what remained of its role on the world stage. The new minister, the civil servant felt, was not long for the Number Two job, and when he was at the top, things would change. An old wind blowing through the corridors, someone had remarked. "Thank you, Minister," he said again.

John Kenshaw-Taylor watched the man leave, staring for a few moments out of the window, looking through the darkness toward Buckingham Palace, then turned back to his desk. John Kenshaw-Taylor's mind was the epitome of clarity and logic. He took pride not only in organising to the last degree whatever he was doing, but in sticking to it, whether in the day-to-day management of his personal affairs, or the advancement of his political career.

It was seven fifteen. He picked up the telephone and dialled his home in the country; the phone rang for thirty seconds before his wife answered. "Samantha, darling, it's me." They talked for ten minutes about what she had done that day, what he had done. That evening, because of his commitments in London, she was due to open the Christmas fayre at the village hall in his stead; tomorrow, she reminded him, the children would be home from school. He assured her he would be back by the following afternoon, and that he was looking forward to Christmas. She said she was already late and would have to go. "OK, darling. Love you. Bye."

He put the phone down and turned his attention to the despatch boxes. Three to get through. He already knew what they contained, worked out his timetable for the evening. One hour on the first box, the reception he had to attend for fifty minutes, a couple of hours in the flat to finish off the other two. Thank God, he thought, he wasn't still at Energy, the midnight meetings about the miners' strike, the problems about the instability of North Sea oil prices. The move had come just at the right time, and to the right department, kept him away from the law and order problems at the Home Office and the financial worries at the Exchequer.

He was in an enviable position, he knew, not just because he was in the Foreign Office, but because of his position within it, aware that he would look back on these days with just a tinge of nostalgia. His hands were on the first trappings of power, real power, but he was still far enough from that power not to be encumbered with its disadvantages. He could still take his wife to dinner, could still go Christmas shopping with the children without the armed bodyguards who were always just a pace away from his senior colleagues. He could ask his driver to wait for him, or he could tell the man to drop the despatch boxes at his flat and make his own way home.

He shut his mind off and opened the first box.

At eight thirty, precisely according to the schedule he had mapped out earlier, he finished the box. At eight forty-five his driver dropped him at the reception and continued to Pimlico where he left the two remaining boxes at the minister's London flat.

John Kenshaw-Taylor stayed at the reception until twenty minutes to ten. Pimlico is five minutes from Westminster by car, fifteen by foot. When the Foreign Minister arrived at the flat it was eleven thirty.

THE TEMPERATURE IN ROME was minus three and falling; it was also wet, the blanket of rain sweeping across the runway, sounding like the roll of kettle drums as it cascaded off the metal roof of the terminal building.

The TWA jumbo was thirty minutes late, delayed by an air traffic control dispute. Abu Nabil hurried through immigration and customs, showered, shaved and changed his clothes in the gents toilet, made a telephone call to the hotel in the city centre explaining that he had been delayed, and was asked to attend as quickly as he could. On the cab rank outside he picked up a taxi, told the driver there was an extra tip for him if he could get to the city centre in record time, and settled back into his seat. The traffic was heavy, he did not feel it was the best preparation for the meeting ahead.

He arrived at the hotel thirty-five minutes later, tipped the driver well, and was shown immediately to the suite on the fifth floor. Sheikh Saeed Khaled was waiting. Nabil apologised for being late, Khaled in turn apologised that he had little time to spare that day and had to leave the hotel for an appointment in thirty minutes. Breakfast arrived two minutes later.

Whilst Khaled poured them both coffee they discussed the outline of their London meeting, concentrating on the sheikh's suggestion that Nabil needed what they had called a friend, as well as the friend who would influence that friend.

"That is why I have come to see you again," Abu Nabil brought the conversation into focus.

"You mean you have found the friend you were looking for?"

"Possibly."

"Who?" asked Saeed Khaled. Both men knew they had little time.

"I am told that Henry Armstrong will be the next major United States Foreign Affairs negotiator and that he has a special interest in the Middle East."

Khaled smiled, nodding his head. "I wonder who told you that." He drew his hands together and rested his chin on them. "You're probably right. Henry Armstrong has the right connections, the right ambitions. Who will influence him on your behalf?"

"The British Foreign Minister, John Kenshaw-Taylor."

The choice did not appear to surprise Khaled. Nabil began listing the details contained in the brief Ahmad Hussein had given him in New York, but Khaled interrupted. "I know him. We met during the oil discussions before he was moved to the Foreign Office. How are they connected?"

Abu Nabil explained the Jacksonian Institute link.

"There is one thing about John Kenshaw-Taylor," Saeed Khaled said slowly and carefully, "that you should know." Nabil noted that the sheikh still had not passed comment on his choice and feared he was preparing the ground for a rejection. "One thing," continued the sheik, "that might make him an ideal target, but which might also prejudice you against him."

"What is it?"

"Think of the betrayal of your country," Khaled instructed him. "Think when the betrayal started."

It was ironic, Abu Nabil had already thought, and probably inevitable, that the man he had chosen to help his people return to their homeland should be the Foreign Minister of the imperial power which had played such a role in their original exodus from it.

"Most people would say the United Nations decision of 1947," he began. "They would be wrong. It actually began in 1917. The Balfour Declaration. The first open support by the British for the idea of a separate Jewish state."

Khaled looked at him again. "John Kenshaw-Taylor has a very long political pedigree. His father was in politics, his father before him."

"I knew he came from a political family."

"Did you know his grandfather was a senior advisor to Balfour?"

"No," said Abu Nabil, "I did not."

He sat silently, remembering the terms of the support, remembering the way his father had taught him to despise what the Declaration had done to his country and people.

"Why did you choose him?" asked Khaled.

"Because he is ambitious."

"Some who know him would say he is too ambitious for his own good," said the power broker. "He is a good choice."

Abu Nabil sensed his relief. "What else is there to know of him?" He did not know what answer he expected, only knew that he had not expected the answer he received.

"I don't know," said Khaled, sitting back, remembering the first time he had met Kenshaw-Taylor, the many times they had observed each other prior to negotiations, the informal conversations in the receptions after. Something about the man, he thought, something they might be able to use. "I don't know," he repeated, "but I will find out."

3

THE COLOURED LIGHTS were shining brightly, even though it was only four in the afternoon, the pavements were crowded. Enderson could smell the roast chestnuts on the corner of the street. It was, he could not help thinking, as Christmas Eve used to be, as it should be.

The children were tugging at his sleeve, forgetting that his left arm was in a sling. It still hurt, where it had been burned and torn, where the surgeon at the Queen Elizabeth Military Hospital in Woolwich had pulled it together and informed him that it was to be checked every month until it was healed. Jane was in front of him, struggling under the weight of the turkey. In his one good hand he carried a bag of food and wine.

"Dad," said his children, "come on, Dad, you know what, Dad." His wife pretended not to hear. "Look, love," he suggested, "you'll want to get the turkey started. Why don't you go home and the kids and I will finish here." His wife smiled. "OK, but don't be late." She watched as Enderson and the children turned back down the pavement and headed for Chadds. "Great, Dad, great," she heard the boy say. "About time," said the girl.

The ground floor of the department store was crowded: he followed the children, protecting his arm. Two weeks in a sling, he had been told, then a plaster. It would not affect his work, the surgeon had said, as long as he took it carefully, as long as he came back for the monthly checks. They reached the perfume counter, he watched as the children worked out the prices, how much they could afford, then bought their mother her Christmas presents. "You want them wrapped here or shall we do it when we get home?" He already knew the answer. "When we get home, Dad." It was his first Christmas with them for three years.

By the time they left the store it was four thirty. "Can we have a Wimpy, Dad?" He knew it was a conspiracy against which he could not win. "OK," he conceded, "you can have a Wimpy." On the way they passed a news-stand, he bought a copy of the *Evening News*, tucked it under his arm, and followed the children.

The Wimpy bar was quieter than he would have thought; they sat at a table near the window: the children ordered burgers and coke, he asked for a tea and began to browse through the paper. At the third table to their left, his back against the wall, was a tramp, he had just finished a plate of chips and was eking out his cup of tea. The music in the bar was seasonal. Enderson remembered when he had last sat in a Wimpy bar, what the music had been then, was glad that the food arrived. The tune changed, he recognised the words. On the table to his left the tramp had finished his tea; in the corner of his eye Enderson saw the waitress approach the man, assuming, he did not know why, that she was going to ask him to leave. She reached across the table and gave him another cup of tea. In the loudspeaker in the ceiling he heard the words of the tune.

"They said there'd be snow at Christmas,
They said there'd be peace on earth."

He looked out the window at the sky. No snow, he thought, remembering the boy in Belfast, the bombings and killings in Europe, the assassination on the motorway near Heathrow, not much peace on earth either.

He turned to the foreign page of the newspaper. In the right-hand column was an item from the Reuter's office in Bonn which a desperate sub-editor had used to fill up space. The piece was headed "Christmas terror alert in Germany". The West German terrorist leader Klars Christian Mannheim, it said, convicted on three bombing charges, had announced that from the New Year he would go on hunger strike in support of demands for greater civil liberties in the country's prisons.

On the table to his left the tramp was warming his fingers round the cup of tea. "Look, Dad, look." His son was pulling at his coat, drawing his attention to a woman in the street outside, trying to push a Christmas tree into the boot of her car. He began to laugh. "Can we have another drink, Dad?" The woman closed the door, cutting off the top of the tree. He called the waitress.

"Two more cokes, please."

She saw what they were laughing at, saw that the tramp had also seen. "Why not?" she began laughing with them. "After all, it's Christmas."

Enderson thought of the newspaper article, the man who would begin to die in the New Year. "Why not," he smiled back. "It's Christmas."

4

JOHN KENSHAW-TAYLOR sat back in his chair and sipped the malt whiskey. He had been shooting since seven and polished off the despatch boxes after lunch. The house was quiet, the children would not be back from the party till six. In the kitchen, the nanny was preparing tea, at the table behind him his wife was wrapping presents. "These killings in Europe," she suddenly asked. "This man who said he will go on hunger strike. It won't affect you, will it?"

John Kenshaw-Taylor sat forward, threw a log on the fire, and poured himself another drink. "Shouldn't think so, darling," he said confidently.

5

THE NIGHT AIR WAS WARM, much warmer than Yakov Zubko had ever expected in Moscow. He stood in the window and breathed it in. It was going well, he thought, better than they could ever have hoped; he had found a job, not as good a job as others with his qualifications would have expected, but a job. They had even been promised a house.

He walked through to the children's room, opening the door quietly so that he did not wake them, and looked at them, hearing the sound of their breathing. In the kitchen Alexandra heard the singing from the street below. That afternoon they had been shopping; there had not been enough money and they had bought nothing for themselves, just a present each for the children to show to the friends they had made. It did not worry her.

She left the kitchen and walked into the corridor, saw her husband looking into the children's room, saw that he was oblivious of her. He was a good man, she thought, remembered, for the first time since they had arrived in Israel, how he had worked for them, stolen for them, how he had got the money for their tickets to Vienna. Remembered her reaction when he had told her about the unmarked car at the top of Dmitrov, about the quiet voice that had told him to run for them all.

Slowly, quietly, she crept forward, slid her arm through his, and kissed him.

BOOK
THREE

CHAPTER ONE

1

AT HALF PAST SEVEN on the morning of Friday, January 4th, Klars Christian Mannheim began to die.

He had woken at five, alert and fresh. The depth and soundness of his sleep that night had not surprised him. The sleepless nights had been before, when he was in doubt, when he was still turning the decision over and over in his mind. The night before, however, he had gone to bed knowing the only issue which remained was the execution of that decision.

Execution had never disturbed Klars Christian Mannheim.

From five until seven thirty he had sat on his bed, enjoying the silence. It was strange, he thought: for three years now he had hated the silence, hated those who had imposed it upon him. Now it was a strength, now it was the authorities who waited. Ever since he had made his announcement on Christmas Eve. And each day he did not start, each day he took food, they relaxed a little, breathed a little more easily, convinced themselves a little more that he lacked the resolve to die for his cause.

They were wrong.

Klars Christian Mannheim was a man of precision. The date of the commencement of his hunger strike, therefore, was not a matter of chance but of calculation.

He was twenty-eight years old and weighed sixty-eight kilos. On a diet of water, he had worked out, he would lose approximately ten kilos in the first twenty days, most of which would consist of water contained naturally within the body. After that the rate of weight loss would slow as the body used up its supply of fat before the crucial phase when it was forced to draw on its own tissue, first the muscles of his arms and legs, then of his heart, and finally the muscles of his chest. At this stage, he knew, his breathing would begin to be affected.

Klars Christian Mannheim also believed in self-determination, man's ability to control his own life and, in his case, his own death. Others, he knew, would calculate the number of days he would take to die, as he himself had calculated the figure, and would build into it a margin of error.

He himself had rejected this. He had calculated the number of days it would take, and determined that he would sustain his hold on life for that period precisely, no more or no less.

He would die exactly twenty nine years after his mother had brought him into the world.

The door opened and the warder brought in his breakfast. Klars Christian Mannheim did not bother to look up or to thank the man; the guards were, in any case, under strict instructions not to talk to their high-security wards, to avoid all forms of communication, even eye contact. When the man collected the tray twenty minutes later only the water had been consumed.

At nine thirty that morning the lawyer representing Klars Christian Mannheim issued a press statement on behalf of his client, spelling out a list of demands and stating that, unless they were met, his client had that morning begun a fast to death.

One hour later, a bomb exploded beneath the perimeter fence of the NATO military school in Oberammergau. At precisely the same time a second bomb exploded outside the NATO headquarters in Brussels. Damage in both cases was minimal: what attracted the attention of the press, however, was that in both cases investigations showed that the bombs had been planted the night before. And in both cases the communiqués claiming responsibility were signed by a group bearing a name which was new to international terrorism: the Commando of the Martyr Klars Christian Mannheim.

2

THE FIRST FROSTS of winter were settling in the courtyard below the window. In the training camps where he had spent the past days, in the mountains where the camps were hidden, the snow had been on the ground for two weeks. Now Damascus would feel its bite.

It had started, he thought, just like the snow, slowly and inevitably: the military campaign, the two men he hoped to ensnare in the tangle of Middle East politics, the first assassi-

nation in London, the sustained, deliberate build-up through
Europe, the clues and connections for the authorities to spot,
to feed to the press, for the press to tell the people, for the people to begin to worry, to put pressure on the authorities, for the
authorities in turn to feel the tightening of the screw. Then the
hunger strike. And now the beginning of the next stage, the last
link in the chain.

He wondered how he should tell Walid Haddad, how he
would explain the job, the possibility that Walid Haddad would
not necessarily return from it. He did not know it then, would
not know it for days, even weeks, but he would remember the
moment, remember it the next time he stood at the window and
wondered how he should tell Walid Haddad.

He heard the knock on the door and turned back into the
room as Issam Sharaf entered with the man he had sent to
London, welcoming them both, offering them chairs and a
coffee, both men sitting down, accepting.

Walid Haddad waited, feeling the liquid warm him, and
wondered why he had been summoned.

"A good job in London," said Abu Nabil.

They had already discussed it. Walid Haddad wondered
again why he had been summoned, knew why he was always
summoned. "It was as you said. Little security, he was wide
open." He shook his head, remembering the final security
lapses on the part of the driver, not mentioning the minutes on
the motorway from the airport.

"There's another job."

There was always another job, Walid Haddad thought.

"It's important," continued Abu Nabil, "very important."
He chose his words carefully, meaning what he was about to
say. "In a way, it's the most important job we have ever done."
He looked at Walid Haddad. "I would like you to take charge
of it."

Walid Haddad knew they expected his first reaction would
be to ask what the job was. "Where is it?" he asked.

"It depends. Partly your choice. Probably, almost certainly, Europe."

"How dangerous?"

"Very dangerous."

The first suspicion of what it was crossed his mind. "Who
else will be involved?"

Abu Nabil gave him the part of the answer that concerned him. "Your decision. A team job. I imagine you will decide yourself plus three or four others."

The suspicion was growing, taking shape. "What conditions?"

"On the team you choose? Only one condition, one of the team must be a West German."

"Why a West German?"

"Because we will be making demands of the West German government."

He knew what it was. "When?" he asked.

"Ten weeks, possibly eleven."

The hunger strike, Walid Haddad thought, the hunger strike that had started that morning, knew for certain what the job was.

"What is it?" he asked at last.

"A hijack," said Abu Nabil.

3

THE FIRST SNOWS of the year had settled on the sides of the hills surrounding the city, laying its blanket over the valleys and moorlands where they had their secret places. The ground was already hard with frost, the cold in the air took his breath away. He wondered what it would be like in the Brecons, in the disused quarries and the forgotten valleys where he and his men would practise their craft.

He left home at seven thirty and began the ten minute drive to the barracks on the southern side of the city. It was his first day on duty since he had returned from Northern Ireland, it was also the first day for as long as he could remember that he would return home when he came off duty that night. He turned out of the road and began the drop into the city. Jane and the children were still on Christmas holidays, they had booked seats for the pantomime that evening. The traffic was light, he crossed the bridge over the river, turned right at the post office and began the drive along the edge of the barracks, the wire of the outer fence glistening in the cold of the sun. The man at the main gate looked into the car as he stopped. He knew what was going to happen.

"It's the bloody pin-up boy," the man joked. "Can I have your autograph?"

"Sod off," Enderson told him.

The barrier lifted and he drove through.

THE KEY NUMBER in the organisation of the Special Air Service, ever since its inception by David Stirling in the deserts of North Africa in 1941, is the number four. The regiment is divided into four active service squadrons named Sabre squadrons. Each squadron is, in turn, divided into four troops; each troop in turn, is divided into four patrols; each patrol is made up of four men. Each Sabre squadron is an entity in itself; there are, therefore, in principle at least, a minimum of four tours of duty in which the SAS may be engaged at any one time. Three of those are normally overseas, and in recent years the fourth has been British-based. It is the anti-terrorist duty. Other circumstances permitting, each squadron takes that duty in turn, with the in-built precaution of an over-lap period during which the outgoing squadron remains in place while the incoming squadron begins its training and familiarises itself with the places and locations in which it might be called upon to operate.

That morning Graham Enderson's squadron went on anti-terrorist duty.

4

WALID HADDAD sat in the darkness, the windows and doors closed, his shoulders hunched and his hands clasped tight in front of him.

Leish ya'Allah a hijack? Why in the name of Allah a hijack?

The thought crossed and re-crossed his mind. He moved his legs slightly, easing the pressure on them, and pushed himself even deeper into the chair. He had been like this, locked into himself, for the past four hours, even since he had returned from the briefing with Abu Nabil.

The concentration was consuming him. He eased himself forward, searched for the small lamp on the floor at the side of the chair, switched it on, and made himself coffee.

There *were* hijacks, of course, often bloody, always spectacular, and there were groups who would carry them out. But
they were the small groups, the fringe groups, who believed in
violence for its own sake, not as a means to an end. He sat
down again, leaving the light on, placing the cup on the arm of
the chair. Hijacks were no good if they made you enemies, if
they lost you friends. Abu Nabil had long seen that, used it as
a criterion against which to judge every action on which he sent
his men, quoted it when he had vetoed the many ideas that were
placed in front of him.

So why a hijack? he thought again.

It was getting cold. He stood up, pulled on a sweater, and
slumped back into the chair, pushing the reasons for the hijack to the back of his mind, turning his attention to the logis-
tics, concentrating on the two basic requirements that were
within his responsibility: how the hijack would take place, and
where.

The two could not be separated, he was aware, separating
them anyway, studying each in turn, beginning with the second.

Europe, Abu Nabil had said, almost certainly Europe. Definitely Europe, Walid Haddad thought, if a West German was
to be in his team, if the West German government was to be the
target of their demands. All the big hijacks of the past had
started in Europe, he remembered. It was good for the public-
ity, the ease with which the television people could get their
pictures out, the images without which the hijack would have
no impact. Bad for everything else, he also remembered, especially the security. With the exception of Athens, most airports in Europe were tight, not water-tight, but tight. He
wondered if he could turn the fact to his advantage, and began
to reflect on what, in his mind, he already thought of as the
Dubai factor, knowing that he would return to it, switching his
attention to the other requirement.

Getting his team on the plane would be simple, they would
have no difficulty posing as ordinary passengers, using false
identities and passports. The problem was how to get their
weapons and explosives on with them. Not just pistols, he
thought, not just inflight perfumes and spirits splashed round
the cabin in the hope they would ignite. The weapons and explosives had to be good, the best. Not only that, they would
have to be seen to be the best.

There was no sense, he had already decided, in hoping he could pick up additional materials half way through, stop for refuelling in, say, Libya and trust that Gadafy would supply him with what he needed. Gadafy aside, it was too obvious, with too many political as well as military complications. It had also been done before, it was one of the things they would expect, and the only way the hijack would succeed, he admitted, the only way he would get through it, was if he always did what they did not expect.

Not *always*, the thought came into his mind, it was not correct that he should *always* do what they did not expect. Sometimes he would do what they expected. Or would appear to do what they expected. He thought again about what in his mind he referred to as the Dubai factor and began to analyse why he had always thought it was important, how he had always known that one day he would use it.

In December 1984 a group of Shi'ite Moslems had hijacked an airbus of Kuwaiti Airlines en route from Dubai to Karachi and diverted it to Teheran. The hijack had ended six days later when they were overpowered by the Ayatollah's security police dressed as doctors and mechanics. What had attracted his attention, however, was not the way it had ended, despite the fact that it had previously been assumed the Khomeini supported both the hijackers and their cause, nor even the period of waiting in the middle, but the day on which and the circumstances under which the hijackers had boarded the aircraft. It was that which had established itself in his mind as the Dubai factor.

He rose from the chair and made himself a fresh coffee, wondering how he could use it, if they had also seen it, wondering if they would see how he was using it. It was interesting, he was thinking, that he was not just considering those against whom he was being sent, but also those who would be sent with him. He knew they would see it, that it was their job to see it, and began to calculate how he could use that fact against them.

It was one in the morning when he left the room and went to bed. The last image which passed across his mind before he fell asleep was the driver from Heathrow, the coachload of children covering the Granada, the bomb attached to the fuel tank of the car, the transmitter which would activate it wrapped in the newspaper on the seat beside him.

And the face, he did not know why he should remember it, the face of the man in the photograph on the front page of the newspaper.

5

THE BRIEFING BEGAN at eleven, and the equipment was issued at twelve. While on the anti-terrorist duty, as well as the two-week period when the squadron which would take over from his were being trained up, Enderson would be on twenty-four-hour call. His equipment, the assault suit, the gas-mask with the built-in radio, the Heckler and Koch MP5K sub-machine gun, his small arms, the stream lights and stun grenades, as well as his body armour, would be kept in place in the special rooms in the center of the barracks at Hereford. When the units were on red alert, he and his men would sit in the rooms fully geared; when he went home each evening, and when he came to work each day, he would carry with him a small hold-all with his personal items in it, as well as a Browning hand gun. He would also take with him wherever he went a bleeper, starting with the pantomime that night.

By five o'clock it was dark, Enderson left the barracks and drove home. The house was warm and bright, the Christmas decorations still in place, the tea on the kitchen table.

"What's that?" his wife asked, looking at the hold-all.

"Something from work," he replied vaguely. "Where are the kids?"

"Getting ready."

He went upstairs, locked the hold-all in the wardrobe at the foot of the bed, and changed.

The pantomime that evening was "The Gingerbread Man", the theatre was crowded; Jane did not query why he took the bleeper with him, nor did she ask again about the hold-all, assuming she would become accustomed to it. She did, however, object when the bleeper was checked at six o'clock the next morning, waking her up, groaning as Enderson told her it was routine.

"Every morning at six?" she asked incredulously.

"Every morning at six," he confirmed.

JOHN KENSHAW-TAYLOR selected a log from the wrought-iron basket inside the inglenook and placed it on the fire. The lounge was warm; he loved the smell and sound of wood burning, the sparkle of lights from the chandelier in the centre of the ceiling. On the oak beam which spanned the massive fireplace stood a glass of his favourite malt. Christmas, he thought, had been good, very good, made even better, he could not help admitting to himself, by the rumours of despondency which had filtered through from the other ministries, worries at Central Office about the fall in popularity ratings, and concern at the Exchequer about the gradual but persistent fall in the value of sterling, the acrimonious sessions in his own previous department about his successor's failure to find the means to a settlement of the oil dispute which was increasingly being seen as the major underlying cause of the weakness of the pound. In two days' time the new Energy Minister would fly to Zurich for the latest round of oil negotiations. It would not, John Kenshaw-Taylor felt, be a successful trip. As a member of Her Majesty's government, he reflected, reaching for the malt, he could take no pleasure in such a failure by a fellow member of government, especially one who, like him, had been short-listed as a potential leader of the party within the next decade.

The door opened and his wife came into the room. He stood up, told her how lovely she looked, and poured her a sherry. "Thanks for a really lovely Christmas, darling," he said. "I've really enjoyed it." They stood looking at the fire. "Pity it has to end," he added. "Pity I have to be away for a few nights."

The first guests arrived five minutes early, the last a mere ten minutes late. The people he and Samantha had invited were those whose company he enjoyed, a merchant banker, a barrister, a shooting partner, rather than those, like the chairman of the local Conservative Association, whom he felt compelled to entertain regularly in order to protect his constituency base. They were, however, not without influence, both inside and outside the party.

The dinner, he insisted, was simple and straightforward, though he did concede that it had been tastefully prepared and presented, joining his guests' demands that cook should leave the kitchen to receive the accolades personally. Thinly-sliced raw salmon, marinated briefly in a mix of fresh lime juice, crushed coriander seed and olive oil from a recipe he had picked up in a little *auberge* he knew in the South of France, with a *Riesling Clos Ste. Hune* 1976 vintage. Pheasant Souvaroff, the game shot by himself and hung for two days and no more (Kenshaw-Taylor did not stand on the custom of hanging a bird till the flesh was falling from its bones), with a purée of celeri-ac, a mélange of carrots and leeks, and almond potatoes, plus a 1978 vintage *Chateau Rayas*. And tartlet with kiwi fruit and raspberry sauce, accompanied by a *Schloss Vollrads Trocken-beerenauslese* by Graf Matushka-Greiffenclau, whom, he happened to mention, he had met at Claridges in the autumn. When they had finished he suggested they try a Stilton he had bought for Christmas but which he judged had not come right in time, ignoring their protests when he fetched a 1960 *Quinta do Noval* from the cellar.

The party finished at one. They told cook she could do the washing up in the morning and went to bed.

"You know, darling," his wife said as they went to sleep. "I have a feeling this is going to be your year."

7

Two MONTHS after they arrived in Israel, Yakov Zubko and his family were given their new home. It wasn't big, the social worker from the Jewish Agency told them when she called them to her office, and it wasn't in the city, yet she believed them when they told her it didn't matter, that at least it was home.

The following weekend Yakov Zubko took his family to see it. They rose at five, Yakov making breakfast and tidying the flat while Alexandra packed them sandwiches as she had done the day they began their journey out of Russia. The social worker had suggested she come with them but had not been surprised when they declined her offer. We, the family Zubko, managed to leave Russia, they told her and we, the family Zubko, can find our own way to our home.

They caught the bus before the sun was up, leaving the city and travelling east, the morning still cool, passing through Ramla and Jerusalem before turning south toward Hebron. They had been out of Tel Aviv before, had knelt at the Wailing

Wall and stood in silence at Yad Vashem; but today was different. When she did not have to hold her daughter, Alexandra squeezed Yakov's hand.

The main street of Beita was long and winding, climbing gently up a hill, then falling away on the other side. At the foot of the hill was a field, opposite it an orange grove; in the middle of the hill the street broadened into a square. It was almost mid-day when the bus stopped and they stepped down, the men and women watching them from the wall of the well in the centre of the square. It was poor, thought Alexandra, even after all the money that had been poured into Israel, it was still so poor.

The house was half way up the street, on the right, fifty yards from the well. They waited at the door while Yakov Zubko felt in his pocket and produced the key. She did not know it, but he had held it tight in his hand since they left the flat in Tel Aviv that morning. The women at the well were still watching. He slid the key in the lock, turned it gently, and pushed the door open. The smell inside was musty, the floor was covered by a thin layer of dust. Small, he thought, it was so small: two rooms upstairs, two down. Smaller than the Jewish Agency flat in Tel Aviv, smaller, almost, than the flat in Moscow. He looked round, feeling the disappointment, wondering suddenly whether it had been worth it, what they should do. Then he stood aside and let Alexandra past, looking at her face, wondering what she would feel, how he could console her, what he could say to her.

"It's so big, Yakov Zubko," she turned to him. "So very big, I can't believe it. It's wonderful." She pulled the shutters back, letting in the light. "We can make curtains, put a chair here for you, one there for me, a bench for the children. I can put flowers on the table."

Yakov Zubko was singing, dancing, whirling round the room, the dust rising in clouds from his feet, Alexandra was looking in amazement, then joining in, singing with him. He came round the room, took her by the waist and began the *hora*. The children were watching, he picked up his daughter, gave her to Alexandra, picked up his son, held him in his arms, danced with him. The children knew the words, began singing with them.

In the street outside, the neighbours heard and smiled.

Two weeks later they moved in. The neighbours saw them get off the bus and begin the walk up the road, the one suitcase between them. As they left the square one of the men stepped down the street, and met them. "Welcome, the family Zubko," he said, shaking each by the hand. "Welcome to Beita." He took the case and walked up the street with them, the others crowding round. At the door they stopped while Yakov Zubko found the key and gave it to Alexandra. They waited, standing back, watching to see how she would react. She opened the door. The house was bright and clean; in the kitchen were a table and four chairs, in the small room to the side there was a carpet on the floor, in the rooms upstairs were beds and cupboards. Alexandra did not know how to thank them and they did not expect her to.

The following morning Alexandra took their son to the small schoolhouse at the side of the square in the centre of the village. The same day Yakov Zubko started work as a fitter at an engineering workshop on the other side of the hill. Each morning after that he walked to work as he had walked to the metro in Moscow, each lunchtime and evening he walked home. The difference was that, for the first time in seven years, he did not have to lie and cheat and steal for Alexandra and the children. Each day the neighbours watched, how Alexandra settled in, how Yakov worked. Some émigrés, they knew, expected too much, demanded too many things: Alexandra and Yakov Zubko did neither. Three weeks later, when Alexandra announced that she was with child, they organised a *mesiba* on her behalf. It fell to their son to point out that he and his new brother or sister would share a birthplace. At first they did not understand. It was only then that he reminded them where they lived, of the secret name they had given to the labour ward in the maternity hospital in Moscow where he had been born, the name of the place less than six kilometres away. It was not the exact spot where they lived, he admitted, nor even the place where his brother or sister would really be born, but, he insisted, it was close enough. The town of Bethlehem.

The only thing missing in their lives, the only thing which caused them sorrow, a great and unending sorrow, was that their beloved brother Stanislav and his wife and children were still in Russia.

8

THE LIGHT IN THE CELL was on. The light in the cell was always on. Klars Christian Mannheim lay on the bed in the corner and ignored it. The cell was totally silent. He wondered what sounds were outside, in the streets, outside the prison walls, even in the corridor outside his cell. It had been a good Christmas, he thought, the best for years, the best since they had captured him and locked him up. And the New Year, he knew, would belong to him.

The gnawing in his stomach refused to go away. He made himself think about it, what it would be like later. Now was nothing, he told himself, a minor irritation, the first reaction of a body that was over-pampered and over-fed. Later he would know what it was to suffer.

His mind began to drift back along the path he knew he would think of almost endlessly in the torture to come: his first action, his first killing, the moment he had joined the group. The happy, balmy days at university, the first time he had made love. His schooldays, the evening he had kissed his first girlfriend. His parents, especially his parents, the days as a child when they had worked for almost nothing simply to survive, the roots, he thought, of his political convictions. The corner of the room where he had been born.

It was the fourth day of his hunger strike. In sixty-five days it would be his birthday.

9

JANE ENDERSON saw the children off, left the house and drove to school. It was cold, she wondered what it had been like when her husband had caught the train to London two hours earlier. It would be his second appointment with the doctors at Woolwich, she knew the arm still hurt him, especially when he played with the children, but it was getting better. She turned through the gates and began to think about the boy whose life he had saved, about the boy's mother, what the woman had thought on that terrible night, what she thought now, whether she even remembered Grah. She thought about him again, where he was, what he would be doing. It was his second night away since he had come back from Northern Ireland, the other time had also been when he had gone to Woolwich. Strange, she reflected, how she was getting used to having him home, even this way, even with the hold-all in the wardrobe at the foot of the bed, even with the shock of the bleeper being tested every morning at six.

She had time for a cup of tea, then began her first class. Jane Enderson had always wanted to be a teacher, even after nine years she still enjoyed it, especially now, especially, she did not realise, that Grah was home in the evenings. The class was waiting for her, their books already open. Most of the children were bright and keen to learn, most of them enjoyed this class in particular, partly because she was a good teacher, partly because they were border country, almost Welsh, and felt a hidden affinity towards the dead genius. She knew they liked reading, knew she enjoyed listening to them.

"Helen James." She chose the pupil with the best voice and thought of Grah. The girl picked up her book, stood up and cleared her throat, her voice small and clear, a gentle, almost magical mix of Welsh and English West Country, and began to read.

10

JIMMY ROBERTS left the flat in Earls Court and took the Piccadilly line to Covent Garden. Even though it was the end of the rush hour, the train was still crowded; he managed to find a seat and settled down. Each day, he took the same train, each day the active service unit followed the same routine. Four hours at work, then home. Recce the locations they would some day be called upon to bomb, prepare the reports that were sent across the water, study the files of the people they had been ordered to target, research them, build up the dossiers on them. The hours at work broke the pressure and gave them some spending money in addition to the wages they received each month. It also made them respectable. The IRA had learned a great deal since they had sent the sleeper units over in the seventies.

The train pulled into Gloucester Road.

The weather was cold and uncomfortable; he found himself
thinking of San Francisco, the roll of the hills down to the sea,
the sun in the summer, the skiing in the winter. Opposite him,
a woman was reading *Harpers* magazine.

The doors began to close.

Three weeks, he found himself thinking, since he had taken
the call in the public telephone kiosk, since the brief coded
conversation with the Arab he had been told to call Peter. Three
weeks since he had pulled on the surgeon's gloves, the rubber
thick enough to conceal his fingerprints but thin enough, delicate enough, for him to still feel the mechanism of the bomb
with his fingertips. Three weeks since he had placed it in the left
luggage locker at Euston station and taped the locker key behind the cistern in the pub in Charlotte Street. He had wondered then why the IRA were helping the Arabs, remembered
the moment he had heard the news about the assassination on
the motorway from Heathrow, the speculation that followed,
the fear that the extremists from the Middle East had teamed
up with the Irish. Good, he thought to himself, the whole thing
had been bloody good.

The train moved off.

Enderson put his overnight case on the floor, behind his legs.

The woman on his left was reading *Harpers* magazine. He
began thinking about the Heathrow bombing, knowing there
was no reason to think about it except that it was his job, except that some day he might have to face someone like the man
on the motorway from Heathrow. The man had made one
mistake; he wondered if he had known when he had done it,
why he had done it. The airport bus full of children. A miracle
really, the driver had been telling someone, been overheard by
an alert policeman, if the stupid bastard hadn't pulled in front
of them and made him brake he would have been alongside the
Granada when it blew up. He had remembered the number,
enough of the number to trace the car to the hire company, to
trace the bomber to the Holiday Inn in Swiss Cottage. And no
further. No fingerprints, no clues. A false name through which
they had been able to trace back some of his travel movements, but then nothing. The bomber had known, Enderson
thought, had known after the killing that they would trace him,
had not used the same passport when he left Britain. No mistake, he realised he had known all along. He wondered why the
man had taken the risk to save the children.

The train pulled into South Kensington.

The woman who had been reading *Harpers* magazine stood up. Jimmy Roberts watched her go, looking at her legs, seeing the man next to where she had been sitting, registering him the way he half-registered everyone else in the compartment. Then he stopped looking at the woman, partly because the doors closed, partly because she didn't have good legs anyway, and wondered why he looked again at the man.

A trigger, thought Enderson, the Heathrow bomb had been a trigger in more ways than one. He began to go through the list of incidents that had followed the killing, almost as if the groups which had carried them out had been waiting for a sign.

The eyes, thought Jimmy Roberts, something about the eyes.

The train was gathering speed, disappearing into the tunnel.

The hunger strike in West Germany, thought Graham Enderson, the incidents which only began after it, the apparent sharing of weapons and explosives.

The eyes, Jimmy Roberts was still thinking, something about the bloody eyes.

Joint communiqués before the hunger strike, thought Graham Enderson, all signed by one group after, the Commando of the Martyr Klars Christian Mannheim.

He knew where he had seen the man before, remembered the fear he had felt then, sensed the sudden excitement he felt now.

Almost as if it was planned, Enderson thought, too obvious to be anything else.

The train began to slow down, emerge from the tunnel. Knightsbridge.

The drinking club in Belfast, Jimmy Roberts knew. The bastard on the end of the line of squaddies who had torn the place apart. The day after he had seen his granny laid to rest. The bastard he had known was up to no good.

So why so obvious, Enderson thought; he knew there was a reason, that whatever the reason it was sending the security people and politicians into a frenzy.

Roberts knew what he was, who he was, wondered only what the bastard was doing in London.

Perhaps that was it, thought Enderson, perhaps that was the whole purpose anyway, to let them all know, to put the fear of God into them all. He thought again of the man who had started it at Heathrow.

The train stopped. Enderson stood up, picked up the overnight case and stepped off. Jimmy Roberts watched him, unsure what to do. Graham Enderson paused, looking for the exit signs. A waste, Roberts thought, what a bloody waste. Looked at the man, was convinced. Saw him beginning to walk along the platform, the doors closing. Knightsbridge, he thought, remembered the targets, the hour after bloody hour the ASU had spent boring themselves silly over the goddam targets, the locations, the nearest tube stations to them. He was moving, fast, knocking somebody out the way, the doors almost shut. He stuck his foot into the space between them, felt the shudder as the power of the doors tried to jerk them together, and pulled them open. Knightsbridge, he thought again, cursing his own stupidity, bloody Knightsbridge.

Enderson picked his way along the platform to the escalator, at the top he searched in his pocket for the ticket, left the tube station, and turned left.

Jimmy Roberts followed him, watching as he stopped for the traffic at the point where he would cross the road if he was going to the barracks overlooking Hyde Park, where he would go straight on, skirt behind Harrods and go to the address in Hans Place if he was the man Jimmy Roberts believed him to be. He stayed back, afraid the man might recognise him as he had recognised the man, hoping he was right, remembering the drinking club off the Falls, what he had thought then, that the bastard at the end of the line of squaddies hadn't cared a damn about the people they were questioning, only about the lay-out, about which doors led where, about the ways in and out.

The traffic cleared. Graham Enderson walked behind Harrods, and went to the address in Hans Place.

The American watched as he went in, remembering in general terms what was inside: the reception and lounges on the ground floor, the bar and dining room on the first, the bedrooms above. Not one of the expensive London clubs, but one of the most exclusive. It was for that reason, because of the people who were allowed to go there, because of what its name implied, that they had the club on their list. For the day the orders came from Belfast, for the day they bombed the shit out of London.

Graham Enderson checked in, left his overnight case, and went back to the tube station. Jimmy Roberts watched him leave. Not on duty, he thought, if the bastard was on duty he would be getting off at Sloane Square, not Knightsbridge, would not be on duty if he was staying at the club.

Graham Enderson had two hours before he was due at the hospital. He took the Piccadilly and Northern lines into Charing Cross, and bought a ticket for Woolwich Arsenal.

Jimmy Roberts followed him to the underground station and watched him go down. No point tailing him any more, he thought; he knew where he was staying, knew he would be back that evening. Every point, he cautioned himself, in *not* tailing him.

The first doubt hit him: suppose he was wrong, suppose the man was not whom Roberts thought he was. He told himself to calm down, work it out, and went to a café on Sloane Street. Of course the bastard was who he thought he was, the bastard was staying at the club, and only bastards like that stayed at the club. He relaxed and began to think what he could tell the men in Belfast, how he could provide the evidence they would require, how they in turn could identify the bastard for the moment they would take him out. Of that one thing Jimmy Roberts was sure, that the men in Belfast would decide to take the man out. In the centre of London. The propaganda value was too great not to.

He knew what he would do.

The flat in Earls Court was empty. Jimmy Roberts collected a camera, a 100-300 mm zoom lens, and two rolls of Tri-X 400 ASA black and white film. By one o'clock he was back in Knightsbridge.

The hospital treatment took longer than Graham Enderson had expected. By the time he returned to the club it was nearly seven and already dark. At least, he thought, it justified his decision to stay overnight in London. He telephoned Jane, said goodnight to the children, and went out for supper.

Jimmy Roberts knew the light level had been too low even before he began developing the film in the darkroom they had built in the bathroom of the safe house. He watched for the image as he slid the sheet of printing paper into the tank and saw it appear, was unable to distinguish any identifying features and knew he would have to go back in the morning.

THAT NIGHT Jane Enderson dreamt about the poem for the first time. That night she heard the girl's voice over the Brecons for the first time. "Helen James," she was saying, feeling happy, choosing the pupil with the best voice, "would you like to read?" The girl was standing up, clearing her throat, her voice small and clear, an almost magical mix of Welsh and English West Country.

"'Do not go gentle into that good night'" she was saying, "by Dylan Thomas."

Jane heard the voice, so still, heard the words, so soft and gentle, so angry. Not all the words, not the words of each verse, just the words of her favourite verse, the words of the last verse.

"And you, my father, there on the sad height,
Curse, bless, me now with your fierce tears I pray.
Do not go gentle into that good night.
Rage, rage against the dying of the light."

She tried not to listen, tried not to see her husband's face, tried not to remember what she had taught the children, that the poem was about death, that the poet was pleading with his father not to die. She was thinking of her own father, thinking again of the father of her children, trying to tell Grah, to speak to him, his face fading. She was trying to shut the words from her mind, the voice faint, dying, finishing the poem, the image of her husband growing stronger. She felt the relief. In the darkness the girl called Helen James began to read again.

SEVEN AND A HALF hours later Graham Enderson left the club and caught the 125 from Paddington; between Hans Place and the main line station Jimmy Roberts managed to snatch three photographs of him. He had developed and printed them within the hour. At nine thirty he began the process of notifying Belfast.

11

THE FIRST INFORMATION Walid Haddad needed in order to consider how he could implement what he referred to as the Dubai factor reached him from Europe six days later. Within twenty-four hours he had collated the material, sifted through it, and come to his first decision.

There were three cities in Europe within the time period which Abu Nabil had indicated, from which he could launch the hijack using the method he had devised. He checked the flights from each in the ABC guide. There were none either of the type he needed or at the time of day he required, from the first city on the list. He eliminated it and turned his attention to the other two in turn, remembering the security at each. The flights at both were good, the timings almost perfect. Even the Dubai factor, he thought, not just an example of the Dubai factor, an almost exact replica of it. It was an omen, he decided, an indication that the hijack would go well.

He would need to confer with Abu Nabil, check both locations, review the security at each, allow Nabil to make the final decision of which city would be the target, knew already which one he would choose. He finished the coffee, telephoned Nabil's headquarters, and arranged a meeting, coding his request. Even in a supposedly friendly country, especially in a supposedly friendly country, the secret police were always the secret police.

The meeting began ninety minutes later and lasted five and a half hours. Walid Haddad was examined and cross-examined by both Abu Nabil and Issam Sharaf on his basic approach to the hijack, the options of the two cities where it would begin, and the arrangements he would have to set in motion, as a matter of priority, in order to begin to obtain the information he would need for the plan he had devised to get his weapons and explosives on board. When he had completed his cross-examination Abu Nabil chose the city Walid Haddad had known he would choose.

The following morning Walid Haddad left Damascus, travelling under the third false passport he had used on the operation. His first destination was Abu Dhabi, where he changed planes and passports, then Madrid, for no other reason than the fact that there was a direct flight from Madrid to the city in which the hijack would begin. He did not want to fly there direct from a Middle East airport.

It was time to be that careful.

12

THE HAZE OF LIGHT protected by the steel mesh in the ceiling above him was blurred. Klars Christian Mannheim tried to focus his eyes on it, seeing the way it danced in front of him, changing colours, the shapes it assumed becoming more and more grotesque. In the last eight days he had lost three and a half kilos, in the last eight days there had been four more bombings and two more shootings. In his home town of Gaggenau the priest who had baptised him almost twenty nine years before said a secret prayer for his soul. In the forensic laboratories in Bonn and Paris, Brussels and Rome, the scientists confirmed the tell-tale links connecting the explosives and weapons being used in the spiralling violence which was sweeping Europe and passed their grim findings to the politicians.

In the prison to the north, the three who would be next to announce their hunger strike felt the fear growing in them and realised for the first time the enormity of what they were about to do.

The light in the ceiling stopped moving. The door opened and the warder placed the tray of food on the floor. When he came back thirty minutes later only the water had been consumed.

13

AT TEN THIRTY that morning, when the international oil conference opened in Zurich, the pound stood at one dollar twenty-six cents; by close in London, with reports of major disagreements in Zurich, it had fallen almost two cents; when trading ceased in New York five hours later, the pound was down to $1.23. At eight o'clock that night, behind the sanctified walls of the City, there was the first talk of a sustained decline in the value of the pound, the first suggestion that, unless such a slide could be halted, it might well degenerate into a major run on sterling. At nine o'clock that night the Prime Minister, on the advice of the man she had personally appointed Governor of the Bank of England, considered adding the problem of the falling pound to the agenda for the cabinet meeting in two days' time. At ten o'clock that night, in his hotel suite in Zurich, Sheikh Saeed Khaled saw the first outlines of the plan for which he and Abu Nabil had agreed to search at their meeting in Rome.

For five hours the next day the pound held steady. At two in the afternoon the oil meeting in Zurich broke up in disarray; when London closed four hours later the pound was below $1.20 and falling. By the time the Prime Minister confirmed the subject of sterling for the following day's cabinet meeting, Saeed Khaled was already in his suite at the Hilton.

14

JOHN KENSHAW-TAYLOR left the Foreign Office at nine thirty and walked the hundred yards to Downing Street. The barriers at the end were in place, a small crowd of sightseers waiting expectantly. The duty policeman recognised him and saluted. Kenshaw-Taylor smiled back, knowing that the crowd would ask who he was and that the policeman would tell them.

There were two television crews outside Number Ten, one from BBC, the other from ITN. General shots of ministers arriving, he thought, assuming they wouldn't bother with him, just the big names, especially those connected with the pound. He had checked with the City before he left, even since opening that morning the pound had slipped another half cent, partly because peace moves on the industrial front had ended in stalemate, but primarily because the latest round of oil price discussions had broken up in Zurich late the previous afternoon with nothing approaching the agreement that had been expected of it.

The cabinet committee started at ten. Item three dealt with terrorism, the Home Secretary reporting agreement with European security chiefs for a top-level conference to be held in two weeks' time, a response which John Kenshaw-Taylor considered inordinately and typically weak, but which he did not state for the record. Item five was the state of the pound. Kenshaw-Taylor again said nothing, allowing his silence to distance himself, albeit indirectly, and in a manner which would antagonise neither man, from the Chancellor, who was taking a general hammering on the weakness of the pound, and from the minister who had taken over his job at Energy, who was taking a very specific beating on the failure of the oil ministers to reach even a temporary agreement in Zurich, from where he had returned fourteen hours previously.

When the meeting broke up at one, Kenshaw-Taylor engineered his departure so that he and the new Energy Minister left together.

"What the hell's going on?" he asked half out of interest, half out of pleasure. He was one rung of the ladder ahead of the other man; both had been given their first ministerial jobs in the same cabinet reshuffle but he had entered Parliament four years after the other.

"God knows," the other admitted, "the bloody Arabs won't make any concession at all."

They began to walk down the stairs.

"Who's the problem?" Kenshaw-Taylor asked, not really interested. "Yamani?"

"No," said the other man. "He's trying his best, as he always does. The problem is not who's making the running inside the conference, but who's pulling the strings outside."

They reached the hall.

"So who's the fly in the ointment?"

"Saeed Khaled. Don't know what's come over him. When I took over from you he seemed on side, not friendly but on side. Then just before Christmas, when we had the talks in London, he changed. He's been a real bastard ever since."

They left Number Ten and walked past the television cameras. "Want a lift?" the Energy Minister asked.

"No thanks," said John Kenshaw-Taylor. "I'll walk."

He checked with his office, then strolled down Whitehall to the House. His Parliamentary Private Secretary was waiting in the Pugin Room; Kenshaw-Taylor tried to see him every day, keep him in touch with affairs at the ministry, keep himself in touch with affairs at Westminster. It had been a surprise to some when the minister had asked the man to be his PPS, though not so unexpected to those with a longer vision. The

PPS was popular among the new Tory intake, the group who were powerless now but who would constitute the backbone of the party when it voted for a new leader in five or ten years' time.

The bar, overlooking the Thames, was not busy, it was too early in the year for most MPs to be back from the Christmas recess. They had one drink then went to the Members' Dining Room for lunch.

"How did it go this morning?" the PPS asked.

Kenshaw-Taylor shrugged. "OK, for some. The Home Secretary bumbled on about terrorism. The Chancellor was in trouble over the pound." He remembered the conversation with the new Energy Minister. "Charles wasn't too happy either. Taking a bit of a bashing because of the oil talks."

His PPS seemed interested. "Why, what's the trouble?"

"Seems the Arabs have suddenly got on their high horse, started digging their heels in."

"Who's the culprit this time?" The exchange was light-hearted.

"Saeed Khaled." Their food arrived.

"Funny that," said the PPS, "Khaled was only talking about you and Charles last night."

Kenshaw-Taylor was intrigued. "What do you mean?"

"Apparently he was saying that since Charles took over, any hopes of a settlement have gone out the window. Not in control of his subject, those were his exact words, not able to grasp what the hell the Arabs were talking about."

Kenshaw-Taylor waited.

"Apparently he thought it was a great pity you'd moved on."

"Why?"

"Seems he reckoned you and he got on together, understood each other."

It had never occurred to John Kenshaw-Taylor that this had been the case. "How do you know?" he asked.

"A friend in the City was telling me this morning."

"How did *he* know?"

The dining room was filling slowly.

"He's a bit of a fixer, good connections in the Middle East, knows Khaled better than most. They had dinner together last night."

The first seed had been planted, was taking root, growing. "Khaled's in town?"

"Apparently."

"Business?"

The PPS shook his head. "Private, apparently." He finished his food. "Wouldn't have thought he would have come for the Harrods' sale. Must go."

It took John Kenshaw-Taylor ten minutes to confirm where Sheikh Saeed Khaled was staying in London and another five to ascertain the Prime Minister's movements over the next twenty-four hours.

The sheikh, when he called him at the Hilton, was out. His secretary said he would be back in thirty minutes and asked if he could return the minister's call. Kenshaw-Taylor gave him the number of his direct confidential line and planned what he would say. He was dictating a memo on Namibia when the call came through; he asked his aide to leave and waited to be connected.

"Sheikh Khaled, thank you for returning my call."

"The pleasure is mine. How nice to hear from you. It must be three months since we last met, congratulations on your new post. To what do I owe this honour?"

"I heard you were in London, and as we don't see much of each other these days, I wondered if you would care for dinner some time."

"Unfortunately," said Khaled, "I leave tomorrow afternoon and I already have arrangements for this evening." Kenshaw-Taylor saw the chance slipping away. "As you say, however," continued Khaled, "we seldom have the chance to talk, and I would welcome the opportunity to cancel what I was doing tonight. The people were very boring anyway. As long," he joked, "as we don't get bogged down in a discussion over oil price structures."

"I agree," Kenshaw-Taylor returned the humour.

"Public or private?" asked the sheikh. The conversation had become serious again.

"Private," said the Foreign Minister.

"In that case," said Khaled, "it would be my pleasure if you would dine with me here. Shall we say eight?"

"Eight would be fine," agreed John Kenshaw-Taylor.

He put the phone down and considered what he was doing, what he was about to do, then he called his aide back and continued the dictation. When it was finished he asked his secretary to cancel the three meetings he had for that evening, and to rearrange the other aspects of his timetable. At six he took sherry with his principal advisors, then returned to the flat in Pimlico and spent half an hour in the bath planning his strategy. He arrived at the Hilton at eight precisely.

Saeed Khaled received him in the same eighth floor suite in which he had entertained Abu Nabil. Dinner was served at eight thirty, they finished at ten: between courses they had discussed, amongst other things, the stalemate within OPEC, the sheikh being remarkably frank, Kenshaw-Taylor thought, both about the decision-making within the Zurich oil conference and, even more to the point, the manoeuvring which took place outside it, as well as the problems of the pound. When Kenshaw-Taylor pressed him on the subject, Khaled was forced to concede his sympathy with the plight in which the British government now found itself.

The table was cleared and the two men moved into the lounge, relaxing with a cognac in the large armchairs in which the sheikh and Abu Nabil had held their first discussion before Christmas.

"The problem," suggested Kenshaw-Taylor, "is not simply that the pound is under pressure, but that it's under pressure from two sides at the same time." He sensed Khaled was relaxed, knew it was time to press him, to capitalise on the concessions the Arab had appeared to make over dinner.

Khaled picked up the cigar box on the coffee table between them and offered it to Kenshaw-Taylor. He accepted, selecting a Haut-Brion and rolling it between his fingers, allowing the sheikh to note his appreciation of it. Khaled passed him the lighter and took one for himself. "Agreed," he conceded, "but we can't do anything about the dollar."

Kenshaw-Taylor picked up the use of the single word "we", recognising the opening he had been seeking to engineer. "No," he said, "but we can do something about oil." The words were carefully chosen, apparently objective, underneath totally subjective, as if he and Khaled faced the same problem, as if he and Khaled were allies. He waited for the response.

"Agreed," said Khaled again.

Kenshaw-Taylor eased on the pressure. "It needs solving for everyone's sake."

"But particularly for yours." The sheikh watched as the smoke from his cigar curled towards the ceiling.

The Foreign Minister knew when to advance, when to retreat. "At the moment," he smiled.

Khaled laughed, appreciating the answer, and refilled their glasses. "The basic problem," he suggested, "is that some countries are failing to keep to the production quotas and that the main offender, Nigeria, produces light crude, which makes it even more difficult for the rest of us. Until you can persuade the Nigerians to police their production as others are policing theirs you will never get the agreement your government needs to stabilise the pound."

It was the first time the Arab had taken the lead in the conversation, Kenshaw-Taylor thought, realising the significance.

"Agreed," he used the single word Khaled had used before, knew also that the sheikh was correct. In 1983, in an attempt to counter the mounting crisis in the oil industry, OPEC had opted to place a ceiling on oil production, with member states agreeing to country quotas within this. Some, however, had continued to over-produce, one of them being Nigeria. Britain, though not an OPEC member, had become involved because the crude oil which it and Nigeria produces is light and sulphur-free, which is cheaper to process and therefore more in demand, and which yields more light products, which are themselves easier to sell than the heavy fuel products which other nations produce.

"As you say," continued Khaled, "the problem is Nigeria."

Kenshaw-Taylor knew that he had not said it, that he had the man on the run. "The problem," he agreed, "is Nigeria. Until *they* agree, *we* can't agree. Until they control production and agree to a common price, we can't afford to be undercut by them."

Khaled took a long time to reply. "But if there was a way we could get Nigeria to agree, and to stick to it," he said suddenly, as if the idea had only then occurred to him, "would your government also agree?"

John Kenshaw-Taylor knew Khaled was about to make an offer, that he had forced him, persuaded him, into it, sensed that an agreement on oil prices and thus the saving of the pound was his for the taking.

"Yes," he agreed on behalf of Her Britannic Majesty's Government, savouring the feeling, "How?"

"There are a number of ways." Khaled was hesitant. As if, John Kenshaw-Taylor thought, he was suddenly aware that the

Foreign Minister had made him concede too much, got too much out of him already. "Nigeria will obviously want certain things in return for an agreement, things which the British government might well be in a position to achieve. With a little pressure in certain quarters," he added.

Kenshaw-Taylor took another sip of the cognac.

"Except," said Khaled, "there is a problem."

Kenshaw-Taylor felt his optimism collapse.

"Your present negotiator." Khaled leaned forward, sharing a confidence, his voice lower. "I know you are colleagues, that you are members of the same government, but he simply doesn't have the stature."

The Foreign Minister liked the word, would roll it over in his mind later. "I know what you mean," he said.

"In ten days' time," said Khaled, "OPEC is due to discuss the oil pricing system again. Non-OPEC representatives will also be there. I will be present. It might be prudent if you were also on hand."

"Where?" asked the Foreign Minister.

"The United Nations. I know it will be difficult to arrange."

"It won't be a problem," Kenshaw-Taylor thought quickly, "I can be in New York in a private capacity."

"How?" He could see that Khaled was intrigued.

"I can arrange to speak at the Jacksonian."

He knew that Khaled himself had spoken there, that he was impressed.

"You don't have much time."

"I know Henry Armstrong," said Kenshaw-Taylor.

"Splendid," said Saeed Khaled.

For the next hour they discussed the tactics they would adopt, the pressure Khaled would bring to bear on the Nigerians, the inducements Kenshaw-Taylor would offer those who were in a position to concede what the Nigerians would demand.

When Kenshaw-Taylor rose to leave, Saeed Khaled walked with him to the lift. "It will take careful management," the sheikh suggested, "we cannot be seen to be working together."

John Kenshaw-Taylor knew what he meant. "Don't worry," he said. "Nothing will be as it seems."

15

THE PRIME MINISTER was halfway through a working breakfast when Kenshaw-Taylor telephoned Downing Street at seven the following morning. It was, he had established, a good time to approach her. She had risen at six, already done an hour's work and was due to leave London at eight to open a factory in the North-East.

"Yes, John." The voice was firm but friendly.

He apologised for troubling her at such an hour, especially when she had a busy schedule, but he needed to clear something with her in order to avoid any inter-departmental misunderstanding in the future. She waited for him to explain, deliberately not asking why he had not gone to the Foreign Secretary, knowing there would be a reason. It was simply, he went on, that he would be having lunch that day with Saeed Khaled, if not lunch than a quick meeting that morning before the sheikh returned to the Middle East.

"I thought that Khaled had returned home after Zurich," she said non-committally.

"Apparently not. He's in London at the moment."

"Not your department, John," the Prime Minister cautioned. "Not since last October."

"I appreciate that, Prime Minister."

"When did you say you were seeing him?"

"Probably lunch, purely personal of course."

"Of course."

CHAPTER TWO

1

JOHAN STREISSMANN had first become aware of the relationship between politics and violence when, at the age of seventeen he had heard with disbelief the news that three members of the Baader-Meinhoff terrorist group had succeeded in committing suicide in the safety of their high-security prison cells after the unsuccessful hijack of a Lufthansa airliner in October 1977. Even as a schoolboy he had refused to believe the confirmation, by an international panel of experts summoned by the West German authorities, that they had not been executed in their cells. In 1981 he had taken part in his first anti-nuclear rally. In 1982 he had received a broken nose when police broke up a demonstration in which he was taking part. In 1983 one of his lecturers had lost his job under the Berufsverbot system whereby those with suspect political records risk losing employment in state institutions. In early 1984 two of his closest friends at university had dropped out of classes and disappeared from his life; when they returned towards the end of the year he had formed a distinct impression, though they did not discuss it directly, where they had been. By the beginning of 1985 Johan Streissmann was psychologically and politically prepared to take the step from the politics of conventional protest to the violence of revolution.

Johan Streissmann was also a computer expert.

On the evening of Tuesday, January 22nd, he returned to the department of applied mathematics at the university where he was a post-graduate student and entered his study.

He had not thought it strange when, two nights before, the friends who had vanished for six months the previous year had made the request of him, had not even questioned why they wanted the information. He had always known they would come to him, he would think in retrospect.

The room was silent. He settled at the keyboard and began typing the codes, playing with the computer, seeing the barriers, meeting the series of obstacles as they presented themselves, typing in the security codes which would overcome them. It was a game he had played before, many times. Before, however, that was all it had been, a game. Now he knew, or at least suspected, it was more than that. The connection took less than three minutes, when he was inside he typed the final instruction and waited as the paper began to spill from the print-out.

The codes had been easy to obtain, they did not, after all, match the level of security classification of the bank codes for which he had exchanged them with the other hackers. And the exchange of codes was all part of the game amongst computer experts like himself. Even now, he thought, the others would be delving into the secret accounts of the bank systems the codes of which he had given them.

One and a half hours later he had obtained the full computerised flight details within Europe for the period January 1st to March 31st of all aircraft operated by the major carriers, including both scheduling and servicing details, as well as information on where each aircraft would be refuelled, cleaned and re-stocked with inflight food and drink. When he switched off the computer there was no record of the penetration of the system at any of the five data banks to which he had gained access that night.

At eleven minutes past nine the following evening he caught the Italia Express to Rome, travelling first class as he had been instructed and carrying the print-out in a large case, arriving the next day. He took a cab to the Hotel Giulio Cesare, on the Via degli Scipioni, again as instructed, checked in and waited for the telephone call.

It came at three. He left the hotel, taking the print-out with him, and walked to a café off St Peter's Basilica, sitting at the table nearest the door, and ordered a beer. Fifteen minutes later he was joined by a woman; he finished his drink and followed her to a second hotel, on the Via Veneto; she escorted him to a room on the third floor, introduced him to the man who was waiting for them, and left.

Walid Haddad shook his hand, and invited him to take a drink. Johan Streissmann asked for a beer; the fact that his host was of Middle East appearance did not surprise him. For the next two hours he explained the information contained in the print-out, flattered by the way the man reacted to his technical expertise, protesting modestly that the codes to the information did not enjoy a particularly high security classification, agreeing at last when the man told him what an excellent job he had done.

By the time they were finished it was dark outside. "Have you been to Rome before?" asked Walid Haddad. "It's a beautiful city."

Johan Streissmann admitted that he had not.

"In that case," suggested the Palestinian, "perhaps you would like Marina to show you around?"

When Johan Streissmann returned to his university department the following Monday, there was no evidence whatsoever that he had been out of the city that weekend. He had, however, in two short nights in a hotel bed in Rome, taken one more step along the road to international revolution.

2

THE DOOR was in front of him, close in front of him. Stand-by, he was thinking, stand-by, stand-by. He was rocking forwards and backwards, in time with the words, the one man at his side, tight against his left side, the other two behind, tight behind, pushing against him.

"Sixty seconds," Graham Enderson heard the voice in his earpiece. "Sixty seconds and counting down." Stand-by, he was thinking, stand-by, stand-by. The gas-mask was hard round his face, the streamlight on the barrel of the sub-machine gun, the body armour enclosing him, protecting him. Stand-by, stand-by. The men behind him leaning forward, pushing him harder. "Fifty-five seconds." Stand-by, stand-by. He went through the routine again: how he would open the door, how the stun grenades would go in, what he would do, what they would all do, in the vital seconds after they followed the grenades. "Fifty seconds." Stand-by, stand-by. Four gunmen, they had been told, four gunmen and three hostages, one of them a woman. They knew the lay-out of the room, where the surveillance equipment had told them the gunmen were positioned, where the hostages were located. Roughly, he thought, only very roughly. "Forty-five seconds." He checked the gun and adjusted the gas-mask, thought about the gunmen, about the hostages, where they were supposed to be positioned, how they

might get in the way. "Forty seconds." Stand-by, he was
thinking, rocking, stand-by, stand-by. Stockholm syndrome, he
was thinking in his subconscious, bank robbery, 1973, first indication of hostage sympathy with gunmen. "Thirty-five seconds." London syndrome, Iran embassy 1980; first example of
religious martyrdom means both hostages and gunmen prepared to die for cause. "Thirty seconds." No one wanted to die
that much, he knew. Stand-by, stand-by. Nobody would want
to die in the split second they had to make up their mind. Stand-
by, stand-by. Door opens right to left inwards, stun it, split
right, maintain arcs of fire, not crossing line. Fourth in checks
behind door. "Twenty seconds." Four gunmen, three hostages. Not sure, they had just been told, not sure any more how
many gunmen, how many hostages, not sure where any of them
were. Stand-by, stand-by. "Ten seconds." Radio silence, total
radio silence. Hand on door, men behind pushing him, pushing against him. Stand-by, stand-by. Open door, stuns in. Go,
go, go, go, go. Seconds, one and a half seconds, before first
effects of stuns clear, before gunman shoot back. First gunman, in front, right in front, finger coming down on trigger,
not where he was supposed to be, not where he was bloody well
supposed to be. Room different, lay-out different. Moving
right, across room, clearing doorway, everyone clearing doorway fast, establishing position. Three-round bursts. Gunmen,
where are the gunmen? Man behind him going left, third right,
fourth left, checking door. Three-round bursts, always three-
round bursts. Gunmen behind door, number four clearing. The
smoke coming at them, the fingers coming down, the room
crashing with the sound of the grenades and the sub-machine
guns.

Silence, absolute silence.

Enderson pulled the gas-mask from his face and surveyed the
room, looking at the position of his men, seeing where he had
gone wrong, where they had gone wrong, where they could
tighten their routine. The smoke was clearing. The four of them
straightened up, looking around, noting where they were
standing, making sure they were in position, making sure none
of them was framed in the doorway, examining the arcs of fire.

The third time that morning they had come through the door,
the fourth day in succession they had practised in the killing
house in the centre of the barracks.

He put the sub-machine gun on safety and inspected the dummies which served as both gunmen and hostages, the plastic bodies of the gunmen shattered by the live rounds the assault teams used, even on exercise, those of the hostages intact.

"Not bad, bit slow coming in, and you almost missed the gunmen behind the door." The second hostage from the right, the one closest to any of the gunmen, got up. "Thought we had you with the one behind the door." It was usual rather than unusual for colleagues to sit in as hostages, one way of sharpening the assault teams, one way of ensuring they made no mistakes. Enderson had himself done it, sat still amongst the dummies, waited for the moment the stun grenades came in and the assault team started firing.

"OK," he said. "Let's set up the room and try again."

3

THE BELL SOUNDED for the end of school. Jane Enderson put the homework books she had to mark that evening in the shopping bag she used and drove home, collecting the children on the way. The weather was cold and wet and they were all glad to get inside.

"What time's Dad back?" asked Christopher.

"Six o'clock, as usual."

It was still strange having her husband home in the evenings, she thought as she made the tea. Not every evening—he had been away on several occasions since he had returned from Northern Ireland—but each time she had known in advance. He had gone away when he said he was going away, and, more important as far as the children were concerned, had come home when he said he would come home.

She began to lay the four places at the table. It was enjoyable having Grah at home, but it was also a strain. It was a disruption to family life when he was away on one of the six-month tours, but they became accustomed to his not being there; in some ways, she made herself admit, it took longer getting used to him again when he came back. She had known, of course, when she married him, but at least before he was either away and operational or he was at home and on leave. Now he was operational and at home: each day he came home with the hold-all, each morning she was woken up by the bleeper.

More than that, she thought. She knew what he did, not in detail, but knew nevertheless what he did, what he was trained to do. He was always at risk, she also knew, but when he was away she had contrived to shut those risks from her mind. She had thought about him, had not stopped thinking about him, but when he was on an overseas tour she had found a strange consolation in not knowing the immediate risks he was facing, not knowing the precise moments he was in danger.

Now, she knew, she would know when he was at risk, would know the precise moments he was in danger.

She heard the car outside and saw Grah coming to the door. The children also heard, and ran to meet him. "Hello, Dad!" They were clambering over him. "Come and see my Lego." "Come and see my doll's house."

She had seen the way he came home sometimes and wondered what he had been doing to make him like that—worn out, drained. He would sit by himself for ten minutes, oblivious to the noise of the house and children around him, as if he had shut himself off from the world. Then he would look up and become a different person.

He took off his coat and carried the hold-all upstairs.

"Dad," said Christopher when he came down. "Why do you bring that home every evening?" She wondered what Grah would say.

"It's to do with my work," he replied.

"What do you mean, Dad?" Children, she thought sometimes, were the most honest, asked the most difficult questions.

"Well, you know carpenters carry things in their bags, and doctors carry things in their bags, those are their work bags. This is my work bag."

The boy nodded his understanding. "What sort of things do you carry in your work bag, Dad?"

Jane waited.

"What sort of things do you carry in your school bag?" Enderson asked.

"Pencils and books and things, and a Mars bar."

"That's the sort of thing I carry in my bag."

The boy smiled. "What, pencils and books and things, and a Mars bar?"

"Sort of," Enderson smiled back at him. "Sort of."

THAT NIGHT for the second time, Jane heard the poem. Not the entire poem, just the four lines of her favourite verse. The girl's voice was clear and still, as if she was reading it from across the valley, as if, the fear was suddenly seizing her, the girl was reading it from across the grave. That night, for the first time, Jane had the dream.

The tunnel was long, filled with smoke, the flames coming at him. Grah was moving down it, eyes sweeping from left to right. Not his eyes, she dreamt, as if he was behind his eyes, as if he could see the destruction around him through the sockets of his eyes. His breathing was deep and rasping, as if it was not his breathing. The voice was guiding him, telling him where to go, what to do. Protecting him. Committing him.

She tried to wake from the dream, tried to take him out of the tunnel, saw the death around him, not sure whether it was his death or the death of another. The hold-all, she knew, the death from the hold-all in the wardrobe at the foot of the bed. He was moving on, the flames coming at him, the smoke engulfing him, as if he was descending into Hell. She heard the voice again, telling him, directing him, the death still around him, wherever he turned, his or someone else's, she was still not sure, knew she could never be sure. He was moving on, deeper into the tunnel, almost to the point where she could no longer see him. The hold-all, she was dreaming, the hold-all which he brought home each evening, the hold-all in the wardrobe at the foot of the bed.

She heard the bleeper and woke up, knew it was six in the morning, remembering they tested the bleeper at six every morning, then she slipped back into a half-sleep, thinking of what he would do, how he would get up, wash and dress quietly in the bathroom, how he would sit by himself in the kitchen for thirty minutes, preparing himself for the day, preparing himself for what he might have to do that day. Then he would bring her tea, kiss her goodbye and take the hold-all from the wardrobe at the foot of the bed. It was the way, she knew, that the morning would start, the way every morning started.

She heard him coming up the stairs.

JIMMY ROBERTS left the power station at four thirty and began the drive back to Earls Court. He had been there since two, photographing it, working out the links and connections, measuring the distances. The installation was part of their surveillance quota for the week: identify and recce the points at which the supply of electricity to London could be interrupted.

He turned onto the North Circular and headed for home.

The hire car had been rented under a false name, using a false driving licence and would be paid for in cash, just in case somebody noticed, and the police decided to trace it back. He had worn gloves in the car, even taken care not to touch the hire form when he had signed it. Too many people had been caught that way, he had been warned, too many connections established because somebody had left a finger or palm print on a car hire form.

By the time he reached Earls Court it was six thirty. The others were already in the flat, one of them was cooking the evening meal, the rest watching television. He took off his coat and went in, sensing immediately that something had happened, not that something had gone wrong, just that something had happened.

"Phone call for you, Jimmy," one of them said. They all knew what it was.

"When?"

"Half an hour ago."

"What did they say?"

"Said they'd phone back."

They began to eat, no one hungry any more. When the telephone rang at eight thirty, the others let him answer.

"Jimmy?"

He did not recognise the voice. "Yes," he said.

"Just phoning to thank you for the photographs of the family, we all liked them very much, it was very thoughtful of you."

He felt relieved more than pleased. "I'm glad I sent them."

"Your cousin was saying you were going to see him tomorrow."

He knew he was being called to Belfast. "That's right," he said. "I haven't seen him for a long time."

"What time were you thinking of leaving?"

Jimmy Roberts knew the times of the shuttles by heart. "Half four," he suggested.

"That's fine."

IN THE KITCHEN of the terraced house off the Falls Road in Belfast, Eileen McDonald finished clearing the supper and began her housework. She had always taken a pride in her home, even when the money was short, always kept it spotlessly clean. Before the shooting she had done the housework during the daytime; after, she had spent three, four hours every day at the hospital, more if they let her, till she knew the doctors by sight, called the nurses by their Christian names. After the shooting she had always finished her housework in the evenings.

In the room upstairs she heard the men talking. She ignored them as she ignored the way they came at night and went at night, just as she tried not to hear what they were saying, what they were planning. Sometimes, though, she could not help but overhear; the walls were thin and the voices loud. Sometimes she could not help seeing the documents and the plans, the maps and the sketches, when she took them the cups of coffee they seemed to drink endlessly.

In the children's ward of the Royal Victoria her Liam would be asleep. He had made amazing progress, the doctors themselves had told her, incredible progress; they had moved him out of Intensive Care at least two weeks before they had expected. A miracle, they had told her, truly a miracle.

She left the kitchen and went into the small room, the chairs and sofa clustered round the fire and television, which she called the front room. It was neat and tidy, even when the soldiers had come through it in the days before Christmas, the days before the shooting, she had got it neat and tidy again after. The Brits, she thought, the stupid bastard Brits.

The kettle was boiling. She went back into the kitchen, made the men their coffee, and took it upstairs.

In the house opposite, she would not have known, there was no longer a man hidden in the narrow confine beneath the roofspace, watching the street, the pub on the corner, her house.

At the crossroads on the outskirts of the city, she would not have known, there were no longer men hiding in the ditch, faces blackened, their secret covered by a bush. In the empty space behind the houses opposite there were no longer men waiting in unmarked cars, hearing the instructions as the IRA planners moved towards the drinking club three doors from her tiny house.

Eileen McDonald came downstairs and made herself a cup of tea.

JIMMY ROBERTS ARRIVED at Aldergrove Airport at twenty minutes to six the following afternoon. He cleared security and walked through the terminal complex, past the hire car desks, to the taxi queue at the side of the car park. There were fifteen people in front of him; on the pavement opposite the airport bus was due to leave. He left the queue, hurried across the road, jumped on, and bought a ticket to the city centre.

The evening had already closed in, snow spitting in the wind. It seemed darker and colder than in London.

In the children's ward at the Royal Victoria, Eileen McDonald helped Liam sit up straight and tucked the paper serviette round his neck. The staff were good to her, breaking the rules by allowing her to stay for tea, sometimes to clear up after. She did not know it, but they still remembered his condition the night the ambulance had brought him to the hospital, still remembered they had not expected him to live, remembered the emergency medical treatment they had seen when they lifted him off the stretcher. The nurse arrived with a tray, Eileen took it from her and put it on the bed.

THE AIRPORT BUS pulled out of the carpark and onto the road. The driver turned right, swung through the roundabout, and began to slow down. Jimmy Roberts wondered why and looked up. In front of the bus he saw the lights of the checkpoint, the soldiers, the automatic rifles hanging from their arms, talking to the driver, waving them through.

EILEEN KISSED LIAM goodnight, tucked the sheets round him, and left the ward. The corridors were dimly lit and quiet; she felt she would never forget the smell of the antiseptic. The night was cold, the snow cutting down from the hills above the city, the street was already empty, only half-lit by the street lights. She pulled her coat round her and began the walk home, the wet seeping through her mack and the cold eating into her neck and shoulders. By the time she reached the house she could barely control her shivering. The men, she knew, were already upstairs. She took off the wet mack, lit the cooker and draped the mack over the back of a chair in front of it. Coffee, she thought, the men would want some coffee; put on the kettle.

THE BUS REACHED the city centre, Jimmy Roberts got up from his seat and stepped down, unsure what to do. He had been given no instructions except the confirmation of the flight he should catch.

"Jimmy." The man had been sitting behind him.

"Yes."

"This way."

He followed the man into the carpark behind the Europa Hotel. Close to the entrance was a Cortina. "Get in." There was a change in the tone. "The back seat." He began to get in, closing the door behind him. Felt the hood going over his head, his arms suddenly pinned behind him. Felt the fear grip his bowels, the air suddenly locked off from his lungs. "Don't worry, Jimmy boy," the same voice said. "Just a precaution. Tonight you're going to meet the big men."

He tried to believe them.

The drive lasted fifteen minutes, too long to be a precaution, he began to think, long enough to be something else. The air inside the hood was growing hotter, he knew he was going to vomit, choke on his own bile. The car stopped, he heard the front door open and someone get out. "OK, Jimmy boy, move it." He was pulled out, across a pavement, and into a house.

THE STEAM was beginning to rise from her mackintosh. Eileen turned it over and moved the chair six inches further from the cooker. The coat had cost her fifteen pounds in the January sales and was the first she had bought for eight years. She heard the front door open and someone come in, and went to the passage to see who it was. The young man in the narrow hallway did not seem surprised to see her. "Don't worry, missus," he said, taking her by the arm and guiding her back into the kitchen. "We're expected."

She heard the noise of someone being bundled into the house and up the stairs, the door banging shut behind him, then the feet running down the stairs and the front door open and shut as whoever it was went out. No coffee, she knew, she should not take the men their coffee, at least for a while. She got up, moved the mack back another six inches, and made herself a cup of tea.

"ALL RIGHT," said the voice, "you can take the hood off." Jimmy Roberts reached up and pulled it off his face and head. The air was hot, filled with cigarette smoke, but without the suffocation of the mask; he wiped the saliva from his mouth and looked around. He was sitting at one end of a table, the top covered with Formica; there were three other men at the table, two on either side, the third at the end facing him. The only light in the room was a desk lamp, trained at him so that he could barely make out the faces of the two men by his side, could not identify a single feature of the man opposite. "Tonight," he remembered the voice in the car, "you're going to meet the big men." He did not know it, but he would not hear a friendly voice for the next thirty minutes.

"The photograph you sent us, Jimmy," said the man he could not see. "You said you had seen him before. Tell us about it."

He began to tell them about the drinking club on the corner of the street, the door opening, the troops coming in.

"From the beginning, Jimmy, from the very beginning. What were you doing there?"

He began to tell them about the time he had to spare before his flight back to London.

"No, Jimmy," there was an irritation in the voice, "tell us what you were doing in Belfast."

He began to tell them about the funeral.

"No, Jimmy. I asked you what you were doing in Belfast."

He was confused, frightened; it was not what he had expected, not what he had come for. He began to tell them about his grandmother.

"But what were you doing in Belfast, Jimmy? We didn't know you were coming, you didn't tell us, didn't ask permission."

He began to ask why he needed permission to attend his grandmother's funeral, stopped himself.

"You're on active service, Jimmy boy. We picked you, trained you, because the man in America said you were good, said you could take orders. We set you up in London, pay you a good wage."

He thought about the files they were keeping, the work they were doing, stayed silent.

"You're having a good time in London, Jimmy." The repetition of his name was deafening, threatening. "A little bit of work here, a little bit there. Not like the boys over here, not like the boys down on the border. You've got it easy, Jimmy. Off to the pub in the evenings, I bet, screwing the girls, telling yourself what a big man you are. And the first time we leave you alone, trust you, what the fuck do you do? You come running here like a bare-assed dog with its tail between its legs."

He knew what they were going to do to him, had heard what they did, even to their own kind, especially to their own kind. His stomach was turning, his bowels began to churn. Not just what they did at the end, he thought, how they did it, what they did to you before.

In the room below Eileen heard the voices and knew the man they had brought in was in trouble. She thought she would watch television, then remembered the set was in the front room on the other side of the passage way and decided she would stay in the kitchen.

"Why didn't you ask permission, Jimmy? Why didn't you ask us if you could go to the funeral?"

He began to reply, admit they would not have given permission, could not hear his own voice.

"Speak up, Jimmy, we can't hear you."

He still could not speak.

"I'll tell you why, Jimmy, because you knew we would say no, you knew why we would say no. You knew you shouldn't have come in the first place. Your old granny would have turned in her grave if she'd known what you'd done."

He knew the man was telling the truth.

"So will you do it again, Jimmy, will you go behind our backs again?"

"No," he replied.

"Why not, Jimmy, tell me why not."

He could hear himself saying it, could not stop himself. "'Cause me fucking granny ain't going to rise from the dead now, is she?"

The man was on his feet, leaning into the light for the first time, pushing the edge of the table hard into his stomach.

"Next time you lose your temper with me, Jimmy boy," he could feel the man's breath on his face, "next time you lose your temper with anybody, just remember one thing."

Jimmy Roberts waited for the sentence.

"Just remember, Jimmy, that you're an American. That's why we brought you over here, trained you up, sent you into London." There was a change in the man's voice. "There was too much of your granny's voice in you then, Jimmy boy, too much of you sounded like a fucking Irishman. Next time you lose your temper, just remember where you come from."

He sat down, not bothering to return to the shadows. "OK," he said, "bollocking over." He pulled out a copy of the photograph Jimmy had sent from London and put it on the table. "Now tell us about this bastard."

In the kitchen downstairs Eileen heard the change in tone and put on the kettle for the men's coffee.

In the small room upstairs, Jimmy Roberts began to recount the story of the man in the photograph, detailing the circumstances of the first time he had seen the man, in the drinking club off the Falls Road, and the next time he had seen him, on the underground in London, describing how he had followed him to the address in Knightsbridge and pointing out why the club was significant, adding that it was already on their target list. The photographs he had taken at night, he explained, were too underexposed, the light conditions being inadequate—he felt he had to justify himself—not himself or the camera. The morning after, he said, he had been in position at six.

"So how can we be sure he's SAS?" asked the man on his left.

Jimmy began to make a suggestion, then the man who had conducted his interrogation took over.

"Three reasons," he said. "First, the way he tagged on the end of any army patrol, that's typical. Second, the place he stayed in London. Third, the fact that he caught the train from Paddington the morning Jimmy got his photo." He looked down the table. "You didn't see what ticket he bought?"

"He didn't," said Jimmy, "he had a return. He caught the eight o'clock Swansea train."

The interrogator turned to the man on his right. "The 125 from Paddington to Swansea stops at Newport. Newport is the nearest station to Hereford."

"So what are we going to do?"

"Get the bastard."

There was a knock on the door. Eileen came into the room with a tray of coffee and biscuits. She moved the photograph out of the way, and put the tray on the table, then she smiled and left. When she was safely downstairs, she went into the front room and switched on the television.

"So what do you want me to do?" asked Jimmy Roberts.

"There are four of you. Familiarise the others with the photograph, then stake out the address twenty-four hours a day."

"What do we do when we spot him?"

"We'll have somebody stand-by in Dublin, there'll be a telephone number where you can reach him at any time of the day or night, he'll be with you in four hours. We'll ship you an M18, it'll be zeroed for him before you get it, so don't go mucking about with it. He won't have time to test it when he gets to you."

Jimmy Roberts nodded. "How long do we stake the place out for?" he asked.

The man looked at him. "As long as it takes, Jimmy boy, as long as it takes."

He rose to leave then had a final thought. "Get your coat on, Jimmy. As this is your last visit to Belfast, your granny would never forgive me if I didn't show you a decent place to drink."

In the front room Eileen heard the men leave; when she was sure they had all gone she collected the cups, washed and dried them, and put them away. She had been in bed half an hour when she remembered where she had seen the man in the photograph.

THREE HOURS after he had received the computer print-out,
seven hours before the West German computer hacker Johan
Streissmann first slept with the woman called Marina, Walid
Haddad left Rome. He was in Damascus eighteen hours later.
It was, according to his timetable, less than eight weeks to the
proposed date of the hijacking.

The meeting with Abu Nabil and Issam Sharaf took place the
following morning. He detailed the European aspects of what
he referred to as the Dubai factor, confirmed the city where they
had preferred the hijack should originate, and spelled out the
information he had gleaned from the computer records, explaining details both of the flight in question and the method
he had begun to set up to get his weapons and explosives onto
that flight. At that meeting the three also discussed the duration of the hijack, the involvement of the media, the range of
drugs he and the other hijackers would need to sustain both
their physical energy and their mental alertness, and the timing of the demand Walid Haddad would make.

That morning, for the first time Abu Nabil disclosed to
Walid Haddad the nature of that demand; that morning, for
the first time, Walid Haddad thought he might live through it.

The meeting lasted six hours. At the end of it, Abu Nabil
asked whether there was anything else.

"Two things," said Walid Haddad.

"The first?"

"I will need access to a Boeing 727."

"I will arrange it. And the second?"

"Is the hijack confirmed yet?"

Abu Nabil knew that Walid Haddad would ask, knew that
he would wait to the end to ask. He thought of what was happening in London, what would happen in New York. "Not
definitely," he said.

"But?"

"But it is now more likely."

For the first time Walid Haddad wondered about the real
reason behind his order to hijack a plane.

THAT MORNING in London, the pound opened weakly at just under one dollar eighteen, within two hours of trading it had slipped another two cents. That afternoon, behind the hallowed walls of the Bank of England, there was the first talk—no more at that stage—of the possibility of the worst sterling crisis in history. That evening John Kenshaw-Taylor arranged the meeting at one of the three London clubs of which he was a member.

IT WAS A JUST IRONY of the imperialistic nature of its foreign policy, thought Jimmy Roberts, that the British government's actions in the South Atlantic should provide the platform from which he and the IRA could launch the assassination of one of the lackeys who maintained that imperialism.

In 1982, as part of the political war conducted around the Falklands campaign, the British government requested that the Argentinian Embassy in London be closed and that the ambassador and his staff leave the country. On his return from Belfast, it took Jimmy Roberts three days to discover that not only was the building still empty, but that it overlooked the address where Graham Enderson had stayed on his last visit to London.

He had briefed the other members of what the Provisional IRA Army Council referred to in its most confidential of discussions as the away team, then set out to organise the surveillance of the club in question. He had found immediately that there were a number of difficulties. The first was the weather: they were required to mount a round-the-clock surveillance. In the day-time it was difficult enough; at night, with temperatures well below freezing, it proved impossible. They had tried a car, but felt conspicuous at the best of times, during the day they were moved on by traffic wardens, at night they felt obvious and exposed. There was also the problem of where to put the car, of not knowing how their target would approach the address. On the previous occasion he had come from the underground station at Knightsbridge, but there were at least three other approaches to the square in which the club was situated.

Jimmy saw the solution on the third day. He had already seen the brass nameplate and noticed the flagpole on the balcony outside the first floor window, but it was only now that he realised why there was no flag hanging from it. He checked the premises to the rear, confirmed there was no back door through which he could enter and went through the front. The lock was surprisingly easy to force and there was no alarm system; he supposed things had been different when the embassy had been in occupation.

The away team moved in that evening, bringing blankets and sleeping bags. Jimmy split the shifts between them, two on, two off, entering and leaving the building at seven in the evening and five in the morning. It seemed fair that the night shift should be shorter. From the position he had chosen there was a clear view to the address where the SAS man had stayed, as well as the various streets which entered the square. When the other members of the team asked him how long the vigil would last, his words were an echo of those he had heard in Eileen McDonald's house in Belfast.

"As long as it takes," he told them. "As long as it bloody takes."

THE DAY AFTER the away team moved into the Argentinian Embassy, a special party was held in the children's ward of the Royal Victoria Hospital in Belfast. Liam McDonald was ten years old. The first his mother knew of it was when she entered the ward with the small basket of gifts and cards from the family and neighbours and saw the other cards on the wall at the head of his bed. Even then she did not realise. At the end of visiting time, as the other parents began to leave, a nurse brought a table to the side of Liam's bed and covered it with a table cloth patterned with Superman. When the ward was quiet, the doctors and nurses brought plates of sandwiches and crisps, and a cake with ten candles round the outside. As they sang "Happy Birthday" she was close to tears, though she did not show it. When the surgeon who had operated on her son held him up in bed to blow out the candles, he managed eight.

"Thank you," she said to them all, "thank you for saving my Liam."

That night, Eileen McDonald thought for the first time about the other man who had saved her son's life and wondered why the men upstairs had his photograph, what they were going to do to him.

8

YAKOV ZUBKO woke at five, beside him Alexandra was asleep; through the window on the right of the bed a shaft of sunlight penetrated the room. He looked at his wife, listening to the sound of their son and daughter asleep in the next room, then looked again at his wife, knowing that when she woke the morning sickness would begin. Another four weeks, he thought, another four weeks and she would be three months' pregnant; in Russia, he remembered, with both their son and daughter, the morning sickness had stopped when Alexandra was three months.

He rose, went downstairs, and dressed in the kitchen so as not to wake them, then he drew a kettle of water and put it on the stove. Quickly, quietly, he made himself breakfast and took Alexandra a cup of tea, it was the only way he could help her start the day, the only way he could help her face the morning sickness. Four weeks, he told her, and she would no longer feel it. He kissed her goodbye and left for work. It was not yet quarter to six.

Alexandra sipped the tea, letting it make her feel better, thinking of her husband. He did not start work till seven, but she did not mind that he left the house early. She lay back, hearing the children, knowing what he would do, happy that he was happy. The sun was warming the room, she could see him now as he reached the square, just down from the house, the school in the narrow street at the side where she took their son every day. He would sit on the wall of the well and drink from its water, then he would walk to the bottom of the hill and dwell for a while in the corner of the field opposite the orange grove. She knew where he would stand, knew there was something special about the place, then he would cross the field and climb the hill called Bethesda, sitting on the stones at the top, looking over the fields to the west, the Jordan to the east, the roofs of Bethlehem beginning to warm in the sun to the north. She finished the tea and pulled herself out of bed.

Yakov Zubko reached the top of the hill and sat on the stones. There was something different, something wrong. Nothing he could see, nothing he could hear, but something happening. He had cheated too many times, lied and stolen too many times not to know. He left the hill and went to work.

The workshop was off an alley way on the other side of the village from where they lived; by the time the others arrived he had put on his overalls and laid his tools on his bench. They did not mind. From the first day he had worked hard, learnt what they taught, asked what he did not know, sat with them when they took their morning break in the sun outside, laughed with them when they laughed at his Hebrew.

The letter arrived at nine.

Alexandra had taken their son to school, then sat on the edge of the well with the other mothers as he played with his friends. It was waiting for her when she returned. She bent down and picked it up, remembering the moment in Moscow, looking at the writing on it. The envelope was stiff, it was marked, "PHOTOGRAPHS, DO NOT BEND" and was addressed to Yakov and Alexandra Zubko, c/o The Jewish Agency, Tel Aviv, Israel. The postmark, she saw, was Norfolk, Virginia, USA. They did not know anybody in Virginia, USA, she thought, sitting at the table, slitting the envelope open with a knife. Inside, handwritten, was a letter from a family called Jefferson, and a second envelope. She skimmed the letter, not understanding it properly, then opened the other envelope. Inside was another letter, this time in Russian, and a photograph.

It showed two families standing outside the station in Moscow, the men staring straight ahead, trying to hide their emotions, the women having the strength not to conceal theirs, the children holding hands, confused.

She remembered the afternoon they had left and began to read the letter. It was from their brother Stanislav and his family, it spoke of how they were, how little Natasha had suffered through the winter, how they were waiting for the warm of the spring to help her asthma, of how they missed Yakov and Alexandra and the children, how they had applied again to come to Israel. She read it twice then turned her attention to the first letter, from the family called Jefferson in Norfolk. They had met Stanislav and his family while they were on holiday in Moscow, it said, and had agreed to post the letter and photograph to them; it said they hoped that Yakov and Alexandra were happy in Israel and that their brother and his family would soon join them.

She put the letter down and looked again at the photograph. It was ten o'clock.

They heard the news at ten fifteen. They had left the workshop and gone into the sun of the courtyard to take their break when the supervisor said he had just heard it on the radio. The Arab mayor of Nablus had been shot, blown up, he wasn't sure; he was in hospital without any legs, they did not know whether he would live or die. The mood on the West Bank, the radio had said, was angry, there was talk of the Arab militants taking their revenge. The Israeli security units were already out, he said, he had seen them in the square ten minutes ago.

Yakov Zubko did not fully understand, partly because of his Hebrew, partly because he had never thought fully of the history of what he cherished as his homeland. When he went home for lunch, the police were still in the square, four men, each armed, plus two vehicles. He looked down the road at them and turned into the house. Alexandra was sitting at the table, he saw she was looking subdued, as if she was uncertain whether she was happy or sad.

''What is it?'' he asked gently, thinking it was to do with the soldiers. She showed him the letter and the photograph.

''They will come soon,'' was all he could say.

When he left the house to return to work, the number of police in the square had doubled.

CHAPTER THREE

1

JONATHAN MATHISON, Jonty to his friends, had, or appeared to have, almost everything, and most of it had either been given him by his father or was a direct result of his father's connections: his accent, his education, his position on the boards of various prominent financial institutions in the City, even, indirectly, his wife, the two families sharing both friendship and financial interests. Jonathan Mathison had also inherited from his father an inclination to over-indulgence, both culinary and sexual, as well as an eye for personal advancement. The only thing his father had not been able to give him was a knighthood.

At six-fifteen in the morning he left his home in Buckinghamshire, was driven to Heathrow and caught the seven-thirty Air France flight to Paris, where he was met by a chauffeur-driven Citroën and taken to his first meeting of the day at the Bourse. He had a working lunch, interrupted only when he telephoned his secretary in London to confirm his appointment at the RAC club that evening, attended a second series of meetings in the afternoon, and caught the five thirty flight back to Heathrow, the time difference allowing him to make the club with ten minutes to spare.

JOHN KENSHAW-TAYLOR left the despatch box at five past three, enjoying a congratulatory nod from the Prime Minister on the way he had stood in for the Foreign Secretary, remained another fifteen minutes in the House and returned to his office. Ministerial question time, apathetic Opposition, the right questions put by the right people on his own side, good briefs by civil servants impeccably delivered, as always, by their favourite minister. The previous afternoon, in contrast, the man filling the job he had vacated at Energy had emerged badly shaken from yet another mauling over his inability to intervene in the oil price dispute which lay at the heart of what was fast becoming the sterling crisis the Bank of England had privately feared. At close that day, the pound would have dropped another almost three full cents against the dollar, as well as losing ground even to other petro-currencies.

THE AFTERNOON SCHEDULE was tight. His private secretary confirmed his meeting at the RAC club that evening and he settled into two hours of discussions on Southern Africa. At five thirty he took sherry with his staff and arrived at the club exactly on time. The squash court had been booked for six forty-five, Jonty Mathison was already changing. Like Kenshaw-Taylor he belonged to the select group who referred to themselves as OEs, Old Etonians. They had gone to the same Oxford college and had maintained the link during the Foreign Minister's period in the City. Jonty Mathison was also on the board of the leading British bank which, in conjunction with a number of American finance houses, was a major lender of money to the government of the country which Kenshaw-Taylor had discussed with Saeed Khaled at their meeting in the London Hilton, the oil-dependent state of Nigeria.

The squash lasted thirty-five minutes, the Foreign Minister winning by two games to one. Kenshaw-Taylor liked winning. As they left the court he suggested they take a sauna: there was nothing his opponent wanted more, he knew, than a gin and tonic, and nothing he wanted less than a sauna. As well as being on top, John Kenshaw-Taylor also enjoyed seeing those beneath him suffer.

The cabin was hot and dry, the Foreign Minister lay on the lower bench, making Mathison sit on the upper, the sweat already beginning to pour off the other man. They talked about their wives and families, Mathison growing redder, panting, enquiring of each other how business and politics were going. Mathison went for a shower, when he came back he told Kenshaw-Taylor to push over on the lower bench. Even there, the Foreign Minister could see he was uncomfortable, that he was only staying because he knew Kenshaw-Taylor had something for him.

"Bad business about the pound," commented the Minister. The cabin was empty.

The banker grunted. He was overweight, the rolls of flesh folded round his stomach. His face was turning red again.

"Nigeria." Kenshaw-Taylor took pleasure in prolonging the other man's discomfort. "Most of the money going into the country is from Saudi, but your bank is one of the major Western creditors."

"Yes," said Mathison.

"Along with the Americans."

Mathison began to take notice. "Yes," he said again.

The Foreign Minister splashed more water on the coals and sat back as the heat swept up at them, waiting for Mathison.

"Why?" the banker asked at last.

Kenshaw-Taylor told him, giving him the details of the plan which he and Saeed Khaled had worked out two weeks before, omitting Khaled's name. Mathison listened intently throughout. "You're serious," he said when Kenshaw-Taylor had finished, unsure whether or not he believed it.

"Yes," said the Minister. "I'm serious."

The Old Etonian hesitated, sweat pouring from him. "The banks will need persuading," he said, "the Americans in particular. What's in it for them?"

Kenshaw-Taylor told him, this time including Khaled's name.

"You can deliver?" There was an astonishment in Jonty Mathison's voice.

"Yes, I can deliver."

"Still difficult," said Mathison, "even with that it would still be difficult."

Kenshaw-Taylor knew why the banker was delaying, what he wanted. "If there's anything else I could do," he suggested.

"A knighthood would help," said Jonty Mathison completely unabashed.

"A knighthood in the next New Year's list," agreed Kenshaw-Taylor.

They left the sauna, took a final cold shower and discussed the details of the arrangements for New York over gin and tonic. On one matter John Kenshaw-Taylor was adamant: that the man who, the following year, would kneel before Queen Elizabeth the Second as Jonathan Samuel Joseph Mathison would not divulge to the Americans who would be present that night either the nature of the meeting or of the offer they would be made. On the same point John Kenshaw-Taylor was totally confident. The man who, the following year, would rise before Queen Elizabeth the Second as Sir Jonathan Mathison, Knight Bachelor, had already decided, for one simple reason, that it was in his own personal interest to meet the minister's condition. As well as receiving his knighthood, the Old Etonian would make a considerable personal killing by being one of only three people in the world who would know in advance the precise moment that the pound would stop falling and begin to climb.

John Kenshaw-Taylor left the club at ten thirty. He was back in Pimlico by one.

2

AT SEVEN THIRTY that morning, when the warder unlocked his cell door and placed the tray of food on the floor beside him, Klars Christian Mannheim saw that, for the first time, the man looked at him. If there had been any doubt in his mind, which there was not, the single glance would have dispelled it. When the warder returned twenty minutes later, only the water had been consumed.

At nine thirty lawyers representing a second group of prisoners announced to the West German news agency DPA that their clients had that morning joined the hunger strike which the terrorist leader had started. The statement, which was reproduced in newspapers in Germany, though not in any of the international press, was treated by both authorities and public in the same way: a belief that Klars Christian Mannheim would not see his hunger strike through to the end, and that when he gave in, they would follow him. If, indeed, they had not already given up.

The group which made its announcement that morning was comprised entirely of women, all young, two in their early twenties, one in her late teens, none of whom had been convicted for anything more serious than taking part in demonstrations against NATO bases in West Germany. For whatever reason, neither of these facts was considered important. Nor was the fact that when she announced her intention to fast to death, the nineteen-year-old had less than three months of her sentence left to serve.

TWO WEEKS AFTER he had taken his first precious cargo to Rome, the West German Johan Streissmann returned to the computer department of his university. The building was quiet. He sat forward in his chair and began to tap the keyboard, feeling relaxed and confident, far enough into the organisation for which he was obtaining the data to be seduced by its intrigue and apparent romanticism, far enough from it to be unmarked by its brutality.

The figures began to appear on the screen. He watched them flitting across the monitor and listened to the chatter of the print-out. At thirty minutes past midnight he switched off the machines, disconnected the print-out and left the room as he had found it, the thick wad of paper in his brown leather case. At one the following afternoon he left his flat on Frauenhofstrasse and began the drive to Switzerland, overnighting, as he had been advised, at a point mid way between the two cities, and arriving in Berne shortly after mid-day. He made his way to the Gauer Hotel Schweizerhof, on the Bahnhofsplatz and went directly, without checking in, to room 369, again as instructed. The woman whom he knew as Marina was waiting for him.

Johan Streissmann began his return drive the next morning. The only difference was that he took with him twenty-five thousand United States dollars donated by Abu Nabil to finance the rash of violence which was spreading across West Germany, taped inside the front passenger door. It had been neither necessary nor expedient to transfer the money in that way; it did, however, give the organisation an opportunity to test another aspect of Johan Streissmann's commitment to the revolution. It also bound him even more strongly to it.

In addition to the money, Streissmann took with him a request for more information from his computer sources, no longer simply for internal European flights, but for certain intercontinental data, specifically for the month of October. When he asked Marina what it meant, she said she assumed they were planning something for the autumn of the year. She was, in fact, in no position to tell him otherwise since it was what she herself had been led to believe.

Three hours before the computer hacker arrived back at his flat on Frauenhofstrasse, the computer print-out he had delivered to Berne reached Walid Haddad in Damascus. He took the material, shut himself off from the world, and began searching through the pages, checking and cross-checking. Six hours later he was satisfied. The same night he visited Abu Nabil and updated him on the information Johan Streissmann had supplied. At that meeting Abu Nabil informed him that he had secured him access to a Boeing 727.

He also authorised Walid Haddad's request that the woman who would place his weapons and explosives on the plane for him begin her work.

4

GENT MUELLER started work on the seventh Wednesday of the year. She found the job the way she knew she would find it. She had checked the local newspapers for vacancies, was not surprised to find that in an area of rising unemployment there were none, and had contacted the airport direct, without success. For three days after that she had watched the gates, working out which women did the job she needed and which amongst the group were the women most likely to help her, following them both when they went shopping after the early shift and when they went home in the evening. On the fourth day she sat near them on the bus to the city centre, making sure she greeted them in a way that ensured they would recognise her again, on the fifth day she met them while they were shopping, on the sixth she had coffee with them, on the seventh they told her they had arranged the job.

The following morning she reported, as instructed, to personnel. The appointment was for nine, she made sure she was ten minutes early, appearing hesitant and nervous. The name she gave was the name on the false identity card with which she had been supplied, the address that of the one bedroomed flat in the block off Landgraffenstrasse to which she had moved three weeks before. Gent Mueller was thirty-two years old, but could pass for ten years older or five years younger without difficulty. That morning she gave her age as thirty-nine and dressed and arranged her hair and make-up to match. She need not have bothered, the only photograph that was taken of her was the one sealed into the identity badge she needed to enter the works and which she was required to wear at all times when she was inside the airport perimeter. From personnel she was taken to the changing room, provided with two sets of overalls, shown her locker, and introduced to the shift supervisor to be shown her job.

That morning Gent Mueller started work as an aircraft cleaner at the international airport at Frankfurt, where the West German national airline, Lufthansa, has its main operational centre.

The women who had found her the job had also arranged for her to work in their shift. The next morning she left the flat at five, walked to the centre, and caught the coach to the gates at the service area of the airport. It was cold and wet. She wore a plain shapeless mack and travelled with her new-found friends. There were two security checks, both of which she had expected and both manned by guards from a private agency, the first at the main gate where they were allowed through after waving their passes, the second at the entrance to the block from which they worked, where their bags were checked. Then she changed in the locker room and had time for a coffee in the canteen before starting work.

The other women worked quickly, explaining the system and pointing out the short cuts. At ten they returned to the canteen for their break; after the hangar it was warm and welcoming. The security guards from the second checkpoint, the position at which their bags were examined, also took their break there. The following day when Gent Mueller came to work she made herself look slightly younger, more attractive.

Gent Mueller was the second daughter of a middle class family from Cologne. Since the age of nineteen she had been associated in an ever more involved and committed manner with the West German Red Army Faction, firstly as a vague sympathiser, then as a courier, finally as a member of the inner core of hard-line activists, for which role she had received training both in Europe and in the Middle East. During that period the women with whom she spent an increasing amount of time never ceased to discuss politics, the environment, revolution; the women with whom she now worked talked of different things, their husbands and families, holidays, what they had done the night before. Unlike the women in the movement, they did not talk of sex in terms of social conflict and exploitation, but in terms of their men's demands upon them, sometimes their demands upon their men. Inside the doors of their lockers they stuck postcards sent by friends on vacation and photographs of husbands or boyfriends, even their children. Only one, the woman they called Jolli, had anything different. It was a picture of a nude male model.

When she had worked with them for ten days Gent Mueller invited the women back to her flat. They had finished the early shift and were getting off the coach in the centre of the city when she made the suggestion, spontaneously, as if she had just thought of it. Two of them were unable to come, but the others accepted immediately. One of them was the woman called Jolli.

The conversation that afternoon was an extension of the conversations they had in the canteen every morning, innocent and innocuous, where their families came from, where their husbands worked. It was Jolli who dropped into the conversation the fact that her husband was on the night shift.

"You're lucky," said Gent, "my old man's at sea. He's been away three months, has another four to go." She showed them the photographs she kept on the sideboard, on the table at the side of her bed, the postcards, apparently from all parts of the world, which were delivered every week to the mail box at the bottom of the stairs.

"Don't you miss him?"

Gent knew it would be Jolli who would ask, knew already what she would reply. "I tell you what I do miss," she said. There was an intonation in her voice that made them all laugh.

The next day, when they took their morning break in the canteen, Jolli introduced her to a mechanic called Rolf. "Rolf sometimes takes me out for a drink in the evenings," she explained while the man fetched them another coffee. "He's got a friend who fancies you." The conversation was direct and between confidantes.

"Who?"

Jolli pointed him out, he was standing in the queue next to the mechanic.

"No," said Gent, "I don't fancy him." The other woman seemed betrayed. "Tell you who I do fancy, though." Jolli leaned forward and waited for the secret. "Him over there, the big one."

Her research had been thorough, the details of the security procedures, the guards whose shifts coincided with theirs, the men who were efficient in their daily searches, the others who looked the women up and down as they checked their bags. "Yes," she said. "I really could do something for him." It was the sort of conversation men have every day.

That morning she began to look for the empty lockers and took the keys for them, putting pictures on them as if they were being used.

The next day Jolli invited her for a drink after work that evening with Rolf and the security man. His name was Kurt and he drove a 1981 Mercedes of which he was excessively proud. At a bar in Voltastrasse, near the main railway station, they drank schnapps, Gent spending most of the time encouraging him to talk about his car, telling him how big she thought it was.

"Do you like it big?" he joked, laughing at the way both she and Jolli looked at each other.

Twice in the conversation he asked her what time she had to be home, what time her husband expected her. She knew Jolli had told him; the second time he asked she mentioned casually that it didn't matter as her husband was away at sea, and saw the look in his eyes.

They left the bar at eleven thirty. Jolli and Rolf waved them goodnight and left in the mechanic's car, the security man unlocked the Mercedes for her and she got in, knowing what he wanted, assuming that he would not return to his own home, seeing after a short while, that he was driving towards Landgraffenstrasse. At the bottom of the block of flats where she lived he asked if she was going to invite him in for coffee. "No," she told him, seeing again the look in his eyes, "not the first time." He leaned across and kissed her. She pulled back, as if that was what he expected, then opened her lips, kissed him more firmly, his tongue searching inside her mouth. She began to move, moaning slightly, then louder, reminding him her husband had been away for three months. He was moving across the seat, feeling her hips beginning to rock, her hands searching for him. "No," she was saying, changing the words. "No, not here."

He drove the car to the area at the rear of the block and switched off the lights. "Come into the back," he told her. She did as she was told. Suddenly, swiftly, he was on top of her,

moving, pushing himself hard against her. She was moaning,
loudly, hands feeling inside his shirt, nails digging into his back,
hips pushing against him, legs opening. He was feeling inside
her blouse, pulling it out of her skirt, fumbling to undo her bra.
She felt his breath and thought of the first lover she had had,
so slim and pretty, the way he had stroked her, caressed her,
made her want him.

The security man was still fumbling with her bra. She moved,
making it easier for him. He was fondling her breasts, firm, the
nipples large.

So many lovers, she thought, so many lives.

He was undoing her skirt, pulling it down, hand searching
the soft flesh between the nylons and suspender belt, feeling
inside her small silk pants, his fingers moving them aside, in-
truding into her. He was pulling the pants down, unzipping
himself, coming into her. "No," she was pulling him onto her,
"please no." He was thrusting into her, moving quickly, feeling her moving under him, taking him, moving with him.
"No," she was telling him, trying to push him off. "I want it
all." She was undressing, pulling off her blouse and bra, letting her pants fall to the floor of the car, unhooking her nylons, peeling them off, feeling the sensation as she exposed
herself, beginning to pull off her suspenders. "Leave them on,"
he told her. She saw his eagerness and did as he said, then lay
back on the car seat, her legs wide apart. He entered her, pulling her up at him. She lifted her buttocks and wrapped her legs
around him. His breath smelt of drink and he had not shaved
since that morning.

He came out of her, breathing hard, towering over her.
"How was it?" he asked. "You said you liked a big one."

"Incredible," she replied, hardly able to breathe. "Absolutely incredible."

"Do you want it again?"

"Yes," she panted, "for Chrissake yes."

The security guard came into her again, pushing hard. The
next morning, when she presented her bag for inspection, he
barely looked inside.

THE FEET MOVED across the concrete, quickly and quietly, through the snow which was settling on the runway. In the trees beyond the perimeter fences, beyond the layers of electrified wire, the rooks settled into the branches, the valleys beyond lost in the cold of a Welsh winter. They reached the plane, the ladders in place, still no noise. The fuselage was cold to touch, the wings slippery where they had iced up.

"Christ," said the man on Enderson's left. "It's bloody freezing."

Near the village of Pontrilas, down the road which sneaked past the site, the postman tried to get his red mail van past Gilberts Hill Wood, gave up and went back for a cup of tea.

"OK," said Enderson. "Let's go through it once again then get inside."

The eleven men clustered round him. Three patrols, four men in each. A Boeing 727 was too big to take with one.

The Boeing 727 has three Pratt and Whitney engines each capable of producing 14,500 lbs of thrust. It carries a payload of forty tons, normally comprising one hundred and forty-four passengers, plus cargo. There are two primary passenger entrances to the plane, one door on the port side in front of the wing, immediately behind the cockpit, the other to the rear complete with steps. There are also seven other points of entry to the plane; three emergency doors, one near the front of the starboard side, one at either side of the fuselage near the tail of the plane, and four emergency windows, two over each wing. According to studies conducted by the United States Delta force at Fort Bragg in Texas, access is also possible through the windows of the cockpit. Tests at Pontrilas had confirmed this but suggested that the equipment and clothing a man would be wearing in that situation, including the gas-mask and body armour at the point of entry, would make such a technique highly difficult.

"Nine entry points," Enderson began, he felt like a steward pointing out the emergency procedures prior to take-off. "We use three, four men for each." They would spend endless sessions debating how the group at each entry point would split, whether the first two would separate, one going right, the other left, or whether they should turn the same way, the two men behind them turning the other.

"Rear port emergency exit. Seats to left ending with row twenty-seven. Rows twenty-nine and thirty to right, three seats on either side, toilet on each side behind the seats."

The wind was cutting across from the Brecon. Had they looked they would not have seen even the outlines of the hills.

"Front starboard emergency window over wing, tight fit, entering by row eighteen." They knew they would have to find out which passengers were sitting in row eighteen.

He turned, facing into the weather. "Front main door, port side, cockpit door on left, opening towards us, toilet opposite, galley diagonally right."

The patrols were waiting. "OK," he said. "Let's get inside."

It was the first time they had practised on a plane, the three patrols working as a unit. They would walk through it, analysing what they were doing, identifying the problems. Only then would they begin the moves in earnest, moving quicker, the dummies in place, their own colleagues sitting amongst them, the diversions going in, the stun grenades preceding their own entry.

Those assigned to the front and rear doors climbed off the wings and placed the practice ladders in position; when they were operational each ladder would be tailor-made for each aircraft, even individual doors on aircraft, the ends covered with foam sponge so that they would make no noise against the metal of the plane. They waited for Enderson's commands.

"Stand-by, stand-by."

They knew what it would be like if they did it for real, when they did it for real, the necessity for the terrifying precision of the diversions, the timings and sequences of the doors opening, the effect and duration of the stun grenades, the chaos and terror inside.

They swung the doors open and moved inside, out of the snow.

THE BOEING WAS PARKED at the side of the hangar, on the side of the airport farthest from the passenger terminal. Walid Haddad drove across the runway, keeping to the route his passenger indicated and stopped the car beneath the plane. It was cold, the wind coming from the east.

Both Walid Haddad and his guide wore the blue overalls of mechanics; the vehicle they drove was an official maintenance car. They got out, turning their collars against the winter, and hurried up the steps, through the main door, and onto the plane.

"You've got two hours," the man told him.

"Plenty of time," said Walid Haddad.

"DOOR OPENS right to left outwards."

Enderson began the walk-through with the men who entered through the front door. "Cockpit door opening toward us. Pilot's seat on left, co-pilot on right, flight engineer behind." In a hijack, they would have photographs of the entire crew, would memorise them before they went in. "Next problem, the toilet." Mile high club, somebody joked; somebody always did. "At Mogadishu one of the hijackers hid in the toilet and fired through the door."

WALID HADDAD opened the toilet door; not much room, hardly any room at all. He knelt on the floor, examining the partitions, the ways the panelling had been fixed. The time factor, he thought, what about the time factor. Once inside the toilet the hijackers would not have unlimited time, and Gent Mueller herself would only have one opportunity to get the material on board. He looked at the screws. Something else to check with the German, the type of screw-drivers he and the team would need for each of the toilets. He assumed they would be the same but would confirm it anyway.

He borrowed a screw-driver from his guide, closed the door and made sure there was enough space to take off the panelling of the wash-stand and to stack it. It was just possible. Then he felt inside the cavity, running his finger behind the lining and the pipework. When he had finished, he replaced the panelling, screwed it back into position and examined the panelling of the toilet, then of the walls. Only when he was totally satisfied did he repeat the procedure with each of the remaining toilets on the plane.

FIRST CLASS, two rows only, two seats on either side of the aisle.

"Officers take this section," someone joked. Even in the plane it was biting cold.

"A lot of legroom," said Enderson. "Somebody could hide there if they wanted."

Economy class, one hundred and forty-four passengers normally, depending on the seating arrangement and the pitch of the seats themselves. Enderson walked through, familiarising himself. "Other ranks and wives," he expected someone to say. No one did. "Assuming that the passengers duck instinctively and keep their heads down," he said, "anybody above seat level should be somebody we're looking for." At Entebbe one passenger had raised his head to see what was happening and had been killed instantly.

They moved on, past the emergency windows over the wings where the second group would enter, working out their arcs of fire, till they arrived at the rear emergency door, the two toilets in the rows of seats behind the last seats. Less of a problem with passengers getting in the way, someone suggested. Unless it was a passenger in the toilet, someone else countered.

"OK," said Enderson. "That's it, let's start thinking about it."

There were few countries outside Britain where they would be called upon to exercise the skills they were about to develop, where they would be allowed to operate openly and officially as an anti-terrorist unit, particularly in Europe and the Middle East, either for reasons of politics, or because other countries had anti-hijack teams of their own.

Conversely there were also countries where they might be asked to perform such a role, for political reasons which were not substantially different. Including one country in the Middle East.

It was even colder.

"One more run through," he said, "then a break."

6

THE SNOW in the streets round Whitehall had turned to sludge. John Kenshaw-Taylor returned from the House at four thirty, confirmed the meeting for that evening, and checked the state of the pound. For the previous two days the fall in sterling had levelled out, the pound holding at just over one dollar thirteen, even climbing slightly at one stage. During that period his reactions had, in theory at least, been two-fold: a strengthening pound was good for the country, but it was bad for the coup he and Saeed Khaled were planning in New York; a weakening pound, on the other hand, spelt potential disaster for the government but without it the New York plan would not even be necessary. He need not have worried. At opening in London that day the pound began to slide again; when he checked that afternoon it was already down a cent.

Shortly before five his secretary informed him that British Airways security had queried whether he required any special measures for his flight to New York the following week; he asked her to inform them that he did not, and dictated a personal note of thanks to the chairman. They were quick, he thought, very quick. The flight had been booked only that morning, after he had received confirmation of his invitation to address the Jacksonian Institute in Washington on the second day of the oil talks in New York, after he had assured both the Foreign Secretary and the Prime Minister that, despite its timing, the visit was purely personal.

At six thirty, following his customary drinks with his senior advisors, he was driven to the club. Jonty Mathison was already in the bar having declined both squash and sauna. For twenty minutes they discussed the arrangements the banker had made for the meeting in New York; at the end John Kenshaw-Taylor asked one question.

"No one, either in London or amongst those invited, knows the real reason for the dinner or what will be offered them there?"

"No," said Jonty Mathison.

"Good."

7

WALID HADDAD was due at eleven. Abu Nabil stood at the window and watched the winter sun shining into the courtyard below. On the desk at his side were the latest newspapers from Germany. He had read them that morning, thought again about the hunger strike, how at first it had been ignored, how it was now taking its toll, the increasing presence of the police on the streets, the analysis by the so-called experts on how much longer Klars Christian Mannheim had to live. And the bombings and shootings, not daily but regular, spreading the fear, tightening the screw. In seven days, he would leave Damascus for New York. It all depended on New York, he thought. Without success in New York all that had gone before would have been in vain.

It was almost eleven. In the courtyard below he saw Walid Haddad arrive and wondered again how he would tell him. Thirty seconds later the hijacker was shown into the room on the third floor.

Abu Nabil crossed the room, welcomed him, and offered him coffee. For the next ten minutes he briefed him on the men and women who were being assembled in the mountain camps, the West Germans and Palestinians from whom he would select his hijack team. For twenty minutes after that the hijacker briefed Abu Nabil on the reports he was receiving from the woman calling herself Gent Mueller; updating him on how she had solved the problem of getting the weapons and explosives past security.

Abu Nabil did not need to know the details. "We all have to make our sacrifices," he said, almost sadly. It was time to tell Walid Haddad. "I think," he said, "you should go home, I think you should go to Ain Helweh."

"Why?" asked Walid Haddad. He knew, had known for four months, had known since the day Yakov Zubko and his family had left Moscow and begun their journey to the West, the day that Abu Nabil had first seen the prediction of the return to the White House of Ronald Reagan, the day a member of the Provisional IRA had first contacted the RUC Special Branch, the day, in the Palestinian refugee camp in the southern area of the Lebanon, that a young doctor had diagnosed cancer in the throat and lungs of an old man.

"I think," said Abu Nabil, "that you should see your father."

It was strange, thought Walid Haddad, that Abu Nabil was sending him to his probable death on a hijack, yet talking to him like a favoured son.

"When?" he asked.

"Now," said Abu Nabil. "You should not forego the opportunity of saying goodbye." He was staring past Walid Haddad as if the hijacker did not exist. "If you have the chance and do not take it you will never forgive yourself." Walid

Haddad realised that Abu Nabil was looking at the single photograph which was always on his desk. "Even those of us who did not have the chance cannot forgive ourselves."

Walid Haddad rose to leave the room. "Thank you," he said simply. As he closed the door behind him, he saw that Abu Nabil was still staring at the photograph.

8

THE STREET LIGHTS barely illuminated the doorway across the square; from the window of what had once been the Argentinian Embassy Jimmy Roberts saw the figures going into the address and tried to distinguish them, knowing that at night, at least in the light snow that was falling, it was impossible. He heard the noise downstairs as the next shift came on duty to relieve them. People coming and going at the club all day, he thought, mainly at lunch time and the evenings, but never the bastard he had first seen in the drinking club off the Falls. He spoke to the two members of the away team who were on the night shift and went to a pub.

During the day the snow had turned to sludge, that evening the sludge had frozen. On the way back from the hospital Eileen McDonald had slipped and bruised her leg. At ten o'clock she finished the housework and went upstairs to bed. Liam was getting better, slowly of course, she had always known it would be slowly, but each day he seemed to have more colour in his cheeks, each day his eyes seemed a little brighter. She had been asleep, half asleep, for almost an hour when she saw the eyes of the man, looking at her from the photograph on the table in the room upstairs, looking at her across her Liam's body. She thought of the night, the moment in the car, the way the man had appeared from nowhere, knew what he was, who he was, knew suddenly what they were going to do to him.

9

WALID HADDAD timed his departure so that he crossed into the Lebanon at night. The road from Damascus to Beirut is long and hard and even in the Syrian-controlled sector, even in the country which acted as host to the organisation of which he was a member; it was closed to Walid Haddad and the likes of Walid Haddad.

He left hunched in the back seat of a Mercedes, the car picking up speed as it passed from the city, maintaining a steady eighty kilometres an hour. The driver knew the road well; he steered with one hand hanging out of the window, the AK47 cocked on the passenger seat beside him. At the point where the road narrows and the grim outline of the mountains stands against the sky he pulled onto a track, following it west, the dust swirling round them, till he reached the point from which Walid Haddad had set out on foot so many times before. Already the cold of evening was draining whatever strength there had been in the winter sun. He wished the man farewell and disappeared into the grey of dusk.

The route was familiar to him. He remembered the men who had been with him the first time, the last time, remembered how some had lived, many died. The dark began to settle; he felt at ease, climbing to the jagged crescent of rocks that marked the eastern rim and listening to the still of the night, hearing in his mind the sounds of hatred which had divided the valley so many times, killed so many of his countrymen, so many others. By two in the morning he had crossed the Beka'a and the hills to the west and was beginning the gentle, dangerous drop to the plain below, the sea only miles away. Here, he knew, was where they were waiting for him; here, he knew, was where they were always waiting for him and the likes of him. Here he was at his most vulnerable, close to his own side, to those who professed to be his own side. The moon was new, its shape barely visible, giving no light, concealing him. He reached the road and heard the men, dropping into the ditch and waiting in the icy water till they had passed.

At five, almost six, he drew upon the outskirts of the city, passing the places where the boys had waited at night for the barrages to fall upon them, the places where he had returned the next morning to pick up the remains of their mutilated bodies. It was growing lighter. He moved on, losing himself in the increasing numbers of people, passing the first of the skeletons, the broken limbs and twisted metal and concrete frames of what had once been buildings. Yet people survived, he told himself, people woke up, went to work, came home, went to bed, made love. Produced the generation that in two decades, one decade, would be pouring out its blood for this wretched piece of land.

By mid-morning he had passed through the city, remembering the most bitter battle of all, in the port to the north, as the Palestinians fought each other, killed each other, in the drive that had sent the forces of Yasser Arafat into the sea. Then, and only then, did he turn south.

The refugee camp of Ain Helweh was no longer a camp, more a city. He passed the outer walls, through the gate marked by the splash of machine-gun bullets in the arch above it and the blackened remains of what had once been a car by the side, picking up the alley ways, turning right and left, the houses close together, the children playing between them, the portraits of the martyrs on the walls.

They had seen him coming.

They were lounged against the wall in the assumed manner of those who had been forced to manhood before they were even children, fanning across the street in front of him, the oldest not yet twelve years of age, asserting the authority of the Kalashnikovs which hung carelessly from their shoulders.

It was like going home, he had thought as he crossed the Beka'a the night before, like a journey back into his own short life. Now he had come face to face with himself.

"Who are you?"

"My father's son."

"Where are you going?"

"To see my father."

"Why?"

"He is dying."

The language was archaic, ritualistic, almost as if it was necessary, almost as if they were speaking in a code only they could understand.

"Who is he?"

"My father."

"Who are you?"

"His son."

They knew who he was, what he was.

"Allah Ma'ak," they told him, "Go in peace."

"Shukran." He returned their respect. "Thank you."

He walked one more block, and went into the house. The old man was on a bed in the corner. The legs of the bed were low so that before he had been as weak as he was now he could rise without help, could fall upon it when his ailing strength betrayed him. The walls of the room were lime green. On them were two paintings; one was of a woman, the other was of a village where the man had once lived and which he still called home.

Walid Haddad stood in the doorway and waited to be invited in. The women at the bed moved back into the shadows as the old man looked up, his eyes blind with cataracts.

"Is that you, my son?" he asked. His voice was low and filled with gravel as the growth sought to tear his words from him before it tore away his life.

"Yes, my father," said Walid Haddad. "It is I."

The old man waved to him to enter, barely able to move his arm from the cotton sheet upon which he lay. Walid Haddad knelt by the bed and kissed his father. He knew that the room smelt of death, that others would say it stank of poverty and desecration. He looked at the old man and knew what his father smelt, what his father heard, knew where his father was.

The old man gestured that he wanted water. The women in the shadows moved forward, offering the son the jug they had filled. Walid Haddad knew it was not what his father wanted, knew what it was that he wanted.

"Excuse me, my father."

He rose, went outside and refilled it.

The old man was waiting for him. The women had seen him like it before, knew he was not with them, did not know where the fever had taken him.

"Is the water fresh from the well, my son?" he asked.

"Yes, my father, it is fresh from the well."

"Is my brother there?"

"Yes, my father, my uncle is there."

"Is he going to market tomorrow?" The women began to understand.

"Yes, my father, he is going to market tomorrow."

He lifted the old man's head, tilted the jug to his lips, and helped him drink.

"Are the oxen in, my son?"

"Yes, my father, the oxen are in. I have fed and watered them."

The old man patted Walid Haddad's hand. "We did well today, my son. Did we not do well today?"

"Yes, my father, we did well today. The field is ploughed and the seeds are in."

"And your mother is preparing the *adas*?"

"Yes, my mother is preparing the lentils."

The old man smiled. The women in the shadows had never before seen him smile.

"She is a fine woman, my son. I remember the first time I saw her, in the orange grove by the field. She was gathering fruit." He was smiling again, nodding his head. "How I courted her, my son, how I married her. How she bore me such a child." His head was still nodding. "She is a good woman, my son."

"Yes, my father, she is a good woman."

The old man moved on the bed. "Give me another drink, my son."

Walid Haddad held his father's head for the second time, tilting the jug and letting the water trickle against his father's lips.

"Ah, my son," said the old man, "there is no water as sweet as the water from the well of Esh Shikara."

He looked round, eyes unseeing. "Where am I, my son?" he asked.

"In the refugee camp of Ain Helweh," Walid Haddad told him.

The women drew back again into the shadows.

"I am dying, my son, and I have nothing to give you." The old man reached out his hand. Walid Haddad took it, held it.

"That is not why I came."

The old man looked at him. "Why did you come, my son?"

"To ask what I could give to *you*."

The old man was drifting away again, nodding his head, smiling.

"What can I give you, my father?" Walid Haddad asked again. "What can I do for you?"

"One thing, my son, only one thing." Walid Haddad knew what he wanted, what they all wanted. "You can deliver me the earth of Esh Shikara."

The women in the shadows knew he had slipped away again, had disappeared into his dreams.

"Yes, my father," said Walid Haddad. The difference in his words was so subtle that the women in the shadows did not notice, so significant that the old man on the bed understood.

"Yes, my father," he said again. "I will deliver you the earth of Esh Shikara."

The women watched as he kissed his father goodbye, then they pulled the sheet over the old man's body and resumed their vigil.

At nine o'clock that night, Walid Haddad left the refugee camp of Ain Helweh, driving south then east in a car he had stolen. Some time after midnight he passed back into Syria, then into Jordan, by four in the morning he had reached the third barrier he would cross that night. At five, as the sun broke from the east, he cut his way through the series of barbed wire fences, crawling backwards across the strip of soft sand that separated them so that the soldiers who would check later that morning would think he had been travelling in the opposite direction, and entered what is marked on the maps as the Israeli military-occupied zone of the West Bank.

10

YAKOV ZUBKO left the workshop and climbed the hill, pausing at the top, enjoying the late afternoon sun on his back, then walked down the street to the house. Alexandra had already collected their son from school and was sitting with him at the kitchen table waiting for his father. As soon as he entered the house, Yakov Zubko could see that the boy wanted to ask him something but that he was unsure whether he should.

It was Alexandra who spoke for their son, standing slightly to the side of him so that he could not see the way she looked at her husband, the way she showed that she was proud of the reason the boy had hesitated.

"Nikki would like a ball," she said, speaking in a way that did not embarrass him. "All the other boys in his class have them, but he is afraid we cannot afford it."

Yakov Zubko looked at the boy for a moment then winked at him. "Of course we can afford it," he said smiling, seeing the expression that came upon his son's face.

That evening, before it closed, they went with him to the shop just below the square, where the other boys had bought their balls, watching as he chose a blue and white one from the cardboard box by the door, smiling as he paid for it with the money they had given him. That night, when they kissed him goodnight, he was holding it tight in his hand.

11

THE DAY THAT Walid Haddad began his journey to Esh Shikara, Gent Mueller boarded, for the first time, the Boeing 727 on which she knew she would one day place the weapons and explosives concealed behind the panelling of the bath in her flat.

Jolli was with her, talking about the mechanic called Rolf, asking her if what Rolf said about the security man was true. When they had finished cleaning the plane, they went for coffee; at the last moment Gent remembered she had left something on board. She waited till she was alone, then walked down the aisle. A hundred and forty-four passengers. She could see them, hear them, frightened and desperate, unsure what was happening, what was going to happen, not knowing whether they would live or die. The fat ones, the thin ones, the ones who would scream in terror, the ones who would be silent with fear. She saw the hijackers, did not know who or how many, wondered what they would be thinking, how they would be reacting under the pressure. Wondered whether they would win or whether they would lose.

The plane was quiet.

She walked into the flight-deck, three man crew, she knew, the pilot in the left seat, the co-pilot in the right, flight engineer behind. She wondered who they would be, how they would react.

The plane smelt clean and fresh, she walked back to the cabins, imagining the sweat and vileness of the bodies, the excreta blocking the toilets, the vomit of the children, the sanitary towels of the women.

It was almost the end of the coffee break. She went to the toilets where it would begin, the places she had been ordered to conceal the weapons and explosives. Not much time she thought, not much time to undo the screws, assemble the weapons, re-pack them in the wrappings that would disguise the smell if dogs were brought on to check the plane, tape them to the wall, place the explosives, similarly wrapped, alongside them. She wondered who would collect them, who would use them. Who would be the heroes, who would be the martyrs.

It was time to leave.

She went back to the canteen, wondering when they would tell her, thinking about the moment she would go to the mail-box at the foot of the stairs and find the postcard from the husband who did not exist, the postcard with the code on it.

That night she allowed the security man to come to her bed, told herself, as he took her, that the following morning she would begin to bring the weapons and explosives into the air-port, the guns broken down, the explosives carefully wrapped, concealed in the false bottom of the bag she carried or close to the parts of her body the security man was even now violating, consoled herself that the following morning she would begin to store them in the lockers she had selected.

His bodyweight was smothering her: she told him how much more she wanted him and wondered how much longer she would have to endure the pig.

12

THE STREET WAS QUIET, the sun already warm; Yakov Zubko sat on the side of the well, looking down at the water. There was no water, he had heard them say, as sweet as the water from the well of Beita. It was six o'clock. He walked down the street, past the orange grove and the field opposite, and climbed the hill called Bethesda, looking north, feeling the first anxiety. In the distance, to the east of Jerusalem, a spiral of smoke was rising in the thin blue sky of the early morning. He knew what it was, had seen the burning the night before, on his neigh-bour's television set, began thinking of the police who had been in the village the previous day, wondering whether they would be back, hoping—he did not know why—that they would not.

THE BUS WAS CROWDED, rocking under the weight of its load. Walid Haddad had boarded it two hours earlier, when the sun was still growing warm and the empty road made him feel isolated and exposed. Gradually, however, as they travelled south, as the bus filled up and the roads grew busier, he had begun to feel safer. Not safe, but safer. After two hours he changed buses, taking one that would bring him closer to Esh Shikara.

It was dangerous at any time, he knew. The Israelis were always on the alert, needed always to be on the alert, against the gunmen who slipped across the border at night, against the gunmen in their midst, but today even more so. He had heard the news at the bus station, the Arab mayor with his legs blown off, the retaliation, the retaliation against the retaliation. He knew what would be happening, where it would be happening.

THE POLICE PATROLS left at eight, three Land-Rovers, each with four men. The captain in charge was twenty-three years old; the night before he had been facing the stones and bricks of the Arab youths, waiting for the bullets from the militants, today he and his men had been re-deployed. He was unsure whether or not he was sorry, he liked the adrenalin of the riots, did not even mind the risks. He forgot about it and told the driver to pull off.

ALEXANDRA ZUBKO rose at six, fighting off the morning sickness, then she tidied the kitchen and got the children out of bed. They left at eight and walked down the street to the school, her son clutching the blue and white ball his father had bought for him the night before. Alexandra smiled as he joined his friends, bouncing the ball, then she kissed him goodbye and returned home.

WALID HADDAD watched as the bus left the city, remembering the first time he had been there, the first time his father had taken him to see the Mosque of Omar. The road had been different then, lined with men leading their donkeys, the animals piled high, heading for the market place close by the shrine where the tourists now came for what they called Easter. The bus passed the turning for Ramat Rahel and he saw the signpost to the place his people called Beit Lahm.

THE VILLAGE WAS QUIET. The only sound, other than the crackling of the radio, was the singing of the children in the school by the square. The captain wondered why they had been sent to Beita; he told the driver to park at the top of the street and settled back for a quiet day.

THE BUS to Beit Lahm arrived at eleven. Walid Haddad got off, left the town and headed south. The village was four kilometres away, perhaps five; in front of him, rising up, he could see the hill called Balama. The road was dusty, the day getting hotter. A truck passed him, throwing up a cloud of dust, he turned his head so that it would not blow into his eyes. Thirty-five minutes later he reached Esh Shikara.

It was as he remembered, larger perhaps, more houses creeping down from the square, but also smaller. He supposed it was because the last time he had seen the place he had only been six years old. Before the Palestinians had moved out and the others taken their place, changed the name.

On the left was the orange grove where his father had first seen his mother, where Walid Haddad had played as a boy. He walked off the road and into the trees, breathing in the smell, feeling the fruit on the branches. Still too early to ripen, he remembered, knew how it would taste anyway, that it would have tasted as he always remembered the fruit of his village.

The light was dappling the ground beneath the trees; he stood up and walked to the field on the other side of the road, the heat haze rising across it, screwing up his eyes against the sun. In that far corner he thought he could see the man, his son at his side, taking the bread and cheese which was their mid-day meal, the oxen standing patiently in the plough. The father had strong arms, strong hands; when they had eaten he took the boy to the plough, controlling it, guiding it, as the boy struggled to learn its skill.

It was five minutes to twelve. In the police post at Bethlehem a man reported he had seen a stranger get off the bus from Jerusalem and walk towards Beita. It was a quiet day, despite the trouble in Nablus, the sergeant wondered why the man had singled out the person from the thousands who came to Bethlehem at all times of the year, and made a note to pass it to the patrol in the village.

Slowly, carefully, Walid Haddad scooped the earth from the field and poured it into the two bags he carried with him. The earth he chose was from the corner near the hill. When the bags were full he knotted them at the top and tied them round his body. It was twelve o'clock.

In the workshop Yakov Zubko switched off his machine and prepared to leave; he was always glad that he could see Alexandra and the children for lunch, was even more glad today, because of the photograph from Moscow, because of the trouble with the Arabs. In the house at the top of the street Alexandra finished laying the table and began to prepare her daughter for the walk to school to collect her son. In the room three hundred metres away, the small boy clutched his ball and thought of playing with his friends by the well in the square while he waited for his mother. In the police station in Bethlehem the sergeant remembered he had to radio the unit in Beita.

WALID HADDAD left the field, climbed over the ditch, and began to walk up the road to the village itself, past the first houses, those that had not existed when he had been a child, into the old part, towards the square and the well. In the kitchen Alexandra covered the food and began to leave. In the schoolhouse by the square the cluster of small boys ran from the door and began to play in the sunshine round the well. In the police station in Bethlehem the sergeant rose from his desk and walked to the radio.

The well was as it had always been—deep, the coolness rising from it. He thought of the night before, the room in the refugee camp, how even his father remembered the sweetness of the water. He leaned forward, dropped the bucket, hearing the splash as it struck the water, and began to pull it up. In the square around him the boys were playing as he had played. He dipped his hand into the bucket, tasting the sweetness. Slowly and carefully he began to pour the liquid into the water bottle he had brought with him from Ain Helweh. The boys by the well were playing ball. It was five minutes past twelve. In the workshop Yakov Zubko picked up his coat and turned for home. In the house at the top of the road Alexandra closed the door behind her and began to walk down the hill. In the police station in Bethlehem the sergeant made his call to the patrol in Beita.

Walid Haddad let the bucket fall back into the water, screwing the top on the water bottle, and looked at the boys, making sure the top was tight, making sure nothing would leak, making sure that not one single drop would leak. On the other side of the village Yakov Zubko was half way up the hill. At the top of the street Alexandra held her daughter's hand, and pointed out her son, saw him playing with the blue and white ball his father had given him the day before.

Walid Haddad began to put the water bottle in his pocket.

In front of Alexandra, the captain acknowledged the radio message and told the driver to inspect the road from Bethlehem. In the corner of his eye Walid Haddad saw the ball bouncing.

Bouncing away. Blue and white ball, he thought. The small boy running after it. At the top of the road the driver started the engine. Bastards, he thought, Palestinian bastards. The ball bouncing. Move it, the captain told the driver. The ball still bouncing. The driver was young, too young. He smashed the Land-Rover into gear and jammed his foot on the accelerator. On the other side of the hill Yakov Zubko was almost home.

"No." The scream went on for ever. Alexandra's scream. Cutting into the minds of those who heard it. Cutting into Yakov Zubko's mind. He was running, dropping his coat, running for his son's life. Knew already what it was, knew already it was too late. The fear biting him. "No, for God's sake, no." The neighbours heard the scream, the horror in it, the despair. Dropped what they were doing, began to run. Knew it was too late, knew they would not stop him. The ball bouncing. Yakov was running, almost to the top of the hill, almost to his son, his beloved son. Alexandra had her daughter in her arms, was running, past the captain, past the rest of the patrol. The ball bouncing. Knew it was too late, knew it was the end of everything. Heard the thump. The single sickening thump. On the other side of the hill Yakov Zubko heard it. Alexandra covered the last fifty metres. Screaming, not hearing her own screams, hearing only the sound as the Land-Rover struck the body. The man was rolling over, the small boy clutched in his arms, protecting him, saving him. His coat and shirt torn where the Land-Rover had struck, the black and purple on his body already beginning to show. The boy too frightened to cry. Alexandra took her son, wrapped him close to her. At the top of the hill Yakov Zubko saw his wife, saw his son was alive, ran to them. "I saw it," someone was saying. "I saw it all. He saved the boy's life, pulled him from the wheels of the jeep." Alexandra was crying, with relief, with fear, looked for the man, did not see where he had gone. Yakov Zubko had reached them, held them, held his precious wife and daughter and his oh so precious son.

Walid Haddad left the village, and began walking down the road towards Bethlehem. His arm and shoulder were numb with pain, he could feel the bruising where his coat had been torn. In the distance he saw the Land-Rover, stopping and turning, the men getting out, coming towards him. Stopping those they passed, checking their identity papers. He looked to the orange grove on the right, the field to his left, knew he had to keep to the road, that if he stepped off the road they would suspect him. Knew they were looking for him. He turned back, remembering the other ways out of the village, began walking again up the road towards the well. In the square Yakov Zubko was gathering his family to him, comforting them. "That's the man," he heard someone say, "that's the man who saved the boy."

Walid Haddad saw the man coming towards him, the crowd of people with him, the police behind them, moving towards him as the police to his rear were him, the police behind them, moving towards him as the police to his rear were moving towards him, checking papers, confirming identities, cutting him off. He glanced to his right, saw that the street was sealed off by a Land-Rover. One last street, he thought, one last way out, confirmed that it too was sealed off.

IN THE SINGLE ROOM in the refugee camp of Ain Helweh the old man moved on his bed and felt the pain in his body. The women in the shadows knew he was near death. "How much longer, old man?" one of them asked, the tenderness in her voice. She could barely hear his reply. "As long as it takes," he said, "as long as it takes my son to deliver me the earth of Esh Shikara." They knew he was delirious and gave him water.

YAKOV ZUBKO stepped forward so that he was facing the stranger.

"You are the man who saved my son's life," he said.

The stranger looked at him. "He is young," replied Walid Haddad. "He has many years to live, many reasons for which to die." He thought of the boys in the trenches outside Beirut waiting for the artillery shells to fall upon them. "Nobody should die when they have so much before them."

Something about the stranger, thought Yakov Zubko, something about his eyes. Behind him he heard Alexandra, still crying. He looked at the stranger again, past him, down the road, saw the police coming towards them, stopping everyone, checking their identity papers. Looked back at the stranger, did not see him, did not see the street in Beita. Saw himself, in the road outside the house of Pasha Simenov in Moscow on the morning the American woman had given him the black market goods which would buy them their tickets to Vienna. He was no longer himself, no longer Yakov Zubko looking at the stranger who had saved his son's life. He was Pasha Simenov looking at Yakov Zubko. He remembered how the man pretended to ignore him, warned him. Saved him.

In front of him a small boy, a friend of his son's, was tugging at the stranger's coat, trying to attract his attention.

Yakov Zubko turned away, saw the look in the man's eyes as he turned away, went to Alexandra, took their son from her and gave him to the stranger.

"I cannot thank you enough," he said. "I can at least ask you to eat at my table."

The small boy was still tugging at the stranger's coat. Yakov Zubko turned back up the hill, the neighbours watching.

The house was on the other side of the line of police. Walid Haddad held the child and began walking with Yakov Zubko up the hill towards the police, the captain stepping forward.

"We are taking lunch," Yakov Zubko stood between the captain and the stranger. "The man who saved my son's life from your Land-Rover and I are taking lunch."

The captain looked at the stranger, "I'm sorry," he said suddenly. "Well done."

Yakov Zubko moved on, his wife and family with him, the neighbours smiling, patting the back of the stranger in admiration and thanks, afraid to touch him too hard, afraid to hurt the shoulder he had injured. At his side the small boy at last caught the man's attention.

"Your water bottle," he said, "You left it at the well."

THE HOUSE WAS SMALLER than Walid Haddad remembered it.

Alexandra led them into the kitchen and poured water for their hands, moving the chairs for them so that they could sit down, remembering the night she had waited in Moscow for Yakov Zubko to return home, the children on either side of her, the papers she had received from the office on Kolpachny Lane on the table. The symbols of the Feast of the Passover spread around the papers.

One symbol above all, she now thought, the spare plate and wine glass for the stranger who might come alone.

Walid Haddad looked around the room: a stove in the right hand corner, a dressing table against the wall, four chairs round the table in the middle. The food on it was barely enough for the family. He sat down where he was offered and saw they were a chair short, knew nevertheless that he should not refuse their offer to share their lunch with them. Alexandra left the room, went outside, and returned with a chair she had borrowed from a neighbour. They waited till she was seated with them.

Yakov Zubko lowered his head and began to say grace. Walid Haddad looked at the man, at his wife and children, turning his face so they would not see he did not know the words. When he had finished, Yakov Zubko broke the bread and gave the first piece to the stranger.

"My name is Yakov Zubko," he introduced himself. "This is my wife Alexandra and these are our two children. Soon," he said proudly, "there will be a third." Alexandra blushed slightly. "What is your name?" she asked Walid Haddad.

"David," he lied.

The food was simple but good. Walid Haddad ate slowly, enjoying it. Alexandra poured him a glass of water. "From the well," she told him, "we always get the water we drink from the well, it is so sweet."

The children began to tell him how long they had lived in the village, how they had arrived, where they had come from, where they had been born.

"But," said the boy whose life he had saved, "I was really born in Bethlehem."

Walid haddad looked puzzled, smiling as the boy explained about the name they had given to the room in the hospital where he had been delivered, the name of the place in the land they thought they would never see. "Where were you born?" he asked when he had finished.

Walid Haddad looked at him. "I was also born in Bethlehem." He used the name the boy had used. "At least, near Bethlehem."

He passed over the subject, asking them about Moscow, how they had left, how long they had been required to wait. Yakov Zubko told him, listening while Alexandra related the story of the morning the letter from the OVIR office on Kolpachny Lane had arrived, how she had been afraid to open it, how her husband had stolen and cheated for them so that they could eat, so that they could come to Israel.

When she had finished, Yakov Zubko rose from the table, took the photograph which had arrived from Norfolk and handed it to Walid Haddad.

"This is the day we left," he explained. "This is the station we left from."

Walid Haddad sensed the sadness in his voice. "And the people with you?" he asked.

Yakov Zubko remembered again the moment they had said farewell. "Also the family Zubko," he said at last. "My brother Stanislav and his family."

He put the photograph on the table, pointing out Alexandra and himself, pointing out their children, pointing out the others.

"This is my brother Stanislav," he said, "this is Stanislav's wife, Mishka, his son Anatol and his daughter Natasha." He told him about Natasha, how she struggled to pull each breath into her lungs.

"Do they want to come to Israel?" asked Walid Haddad.

"They have tried," said Yakov Zubko, "but they were refused. Now they have applied again."

The son of Yakov Zubko asked if he could show the man called David his room. Alexandra looked at their guest. "If he wants to see it," she said.

The stairs to the bedroom were narrow, Walid Haddad had to duck his head under the beam, half way up, where the stairs turned on a small landing to the left. He remembered when he could not touch the beam, even when he stood on tiptoe, remembered the day he had first touched it.

The boy's bed was in the corner. The window in the wall opposite was open, the breath of air coming in, the sunlight playing in the room.

"That was where I had my bed." The words had come out before he knew he had spoken them.

The boy looked at him. "You lived here?" he asked.

"Yes," said Walid Haddad, "I lived here." He realised that Yakov Zubko and his wife were on the stairs looking at him.

"This is the room where I was born," he said simply.

He turned to face them. "You must go?" Alexandra asked him, remembered the spare plate and wine glass for the stranger who came alone.

He knew she understood. "Yes," he replied, "I must go."

"Have you far to travel?"

Walid Haddad looked at them both. "Yes," he said, "I have far to travel."

"Then I will prepare food for you."

He sat playing with the children while Yakov Zubko cleared the table and Alexandra wrapped two slices of matzo and gefilte fish and handed it to him. From a bowl on the table Yakov Zubko gave him an orange.

"From the grove by the field," he said.

Walid Haddad thanked them and left.

At eight that evening, on the bus north from Jerusalem, he took the package from his coat pocket, unwrapped it, and began to eat. He did not know, but the woman sitting two seats behind him, alarmed by the Nablus scare, had been looking at him, growing suspicious of the tear in his coat, trying to decide about him. When she saw him take out the matzo and eat the gefilte fish she knew she had been wrong. Only a good Jewish boy would eat matzo and gefilte fish on a bus, only a good Jewish boy whose mother had wrapped it for him and who said grace.

At eleven that night, as the moon rose above the line of the Jordan and the fires of Rajib burnt in the distance. Walid Haddad crossed back under the wire at Kureiyima. The bruising on his shoulder and side were paining him, making it difficult to ease his body through the narrow hole he cut for himself. As he wormed through, a single needle of the barb penetrated his jacket and his shirt. When he moved forward, it tore open the plastic bag strapped to his back.

Half a mile beyond the fence, half a mile into Jordan, he stopped, crouching in the cover of an olive tree, and ate the last of the food Alexandra had prepared for him, keeping the orange which Yakov Zubko had given him in his pocket. It was only when he began to move off again that he discovered the container on his back was torn. He stopped again, took off his coat and shirt, and examined the bag. It was empty. In the sky above him the moon passed behind a cloud. It was ironic, he thought, that just as they had taken the land from his father during his life, so they had sought to deny it to him even at his death.

He checked the other bag. It was still full.

CHAPTER FOUR

1

JOHN KENSHAW-TAYLOR left Whitehall at five thirty and took the seven o'clock Concorde to New York, arriving at John F. Kennedy at ten minutes to six Eastern Standard Time, the special clearance which the British Embassy had arranged enabling him to catch the next shuttle to Washington. He was in his room at the Ritz Carlton by ten past eight. He showered, then made three telephone calls: the first was to the City banker, Jonty Mathison, confirming for the second time the details for the following evening, the second was to Sheikh Saeed Khaled at his private suite in New York, the third was to the offices of the British ambassador to the United Nations, also in New York. He identified himself and was immediately transferred to the meeting where the British negotiating team at the oil talks was locked in an analysis of the day's lack of progress.

The fears, expressed initially behind the closed doors of the Bank of England, that the previous slow decline of the pound might, unless halted, degenerate into a rapid and uncontrollable slide and the worst sterling crisis in history, were proving ominously well-founded. At opening in London that morning, the pound had stood at a little over one dollar ten; by midday it had slipped to one dollar eight. When John Kenshaw-Taylor had left Heathrow that evening, it was trading in New York at just under one dollar five. There was even talk of the fall not levelling out until the pound reached parity.

The Foreign Minister waited patiently while the connection to the conference room was made then was briefed by the man who had replaced him at Energy, offering any help he could whilst he was in America, despite the fact, which he took pains to emphasise, that his visit was in a purely private capacity.

He left his hotel at eight forty-five, at nine fifteen he sat down to dinner with the man who had arranged the invitation to the United States, the man who, according to the confidential reports Whitehall had now begun to receive from its man in Washington, was about to become the individual who would guide American foreign policy through the years of the second Reagan administration, the man the Palestinian industrialist Ahmad Hussein had identified three months before as Henry Armstrong.

Abu Nabil arrived in New York three hours after John Kenshaw-Taylor. It was warmer than on his previous visit. He took a cab to the Plaza Hotel, checked in, bathed, and made his way to his first appointment.

The meeting with Saeed Khaled took place, as did all their discussions, under conditions of the utmost secrecy and security; it began forty minutes after the British Foreign Minister had made his own private call to Khaled and lasted a little over an hour. For twenty-five of those minutes Khaled went through the details of the next thirty-six hours, the strategy he would adopt to guarantee that the next day's oil discussions would not reach agreement and the two meetings he and John Kenshaw-Taylor had confirmed for the following morning. During that time Abu Nabil listened carefully, hardly speaking, the feeling growing in his mind that Saeed Khaled was holding something back, that Saeed Khaled would tell him at the end.

"There is one more thing," Khaled said at last, "one more thing you should know about John Kenshaw-Taylor."

"Why did you choose him?" he had asked Abu Nabil at their meeting in Rome.

"Because he is ambitious," Nabil had replied.

"Some who know him would say he is too ambitious for his own good." Khaled had agreed. "He is a good choice."

"What else is there to know about him?" Nabil had asked.

"I don't know," Khaled had replied, "but I will find out."

Had not known then, had only discovered later, that the British Foreign Minister's flat in Pimlico was fifteen minutes by foot, five minutes by car.

Had not known then, had only discovered later, that on the same day of the Rome meeting Kenshaw-Taylor had ordered his driver to drop him at a reception and to take his remaining despatch boxes to the flat. Had not known then, had only discovered later, that the minister had left the reception at twenty minutes to ten and arrived at the flat at eleven thirty.

Had not known then, had only discovered later, that on the evening John Kenshaw-Taylor had made his first approach to the British banker who would arrange the dinner with the

American bankers in New York in return for a knighthood, the
Foreign Minister had left the club where the meeting had taken
place at ten thirty and returned to Pimlico at one.

Sheikh Saeed Khaled told Abu Nabil the final detail about
John Kenshaw-Taylor.

Nabil had expected it, knew he would have been surprised if
there had not been such an indiscretion; knew, at the same
time, that he was surprised. Not at the indiscretion, at the nature of it. Abu Nabil, author and perpetuator of terrorism was,
in his way, a conservative, a man of almost puritanical morals.
The bastard, he thought. "Interesting," he said. He did not ask
Khaled how or from whom the information had been obtained.

"Can we use it?" He knew they could use it, how they would
use it, the conditions that would have to be met in order for
them to use it.

"It all depends," said Saeed Khaled.

"It all depends," agreed Abu Nabil.

By the time he left the meeting, it was almost nine. He returned to his hotel, unpacked his case, hung his clothes neatly
and tidily in the wardrobe, and placed the chess set he had
brought with him on the table at the side of the bed.

The only thing missing from the bedroom was the photograph he had left in Damascus.

2

HENRY ARMSTRONG'S Washington penthouse was situated in
the Watergate complex. From where he stood John Kenshaw-
Taylor could see across the Potomac to the lights of Rosslyn,
the black of the Parkway downstream, and the blaze of colour
of National Airport. They had finished dinner and were taking coffee in the lounge. The conversation that evening had
ranged over a variety of issues; now they drifted back to the
subject of the conference at the United Nations and the relationship between the oil producers' inability to agree on a new
price structure and the almost catastrophic fall in the value of
the British pound.

"The problem," suggested Henry Armstrong, "is that even
if they all agreed it would only be five or six months before they

disagreed again, so that any agreement would only be in the short term.''

"Correct," said John Kenshaw-Taylor. "But even a short-term agreement would be enough to halt the fall of the pound. And by the time the major oil producers fell out again, I imagine the dollar would have begun to fall for US domestic reasons, so the pound would be able to survive anyway."

It was a replica of the conversation the Foreign Minister had had with Sheikh Khaled in the Hilton Hotel in London.

"Probably," said Henry Armstrong. "But can your man pull it off?" He named the minister who had taken over the British negotiations from Kenshaw-Taylor.

"No," said John Kenshaw-Taylor. "Our man won't pull it off." There was a change in the grammar, a double meaning in the statement, which Henry Armstrong knew he was meant to recognise.

"I'm glad to be able to invite you to Washington at this time of year," he said, inviting an explanation.

"I was very glad you were able to."

Armstrong knew when to let a point pass. He rose, went to the percolator, and poured them another coffee.

"I hear rumours," said John Kenshaw-Taylor, almost casually, "that the president might be about to appoint a new foreign affairs negotiator."

His host put the cups down. "I hear the same rumours," he replied, walking to the cocktail cabinet and fetching them each a large brandy.

"The president would only choose a man he knew could deliver," said Kenshaw-Taylor. They both knew it was meant as a compliment, both knew that the response to it was meant as an offer.

"And the man the president chooses would in turn choose friends he knew could deliver," said Armstrong.

It was a replica of the conversations Abu Nabil had had with Ahmad Hussein in Paris and New York, and with Saeed Khaled in London and Rome.

Henry Armstrong raised his glass. "To success in the oil talks," he proposed.

"To success in US foreign policy," said John Kenshaw-Taylor.

THE BRITISH Foreign Minister returned to his hotel at one and was awake again by four, partly because his body had not adjusted to the time change, partly because he would have woken at four anyway. He spent ninety minutes finalising his notes for the seminar he would give that morning then went for a walk. He had breakfasted by eight, checked the financial news from London, noting that the pound had dropped another one and half cents, and left the hotel by eight thirty. His performance at the Institute, chaired by Henry Armstrong himself and attended by key members of the Washington diplomatic élite, earned him a standing ovation. By the time he caught the shuttle to New York the first reports were coming in of a near-total breakdown in the oil talks. There were even suggestions that the conference would not last its planned three days.

The official limousine was waiting for him at La Guardia. He took it to his hotel, showered, then asked to be driven to the United Nations headquarters on the East River, making his way immediately to the suite of offices which the British delegation were using. Most of the advisors he knew from his own days at Energy; they seemed dejected, even more so than he had anticipated. In London, they told him, the pound had plummeted to within three-quarters of a cent of parity with the United States dollar. The man who seemed most depressed, the foreign minister noted, was the cabinet colleague who had replaced him at his old department.

"No hope at all," he confided to Kenshaw-Taylor. "The PM's screaming down the phone, telling me what it's doing to the pound. Don't want your old job back, do you?"

Kenshaw-Taylor expressed his sympathies. "What's the problem?" he asked.

"Bloody Nigerians. Saying no to everything. Everybody else will agree if they will, but they won't."

"Anything I can do?"

"Thanks all the same, but I don't think there's much any of us can do. We're meeting people tonight, of course, trying to bend a few arms, but nobody can budge the Nigerians."

The ambassador had joined them.

"What about the Arabs?" asked Kenshaw-Taylor. "What's their position?"

"Not much help," said the ambassador.

"I don't suppose there's anybody either inside or outside the conference they would listen to?" He sowed the thought carefully.

"Only Saeed Khaled," said the ambassador.

"Any point having a word with him?"

"Not really."

"Wouldn't do any harm, though," suggested Kenshaw-Taylor. "Where's he staying?" The ambassador asked an aide to get the Foreign Minister Sheikh Khaled's telephone number. The ambassador, Kenshaw-Taylor was aware, was a personal appointee of the Prime Minister.

Five minutes later the official returned with the New York telephone number of Saeed Khaled. "Good luck, sir," he said, handing the minister the sheet of neatly-folded paper, the number inside. There was a way the man said it which Kenshaw-Taylor noted, the smack, the faint but unmistakable smack, of Empire. He liked it.

Thirty minutes later he telephoned Khaled as arranged, confirming the arrangements for that evening, confirming all was in order.

For the first time since he had launched the plan John Kenshaw-Taylor began to think he could pull it off, for the first time he began to wonder what else he could persuade Saeed Khaled to deliver.

"The president would only choose a man he knows can deliver," he had complimented Henry Armstrong less than twenty-four hours before.

"The man the president chooses will in turn choose friends he knows can deliver," Henry Armstrong had offered him.

For the second time that afternoon, he liked the feeling.

THE DINNER which the City banker and Old Etonian Jonty Mathison had arranged with his American counterparts was at eight thirty. Saeed Khaled's engagement with the Nigerians was due to begin fifteen minutes earlier. At six Abu Nabil had his second meeting with Khaled, both men were quiet and anxious. "How is he?" asked Nabil.

"He is enjoying the taste of power," replied Khaled.

"How will he react after tonight?"

Khaled remembered the lessons his father had taught him. "In life," he said, "there are two types of men. Those who dream of something, and who, if they achieve it, are satiated beyond their wildest dreams.'' Abu Nabil waited. "And the other sort,'' said Khaled, "for whom the act of satiation merely creates an even greater need.''

"Will Kenshaw-Taylor be satiated?''

"No,'' said Khaled, shaking his head. "He has tasted his first power, he will never be satiated.''

"Will it work?'' asked Nabil. It was the first sign of weakness he had exhibited.

"It might,'' said Khaled, "it might just work.''

"The Nigerians,'' asked Nabil. "Will they accept what you will offer them?''

Khaled thought for several moments before he replied. "Probably,'' he said at last.

"Only probably?''

"Only probably,'' replied Saeed Khaled.

THIRTY MINUTES before he was due to dine with Sheikh Saeed Khaled, the chief Nigerian delegate to the oil conference received one of the many visits that were made in New York that evening as politicians and diplomats lobbied both friend and foe alike. The Nigerian's visitor, however, bore an invitation that was more indirect, and at the same time more direct, than any other delivered that night. It was, simply, that the organisation which the visitor represented understood that the delegate was about to receive an offer which would, in one stroke, solve the OPEC crisis and, at the same time, relieve the foreign debt burden under which his country was struggling. It was in the chief delegate's best interests, suggested his visitor, that he look upon the offer with the reason and fairness which it deserved. The chief delegate had no personal experience of the organisation which his visitor represented. He did, however, know of its reputation.

AT EIGHT FIFTEEN PRECISELY, Sheikh Saeed Khaled sat down to dinner with the chief Nigerian delegate and his senior advisor. Exactly fifteen minutes later, John Kenshaw-Taylor welcomed the élite circle of American bankers whom Jonty Mathison had invited on his behalf.

He had met only two of the five before, shaking hands with them as if they were old friends, and was then introduced to the other three by the London banker who knew that a knighthood, plus a considerable personal fortune, rested entirely on a successful outcome of the evening's negotiations.

At four o'clock that afternoon, at a time when others were desperate to sell their holdings in the British pound, Jonathan Mathison had bought, with money he did not possess, five million pounds' worth of sterling. If, as he both calculated and fervently prayed, the night's negotiations succeeded and sterling rose to one dollar twenty-five within the next two weeks, he would make a killing of one and a quarter million pounds. If, on the contrary, the night's negotiations did not succeed, he had already decided that he would desert both his wife and his country.

John Kenshaw-Taylor made his first move shortly before twenty minutes to ten. Gently, subtly, apparently without significance. They had finished the first two courses, and were about to begin the third; the range of wine had been particularly commented upon by his guests. He liked to think he had arranged it that way. They had discussed, as they were bound to discuss, the problem of the pound and the future of the dollar, and agreed that although they as bankers enjoyed a short-term advantage from the strong dollar, their long-term future lay in the stability of the international monetary system as a whole. They had also agreed that the OPEC crisis did little to help that stability. Nigerian intransigence, they had been briefed by inside information, lay at the heart of the matter. And the Nigerians—they also had been briefed—would not budge.

"There is one thing that would move them, I suppose," said the Foreign Minister quietly. There was a stir round the table: the conversation to that point had been political, theoretical, now it had changed. Kenshaw-Taylor saw by their reactions, the way they had stopped drinking, that they knew he was serious. The two waiters were close to the table, he called them over and told them he would send for them when he needed them, aware that the bankers could hardly wait till the two had left the room.

"What would move them?" The speaker was the most senior banker present.

Kenshaw-Taylor knew when he had to stall, when to hit hard. It was something he had learned from his father. "Nigeria's problem," he said, "is that most of their international loans are oil-related, mainly from Saudi Arabia. They would give way if there was an increase in non-Arab loans into their country."

The silence seemed to last for ever.

"Impossible," one of the bankers responsible for scheduling the repayment of existing Western loans to Nigeria began to say.

"Difficult," Kenshaw-Taylor replied carefully, "but not impossible." He looked round the table at each of them in turn. "The decision, after all, lies with you, and you alone."

He saw the way they looked at each other, the moment they began to realise that seated round the table that evening were the major decision makers of the leading non-Arab international creditors to Nigeria, the moment they saw that no one else was present. The moment they remembered where he had been that morning, remembered that he was reputed to be a close personal friend of Henry Armstrong, remembered what the future held for Henry Armstrong. A private visit, their host had said. At the same time as the oil talks.

"What's in it for us?" The question was as blunt as it was necessary.

"A great deal." He tantalised them, led them on. "It could not be done immediately," he said, "and if it ever got out there would be hell to pay."

What exactly?

"The transfer to your institutions of a substantial amount of Arab monies currently held in other banks, at a rate of interest below the market rate, for an agreed minimum period."

He saw the looks on their faces.

"How much and how long?"

"To be agreed between you and them."

"When?"

John Kenshaw-Taylor knew he would enjoy the moment. "Tonight," he said simply.

For the second time in five minutes the silence round the table seemed to last forever.

"Who would guarantee it?" It was the banker who had said an expansion of credit to Nigeria was impossible.

"Who would you like to guarantee it?" Kenshaw-Taylor knew who the man would choose.

"Sheikh Saeed Khaled."

"I could try," said John Kenshaw-Taylor.

He rose from the table, went to a room off the main suite, and telephoned Khaled's direct number, it was answered by an aide. Kenshaw-Taylor asked for the sheikh, not identifying himself, and waited, wondering again whether even Khaled could deliver. He heard the sheikh's voice, told him that the bankers had agreed and felt the relief as Khaled told him that the Nigerians had also agreed. Then he put the phone down and returned to the dining table, aware of what they had been saying during his absence, sensing by the way they were looking at him that they did not think he could pull it off but hoping that he had.

"Well?"

He folded the napkin and placed it neatly on the table. They knew he had failed. "The meeting is in half an hour," he said. "I suggest we forego coffee."

THE OIL MINISTERS reconvened at ten, the delegates looking grim-faced as they arrived, not stopping to comment to the press. Although the conference was scheduled to finish at three, it was not expected to last that long. At ten thirty the first leaks started; by eleven they had become a deluge. In London the first suggestion of a breakthrough came an hour and thirty two minutes before the market closed; in that time the pound leaped two and a half cents; by close in New York it had gained another two. At four in the afternoon Eastern Standard Time the British Energy Minister gave a formal press conference receiving the acclaim for settling the crisis. It did not bother John Kenshaw-Taylor. Fifteen minutes before he had received a personal call from the Prime Minister.

ABU NABIL left the hotel and walked the eight blocks to the meeting with the businessman Ahmad Hussein. It was warmer than their first meeting in Paris, he thought, much warmer than the meeting in New York which followed it. The other man was waiting for him.

"Thank you," said Abu Nabil simply. "The man you chose for me was the right man."

JOHN KENSHAW-TAYLOR returned to his hotel at four-thirty. The British team at the United Nations had arranged a reception at eight. He would attend for an hour then go on to a private, more discreet function with Khaled. He went to his room and opened the door. In an ice-bucket on the table at the side of the bed stood a bottle of champagne, delivered by room service. There were four sentences on the note which accompanied it:

One hell of a private visit. Glad to be of help. Congratulations.
From a friend who knows his friends can deliver.

Kenshaw-Taylor opened the bottle, poured himself a glass, and made three telephone calls. The first was to Henry Armstrong, the second was to his wife, the third was to the parliamentary private secretary who had first mentioned Sheikh Saeed Khaled's words about him in the dining room at Westminster, instructing him to arrange an off-the-record briefing about the series of secret meetings, and his role in them, with the political correspondent of the *Sunday Times*. The paper has an ABC circulation of one and a quarter million, less than a third of the overall sales of the more popular Sunday papers; a substantial number of those, however, were people he considered to have influence, in the press, the City, in industry.

And three hundred and ninety-one would be Conservative Members of Parliament who would one day vote for the leader of the party.

He poured himself another glass of champagne and began to run a bath. He had hardly slept since leaving London forty-eight hours before, but he felt alert and fresh. The change of time zone helped, plus the adrenalin of the oil price deal. He bathed, dried himself briskly and poured himself a third glass. Pity his wife wasn't with him, he thought, taking another sip, pity he wasn't in London.

IN HIS HOTEL ROOM fifteen blocks away, Abu Nabil wondered how John Kenshaw-Taylor was reacting to his OPEC triumph, how he would react to what they would offer him later that evening, wondered also about the man's indiscretion, the man's other weakness.

In the aircraft hangar in Germany, Gent Mueller finished work, and prepared herself for the demands the security man would make on her body and soul that night. In the hospital ward in Belfast, Eileen McDonald kissed her son goodnight and thought about the man in the photograph. In the empty shell of the Argentinian embassy in London, Jimmy Roberts' away team began the twenty-sixth day of their stake-out. In the loneliness of his cell in Stammheim Prison, the hunger-striker Klars Christian Mannheim slipped one more day closer to death.

3

WALID HADDAD walked quickly and quietly, his shoulder and side still hurt and he was tired from lack of sleep, not having rested since he had left Ain Helweh. He turned off the road that served as the main thoroughfare of the camp and began to descend into the maze of side streets. On the corner where they had stopped him two afternoons before, the boys with the rifles across their shoulders let him pass. It was almost night.

The old man looked up, sensing the figure in the doorway, knowing that although his path had been long and hard he would soon embark on an even longer journey.

"Is it you, my son?" he asked.

"Yes, my father, it is I."

"You have been away, my son. I have been waiting for you."

Walid Haddad crossed the floor and knelt by his father's bedside. The old man had grown smaller, weaker, even in the two days he had been away. The eyes were blinder than they had been before, the breathing more shallow. He took the old man's right hand, the hand that had guided the oxen across the fields of Esh Shikara, the hand that had held the woman called Leila on the day they had married, the hand that had first touched him, when he had entered the world in the small room in the house at the top of the hill.

There was no strength left in it; the muscles were dead, the skin withered and dry, the bones old and brittle. Walid Haddad felt in his pocket, took out the orange Yakov Zubko had given him, and curled the fingers around it. Slowly, painfully, the old man raised his other hand, transferred the fruit to it, and stroked it with his fingers.

In the shadows, the women watched. The old man pressed what remained of his finger nails into the skin of the orange, and began to peel it, his entire body shaking with the effort, till he removed one single segment, and passed it into his mouth.

A smile came upon his face, a thin smile, so thin it could hardly be seen in the grey of the journey that was almost upon him. He knew why his son had left him, where his son had gone.

"Ah, my son," he said, "there is no fruit as ripe as the fruit of the groves of Esh Shikara."

Walid Haddad remembered the man who had given him the orange.

From his pocket he took the water bottle, unscrewed the top and lifted father's head, tilting the metal rim of the bottle till it rested on the old man's lips, allowing the cool of the liquid to trickle through the lips and into the mouth.

"Ah, my son," said the old man, "there is no water as sweet as the water that comes from the well of Esh Shikara."

Walid Haddad remembered the boy with the blue and white ball, the other boy who had retrieved the water bottle for him, the family of the man who had saved his life, the faces of the brother and his family still waiting in Moscow.

The old man's head fell back. Walid Haddad placed the top back on the water bottle, put the bottle on the floor and reached inside his shirt for the bag strapped to his body. He removed it, undid the string that tied the neck of the bag, and knelt again at the bedside, feeling the sorrow sweeping down upon him, knowing that his father was about to begin the journey, knowing that no matter what the pain and tribulation of this world, he did not want him to leave it.

The old man's blind eyes were looking at him, seeing him. Slowly, gently, he took again his father's hand and guided it into the bag, watching as the fingers searched their way across the earth in the bag, into the soil, watching the pain in the old man's face, the strain in the wasted muscles. Slowly, so slowly he was barely moving, his father dug his fingers into the bag, deeper and deeper, feeling the moist of the earth on his palm and the rough of the soil beneath his finger nails. The pain on his face was increasing, not the pain of death or despair, the pain of strength and determination. Slowly, even more slowly, till the effort was racking his entire body, he closed his fingers round the earth and withdrew his hand from the bag, bending his arm, pulling his hand, in one final supreme effort, closer to his face. The fingers opened, he raised his head, shaking again with the effort and held the earth against his mouth, his nostrils. Felt it, smelt it. Closed his fingers around it.

"Ah, my son," he said, "there is no soil as rich as the soil of the fields of Esh Shikara."

Walid Haddad thought of the morning before, the haze across the field, the man and boy he thought he had seen in the corner of the field. He knew his father had started upon his journey.

"No, my father," he said, "there is no soil as rich as the soil of the fields of Esh Shikara."

The old man looked past him, to the women in the shadows. "My son has delivered me the soil of the fields of Esh Shikara," he said. His head returned to the pillow, the right hand across his chest. Walid Haddad leaned forward, seeing that the pain was no longer on the face of his father. He kissed the old man on the lips and stepped back. The women moved forward, shutting the eyes, trying to open the fingers of the right hand so they could cross them in the sign of peace, could not prise them apart. The fingers were closed in the grasp of youth, the hand was the hand of the young man who had toiled in the field at the foot of the hill once called Balama, who had beheld the young woman in the orange grove at the side of the field, who had wedded her, given her the seed of his only son.

"You will not open his hand," said Walid Haddad. "You will never open his hand."

The women turned to him for explanation.

"He will never let go. He is like us all."

They still did not understand.

"My father is holding his land," explained the hijacker simply.

THEY BURIED THE OLD MAN that night, in the place where so many now lay. They were few in Ain Helweh who knew him, outside his immediate family, even fewer who had attended him in his last days. There were, after all, twenty thousand men, women and children crowded inside its walls, and the old man had been sick, had not walked the streets, for as long as the

women could remember. Yet that night the *fedayeen* sealed off
the camp totally, that night the guards on the entrances were
doubled, trebled, the cars pulled across the openings, the machine guns in place, the Kalashnikovs cocked and ready. That
night the people of Ain Helweh moved silently through the
narrow streets that were their home. That night, as the crescent of the new moon rose above the hills to the east, they filed
past the sheet on which the old man was laid, his face and body
so eaten by the cancer that they were hardly recognisable. As
each passed they paused to look at the face of the father who
had waited for his son to return. As each of the *fedayeen*
passed, the rifles on their arms, they looked in wonder at the
strength with which the old man held his right hand closed. As
each father passed he explained to his son the treasure that the
old man clutched to the frame that was once his chest.

That night the story was born of the son who had delivered
the earth of Esh Shikara back to his father.

That night the legend took root of the fighter who had delivered the land of Palestine back to his people.

That night Walid Haddad knew that it no longer mattered
whether he lived or died, as die he must. Some time that night,
he was not sure of the exact moment, he knew that he had
nothing to give his people, that the only thing he could give his
people was his life. Not just his life, but the manner of its
passing.

That night, as the Kalashnikovs crashed into the sky and the
children who would be the martyrs of the future lay awake and
thought of what they had just witnessed, Walid Haddad left his
father for the last time and went himself into the darkness.

4

THE DINNER with Saeed Khaled and John Kenshaw-Taylor was
at nine thirty. Abu Nabil dressed slowly, contemplating how
Khaled would play it, how Kenshaw-Taylor would react.
Everything, he was aware, depended on what would happen,
what would be agreed, in the hours between now and breakfast. He thought of those already committed, the hijacker
himself, Walid Haddad, Gent Mueller, groaning under the security man, the teams already training the secret desert places

of the Middle East, the hunger-striker Klars Christian Mannheim who had eaten less in the past eight weeks than they would
leave as crumbs from their bread that evening. All dedicated to
one supreme act, all dependent on how John Kenshaw-Taylor
would react that night.

He knotted the bow tie, pulled on his coat and left the hotel.

JOHN KENSHAW-TAYLOR had difficulty extricating himself
from the reception. Partly because the ambassador had hinted
at the minister's role in the negotiations which had led to the oil
price agreement and he had found himself the centre of attrac-
tion, primarily because one of those who had expressed greatest interest in those negotiations was a reporter from the *New
York Times* who had suggested that he brief her over dinner
after the reception. He left at nine forty, mentioning that she
should phone him at his hotel to arrange something later, the
ambiguity deliberate.

The limousine which Khaled had sent for him was waiting.
Kenshaw-Taylor got in, thinking about the *New York Times*
reporter, and sank back into the seat. For one moment, as they
dropped out of the lights of central New York, towards the
backstreet of Fifth and Second where the restaurant was situated, a neon sign above the door and the garbage cans stacked
against the building next to it, he feared that something was
wrong, that the car was not from Khaled. Only when the driver
showed him inside and he saw the sheikh rising to greet him did
he relax.

His eyes began to adjust to the darkness. The restaurant was
large, well decorated with velvet drapes on the walls; there was
a hum of confidence, of affluence, about the place which he
had not expected from the outside. Khaled watched him, waiting till he saw the change of expression in the eyes then he took
Kenshaw-Taylor by the arm and led him towards a table in the
corner, half concealed by the drapes. "This," he explained, "is
a very special place, few people are welcome here. People who
are leaders. Normally only Arabs."

At the table Abu Nabil heard the words and remembered the
game of *tawli*, waited for the first apparently innocent move.

"You," Khaled told Kenshaw-Taylor, "are the first non-
Arab I have ever brought here."

They reached the table; for the second time that evening John Kenshaw-Taylor was surprised. At the table were five more men and three women. The men were dressed in dinner jackets: one was older, in his mid fifties, a second in his late thirties, the other three in their twenties. The three women were in their early twenties, one was black, the other two were white. All three were expensively though tastefully, even conservatively, dressed; all three were also extremely attractive.

Saeed Khaled introduced Kenshaw-Taylor to each in turn, referring to the minister as his "friend", starting with the oldest of the men, introducing Abu Nabil as his political advisor, the second oldest as his economics aide and apologising for the presence of the others.

"The bombings and shootings all over Europe," he explained. "As I am not known as a militant, as a sympathiser of the men of violence, I have to take them with me." He looked at the women. "The boys are younger than I am, sometimes I have to allow them their relaxation."

Kenshaw-Taylor smiled his understanding and thought about the reporter from the *New York Times*. "The situation in Europe is getting out of hand," he agreed.

The *arak* arrived, Khaled raised his glass. "Do such things affect you at all?" he asked. Too quick. Abu Nabil felt, too early, then relaxed, realising it was only an extension of an innocent conversation, seeing that the minister enjoyed being asked.

"Not directly, no," Kenshaw-Taylor said, sipping the drink. "I've managed to steer clear of it so far." He did not mind being indiscreet, especially when it did not matter or when he could use indiscretion to impress others. "When I left the Energy job there was a suggestion I might take over at the Northern Ireland Office." He put the glass on the table. "Thank God that was all it was, a suggestion. Imagine having to be tailed by bodyguards for the rest of your life." He realised he might have offended the man who was attended by three such young men.

Khaled laughed. "I agree with you," he said.

Abu Nabil sat back, watching the trap already being set, waiting for the first move.

Saeed Khaled waved to a waiter, and spoke to him in Arabic. A few moments later an older man appeared. Khaled spoke to him, again in Arabic. The man who had been introduced to Kenshaw-Taylor as Khaled's political advisor leaned across to the minister, smiling at the three women who were talking to the guards.

"The owner," he explained. "The sheikh is telling him that he wants him to meet a special friend of his. The owner is saying that he has never seen a European here before, but that if you are a friend of Saeed Khaled's then you are a friend of his."

Khaled stood up, walked round the table, and introduced Kenshaw-Taylor to the owner. The man said something in Arabic. "He says he is most honoured that you have come. He hopes that you will enjoy his food, however meagre it is, and that you will come again."

Kenshaw-Taylor was beginning to enjoy himself. "Would you tell him that the honour is mine, not his, that he should be so kind to me."

Khaled interpreted. The proprietor spread his hands in pleasure and said something else. "He asks you to excuse him," said Khaled, "he says he would like to prepare a *meze* for you, but asks your forgiveness as it will take some time."

"Tell him I would be more than happy."

They sat down again, the owner bustling away, the pride reflected in his face, in the way he was suddenly snapping his orders to his staff, Khaled ordering champagne.

"When you are Foreign Secretary," he leaned close so that only Kenshaw-Taylor could hear, "perhaps when you are something else, you had better not say that Saeed Khaled brought you here, or they would think you were an Arabist."

John Kenshaw-Taylor smiled. "I am already an Arabist," he confided, meaning it in the traditional sense, the sense of being an expert, not necessarily a sympathiser, confident they knew what he meant. "My father, and his father before him, were the same."

He saw Khaled's eyes light up and began to tell them about his father's service in the Middle East, his grandfather's before that, remembering the places, the smells, the excitement of the trips to the far-off places during vacation from prep school. Even the bodyguards had stopped talking among themselves, he realised, had stopped looking at the girls and were listening to him. It was a long time since he had spoken about it, even inside his own family, he thought of his father and grandfather, how they would react if they could see him now, how they would wish to be where he was now.

"Do you envy them?" Saeed Khaled suddenly asked.

In the shadows Abu Nabil watched, the pattern developing, moving faster. Ever so slightly, but faster. Waited for the reaction, remembering how much depended on that evening, remembering again the words of the old man at the *tawli* table in Damascus.

"Yes," John Kenshaw-Taylor heard himself saying. "I suppose I do." It was a truth he had never before considered, at least not consciously, the truth that lay at the heart of many of his motivations and ambitions.

"Why?" It was not a cross-examination, more a discussion of a sacred subject between friends who had just discovered it was a matter about which they cared equally deeply.

John Kenshaw-Taylor knew they were all watching him, especially the women, especially the one woman. He thought for the briefest of moments about the telephone call from the *New York Times* reporter, about what he should do.

"I suppose," he answered at last, "that I envy them because they are part of an era, a history, which I admire and which can never be repeated."

Khaled called the waiter to pour them more champagne. "And that is why you chose the Foreign Office," he suggested.

Kenshaw-Taylor took the glass, laughing. "It wasn't quite a question of me choosing the Foreign Office," he was modest enough to admit, "more a matter of it being offered." He recalled the corridors, the sense of time immemorial, the aroma of power that still pervaded the building. "but if I had had the choice," he conceded, "I would have chosen the Foreign Office."

"I envy you," said Saeed Khaled. Kenshaw-Taylor knew he meant it.

Abu Nabil saw and smiled to himself.

The table was cleared and the owner brought the *meze*, placing it in front of them and waiting as Kenshaw-Taylor sampled each dish in turn, seeing the way he reacted, the way he enjoyed it, receiving his thanks with pleasure and pride. Kenshaw-Taylor knew the woman was looking at him again and realised he had been at the table over an hour.

"But a man like you must feel a frustration." The words were subtle, carefully chosen, focussing attention on his guest, picking him out as an individual.

"How do you mean?" he asked.

Abu Nabil waited. "Fifty years ago, a hundred years ago, a man like you would have had such power, so many areas in which to exercise it." The same subtlety again, the same pointing to him as an individual. "There was an empire to run, great decisions to be made." Kenshaw-Taylor suddenly felt that Khaled had something more to say, was inhibited by the presence of the women. "The only thing your Foreign Office has done for the last three, four, decades is to rule over the disestablishment of that empire."

It was what Kenshaw-Taylor's principal advisor in the Foreign Office himself thought as they took sherry in the evenings. "Perhaps frustration is inevitable," he replied diplomatically, sensing again that his host wished to say something more.

"Ladies," said Khaled, "would you mind leaving us for a moment. Five minutes, no more." John Kenshaw-Taylor waited. Abu Nabil sat back, noting the way the minister watched the women, the one woman in particular.

"How did you manage it?" Saeed Khaled asked when the women had gone.

It was now what Kenshaw-Taylor had expected. "Manage what?" he asked.

"The American bankers." Khaled's voice was low. "I don't mind admitting, now it's over, that when I sat with the Nigerians last night, I never thought you could pull it off. When you phoned, I knew it was to say the bankers had said no."

Each move a part of the game, Abu Nabil thought, each move a game in itself.

"How did you manage it?" Khaled asked again. "How did you play them?"

Kenshaw-Taylor considered how he should answer. "Your money helped," he suggested. It had only been possible because of the transfer of the Arab monies, he knew, but Khaled was correct in that the money had only been one factor, that it had also been the way he had played it.

"A friend," he adapted the words of Henry Armstrong, "you need a friend you know can deliver, then you can convince anybody to do anything." Saeed Khaled nodded. Closer, thought Abu Nabil, they were getting closer. The women came back and sat down.

Kenshaw-Taylor stood politely, wondering for the first time which of the bodyguards would have which of the women, how, he suddenly thought, they would have them, wondering if the American reporter would phone his hotel, how long she would continue to phone. He began to think of leaving a message saying he would be late but that she should keep phoning, even leave her number, began to think he should ask to use the telephone.

The flat in Pimlico, Abu Nabil was thinking, five minutes from Westminster by car, fifteen minutes on foot.

Khaled spoke to his escorts in Arabic, they pushed their chairs back and began to get up.

"I have told them they can go, that I am among friends," he explained to Kenshaw-Taylor.

The women began to rise, a waiter hurrying to fetch their coats.

The man who had been introduced as the sheikh's political advisor whispered something else to them. The guards looked at Saeed Khaled and waited till he agreed. Kenshaw-Taylor wondered what was happening, what was being said.

The waiter appeared with the coats. The guards took two of them and spoke quietly to the woman who had been looking at the Foreign Minister. She looked in turn at the political advisor and sat down, smiling at the man. Kenshaw-Taylor watched the bodyguards and other women as they left. Three on two; he was imagining what they would do, how they would do it, thinking again about the telephone call to his hotel.

"This week was good," Saeed Khaled interrupted his thoughts. "This week was very good. I propose a toast." He held up his glass. "To success," he said. "To friends who deliver."

"To friends who deliver," said John Kenshaw-Taylor. He could see the way the political advisor was looking at the woman.

"Would you excuse me a moment," he said. "I have to make a telephone call."

The telephone was behind the bar. He called the hotel and asked if there were any messages for him.

"One call, sir," said the telephonist. "No message other than that they would call back."

It could mean anything, be anybody, he thought. "He or she?" he asked.

"I'm afraid I don't know, sir."

He left a message, saying that if anyone called they should be asked to leave a number and he would return the call, then walked back to the table. The men Saeed Khaled had introduced as his two advisors and the third woman were getting up. He thought they were leaving but was told they were going to play backgammon in the rear section of the restaurant. He watched the way the woman walked, envying the Arab who would have her that night, hoping the reporter would call again.

It was the first time that evening that he and Khaled had been alone together. They drank one more glass of champagne and called for coffee. It was two in the morning, seven in London. Kenshaw-Taylor felt fresh and alert, even though he had slept less than eleven hours in the past three days.

Khaled was sipping his coffee, looking intent. "Would you mind if I asked your advice on something?" he said at last.

Gently, thought Abu Nabil at the backgammon table, very gently.

"Of course not."

"We talked earlier of the bombings and shootings in Europe. As you know, there were two more today."

Kenshaw-Taylor did not know. "Yes," he said, "I heard."

"It is possible that I am about to become involved."

Kenshaw-Taylor looked up, horrified. "Your bodyguards," he asked immediately. "Why did you let them go?"

Khaled shook his head. "Thankfully," he said, "I am not a target. At least as far as I know."

Kenshaw-Taylor waited.

"There is a theory amongst various intelligence agencies," said Khaled, "that the bombings and killings are not unrelated. There is also a theory that the Middle East is about to be involved."

Kenshaw-Taylor was intrigued. "How?" he asked.

"We think there is going to be a hijack."

Kenshaw-Taylor leaned closer. "You think or you know?" he asked succinctly. They both knew the importance of the difference.

Khaled answered his question obliquely. "All I know," he replied, "is that a number of prominent Arab politicians and diplomats have been approached and have been asked, if there was a hijack and a negotiator was needed, who they would nominate. They have nominated me."

In the next room Abu Nabil could sense it, feel it. Gently, he pleaded, for the love of Allah, gently.

Kenshaw-Taylor knew what Khaled was going to ask him. The president will choose a man he knows can deliver, he had complimented Henry Armstrong two nights before. That man will, in turn, choose friends he knows can deliver, Henry Armstrong had replied.

"What do you want to ask me?" he said.

"I was contemplating whether or not I should accept."

The reply shattered him. He felt himself sag, almost physically, struggling to pick himself up.

Perfectly, thought Abu Nabil, absolutely perfectly. John Kenshaw-Taylor overcame his disappointment. "I think you should accept."

Khaled considered the reply. "You don't think it's immoral," he queried. "You don't think I should do something about preventing the hijack?"

It was the question Kenshaw-Taylor had put to himself in the split second he thought that Saeed Khaled was going to ask him to be the European negotiator in the impending hijack.

"What do you know about the hijack!" he asked. "Do you know when or where it will take place, who will do it, who will be the victims?"

"No," conceded Khaled, "I don't."

Almost there, thought Abu Nabil, they were almost there.

"In that case I don't see it's immoral to agree to be a negotiator."

Saeed Khaled nodded his appreciation. "In that case," he repeated the first words of Kenshaw-Taylor's last answer, "I wonder if you would mind if I asked you something else?"

The Foreign Minister felt his excitement rise again.

Is he satiated? Abu Nabil had asked. No, Khaled had told him, he has tasted power, he is insatiable.

"Of course not," Kenshaw-Taylor said.

Khaled looked hard at him. "If there was a hijacking, and if there was a need for a major European negotiator, I wonder if it would be in order to suggest the British Foreign Minister, John Kenshaw-Taylor?"

John Kenshaw-Taylor sat back. "I think it would be most in order," he said.

At the backgammon table Abu Nabil knew it was done.

"Who else knows?" asked John Kenshaw-Taylor.

"No one else."

"In that case," Kenshaw-Taylor took the initiative, "I suggest we keep it that way."

"Without telling even our own people?"

"What can we tell them?" countered Kenshaw-Taylor. "What sort of reaction would we get if we went to them with the details of this conversation?"

"You're absolutely right, of course," Khaled conceded.

Kenshaw-Taylor knew he was absolutely right. "One other point," he suddenly thought. "Is there likely to be any British involvement, either through the plane, the passengers or anything of that nature?" The premise, they both knew, had changed. Before they had merely been discussing a theoretical hijack, now they were building their own requirements into it.

"I don't know, but I don't think so. Why?"

"If there isn't, it might be difficult for me to become involved."

"Damn," he heard Khaled swear softly.

The two advisors and the third woman returned from the backgammon tables. Kenshaw-Taylor knew by their faces that they had lost. "Don't worry," he said. "I'll think of something."

It was almost three; they began to leave, the waiters fetching their coats, and walked outside. John Kenshaw-Taylor thought about the reporter from the *New York Times* and hoped again that she had left her telephone number.

The two limousines were waiting. One, he assumed, was Khaled's, the other was the car which had collected him from the British reception at the United Nations. The driver saw him coming, and opened the door for him.

"You're at the Waldorf-Astoria?" asked Khaled.

"Yes."

"In that case, perhaps you could drop the lady off?"

The man he thought was going to have the woman that night was already getting into Khaled's car. "I don't mind if she doesn't," replied Kenshaw-Taylor. The response was delivered as a joke; they both knew what each meant, he thought, both knew that they understood each other.

They shook hands, the woman beginning to get into his car. The solution struck him, the solution and the bonus.

"Jordan," he said. "If it ended in Jordan I would have reason to be involved." His brain was working quickly. "Jordan," he repeated, "then I could bring in the SAS."

"Jordan," confirmed Saeed Khaled, "then you can bring in the SAS."

IN THE SOLITUDE of his bedroom Abu Nabil closed the chess set and thought through the events of the past twenty-four hours. It had been a good day, a very good, but by now it would also be a bad day. He thought of the woman who he knew would already be in Kenshaw-Taylor's hotel room, the woman the Foreign Minister had thought all evening was for someone else.

Something about Kenshaw-Taylor, Saeed Khaled had told him in Rome, something he did not know, something he would find out. Something Saeed Khaled was holding back, he had thought when they had met in New York, something Saeed Khlaed had eventually told him, something that he should know about John Kenshaw-Taylor.

The woman had been well paid, of course, extremely well paid, and they would pick up the clinic bills if things got out of hand, but he still regretted what she was about to endure.

He switched off the light, knowing he would not sleep. For a man who sanctioned violence as a matter of routine, Abu Nabil was remarkably puritanical. He had never believed in violence for its own sake.

CHAPTER FIVE

1

JIMMY ROBERTS saw him at seven minutes past five, turning left out of Handel Street, moving slowly along Herbert Crescent, stopping every few yards. He could set his watch by him, as he could set his watch by the twenty or so other people whose movements he had come to know since the unit had begun its vigil from the former Argentinian Embassy. The milkman stopped outside number thirty-six, delivering the bottles to the even numbers between thirty and thirty-four then moved on. His routine had been the same since the day they had moved in. Jimmy Roberts sat back and waited for the bastard he had first seen in the pub in Belfast.

EILEEN MCDONALD woke at six thirty, Eileen McDonald always woke at six thirty no matter the day of the week or the time of the year. Beside her, her husband was fast asleep. He was a good man, she thought. Violent certainly, but never to her, never to those for whom he cared; only to those who opposed him and his politics. She had supported him, told him he was right, partly because he was her husband, the father of her son, partly because she knew he was right. Except that sometimes she had grown tired. Not of him, not of the cause in which he believed; tired of being a wife and mother in an oppressed group in a land of occupation. Each day she woke with the same tiredness, each day she got out of bed and carried on as the day before. Each night she went to bed just a little more tired.

The morning through the thin net curtain was brighter than yesterday, she thought, each day lighter than the previous one. If anything made her happy it was this: that the winter was ending and she would soon have her Liam home. She missed him, missed the sound of his breathing in the next room in the mornings, missed the shoes, scuffed at the toes, in the narrow hallway, missed the times he had been good, even missed the times he had been bad. No other children, she thought, getting out of bed, taking care not to wake her husband. Only Liam, then the second pregnancy, almost immediately, and the miscarriage. And no more children, even though they were good Catholics.

The kitchen was warm, she began to make a pot of tea. At least, she thought, there had been no dream last night, no eyes staring at her as the hands stemmed the flow of her son's precious life blood, the same eyes staring at her from the photograph she had seen on the table upstairs. The night she had waited in the kitchen, the night they had brought in the man in the hood.

She had not dreamed the dream, she thought, but now she was thinking it. The tea was ready. She began to wonder whether the eyes would stop looking at her after they killed him.

THE SCOUT HELICOPTERS took off at ten, disappearing into the sky to the east, the Range Rovers following them at twelve, four men in each, the springs of the vehicles reinforced to bear the weight of equipment that was loaded into them, the aerials bristling from the roofs, bending in the wind as the convoy left Hereford then turned south and finally, like the helicopters, east. The anti-terrorist teams never left Hereford unless they were fully operational; they left behind them a second squadron, the one from whom they had taken over the anti-terrorist responsibility, on ten minute stand-by.

Enderson watched them go and cursed his luck. The monthly exercise, the climax of their training, this time a hijack at Stansted airport in Essex.

Then the doctor had said he needed him at the hospital in Woolwich, told him the only day he was free was the Monday, that after that he would be out of the country. Enderson had tried to put it off but been ordered to go. Only an exercise, they had told him, there would be plenty more.

At least, he thought, it was a nice day. He watched the last of the Range Rovers pull out of the barracks, went home, and took Jane and the children for a walk.

JOHN KENSHAW-TAYLOR dined early, finishing by five, and checked his overnight bag. The evening was still an hour off setting, the drive would be swift and pleasant. He took coffee in the conservatory, shutting the door so he could not hear the nanny in the kitchen, and sat reading the *Sunday Times*. Opposite him his wife was reading the colour supplement.

The political correspondent had done a good job. He had, after all, received a good briefing. The phone had rung all day with congratulations, sometimes from colleagues he had not previously assumed would vote for him in the future. He finished the coffee, kissed his wife goodbye, and left the house.

He had only heard about the exercise the day after he had returned from New York, had been assured it was only routine, nothing to get excited about, but had arranged nevertheless to be on it as an observer. It always paid to see things from the sharp end, he thought.

He arrived at Coggeshall at nine and checked in to the White Hart. There were other, bigger hotels in Cambridge, but the drive from the village to Stansted was only twenty minutes and he was, after all, an Oxford man.

JIMMY ROBERTS heard the key turn in the lock and the footsteps on the stairs to the first floor. The other man checked and grunted a greeting to the two men coming into the room. It was nine thirty. They talked for ten minutes then Jimmy and the man with whom he had been on watch let themselves out, went to the pub off Sloane Street where the drink was cheap and the food was good, staying till closing time, then returning to the embassy. He had almost lost count of the number of days they had been waiting.

EILEEN MCDONALD watched television till eleven thirty, switched off the set, tidied the room and filled the kettle for the morning. At fifteen minutes to twelve she went to bed, kneeling to say her Hail Marys and thanking the Holy Mother for watching over her Liam. She had always gone to bed earlier, been asleep by ten thirty, but going to bed later meant she had less time to sleep, less time to dream. She pulled the bedclothes over her and prayed to the Virgin to keep the eyes from her that night.

GRAHAM ENDERSON had been asleep two hours when his wife heard the foxes on the hills over the Brecon. She knew what was going to happen and tried to shut out the noise, to seek refuge in sleep. The moon was full, the light streaming in through the curtains. She tried harder to sleep, knew what would happen when she did sleep. Saw the face, fresh and innocent. Heard the voice, clear and still.

> And you, my father, there on the sad height,
> Curse, bless, me now with your fierce tears, I pray.
> Do not go gentle into that good night.
> Rage, rage against the dying of the light.

She thought about the man, kneeling by the deathbed of his father, remembered how she had taught the children what the poet had meant by the words, remembered how she had always felt that for her they would mean something else, how she had wondered whether she would ever know what the other thing was.

She was deeper into her sleep, the voice was fading over the hills, the dream beginning.

The tunnel was long, filled with smoke, the flames coming at him. He was moving down it, eyes sweeping left to right. Not his eyes, she was dreaming, it was as if he was behind his eyes, as if he was looking through their sockets.

He was moving on, the voice commanding him, directing him, the death around him, she was not sure whether it was his death or the death of another, the death from the hold-all in the wardrobe at the foot of the bed.

The bleeper, she thought, she was praying for the bleeper, knew it was the only way the dream would end, knew it was the only way the new day would begin.

THE MOON WAS SHINING through the curtains, casting patterns on the wall. Eileen McDonald watched them forming and re-forming as the curtains moved. Beside her, her husband lay asleep; she could hear the rhythm of his breathing. She tried to sleep, knowing what would happen when she did, beginning to see the face in the patterns of the moon at the foot of the bed, the face of the man in the street outside their home, bending over her Liam, pulling his body together, the face of the man in the photograph the American had brought from London. She knew he was an American, had heard his voice as the men had left. The curtains stopped moving, the pattern on the wall was still. The eyes were still looking at her.

JIMMY ROBERTS saw him at seven minutes past five. Turning left, out of Handel Street, moving slowly along Herbert Crescent, stopping every few yards. He could set his watch by the milkman. The cleaner woman would be next, then the postman. After him the square would begin to get busier. He left the window, switched on the kettle, and made a cup of coffee.

GRAHAM ENDERSON left the house at seven, drove to Newport and caught the eight ten to London. He would stay at the club that night, he had told Jane, and return the following morning. The train was ten minutes late but it did not worry him, he would still have time to leave his case at the club before going to the hospital. The train pulled into the station; he thought about what was about to begin at Stansted and got on.

2

THEY KNEW when it was coming, heard on air traffic control before they picked up the noise, the soft rumble in the sky, as the plane banked gently and began its approach into Stansted. Unreal, of course, they all knew it was unreal, knew that normally they would not be waiting, that normally they would be reacting. There was still a tension. In the main terminal building, the late winter tourists were queuing to board their package flight to Majorca, unaware what was happening, unaware of what was about to happen. Even those waiting unaware. Kenshaw-Taylor stood up, mug of tea in hand, and looked out the window, across the expanse of the runway, senior officers and observers only in the room. He had no idea of what was to happen, knew no one had. The other thing he did not know was the full extent of that lack of knowledge.

In the mist in front of him he saw the shape of the Boeing, steady, flying straight, air traffic control talking the pilot down. The wheels skidded onto the concrete and the plane slowed down.

"Golf Bravo India, this is Stansted Tower, proceed via taxiway one to stand twelve and wait further instructions." He saw the mistake the controller had already made, the suggestion that those on the ground would be issuing instructions to the hijackers.

"I'm sorry, Bravo India, proceed via taxiway one and await further communications."

Another mistake, he thought, the man should not have apologised, should not have drawn attention to the error. He looked across the concrete to the Boeing: a hundred and twelve passengers and crew on board, they had been told, the plane two-thirds full, plus four hijackers.

For the briefest of moments he remembered the moment he had accepted Saeed Khaled's offer in New York. Theoretical, he had told himself after, purely theoretical, knew it was not. He pushed the thought to the back of his mind and concentrated on the exercise.

"Golf Bravo India, proceed via taxiway one to stand twelve."

A soldier in a combat jacket, longish hair, no identification on the jacket, pushed past and began connecting a series of circuits and switchboards into the main system of the room behind him. A Home Office technician was wheeling in the video monitoring screens, another testing the communication links to the COBRA room beneath Downing Street. In front of them the plane rolled past stand twelve and disappeared behind the terminal building.

"Golf Bravo India, I said stand twelve."

"Listen to me." They heard the voice of the hijacker for the first time. An exercise, he thought, it was only an exercise. "I'm in charge, I tell the pilot what to do. I tell you what to do. Understand?"

Kenshaw-Taylor looked round the room, the desks prepared, the communications almost set up, the view across the tarmac to where the plane had been directed had been clear and uninterrupted.

There was silence from the controller.

"Do you understand?"

He heard the noise, everybody heard the noise, the sound of somebody in pain. Not the sound of the pain, the long awful unending reaction to that pain.

"What was that?" asked the controller automatically.

"I asked if you understood me," the hijacker repeated. He could still hear the noise, knew they could all still hear it, wondered what the hijackers were doing, who they were doing it to.

An exercise, he thought, for God's sake it's only an exercise, a run-out for the anti-terrorist teams who would go onto the aircraft, take it out. He could hear the noise again, sharper, more horrible. Knew suddenly what they had done to the man, what they were still doing to the man. Saw the looks on the faces of the Chief Constable in charge of the operation, the Assistant Chief Constable who would conduct the negotiations, the Home Office advisors.

"Understood," said the controller, without authorisation.

They were all on trial, Kenshaw-Taylor suddenly realised, not just the people up front, the men who would go onto the plane if and when the order was given. He began to wonder how much was an exercise, how much was not.

"What do we do?" asked the Chief Constable. "Stay here or move where we can see them?" There was another moment of indecision, he was glad he was only an observer. The Chief Constable began to talk with the Home Office advisors.

"Stay here." The voice was from the other end of the room. "Cameras will be in place in five minutes. Then we'll see all we need to see." The major was in the early thirties, Kenshaw-Taylor thought he looked rather scruffy. "In any case," the man continued, "he'll probably move again before the day's up." He turned away from them and spoke into a microphone. "Snipers in position yet?"

"Snipers in position." The reply sounded hollow, echoing through the room.

"OK," said the Chief Constable, "we stay."

At least, thought Kenshaw-Taylor, they had stopped torturing the poor sod on the plane. He remembered it was only an exercise and knew the sounds of suffering from the plane had been a recording.

3

THE TRAIN WAS CROWDED. Graham Enderson bought a second coffee and went back to his seat two carriages from the buffet car. It was going to be a fine day, he thought casually, looking out the window. At Stansted, he knew, the exercise would have begun. They passed the towers of the Didcot power station on the left, thirty minutes to London. He thought again about Stansted.

JIMMY ROBERTS looked at the photograph they kept in front of them. He had memorised it, drilled it into his brain, knew he would remember, knew also there would be a moment when he would be in doubt, hoped he would make the right decision when the moment came. No guarantee, of course, that the man would turn up again, but if he did, if they got him in the centre of London, the propaganda value would be worth the wait, every minute of the wait.

He made the two of them a cup of coffee and went back to the window, just inside the window, so that no one would know he was there.

IN THE SCHOOLROOM in Hereford the children began to leave the morning assembly. Jane Enderson picked up her books and followed them down the corridor and into the classroom. The children were chattering between themselves, it was a sign of the end of winter, she thought, they always chattered this way at the first sign of the change in season. She settled down and began the class. In eight days, she remembered, it would be her birthday.

IN THE STREET in Belfast, Eileen McDonald turned the door mat, beat it, scrubbed the front step and put the mat back in position. She had had few possessions in her life, and she took a pride in those she had. The air was warmer than the day before. She thought of spring and began to plan what she would do with Liam when he came home, where she would take him. The Bellevue Zoo, on the Antrim Road, he had always liked animals. Perhaps even some tea, then home for supper. She went inside, closing the door behind her. It was surprising, she thought, what the first warmth did, for herself, for everyone. She felt happier, more alive, knew it was only partly the new season. Knew it was mainly the latest report on Liam, the fact that the doctors had said he could leave the hospital in two to three weeks.

Knew it was also because she had slept better the night before.

She had only seen the eyes once.

THE OPERATIONS ROOM was bustling with activity, the rows of monitors showing the Boeing, the communications between the plane and the negotiator crackling, the link-ups between the anti-terrorist commander and his units on the ground always in the background.

Kenshaw-Taylor walked behind the people at the desks. The Assistant Chief Constable was talking to the hijackers, telling them he could not get a response to their demands as quickly as they wanted, checking how much fuel the plane carried, talking out his priorities. The Foreign Minister walked on, carefully, not getting in the way, stopping behind the army commander. In front of him, in addition to the monitors and radio links, the man had a display of lights.

"What's that?" asked Kenshaw-Taylor.

The major looked up and saw who it was. "Snipers," he explained briefly. "Four gunmen on the plane, two snipers assigned to each. Others round the airfield, of course. Each of the snipers targeting the gunmen has a link-up with these lights, each sniper will only take his target, and no other. On the barrel of their weapon, each sniper has a button. He pushes it when he has contact, good contact, with his target."

Kenshaw-Taylor looked along the line. All the lights were green.

"Early days," said the major. "Still too early for them to show themselves."

Kenshaw-Taylor nodded. "When would you give the order to fire?"

"Assuming that course of action has been decided upon?" queried the soldier.

"Yes."

"Only when all the lights were red. Only when each of the targets was covered by both snipers assigned to that target."

Behind them the Chief Constable called his first conference of the day.

GRAHAM ENDERSON walked through the ticket barrier at Paddington and caught the underground to Knightsbridge; he knew he was thinking about Stansted, would not stop thinking about it all day. Even his equipment was there, his body armour and his weapons. The team had taken it with them in case they were called out, in case they had to call him on his bleeper to join them in a hurry. That was why he had carried it to London, why the duty officer in Hereford had a telephone number for every place he would be that day.

The doors shut and the train pulled away.

Jimmy Roberts knew he would see him, knew that today was the day he would see him. They changed positions as they changed positions every fifteen minutes, Jimmy to cover the approach from the tube station, Ray to take the others from the west. Today, he thought again, today was the day, laughed at himself; every day he had the same feeling, every day he made himself have the same feeling. It was a game he played with himself, a game he imposed upon himself to make him concentrate. He looked at the time.

The train stopped at Gloucester Road; Enderson changed to the Piccadilly line.

The street was reasonably busy; fifteen, twenty people at any one time, the parking spaces already filled. He went through the routine again, the route the man from Dublin would follow after he had done the job. Jimmy Roberts had worked it out, walked it through, knew that when the time came when the man from Dublin needed it, it would have to be flawless. He looked at his watch again, the minute hand had barely moved.

The train stopped at South Kensington.

A hundred yards, Jimmy had calculated, that was the distance the police normally held the people back, the place they put up the white tape to cordon off an area, a hundred yards minimum. He went through the calculations in the square below, deciding where the white tape should go.

The train reached Knightsbridge, Enderson ran up the escalator and handed in his ticket.

Three minutes, Jimmy Roberts thought, less, more like two. For somebody to phone the police, tell them a man had been shot, for the police to get there. So many police in the area, especially after the Harrods bombing. Not that they would know immediately that it was a political shooting, not unless the man from Dublin took him out on the steps of the building, then they would know right away, then they would come like a bat out of hell. He heard Ray begin to tell him a joke he had heard in the pub the night before.

"That's him." Jimmy Roberts saw him, recognised him immediately, grabbed the binoculars.

"Christ, where?" Ray was reaching for the photograph.

"Just passing number thirty-two. On the right." They knew the street, the numbers of the houses, every detail. He passed the glasses to Ray and picked up the camera.

"Christ, you're right. It's him."

The man was close, getting closer, sixty yards, less. He focussed the lens and began shooting stills of the man. Thirty yards. Twenty-five. Jesus, he thought, if only they had the go-ahead, if only they could do the job themselves. Twenty yards. He wondered if he could do it, should do it, wondered what Belfast would say. The rifle was on the floor, less than three feet from him, he could pick it up without even moving. The man had gone, into the door. No problem, he thought, ten minutes inside, ten minutes as he had done the last time, then out again, up the street to the tube station, return again that night. He thought again about the gun, decided against it. Knew what they would do to him if he disobeyed them a second time, especially what they would do to him if he missed.

"What do we do?" Ray was trembling with excitement.

Jimmy Roberts looked at his own hands, not totally still, he was not totally in control of himself. He knew why he had been ordered to bring in the man from Dublin, knew that the big man in Belfast had been right.

"We wait," he said. "Get a couple more shots of him as he comes out. That way we can tie him to the address, that way we can prove there's no mistake."

Ray nodded. "What then?"

"When he's gone, you stay here, start clearing up, I'll get the photos developed and phone Dublin."

Ray began to ask something else then stopped. The door opposite opened and Enderson came out, turned right, and headed back towards the tube station. Exactly as before, Ray whispered, exactly the same as before. Enderson disappeared from the square. He had the bastard, Jimmy Roberts knew, knew that his wait was over.

He gave the man five minutes then left the embassy. In Brompton Road he took a cab to a shop three streets from the flat and walked the rest. The others were still asleep. He let himself in, woke them, and dialled the number. The phone rang three times before it was picked up. A woman's voice answered. Jimmy waited thirty seconds till the man came to the phone. The code was pre-arranged. Ninety minutes after he had spotted Graham Enderson, Jimmy Roberts was back in the embassy. Ray had stacked the items they had brought with them by the door. There was one lingering doubt on both their minds; Jimmy was glad he had taken the sets of photographs. He pulled the prints he had just developed from the envelope and laid them on the desk beside the first set.

"I think you've got the bastard," said Ray.

"I think you're right," said Jimmy.

THE DISCUSSIONS were going badly. The police officer dealing with the hijackers was not prepared to make any concessions, and the hijackers insisted their demands be met immediately. The Chief Constable's first conference had ended without decision; it was not, in any case, the conference at which decisions would be made. The demands were familiar: the release of what the hijackers called political prisoners, what everyone else called terrorists, and the payment of a substantial ransom. Once and only once during that period had any of the hijackers appeared. At nine fifty, one hour and fifty minutes after the plane had landed, a single figure dressed in black and wearing a hood had come to the open doorway of the aircraft to take the food and hot drinks which the hijackers had demanded. John Kenshaw-Taylor had been standing behind the army controller at the time, had seen the lights change colour, the two lights flicking from green to red. Then the hijacker had disappeared from the doorway and they had changed back.

THE KITCHEN was quiet and peaceful. Eileen McDonald sat at the table, writing out her shopping list with the stub of the pencil she kept in the drawer. She was a careful housekeeper, had learned through necessity how to be careful; each week she budgeted the money her husband gave her, each week throughout the year she managed to put aside a small amount, each week she saved a little more for Christmas. She thought again of Christmas, the Wednesday before last Christmas.

Every thought she had, every sound she heard, brought her back to the day; she wondered if she would ever forget it, tried to push the thought away, tried to concentrate on the shopping list. She had been saving a little more with Liam in hospital, not much more, of course, it was amazing how much she had spent on the little things she took with her each day. She told herself to stop, knew she was thinking again of the eyes of the man who had pulled Liam's little life back into him, the eyes of the man in the photograph upstairs. She finished the list and put the stub back in its place in the dressing table, then realised it was Liam's pencil.

"Holy Mary," she asked aloud, "will I ever forget, will you ever allow me to forget?"

She was almost ready when she heard the knock and her husband answer it, the footsteps going up the stairs to the small room at the top.

The house was quiet. She knew why the visitor had come, even before she heard his words as they shut the door.

"The Yank's spotted the bastard. Phoned Dublin twenty minutes ago. The man's on his way. It'll be done by tonight."

IN THE CLASSROOM of the school in the Welsh border country Jane Enderson put away her books and went to the staff-room for a cup of tea. It had been a good weekend, she thought. She enjoyed having Grah home, even though he had seemed on edge on the Sunday, even though he carried the damn bleeper everywhere. If the weather held, she began to plan ahead, they could go to the Long Mynd next Saturday, watch the gliders, take a picnic.

IN THE HOUSE in Belfast Eileen McDonald put on her coat, picked up her purse and shopping bag, and went into the street. The sun was still shining though she hardly noticed it. Different now, she thought, ever so different now. No different, she told herself, no different at all; she had known all along they were going to kill the man. The only difference now was that they were going to kill him today.

ON ANY OTHER DAY, Graham Enderson thought, he would have enjoyed the train ride, the sun streaming through the window. Any day except the day of the exercise. He looked at his watch, time for the first deadline, the first trick the hijackers would play on the unsuspecting negotiators. The train reached Woolwich, he left the station and decided he had time to walk to the hospital.

AT ELEVEN O'CLOCK, despite the repeated assurances of the negotiators that they were doing all in their power to reach a settlement, the hijackers issued their first ultimatum. If they had not received a satisfactory answer by one, they would kill a hostage, they would then kill a hostage every second hour for as long as the authorities denied their demands. The atmosphere in the operations room was tense, for the second time that day John Kenshaw-Taylor had to remind himself it was only an exercise.

EILEEN McDONALD took one of the black cabs to the city centre and walked to the supermarket; she knew she should shop in the corner shops on the Falls itself, knew she should support them, but the prices were cheaper in the big stores and the journey took her past the Royal Victoria. Everything she did took her past the Royal Victoria. She finished her shopping and began to walk back to the Falls.

Dunville Park was quiet. She sat down, so small and insignificant that not even the pigeons bothered with her, remembering the night again, wondering what she had to do to stop remembering. Her Liam's body, torn apart, the man appearing from nowhere, holding her Liam together, bringing the life back into him. She had thought he was dead, been sure he was dead, had never seen blood so red before. And the bastard Brit had saved his life, held what was left of Liam's tiny bones and flesh and innards together, staunched the flow of the blood. Given him the relief from the pain. There was a telephone kiosk on the corner of the square. One Brit, she thought, just one Brit. She knew they had to kill all the Brits, hated them, had reason to hate them. But surely one Brit would make no difference. Somebody was using the telephone kiosk. Not one Brit, she knew, not one ordinary Brit. She knew what the man was, who he was. Even more reason to kill him, she knew.

Especially in London, especially where he thought he would be safe. The telephone kiosk was empty. She remembered the number, on the notice board above the police stations, the number they could dial if they wanted to inform on their own kith and kin, remembered again the red pouring from the boy's body, the way the man had stopped it, remembered the knock on the door that morning, the footsteps up the stairs, the words before her husband shut the door at the top. Ten pence pieces, the phones took ten pence pieces. She knew she did not have any, did not need to open her purse to check. She got up from the bench.

THE SQUARE WAS less busy, it always seemed less busy in the late morning, would pick up again after lunch. Jimmy Roberts checked that they had left nothing except the M18 at the side of the desk by the front window and the set of photographs on top of the desk, plus the instructions for the departure from the flat after the man from Dublin had done the job. He had calculated how long it would take from Dublin, plus the times the man would need to recce the place himself, work out the approaches, suspected that the man from Dublin had already done so, already passed under their very noses, without the men in Belfast telling him. Another three hours, he decided, four at the outside, and the man would be in position. Plenty of time, he told himself, as long as the bastard he had seen that morning stuck to the timetable. He took one last look round the room and knew he had done his job. Now it was up to the man from Dublin.

THE FIRST BUDS were appearing on the bushes outside the Royal Victoria. Eileen had no intention of going in, but found herself inside anyway, smelling the polish and the antiseptic, walking up the stairs, past the telephone on the landing. She hesitated, realising she had known all along that it would be there and thought about the man, about her Liam, then she walked on towards the ward.

THE RECEPTION AREA on the ground floor was brightly decorated, a bowl of daffodils on the counter: Graham Enderson checked in fifteen minutes early and was referred to the consultant's secretary on the second floor. He told the receptionist he knew the way and went up the stairs rather than waiting for the lift. The secretary was apologetic, the consultant had been called to an emergency operation that morning, would Mr Enderson mind waiting till two?

Enderson knew he had no option. He left the hospital, thought about going to a pub, and went for a walk.

EILEEN LOOKED INTO the ward, saw Liam, knew the staff nurse had seen her by the telephone on the landing, began to pull back.

The nurse smiled, got up from the desk in the middle of the ward and came over. "Hello, Mrs McDonald. A bit early today."

Eileen was thinking of the boy on the ground, the man saving his life. "I just thought," she began to stutter, did not know what she was thinking.

The nurse took her arm. "Just thought you'd pop in to see Liam on the way home from shopping. Go on, then, but quickly, or you'll get me into trouble."

Eileen walked into the ward, past the other beds and stopped at her son's. "Hello, Mum," he said. "You're early today." He still looked white, she thought, still looked so white. She kissed him and wondered what he would be when he grew up. Whether he would be a man of violence like his father, like the man who had saved his life. The nurse was looking at her, she knew the nurse sensed something was wrong, kissed the boy again, telling him she would see him later, and left the ward. The landing was empty. She stopped at the telephones. No ten pence pieces, she knew, there were no ten pence pieces in her purse. Please God may they answer quickly, please God may they not ask her any questions. She knew what she was betraying if she made the call, knew what she was betraying if she did not, glanced back, saw that the nurse was still looking at her.

She turned from the telephone, went into the ladies toilet, locked herself in a cubicle and began to cry.

"Why me, Holy Mother," she asked, "why me?"

THE CLOCK on the wall of the operations room seemed to be standing still. An hour and fifty-five minutes since the hijackers had set the deadline, an hour and fifty-five minutes that had passed so quickly Kenshaw-Taylor had not noticed. Now the last five seemed to be lasting for ever. The second hand completed another circle. Four minutes to go. He heard the voice of the hijacker asking for the senior negotiators to come to the aircraft. It was the first time the Assistant Chief Constable had been in the position; he asked for time to confer. Three minutes to go. The Chief Constable had been through it before, knew the man was being tested, wondered how they were about to test him and gave his consent. Two negotiators, the hijackers repeated, they wished to see the two senior negotiators at the plane, asked who the second would be. It was Kenshaw-Taylor's first experience of a hijack, even an exercise: when the Chief Constable turned to him he had no hesitation in agreeing.

THREE TEN PENCE PIECES, she had had three ten pence pieces all along, knew that she had had them, that she had known she did not need them for the number on the police station wall. She took them out anyway, closed her purse, put it back into her shopping bag, stood up and left the cubicle, remembering at the last moment that she had not flushed it, checking there was no one to notice. The landing was empty, the nurse who had been watching her before had gone. She knew the number she had to call, the number she despised, picked up the receiver and dialled it. Heard the voice immediately, knew it was a Protestant. Could tell by the accent, by the way he breathed. Could smell him, feel him. No ten pence piece, she thought, she had needed no ten pence piece. She knew what she wanted to say, knew that she wanted to share her guilt with someone, even a policeman, even a Protestant. Pass the burden to stronger shoulders. She looked round again, no nurse looking, remembering what they did to people who betrayed them, fearing what her husband would have to do. She wanted to talk to the man on the other end of the telephone, tell him they were going to kill the man who had saved her Liam, tell him about the nightmares, about the eyes that haunted her.

"There's going to be a killing." She spoke calmly, quietly, as if the voice did not belong to her. "This afternoon. A Brit."

The man was asking her a question. She thought she heard footsteps, looked round, made sure nobody could see her, hear her. Who, where, when, the man was asking her. He knew she was telling the truth, was cupping his hand over the mouthpiece, motioning to his colleagues to keep quiet. She thought she heard the footsteps again.

"The Wednesday before Christmas there was a shooting."

It did not sound like her own voice. "There was an army unit there. One of them is going to be killed."

She heard the footsteps again, knew she was not imagining them, began to put down the telephone, realised she had not finished. The footsteps were getting closer. She tried to hurry up, tried to work out what she should tell the man, how she should tell him without his knowing who she was. He was thanking her, reassuring her, asking for more details. Not asking her name, she thanked God, not asking her address. She knew he believed her, was sure he knew she was telling the truth. The footsteps were almost there.

"This afternoon," she said. "London."

The doctor recognised her, smiled at her, went past. She put the phone down and left the hospital.

In the police station the RUC constable reached for the tape-recorder, spun it back, waited to hear the words again. Realised the tape had run out.

THE CAR STOPPED fifty yards from the plane. John Kenshaw-Taylor sat quietly for a moment, drawing a breath, preparing himself, and stepped out. The driver was looking at him, he wondered what the man was thinking. The senior policeman came round the front of the car and stood beside him. Not an exercise, Kenshaw-Taylor thought, it never had been. They moved towards the plane.

A window in the cockpit opened slightly. "What time is it?" asked a voice. Kenshaw-Taylor assumed it was one of the hijackers. For the first time he felt the awful unease that something terrible was about to happen.

"Two minutes past one," said the man at his side.

They were told to step forward, closer to the plane, till they were almost directly beneath the front passenger door, looking up at the cockpit. He could see the outline of the hijacker's head.

"You know what we said we would do if you didn't meet our deadline."

The Assistant Chief Constable was trying to stall, trying to remember what his training had taught him. "As we were saying, I have passed your request to my superiors and am still waiting for their reply."

Wrong answer, thought Kenshaw-Taylor for the second time that day, even though it was the truth, even though he did not know what he himself would have said.

He heard the shot. The single sickening shot. Felt the fear. Looked up. Saw the door open.

The man at his side was beginning to protest. Two hijackers exposed, Kenshaw-Taylor was thinking, could imagine the lights on the monitor in front of the army commander, the green flicking to red. No, oh my God, no. He could see what was happening. In front of him. No, for God's sake, no. Above him, coming towards him. He tried to step back, was fixed to the spot, knew he could not move, knew he could never have moved.

The body hit the ground in front of them, just missing them, the blood splashing over them, staining them, implicating them. The entrails. The head, bloody and smashed where the bullet had torn it apart. Hitting him, rolling in front of him. He could feel the vomit shooting up his throat, filling his mouth. Beside him the negotiator was already vomiting. He reached for his handkerchief, trying to control himself, knew it was too late. Even before he saw that the body was a boilersuit stuffed with offal and the head was a carefully constructed section of a tailor's dummy.

By the time they had returned to the operations room the Chief Constable had formally handed over control of the operation to the army commander.

EILEEN MCDONALD put the shopping bag on the kitchen table and made herself a cup of tea. The house was empty, she knew her husband would be back later, they would all be back later, waiting for the telephone call, for the report on the television news, knew how they would react when there was nothing. Another failure, they would say, just another failure. To them it would not matter but to her it would matter a great deal.

She would not see the eyes again.

GRAHAM ENDERSON reported to the consultant's secretary at exactly two o'clock. At ten minutes past two he was examined for five minutes by the doctor and sent to the floor below for a final X-ray. At fifteen minutes to three he was told what he knew already, that he was fully fit.

"Is that it?" he asked incredulously.

The doctor seemed surprised at his query. "Yes," he said. "That's it."

Enderson did not say that he considered he had wasted the entire day, at the back of his mind was the knowledge that it was not improbable that at some time in the future he would lie on an operating table with the same surgeon bending over him.

He thanked the man and left.

"YOU'RE SURE she was telling the truth?"

The RUC constable who had taken Eileen McDonald's call was adamant. "I'm sure she was telling the truth."

"How can you be so sure?"

"Because she was scared."

"Then how can the British army say that what she says is impossible?" The inspector knew his man and trusted his judgment, knew both from his experience and his instinct that the man was correct, that some time that afternoon a British soldier would be shot to death by the Provisional IRA and that they were powerless to prevent it.

The constable did not reply.

"No tape-recording of the call?" It was the third time the inspector had questioned the man.

"No, apparently we had just run out of tape and were changing over when she phoned. She wasn't on the line for more than twenty seconds, she put the phone down in a hurry before she could finish."

The inspector shook his head, partly in disbelief, partly in frustration. It was almost an hour and a half since they had taken the call and passed the information to the army, three-quarters of an hour since Lisburn had come back to them, querying their information and the reliability of their informant, telling them firstly that there had been no shootings involving British army patrols in Belfast on December 19th and secondly that no members of the Green Jackets, who had been covering the city that day, were now in Northern Ireland, or, specifically, in Londonderry, where the caller had said the shooting was to take place.

He waved for the constable to leave and banged the door in disgust.

6

THE MAN FROM DUBLIN let himself into the former Argentinian Embassy at ten minutes to three; he had arrived at Heathrow ten minutes late at one thirty, caught the Piccadilly line to Knightsbridge, and spent the rest of the intervening time recceing the area, confirming the details he had noted when he had walked the square four weeks before, checking that the embassy was not under surveillance.

The building was quiet; the room from which the away team had mounted its operation was neat and tidy, and with the exception of the box on the floor and the photographs and instructions on the desk there was no evidence that the room had been occupied. A good clean job, he thought to himself, knowing it augered well. He kept his gloves on and examined the square below, noting the address where his target would stay, as well as the various directions from which the target could approach the address, then opened the box. The M18 was as he had zeroed it on the marshes at Soldier's Point. The light outside was good, he thought, looking at the photographs on the desk; he knew the face, was sure of the face, from the countless times he had studied it in Dublin. Whoever had set it up was good, even down to the escape routes, the different ways out, depending on where the target came from, where he decided to take him out. He knew there was only one place he would take him out. Bang on the steps, the men in Belfast had told him, just as he's going into the club; that way there would be no doubt that the Provos knew both who they were getting and where they were getting him, that way the proverbial would really hit the fan. He eased the window open, chose his position, and settled down to wait.

SOMETHING WRONG, the inspector thought, something missing. Or both. He began to go through the file again, the constable's report on his conversation with the woman. The telephone rang; it was the superintendent's secretary reminding him of a meeting in fifteen minutes; he thanked her, telling her he had not forgotten, and tried to remember what it was about. So many things to do, so many reasons not to bother any more with the woman and her bloody telephone call. Something they had got wrong, he thought again, something they had missed. Or both. He knew it was both.

Ten more minutes, he thought, he would give it ten more minutes, then he would forget about it. He turned back to the report, comparing it with the notes he had made on the army response.

"There's going to be a killing." The man who had taken the call said that the voice had been calm, he knew it was not the woman's true voice, that it did not reflect the turmoil she felt.

"This afternoon. A Brit." He began to think that she knew the man personally.

"The Wednesday before Christmas there was a shooting. There was an army unit there. One of them is going to be killed." No shootings involving British units, the army had said, nothing at all on December 19th.

"This afternoon." There had been a fresh element in her voice, the constable had said, as if someone was coming, as if she knew what they would do to her if they caught her. "Londonderry." No members of the Green Jackets who had been covering Belfast that day were now in Northern Ireland, the army had said, specifically Londonderry they had added pointedly, where the caller had said the shooting was to take place.

How did it end, he had asked the man who had taken the call. The woman had been frightened, the constable had confirmed, very frightened, had put the phone down as she was speaking, had not finished.

Ten minutes, he reminded himself, ten minutes then he would forget about it. He reached again for a report and asked for the RUC incident summary for December 19th, shootings or no shootings. British army involvement or not, remembering what the woman had said, what she had not said. Not December 19th, the thought was forming, the Wednesday before Christmas. No difference, every difference. He began to remember the night, the picture in the paper the next day. Knew who the woman was, knew who was going to be killed that afternoon, cursed himself, cursed all of them, for not seeing it, not believing the woman who had called. He was shouting for the constable, reaching for the telephone, telling the switchboard to get

him a number at Lisburn as priority, over everything else, he
was telling her, over absolutely everything else. The superintendent's secretary was on the phone, asking where he was.
Later, he was telling her. Priority, he was still telling the
switchboard, absolute priority.

Perhaps the woman had panicked, perhaps she hadn't put the
phone down before she had finished, perhaps she had told them
all they needed to know. He knew it, was sure of it, wondered
if there was still time. One thing, he was also thinking, one
other thing. The constable who had taken the call came into the
room.

"Your notes on the conversation, the last line."

"Yes."

"She said the killing was to take place in Londonderry."

"Yes."

"She says there's going to be a shooting, she says it will be a
Brit."

The constable was confused.

"She calls someone a Brit, she probably lives in the Falls.
What does that make her?"

The constable was still confused.

"It makes her a Catholic."

The constable could not see the point.

"If she was a Catholic," said the inspector, "she would have
called it Derry, not Londonderry."

"Oh Jesus," said the constable.

THE PHONE RANG, the switchboard told him they were connecting him. He identified himself and asked for the department which served as a front for special operations in Northern
Ireland. It was lucky, he thought, that for six of the years since
Bloody Sunday he had worked in Special Branch. He was put
through immediately, identified himself for the second time and
detailed the call his station had received that morning, adding
his interpretation of it as well as details of the person he thought
was at risk.

"Why the delay?" asked the faceless man.

The inspector explained the army reaction and the official
refusal to accept the call as genuine. "Either they don't remember your lot were around," he suggested, "or they don't
want to."

"Jesus Christ," said the faceless man, neither confirming nor denying that the people the inspector had called his lot had been involved. "What time did you get the call?"

The inspector told him.

"Where's the target?"

"Either London or Londonderry, more likely London." He explained the confusion.

"Give me your number," said the voice. "I'll phone you back."

THE SQUARE HAD CHANGED, the shadows from the trees falling differently as the sun passed across the sky. The man from Dublin checked up and down the streets. People, lots of people, not the right person. Not yet. It did not concern him, he knew he could wait as long as he needed.

THE TELEPHONE in the inspector's office rang, he picked it up immediately.

"Somebody owes you a drink," said the voice, not identifying itself. The inspector knew who it was.

"One of yours?" he asked.

"One of ours," confirmed the voice.

"Which was it, London or Londonderry?"

"London."

"Did you get him in time?" He thought of the woman waiting by the television set for news of a killing.

"We don't know yet. He's by himself. Carrying a bleeper, but the bloody thing's gone on the blink."

THERE WAS A TENSENESS in the operations room, a different tenseness, as if what had gone before was merely a necessary preamble to what was about to happen. The images of the plane on the monitors, different angles, different sizes, long distance and close-up, the front passenger door still open. In the background Kenshaw-Taylor could hear the negotiator talking to the hijacker's spokesman, stalling him, giving the assault teams the time they needed. Around the plane, he did not know where, they were almost ready. In front of the army commander the monitor of sniper lights flickered from green to red and back to green, sometimes two lights red, never more than four, the hijackers being careful, not exposing themselves.

Five minutes to three. The plane had been on the ground almost seven hours.

"Thirty minutes. Alpha and Bravo update." The army commander was speaking quietly, calmly. Kenshaw-Taylor heard the reports from the unit commanders. "Alpha One approaching target. Can see one hijacker." "Bravo One slight hold-up. They can see us on our original line. Am going back."

"Five minutes and we kill another hostage." The words of the hijacker penetrated the room.

"Twenty-five minutes. Charlie and Delta update."

The AT unit commanders on the field radioed their reports. Three lights on the sniper panel flicked to red, five still on green.

"We wish to refuel. Immediately. Then we will take off." There was a decisiveness in the hijacker's voice, the negotiator turned for advice.

"Twenty minutes," the army commander told him, not taking his eyes off the monitors. "Refuelling will take twenty minutes, it might not give us cover." The negotiator was unsure. "Agree if he guarantees not to kill the next hostage," the soldier told him, still concentrating on the monitors in front of him. Four minutes, they all heard the voice of the hijacker, four minutes and another hostage would die. The negotiator confirmed the request, provisional on the hijacker not executing the next hostage, welcomed the agreement from the plane, and ordered a fuel tanker onto the runway.

"No tricks," the hijacker said. "No tricks or we kill *two* hostages."

"Alpha and Bravo update." The commander's eyes were riveted to the screen, his concentration totally on the images in front of him. No one spoke. The fuel tanker stopped in position beneath the wing of the Boeing and the two mechanics stepped from the cab. Kenshaw-Taylor knew something was about to happen.

"Not ours," said the army commander.

He felt the disappointment in the room.

"Twelve minutes."

In the passenger door two hijackers appeared and dropped to the ground to supervise the refuelling. Kenshaw-Taylor saw the images on the screen, and saw they were carrying guns, did not know what sort, saw the lights on the sniper panel, four lights suddenly on red, the others green. In the door above the

tanker a third hijacker appeared. For the first time that day
Kenshaw-Taylor realised that not even the major in charge of
the operation knew what was going to happen, wondered if he
had seen the lights, prayed he had, glanced again at the sniper
panel. Six red, only two green. The last two suddenly blinking, changing, green to red. He looked at the monitors, a second figure in the doorway, the fourth hijacker, looked back at
the sniper panel. Eight lights, all red. Heard the voice of the
operation commander, calm, almost detached briefing the assault teams closing on the plane.

"Targets in vision, standing by. Radio silence."

Enough for the team commanders to know what was happening, thought Kenshaw-Taylor, wondered what would happen in the next thirty seconds, heard the commander talking to
his snipers. Standing by, he was telling them, standing by. The
two hijackers on the ground were secure, he knew the major
was thinking, was waiting for the two in the doorway, looked
again at the lights. Red, he thought, all red. Standing by,
standing by. Now, he thought, for Chrissake now. Felt the
caution. All four hijackers had to die together, at the same
moment; if even one survived, even for a few moments, all the
passengers would be dead. Red, he looked again at the lights,
all red.

"Standing by, looking good, ten, nine, eight . . ."

The telephone at the side of the monitor rang. The man beside the commander picked it up.

"Seven, six, five . . ."

"You boss," the man was telling the commander. "Take it
now."

Five seconds, the voice inside Kenshaw-Taylor screamed,
wait just five seconds. Don't take the call. He was subconsciously still counting down. Four, three, two... The lights still
on, still red. Wait, the voice was pleading.

The army commander was listening to the telephone, not
speaking. "Hold," he told the man on the phone. The lights
red, eight lights all red. Now, Kenshaw-Taylor was shouting silently at him, for God's sake now. He looked again at the lights.
Red, all still red. Now, the voice was screaming, for Chrissake
now.

"Abort exercise. Repeat abort exercise."

Kenshaw-Taylor heard the words, did not understand them, could not understand what the man was doing. Could still see the images, still see the lights.

"Abort exercise. Repeat all units abort exercise."

Kenshaw-Taylor heard the words again, could not believe them, wondered what the men on the ground were thinking, what the snipers were thinking. The images of the hijackers still on the monitors, the lights still red. Now, he was still urging for Chrissake now. No more lights, no more voices.

"Alpha and Bravo stand by for immediate departure. Unit commanders to me immediate. Repeat immediate."

No one in the room spoke, no one in the room knew what was happening or dared to ask. The army commander swivelled in his chair and took the telephone again.

"Two units will be moving in four minutes. Tell me again."

Through the window Kenshaw-Taylor saw the two Range Rovers, appearing as if from nowhere, heading fast towards them. The commander was listening intently, simultaneously issuing orders to the senior policemen at his side.

"Alert Essex police two vehicles travelling at speed down M11, request Met to pick them up at junction four and escort through Central London."

He was concentrating again on the telephone. Outside, Kenshaw-Taylor heard the feet running up the stairs to the control room. The police officers at the army commander's side were waiting.

"Now," the long-haired man next to the commander ordered them. "Move it now." They did as they were told.

Two men came into the room. Kenshaw-Taylor would not have recognised them: they were dressed in black, the gas masks still in place, the weapons and explosives hanging round the body armour, the hoods over their heads. The army commander told the person on the phone to keep the line open, gave the set to the soldier at his side, and turned to the men who had just entered. Kenshaw-Taylor tried to listen but could not hear. Overheard only one question and answer.

"Is the information good?"

"Apparently so. Met police will meet you at junction four, take you through London. I'll arrange unmarked cars for you near the location, and update you as soon as I know anything more." The men were running, not even saying anything else, past Kenshaw-Taylor, out the door. Twenty seconds later he saw the Range Rovers pulling away, engines racing, accelerating towards the exit. Even in the control room he could hear the screaming as the drivers changed up through the gears. He began to ask what was happening.

"Briefing in five minutes," said the army commander. His voice had not changed since he had talked to the unit commanders ten minutes before. He turned in his seat. "Scotland Yard anti-terrorist squad and Home Secretary in that order." He picked up the telephone again. "OK," he said, "They're on their way. What's happening at your end?"

7

IT WAS TEN MINUTES before the afternoon break. Jane Enderson saw the headmaster through the glass window of the door as he paused before coming in to the class room. "Sorry to trouble you," he said, "but there's a telephone call for you."

She knew he disapproved of personal calls at work. "Who is it," she asked, "couldn't it wait till the break?"

"It's a friend of your husband, he said it was urgent."

The first hint of fear touched her. Nothing on the news, she thought, nothing he would have been involved in. He was in Woolwich, at the hospital. The headmaster did not know what her husband did, thought he was a civil servant.

"Thank you," she said. She gave the class its instructions and followed him along the corridor to his office, picked up the telephone.

"Yes," she said, the fear growing. The headmaster had left the room.

"Jane, it's Stewart Marshall." She knew he was the duty officer. "Sorry to trouble you, but I need to get hold of Grah in a hurry. Any idea where I can contact him?" What is it, she thought, what the hell's going on? They knew where he was, they always knew exactly where he was.

"At the hospital, then at the club tonight." The numbness was seeping into her. "Have you tried there, have you tried his bleeper?" She knew she was speaking faster and made herself slow down.

"He's left the hospital and hasn't arrived at the club yet."

"What about his bleeper?"

"I've tried that, it's not working." His voice was calm and friendly.

"What is it, Stewart," she asked. "What's wrong?"

"Nothing." She knew he was lying to her. "If he phones you, tell him to get hold of me immediately."

"Is he in trouble?" she asked.

"No," he lied again, "just tell him to phone immediately."

The headmaster was staring at her through the door. "Nothing wrong, I hope," he said.

She shook her head. "No, nothing wrong."

She walked back down the corridor, saw that the children had left for their break, and sat down in the empty room.

THE BRIEFING, to those at Stansted authorised to be informed, took six minutes. There were no questions at the end. The army commander told them that information had been received that a Provisional IRA gunman was believed to be in London and that his target was a member of the SAS who had just completed a tour of duty in Ulster. He apologised for interrupting the exercise and assured them that the sole function of the two units he had sent to London was to intercept the target before he was spotted by the gunman; all other matters, he emphasised, would be dealt with by the police. The meeting ended at three twenty-one. Two minutes later John Kenshaw-Taylor was updating the Prime Minister on a secure link to the COBRA room beneath Downing Street.

At three twenty-eight a patrol of the Essex police radioed their Chelmsford headquarters that two range Rovers had passed them heading south. They estimated the vehicles were travelling in excess of a hundred miles an hour. At three fifty-five Scotland Yard informed Hereford that their units had picked up the vehicles and were escorting them into London. Late, they knew, it was so late, knew the units would not find the man in time, if they found him at all, waited for the first report of a shooting in Central London. At five minutes past four Scotland Yard received an emergency 999 call reporting that four men had been seen jumping out of two Range Rovers at Tottenham and into Rover 3500 motor cars; the caller said he had once been in the army, he said the men were all armed. Late, they knew, so very late, continued to wait around the operations room, the units drifting in from the airfield, clustering round the telephone. At twelve minutes past four a second emergency call was received complaining that two police cars, followed by two unmarked Rovers, had gone through the traffic lights at Camden Town when they were red and had driven towards Regent Park on the wrong side of the road. All in vain, they knew, it would all be in vain. Waited anyway.

GRAHAM ENDERSON saw him immediately.

He had left the underground at Knightsbridge, passed through the ticket barrier, and was walking up the stairs to Brompton Road.

The man was standing at the top. Enderson knew he was looking for him, knew he had spotted him. The man was wearing a mack, even though the afternoon was warm; under it, Enderson knew the man was carrying a gun, even knew what it was, a Heckler and Koch, short barrel, folding stock, a second gun, a Browning, in his pocket. The man moved towards him. Enderson looked past and saw the back-up, turned down the stairs, wondering what was happening. The man had almost reached him. Enderson knew what he was going to do, moved to the side, away from the people, felt the man against him, took the Browning and slipped it under his jacket.

"Hello, Dave," he said to his number two. "I thought you were at Stansted."

"We were. What kept you?"

"What do you mean?"

"You left the hospital two hours ago, should have been here by four. We thought we would be too late."

Enderson knew the man would explain. "Stopped to buy Jane a birthday present," he said.

"In that case," replied the man with the sub-machine gun under his mack, "I hope you bought her something worthwhile."

IN NOVEMBER 1985 an unarmed London policeman, Simon Tanner, was shot dead close to what was found to be an IRA bomb factory in Earls Court. The following March the British authorities requested the extradition from the United States of an American citizen, James Patrick Roberts in connection with this offence. The preliminary hearings were held in the District Court in San Francisco, where Roberts lived. Lawyers for the defence argued firstly that Roberts was not involved and secondly that the killing was a political act not at the time subject, under the laws of the United States, to extradition. In June 1986 Magistrate F. Stanley Longton granted an order of extradition. The case is still under appeal.

In July of the same year an architect surveying the Argentinian Embassy in London reported to police that he had found a gun in one of the rooms. Checks revealed that the weapon, an M18 automatic rifle, was one of a batch used by European terrorist groups in the outburst of bombings and shootings which had rocked Europe the previous year. Purchase of that batch, cross-checks suggested, had been financed by the Palestinian splinter group headed by Abu Nabil.

BOOK FOUR

CHAPTER ONE

1

KLARS CHRISTIAN MANNHEIM died at precisely six minutes past four on the morning of Thursday, March 14th, 1985. He had been born a little over three hours and twenty-nine years before and he died, as he had planned, on his birthday. There were the same number of people present at both events. In the small back room of the rented accommodation behind the Mercedes factory in Gaggenau there had been the woman who had conceived him and carried him for nine months, and the midwife who had tended her during her twenty hours of labour. In the room in the prison hospital in Stammheim where he had been moved three days before were a prison doctor dressed in a white coat and an armed guard. The only other difference between the two events was that while no one except his mother had taken any particular interest in his entry into this world, an entire nation waited anxiously on the consequences of his passing from it.

On the morning of his birth the midwife had wrapped him in a clean white linen towel and handed him to his mother. On the morning of his death the doctor covered him with a clean white sheet and handed responsibility for him to a pathologist. When he was born, Klars Christian Mannheim weighed three kilos, at the beginning of his hunger strike a fit sixty-eight. When he died he weighed three grammes over thirty-one.

Even before the official announcement, Gent Mueller knew that he was dead; she felt it as she left the apartment, confirmed it when she arrived at the bus station and saw the police car parked by the bridge, when she arrived at work and presented her bag for inspection. The guards at the building had been doubled, the checks were thorough. Even Hans, who had wallowed his way between her legs less than eight hours before, opened her bag and rummaged through it. She was glad she had taken the guns and explosives in days before.

The announcement itself was made at seven. Gent heard it in the canteen as she and the other cleaners downed their coffee

before going to the hangars. She had been expecting it, counting the days, seeing the gradual build-up of police in the streets
as the authorities realised Klars Christian Mannheim was not
going to retreat from his own death. The others ignored it and
turned to another station, preferring the pop music. She
laughed with them, not hearing their jokes, remembering when
she had first met Klars. Remembered how they had trained together, crossed back into Europe together, the only operation
they had carried out together. Remembered her reaction when
he had been caught and sentenced, her thoughts when he had
announced his hunger strike, when the authorities and press
said he would give in before the month was out. Remembered
how she had waited for this morning, knew that soon she would
find the coded postcard in the mail box at the foot of the stairs.

She left the table, went back to the locker room, picked up
her cleaning equipment, and went to the hangars.

Graham Enderson woke at fifteen minutes to six, switched
off the bleeper as soon as it sounded, showered, dressed in the
bathroom so as not to wake his wife and children, and went to
the kitchen. He enjoyed the early morning, the quiet, no matter what the time of year, no matter where in the world he was.
He filled the kettle, made himself a cup of tea, and cooked
breakfast. Early morning in the border country was different,
however. He could hear the birds, pick out the change in their
song as the season changed and the weather began to lose its
cold.

He turned on the radio and listened to the first news bulletin
of the day. The fourth item stated casually, almost unimpor-
tantly, that the West German hunger striker Klars Christian
Mannheim had died that morning in the prison hospital at
Stammheim. He had been on hunger strike for sixty-nine days.

Enderson put aside the breakfast and listened to the report.
The BBC correspondent was being interviewed by the programme presenter, describing the increase in police activity, the
road blocks and traffic checks that were causing chaos with the
morning rush-hour, bearing witness to the fear as the country
waited for what was considered the inevitable backlash of
bombings and killings.

He switched off the radio, remembering the same fear in
Belfast the night Bobby Sands had died, the women on the Falls

banging their tins and saucepans on the ground, waking the area. The waiting the next day, as Sands' body was taken to the small terraced house where his family lived, the fear the following afternoon when they had moved the body to the chapel two hundred yards up the road. The fear that the moment the body was in the earth Belfast would burn.

He poured himself another tea and began eating again. They had been wrong, of course. There had been no violence, no bombings or burnings or shootings to speak of. And it had worked, for the Provos it had worked, there had been nothing to distract from the wave of national and international sympathy that had been born of Sands' death.

And now West Germany, one hunger striker dead, the line of those seeking a similar martyrdom almost endless. And the second group, the next ones to die. No ordinary hunger-strikers, no ordinary martyrs. Just girls, one of them not even out of her teens, with no history of violence, no connection with terrorism. Nothing, he knew, there would be nothing to distract the nation as it waited for the death of an innocent. He finished breakfast, kissed Jane goodbye, and went to the barracks.

WALID HADDAD began his final briefing with the unit which that morning had requested permission to call itself the Commando of the Martyr Klars Christian Mannheim at twelve noon Damascus time. There were three in the group, in addition to himself. He had chosen them carefully, for reasons which he had not necessarily fully explained to them.

Gunter Pohl was twenty-six years old, a member of the Red Army Faction for five years, during which time he had been involved in two kidnappings and three bombings. Pohl was short, with blond hair, and good-looking. He had been in Syria since the beginning of the year. The passport he was to carry identified him as a West German architect, Rolf Heinnemann, with both an office and a residence in Hamburg.

The second male member of the team, Ahsad Kayeh, was twenty-three years old and had grown up in Jordan and the Lebanon, also spending a short period in Europe. Kayeh was not only good-looking, his brief stay outside the Middle East had given him a taste for expensive and slightly extravagant clothes.

The only female in the unit was Salma Sayeh. Even in the training camps she had attracted attention, not simply because of her outstanding ability but also because of her physical appearance. Salma Sayeh was twenty-two years old with light brown skin and sharp piercing eyes, her long hair swept back over her shoulders. She was slim and taller than average. She and Ahsad Kayeh would carry Kuwaiti passports in the names of Alameh and Akache.

The meeting was brief and to the point; each of the three had rehearsed their roles to the point of both boredom and perfection. At the end Walid Haddad asked if there were any questions. The West German Gunter Pohl had the only one.

"What will security be like?" he asked.

Walid Haddad remembered the days and nights he had spent planning the operation, the first time he had seen how he could do it, the first time he had seen what was established in his mind as the Dubai factor.

"Tight," he said, "security will be very tight." He knew they wanted an explanation, that they had a right to one. "On the same day as the hijack, the state president is due to make a formal visit to Frankfurt. Security for that will be massive."

"So why have we chosen Frankfurt, why have we chosen that day?"

"Because all the security will be around the president. When he leaves, they will relax, the bureaucrats will be anxious to get everybody off duty as soon as possible to save on the overtime. When he leaves, Frankfurt will be wide open."

They saw the logic. "Good," said Gunter Pohl.

Two hours after the Commando of the Martyr Klars Christian Mannheim left, Walid Haddad held his second briefing of the day. Ninety minutes later he reported back to Abu Nabil. The coffee was already on the table when he arrived. Abu Nabil had one simple question.

"Is it arranged?" he asked.

"With you," the old man had told him, "nothing is as it seems."

"Why?" Abu Nabil had asked him.

"Because you are more than an Arab," the old man had said. "You are a Palestinian."

"Yes," confirmed Walid Haddad. "It is arranged."

THE BRIEF which John Kenshaw-Taylor had requested from the British Embassy in Bonn reached him at one fifty in the afternoon. He made time to read it between the various appointments he had between two and three, asked for a telephone call to the embassy, and was connected within ten minutes. The ambassador had already been informed of the reason for the conversation, and Kenshaw-Taylor therefore came straight to the point.

"Just want to keep in touch with events in your part of the world. I would appreciate it if you could keep a close eye on things, keep me informed throughout." The line was open, the ambassador knew it was a low level discussion.

"Not a lot happening at the moment," he replied. "One man died this morning, three more went on hunger strike this afternoon. The West Germans have taken a leaf out of the British book and are facing up to the threat."

"Any chance of a cave-in?" Kenshaw-Taylor remembered his dinner with Saeed Khaled in New York, what had been offered to him, what had been accepted.

"No chance at all on the part of the authorities. Touch of the Iron Maiden about Bonn at the moment."

Kenshaw-Taylor knew what the ambassador meant. "When is the next death expected?"

"Just over two weeks."

"Anything to worry about other than the obvious?"

The ambassador knew the Foreign Minister had done his homework. "Perhaps," he conceded. "The next one on line is a girl, with no history of violence. The government here might be in for a rougher ride than with Klars Christian Mannheim, but my understanding is that they won't give in."

It was time to be in the House. He thanked the ambassador, asked him to keep him informed of any developments and was driven to Westminster in his official Rover. He was back by five-thirty, took sherry with his senior civil servants, phoned his wife, managed two hours at the despatch boxes, then went for dinner at the Carlton.

The man who, in the next New Year's Honours list, would become Sir Jonathan Mathison was sitting at the table in the corner entertaining an American. Kenshaw-Taylor exchanged pleasantries with him, wondering precisely how much the banker had made on the exchange rate deal, and went to the table he had reserved.

His own guest was late; he sat back, not relaxing, using the time to reflect again on the offer Saeed Khaled had made him in New York, the offer he had accepted. Some, he mused, would have considered both the offer and its acceptance as being of dubious morality. It was a premise he did not accept: he had long accepted there was no morality in politics, had long concluded there was little morality in anything. He thought again of New York and reminded himself there was no reason why he or his actions should be the exception.

The guest arrived. Kenshaw-Taylor dismissed the thoughts and rose to greet the man. He left the club at ten thirty and was back in Pimlico at ten minutes past one.

IN THE FLAT in Damascus, Abu Nabil thought about the twenty-four hours in New York, the offer that had been made, the one condition that had been placed upon its acceptance. Not a condition, he corrected himself, an addition which had made it possible. Jordan, John Kenshaw-Taylor had said, then he could become involved, then he could bring in the SAS.

He turned away from the window and looked at the photograph on the desk. So many deaths, he thought, so many still to die.

By the time Abu Nabil went to bed that night, Walid Haddad had left Damascus and begun his entry into Europe.

2

YAKOV ZUBKO rose at five, went to the kitchen, made breakfast for himself and a cup of tea for his wife. Alexandra was sitting up in bed; her morning sickness was almost over, every day she felt better, every day she drew nearer to being able to enjoy the child she was carrying. The only sadness in her life, the only sadness in both their lives, was that their dear brother Stanislav and his family were still not with them.

He left the house a little after five thirty and walked down the street, breathing in the freshness of the early morning, feeling that he should not pause in the square, that he should not sit as he always sat on the wall of the well, knowing that he would. They had been sitting the night before, watching the children play, talking to the neighbours about the old people in the village, the fact that there were no old people in the village, talking of when they had first come to Beita, how they renamed it, of the people who had been there before them. His son had been playing with the ball; he had often thought about the stranger who had saved his son's life, had never stopped thinking about him. Had managed, nevertheless, not to consider who he was, what he was, what he was doing in Beita. It had only been the night before, as he and Alexandra had sat by the well with the others, that he had finally admitted to himself that the man who had saved his son's life, who had been born in the room where his son and daughter now slept, was not a friend but a foe, was not a Jew but a Palestinian.

He left the square, walked past the field and the orange grove opposite, and climbed the hill called Bethesda.

THE RESTAURANT which Walid Haddad had selected as the rendezvous point for the hijack team which called itself the Commando of the Martyr Klars Christian Mannheim was on a side-street off Alfred-Brehm Platz, close to the zoo. It was small and discreet, in the dining room on the first floor there were only eight tables, served by two waitresses.

The Palestinian members of the team arrived in Frankfurt within four hours of each other, Ahsad Kayeh via Rome and Madrid, the woman Salma Sayeh via Lisbon and Paris. Both cleared the immigration procedures and security checks at the various airports through which they passed without difficulty, the only thing that the range of officials who dealt with either of them noticed was Salma Sayeh's looks and, separately, Ahsad Kayeh's style of dressing.

Ahsad Kayeh arrived first, took a cab to the Steigenberger Hotel on Am Kaiserplatz, and checked into the suite he had booked from Madrid. The receptionist told him it was lucky he had made the reservation: all other rooms in the hotel, and most in the city, had been taken. When he asked why she explained it was because of the visit by the state president on the Monday. When she asked how he was paying he said it would be in United States dollars.

Salma Sayeh arrived in Frankfurt shortly after mid-day and went straight to the restaurant which was the rendezvous point. Ahsad Kayeh was waiting for her; they ordered food and wine, smiling at the waitress and waiting while she brought the bot-

tle to the table and poured it for them. They were an attractive
couple, she thought, the man handsome and well-dressed, the
woman extremely attractive, probably Middle East. The waitress had barely moved away when Salma Sayeh raised her glass.

"Klars Christian Mannheim," she said.

"The Commando of the Martyr Klars Christian
Mannheim," said Ahsad Kayeh.

The waitress heard, half-heard, was too busy thinking about
their order to take notice, only remembered later when she saw
the news programmes on the television that night, the prepa-
rations for the burial of the hunger-striker. She wondered what
she should do and decided to do nothing, telling herself she had
not heard properly.

When they had finished lunch, Ahsad Kayeh and Salma
Sayeh went to the hotel; after she showered and changed her
clothes they spent the rest of the day familiarising themselves
with the city, then took dinner in the hotel restaurant.

That night they slept together.

That night the computer hacker Johan Streissmann exercised his craft for the penultimate time.

That night Walid Haddad lay awake and went through the
details of what was already set in motion.

It was three days to the hijack.

3

THE TWO PALESTINIANS rose at eight, breakfasted in the suite,
left the hotel at nine and split up. By eleven thirty each had
booked a seat on Lufthansa Flight LH608, Frankfurt to Tel
Aviv, departing Frankfurt at 1920 the following Monday, arriving Ben Gurion at 2345. Ahsad Kayeh was to fly economy,
Salma Sayeh first class. The bookings were made at different
times and at different travel agents, although both tickets were
paid for with United States dollars.

KLARS CHRISTIAN MANNHEIM was buried at ten that morning. There had been no debate about the nature of the burial,
no religious dialogue on whether a death such as his was or was
not suicide; Klars Christian Mannheim had long renounced the
church into which he had been baptised at the age of six

months. His last statement requested only that he be buried near the members of the Baader-Meinhoff group who had died in their prison cells in the single night after the successful West German assault on the hijacked Lufthansa charter jet at Mogadishu eight years before.

The weather was cold, the mist staying longer than the early dawn, hanging like a shroud around the trees which surrounded the graveyard, settling on the lines of mounted police who maintained a vigil round the several hundred sympathisers who attended. The television pictures which dominated the news programmes for the rest of that day did little to ease the tension that was slowly imposing itself.

At ten that morning Gent Mueller did not take the customary break. It was dangerous and she knew she should not have done it, but that morning, when the others went to the canteen for their coffee break, she stood in silence in the locker room.

One hour later John Kenshaw-Taylor received the latest report on the West German position on the hunger strike from the British ambassador in Bonn: there would be no change, the man said, in the hard-line stance which the authorities had assumed throughout.

At twelve o'clock the lawyers acting for the hunger-striker Christina Melhardt announced that doctors had estimated that she herself had less than two weeks to live. For the first time since the second group of prisoners had joined the hunger strike, the full significance of that group began to sink upon the people of West Germany. Christina Melhardt, the lawyers reminded them, had joined the hunger-strike in demand for straightforward civil liberties, she was in no way connected with terrorism. She was, they also pointed out, just nineteen years old; if she had not joined the hunger-strike, she would be due to be released from prison in exactly three weeks' time. Half an hour later the West German government confirmed, for the second time that day, that there would be no negotiations, no concessions, on the demands of the hunger-strikers, even those of the teenager Christina Melhardt.

Graham Enderson saw the video pictures on the lunchtime news bulletins, watching the images of the mourners at the graveside, the mounted police shrouded in mist, the anti-riot police in the streets outside, their visors pulled over their faces like mediaeval warriors, the scenes in the city as the police reacted to the threat, perceived or actual, of retaliation, the lines of traffic at the check points. It was like the fear in West Germany after Mogadishu, he thought, after the suicides in Stammheim, like the fear in Belfast the night after Bobby Sands had died.

It began to come together, the assassination at Heathrow, the bombings and shootings which had followed it, the connections between them, the connections he had always thought had been too obvious, as if they had been planned, the joint communiqués, then the hunger-strike, one dead, the second about to die. The girl with no connection with terrorism, simply her opposition to Cruise missiles in her country. Even the name, he thought, the name that everyone would remember. Christina.

He knew what was happening, what was going to happen, even knew how it would end. A hijack, he was certain, suddenly but positively, they were building up for a hijack.

He even knew who would do it. If the man from Heathrow had started it, he thought, then the man from Heathrow would finish it.

TWO AND A HALF HOURS after what remained of Klars Christian Mannheim was laid to rest, Ahsad Kayeh and Salma Sayeh returned to the restaurant where they had met the previous lunchtime. The waitress remembered them, their clothes and good looks. The West German, Gunter Pohl, joined them five minutes later; he had arrived in Frankfurt the night before, making the last leg of his journey by hire car, and found accommodation in a *pension* near the station. They ordered beer and began talking amongst themselves, ignoring her, confirming their flight reservations. When the waitress came back with the drinks they commented on the number of police in the city, listening attentively when she told them about the state visit on the Monday. Two men and one woman, she thought, the second man not quite as handsome as the first. Someone was calling her from another table, they thanked her and raised their glasses.

"Monday," said Salma Sayeh.

"Monday," said the others.

WHEN THEY HAD finished lunch, the members of the unit calling itself the Commando of the Martyr Klars Christian Mannheim laid the first foundations of the escape route they would use if anything went wrong. The arrangements were simple: a BMW hired through the hotel in the name Ahsad Kayeh was using, and a second vehicle, hired direct from a car rental office in the city using a second passport the West German Gunter Pohl was carrying and left at the airport with a change of clothing for the three of them. When the arrangements were made and the second car was in position, they left it and inspected the departure area of the airport itself. It was as they had expected from their first briefings and rehearsals.

That night they ate together before Gunter Pohl returned to the *pension* in which he was staying and Ahsad Kayeh and Salma Sayeh retired to the large double bed in the centre of the suite at the Steigenberger.

That night Walid Haddad thought through the final details of his plan.

That night the waitress at the restaurant realised what she had heard and seen. Not two men and one woman, she thought, two Palestinians and a West German. She remembered the toast, not just Klars Christian Mannheim, the Commando Klars Christian Mannheim, remembered the other toast, to Monday, what was happening in the city on the Monday. She knew she was wrong but telephoned the police anyway.

It was two days to the hijack.

4

YAKOV ZUBKO woke at five and made tea for himself and Alexandra. The sun was shining through the window into the children's room, when he sat on the bed by his wife he saw she was smiling.

"No morning sickness, Yakov Zubko," she said. "Today I can start enjoying life again."

He kissed her. "Today," he said, "is a good day."

At fifteen minutes to six, later than normal, he left the house and took the route he always took, sitting at the top of the hill, enjoying the morning as he knew Alexandra was enjoying the morning, breathing in the freshness of the air. By the time the others arrived at work he had put on his overalls and started his machine.

Alexandra rose and dressed, taking care not to wake the children, and went to the kitchen. She felt fresh, young again, happy to be with child, happy for them all; when she opened the door and felt the warmth sweep across the room she wanted to sing and dance, felt ridiculous that she should feel that way. Today, Yakov Zubko had said, was a good day, today, she knew, was going to be a day she would remember.

At ten fifteen Yakov Zubko switched off his machine and went with the others to the courtyard outside, sitting on the ground beneath the orange tree which grew from the corner of the building, enjoying the break. They had been there for ten minutes when the telephone rang. The supervisor groaned at his luck, pulled himself up and trudged inside the factory and up the wooden stairs to the small room which served as an office. They could hear him, still groaning, as he picked up the phone. The sun was warm and relaxing.

"Yakov Zubko." He pushed his head out the window, "It's for you."

The warmth of the day drained from him. Yakov Zubko rose, the fear already growing in him, and hurried into the cool of the workshop and up the stairs. Bad news, he thought, it had to be bad news; he tried to work out who knew he worked at the factory, who would call him there. Official, it had to be official; he wondered what he had done wrong, knew what they did to wrong-doers in Russia, wondered what they did to them in Israel. Not today, he thought, not this morning, not the day Alexandra lost her morning sickness.

The supervisor handed him the telephone and left the room.

"Yes." His voice was frail and frightened.

"Yes," he repeated the word, trying to make it stronger, more positive, knowing he had failed. In the house at the top of the street, he thought, Alexandra would be washing the floor, singing to herself. He wondered how he would tell her.

"Yakov Zubko?" The voice was that of a woman.

"Yes," he said, "this is Yakov Zubko."

The voice was distant. "This is the Jewish Agency." He knew again that something was wrong, something to do with the way he and Alexandra and the children had crossed to the West.

"The Jewish Agency in Tel Aviv?" he asked. Outside the men were relaxing in the sun.

"No," said the woman, "the Jewish Agency in Vienna. I have someone who wants to speak to you."

He waited, heard the sounds, the scuffles as the telephone was handed from one person to another. Felt the anxiety in his stomach. Heard the voice he thought he would never hear again.

"*Beshanah Hazu b'Yerushalaim*, Yakov Zubko," his brother told him, "This year in Jerusalem. We are in Vienna, Yakov Zubko, we are coming home."

He was standing still, hardly hearing the words, dancing round the room, shouting, singing. Standing still, standing quietly, listening to his brother.

In Vienna.

"Stanislav, is it you? Is it really you? Are you really in Vienna?"

"Yes, Yakov Zubko, it really is me. I really am in Vienna."

The fear returned. He knew what they did, how they split families, allowed some to come, made the rest stay.

"Mishka," he asked, "Mishka and the children. Are they with you?" He knew they were not, knew by the way his brother delayed, knew Mishka and the children were still in Russia.

"Yes, Yakov Zubko, Mishka and the children are with me. I would not have left without them." He was saying something else, Yakov Zubko could not hear properly, did not want the details, just the confirmation.

"Is it you, my brother," he asked again, "are you really in Vienna?" He heard the sound as the telephone was passed from hand to hand, heard his brother's wife.

"Yes, Yakov Zubko, it really is your brother. We really are in Vienna."

He heard the voices of the children, asking about his own son and daughter; heard, even at such a distance, the sound of the asthma in Natasha's breathing. They were telling him about the toys the woman from the Jewish Agency had given them, were asking what toys his children had.

"When are you coming?" He was excited, so excited.

"Soon. Tomorrow we hope, or the next day." It was his brother again. "There are problems with El Al, they are trying to get us on the next plane."

"We will meet you at the airport." So many things to talk about, too many things to talk about. "Beita is a good place, we will get you settled here, get you a house, a job."

They had been talking for ten minutes when the woman from the Agency took the telephone again, informing him that she would telephone again the following morning when she knew the details of his brother's flight. There was a problem, she repeated Stanislav's words, with El Al, the national airline, which they would normally use, which they had used for himself and his family, were due on strike that evening. They would therefore have to arrange for his brother and his family to come to Israel on another airline.

The strike, she did not know it, the first seeds of which were sown the day Yakov Zubko and his family had left Moscow and begun their journey to the West.

He did not mind, knew it was not important, wanted to ask her again if his brother really was in Vienna, thanked her, and put the telephone down.

In the courtyard outside the men were standing up, stretching, preparing to start work again. He walked down the rickety stairs onto the shop-floor. Alexandra, he had to tell Alexandra. The men were in the doorway in front of him. He felt numb, did not know what to say.

"My brother," he said, nodding his head. "My brother Stanislav."

They knew of his brother, that he was waiting in Moscow.

"My brother," he said again. "He is in Vienna, he is coming home."

The men were looking at him, moving towards him. The phone was ringing again, they were ignoring it, laughing with him, slapping his back. Is he an engineer, someone was asking, he can have a job here. We'll get him a house, get it ready for him and his family. Hope he doesn't start work as early as you, someone else was joking.

"Alexandra," said the supervisor, "you have to tell Alexandra."

"Yes," Yakov Zubko remembered, "I have to tell Alexandra."

The hill was steep, he did not notice, came to the house. The door was open, he could still feel the warmth, the contentment, inside. He stood in the doorway, seeing Alexandra at the table in the middle of the kitchen. She looked up and saw the look on his face, knew what he was about to tell her.

"They are in Vienna," he said simply. "They are coming home."

GENT MUELLER woke at ten, showered, dressed and began to eat the bread and coffee that constituted her breakfast. She felt isolated and alone, had done so ever since the veil of secrecy had been drawn over her and she had been cut off from her friends. Even the flat she called home felt alien; the knives and forks she ate with, the cups she drank from, the postcards from the various ports of call which her fictitious husband was supposed to be visiting, delivered every two weeks to the mail box on the ground floor then stuck haphazardly on the mantelpiece for the security man to see. Even the sheets on the bed on which she allowed the security man to take her. Especially the sheets on the bed.

She rose up from the table, cleared the cup and plate, and began to tidy the flat. That day she would begin the two-to-ten shift. She did not know which depressed her the most, the early shift because it gave her time off in the afternoons and evenings, or the late shift because it gave her the mornings off. They were the same really, she supposed, both gave her time to herself when she could not be herself.

It was the way they had ordered it, which week she should be on early shift, which week on late. When the cleaning rota had allocated her different times they had been firm about it, emphasised how crucial it was that she stuck to the schedule they demanded, made her change her shift, told her it was vital. To everything.

She put the cup and plate in their place and thought for the third time that morning about Klars Christian Mannheim and the girl who would die next, admonishing herself for her own pathetic self-pity, comparing her sacrifice with theirs. Then she pulled on her coat and left the flat. The mail boxes were in a neat row at the foot of the stairs on the ground floor, just inside the entrance. The postman did not deliver the mail on Sundays, and even if there was any during the week, it was when she returned home in the evenings.

She opened the door of the mail box and saw the card.

It was strange, she had once thought, how she looked forward to getting the cards. How she wanted the husband that did not exist to say more than where he was, how she wanted him to write a letter, a long letter, telling her what he was doing, how much he missed her, how long it would be before he was home.

She began to read it and saw the code, knew that the hijack team was in position, knew that that night she would put the guns and explosives on the plane for them. She went back to the flat, burned the postcard, and crumbled the ashes down the sink.

WALID HADDAD caught the 10.16 train with twenty minutes to spare. The early morning rain had stopped and the day was bright and warm. Even in the city he had felt the first touches of spring. He bought a handful of newspapers and checked there was a buffet car.

The front pages of the first two papers were devoted to the security arrangements round the funeral, the previous day, of the hunger-striker Klars Christian Mannheim, with references to the group of three women who had been next to join the hunger-strike, plus a case history of the nineteen-year-old, Christina Melhardt. The front page of the third newspaper was different. It carried a picture of a young woman, no older than a girl, her hair was short and her large eyes had the ring of innocence. "This is Christina," the headline said. Beneath it was the words "Twenty days to freedom, twelve days to death."

The train pulled off; he felt the jolt as the carriages coupled together, then the gentle sweep as it picked up speed. He made his way to the buffet car, bought a coffee, and took it back to his seat. Close, they were so close. He thought about the plane, the weapons and explosives Gent Mueller would put on it, the team who were preparing themselves, the two men and one woman he would not meet until the 727 was in the air.

SIXTY-FOUR MINUTES after the train carrying Walid Haddad began its journey across Germany, the police in Frankfurt made the first move to discovering the presence in that city of the hijack team which named itself after the dead hunger-striker. For the previous three weeks a special task force of detectives had scoured every piece of information, every hint of a threat on the visit the following day of the state president. For the fourteen hours since the waitress at the restaurant in the side street of Alfred-Brehm Platz had telephoned the police, three detectives had been assigned to checking out her story. The waitress's report had been one of thirty-seven which the fifteen strong task force had investigated during the past thirty-six hours. Most of the men and women on the team were tired, some were irritable.

At ten o'clock they assembled for their morning conference; by eleven they had discussed most of the information which had been passed to them. By eleven ten they were prepared to reject the conversations and toasts the waitress had reported. At twenty minutes past, partly out of desperation, partly out of Germanic emphasis on computer efficiency, they switched targets, not switched targets they would think later, as much as extended their field of reference. It was the detective who had interviewed the waitress who made the suggestion.

On the first day she had noticed the couple, he said, the waitress was under the firm impression they had just flown into Frankfurt. Could they not run a check on airline records for the names of people who had flown in that day and run them against hotel records?

A long shot, a colleague commented, not in criticism, but a lengthy process with a lot of work. Why not check those people due to fly out *after* the state visit.

Why not the two together, a third man suggested.

There was a silence in the room. Something else, they all suddenly thought, something they had not even considered. They waited for the man in charge of the task force to say it.

Ulrich Silewski was forty-three years old and had been a policeman for twenty of those years. He suffered from overwork and a department chief who was a political appointee and did not understand the basic treadmill that was a detective's millstone. In the past three weeks he had worked an average of fourteen hours a day, seven days a week. For the past four days he had slept on a camp bed in his office.

"Suppose we've got it wrong." He offered the thought at last. His team waited. "In on Friday, out on Monday. We've assumed that they're here for the state visit, but suppose that's either a coincidence, or they're using it as a cover."

They all knew what he meant.

"Why should Palestinians be involved with a West German if it's only to do with the state president?" asked Silewski's sergeant. It was the question that was suddenly on all their minds.

"A hijack?" said the detective who had interviewed the waitress.

"A hijack," confirmed Silewski.

GENT MUELLER finished her shopping and took the bus to the airport, talking to the other cleaners, thinking about the hijack team. Twice on the way out of the city the bus passed through road blocks, the BMWs slung across the road, the police working in pairs, one man checking beneath boots and bonnets, the second with a machine gun at the ready. The checks at the airport were thorough; she was asked to empty both her bags and unwrap her shopping. At the second security point Hans winked at her as she passed through. She winked back and wondered how the bastard would react when he realised.

The locker where she had stored the weapons and explosives was next to her own: she wanted to open it and check that the Heckler and Kochs were as she had left them, then told herself to calm down. The other women had already changed and were leaving for the canteen; she undressed, pulled on her overalls and checked the schedule on the wall. The Boeing 727 was due in at seven thirty that evening. It was lucky, she thought, that she was on the late shift that day, knew it was not luck, that it was the way they had planned it from the very beginning.

THERE HAD BEEN 380 flights into Frankfurt on the Friday and there were 396 scheduled to leave the city on the Monday. At twelve noon Ulrich Salewski divided the six men he had reassigned to the investigation based on the waitress's report into two teams: the first, comprising four of his task force, were to compile a computer list of all passengers arriving on the Friday and departing on the Monday who might, for any reason, give cause for suspicion; the second, comprising the other two, were to analyse the Monday flights for any that might be considered targets, and to begin computer checks on the passengers of each flight under suspicion.

At six that evening he summoned the task force to his office on the fifth floor. Outside it was still light; he remembered for a moment how he enjoyed the light evenings, the first signals that the winter was over, then pressed on with the briefing. "Of the people who flew in on Friday and who are due to fly out on Monday," he summarised the mass of computer lists on the desk in front of him, "nineteen are under suspicion. Of those nineteen, six stand out, because of either their country or region of birth."

"Why countries *or* regions?" someone asked.

"Because if they are hijackers, they are hardly likely to give their own country of birth." He looked round. "Particularly if they're Palestinian."

Silewski was good, the task force knew.

"Of those six, two stand out."

"Why?"

He looked round again. Why had they chosen his city, he thought, why the hell had they chosen Frankfurt?

"Because of their ages. Because they are of Middle East origin, their flight details say they are Kuwaiti, and because the flight they are booked on is to Tel Aviv. Because they gave no addresses in Germany." He sensed the reaction, aware he had to balance it.

"I might well be wrong. There are four other people who also have strong grounds for suspicion, and several others who also seem to have the right credentials."

They waited for his instructions.

"We don't know for sure that they are up to no good. The only thing we can do is cover them if they are." He looked round the team. "I'll get the list copied. Divide the hotels between you and start checking. Start with the main two suspects. And only deal with hotel managers, we don't want any leaks."

"Who are the two we're after?" It was the detective who had interviewed the waitress.

Silewski knew the names by heart. "The woman is using the name Akache," he said, "the man's name is Alameh."

"You know how many hotels there are in Frankfurt?" someone asked. It was not a complaint.

"I know," said Silewski.

"Any chance of some help?"

Silewski had already asked. "The powers that be," he said, "have decided that financial measures are more important than efficient policing. They're already concerned with how much the overtime is going to cost them, and everyone is already booked up for tomorrow anyway." It was the beginning of the Dubai factor, the element that Walid Haddad had identified when he had begun planning the hijack. "You'd better tell your families you won't be seeing them until tomorrow night. Any questions?"

"One. If they are planning a hijack, why the hell choose a place on a day when they must know the security is going to be as tight as hell?"

Silewski knew there must be a reason. "I don't know," he admitted. "Anything else?"

There was only one more question.

"How far up is this going?"

Everyone in the room knew it was an indication of how seriously the authorities were taking the lead.

"The Chancellor has already been informed," said Ulrich Silewski.

WALID HADDAD had been travelling for seven hours. In midmorning the train had passed through Nuremberg, in midafternoon through Linz. Soon the evening would begin to lose its light. He thought of the same time of day in a plane, the moment when the late afternoon gave way to dusk and the night began to take over, the sky to the east taking on a purple hue while the sky to the west remained blue and clear, till the darkness folded over and reached even the western horizon. He looked out of the window, not seeing the rush of trees, the mill on the riverside, and wondered how many more sunsets he would see.

The team would have made their arrangements, would be out of contact with each other, each of them by himself, and herself. He thought about when he would next see them, in the queue at the airport, one first class, the others in the economy line; thought about the first time they would make contact with each other, on the plane. In the distance he saw the first lights of the city, and wondered how good the police in Frankfurt were.

MARTIN HAUSNER placed his call to the manager of the Steigenberger Hotel at precisely twenty-nine minutes past eight, logging the fact in his notebook and ticking the name of the hotel off the list in front of him. It was the seventh hotel he had called, he had also telephoned his wife and told her he would not be home that evening. She had accepted it without question. It was only when he put the phone down that he remembered they were going to have friends for dinner.

The manger was off-duty, he was put through to the duty manager and explained who he was, saying he would appreciate his cooperation in checking some names. The man was suspicious and asked if there was a number he could phone back. A good sign, Hausner thought, at least the man was careful. He gave the switchboard number, told the man it was in the directory if he wished to check, and his extension. The duty manager came through two minutes later, at the desks around him Hausner heard the rest of the task force going through the same procedure and explained again what he wanted.

"Strictly confidential?" queried the duty manager.

"Strictly confidential," Hausner assured him.

"Are there many names?"

"A few." He wondered if his wife would make the dinner without him.

"Could you wait a minute while I get the computer?"

Efficient, Hausner thought again.

"You're sure it's strictly confidential?"

The detective assured him again that it was.

"OK," said the duty manager. "What are the names?"

"Akache." Hausner read the name at the top of the list, the name of the woman. He could imagine the man tapping the keyboard, the letters appearing on the screen.

"No," said the manager, "no one of that name."

Hausner knew there wouldn't be and read the second. "Alameh." He spelt it out for the man, heard the tapping on the keyboard again, the phone being picked up and looked idly at the list, noting the next hotel he would telephone.

"Salim Alameh," said the manager. "Kuwaiti, checked into a suite here on Friday." Hausner hid his excitement. "Interesting," said the duty manager. "He's paying cash."

"Possibly." Hausner knew he had to be careful, had to be certain. "Would you mind checking it again for me?" The man on the desk opposite knew he was on to something and stopped dialling, looking at him.

The duty manager read the details again.

"One moment please, sir." Hausner cupped his hand over the mouthpiece. "Tell Silewski I've got Alameh," he said to the detective looking at him. He turned his attention to the duty manager at the Steigenberger. "When is Herr Alameh due to leave?"

He heard the tapping on the keyboard.

"At the moment he's due to leave on Monday." The next question was inevitable. "Is there something wrong?"

Hausner knew he could not lie, but neither could he tell the truth. "I'm not sure, sir." The entire team were standing around him, waiting on him; he saw Silewski come out of his office.

"I wonder if you could find out whether Herr Alameh is in or out at the moment?"

"I'll phone reception."

"Don't phone reception." Hausner heard the tension in his voice, and tried to lose it, hoping that the man had not put the phone down already. "I'd appreciate it if you checked yourself without letting anyone know what you're doing."

The duty manager knew there was something wrong. "I'll check myself," he agreed.

Good man, thought Hausner. He cupped his hand over the telephone again and looked at Silewski. "Alameh is at the Steigenberger. He checked in on Friday and is due out on Monday. No record of Akache, but he has a suite, so she might be with him. The duty manager is seeing whether he's in or out at the moment."

Silewski began to ask a question then stopped as the detective put up his hand.

"He's out at the moment. Good." He knew what the other man must be thinking. "Look," he said. "I think it would be a good idea if I popped round to see you." He tried to make it relaxed, Silewski was nodding his head. "You think you ought to contact your general manager, ask him to be there?" Silewski was nodding again. "A good idea," Hausner told the duty manager. "I'll be round in fifteen minutes."

He put the phone down and felt his shoulders drop, partly in relief, partly in triumph.

"Jesus Christ," he said.

THE 727 ARRIVED LATE, due to a delay at Stuttgart, and was taxied into the hangar. Gent Mueller did not see it come in: she had checked with the duty list and confirmed she was one of the three women who would clean the plane, then gone with the others to the canteen while they waited. It was seven o'clock, outside it was getting dark. The other women were talking about a dance the following Saturday evening and asked her if she wanted to come. She said she would, not properly hearing the question, thinking only of the locker in the changing room, the spaces behind the panelling in the 727, of the men and women who were waiting to board the plane.

The security guard saw her and came over to their table. He was discreet, though sometimes not discreet enough; she thought about the ways he had taken her, thought about his fat fingers, the way they had penetrated her, opened her, the beer on his breath. She smiled at him and wondered again what he would think, what he would do, when he knew. The other women were getting up, going to the 727.

"See you after work tonight," Hans said as they rose.

She knew there was no option. "After work," she said.

The vacuum cleaners were at the side of the changing room. She caught up with the others, picked up her cleaner and her bag of equipment, and began to go towards the hangar. It was seven thirty. She felt nervous, only slightly nervous, imagined what the people the following night would be feeling. They were half-way to the hangar when she seemed to remember something, telling the others she would catch them up, then she turned back and went into the locker room.

Please may it be empty, she thought.

There were two women there, on the far side, away from the lockers, they were both smoking. There was no time to wait for them to leave. She reached inside her overalls, felt the key on the chain round her neck, took it off and opened the door.

The weapons were still there, the pistols and the sub-machine guns, the grenades and the explosives, each item wrapped separately in a plastic bag. She wondered why she was relieved they were still there, knew that if they had been found, the police would have left them and waited for whoever came to collect them. That if they were watching, now would be the time they would move in on her.

The women behind were still talking. She tried to remember if she had seen them before and concentrated on the locker. The top of the vacuum cleaner unscrewed easily; she took it off, ignoring the women, removed the paper bag inside, folded it into her pocket, slid the bags containing the grenades and explosives in its place, and put the top back on.

Too long, she thought, she had already taken too long, told herself to calm down, not to rush things. She took the cloths and cleaning rags from the top of the box she carried, placed the bags containing the clips for the sub-machine guns and the detonator cord plus the detonators on the bottom, and covered them with the rags.

Her hands were cold. She felt in control, detached. It was just like the first job, she thought, the nerves beforehand, the welcome, almost dangerous calm as soon as she had begun. The women behind her were getting up, moving toward the door. She undid her coat, unzipped the overalls, and strapped the sub-machine guns to her body using the belts she had placed in the lockers, sliding the ends of the spare magazines into her pants, zipped up the overalls and buttoned up the coat. It was difficult to bend. She closed the door of the locker, picked up the cleaner and the box, and hurried towards the hangar.

It was much colder than the locker room, the other women were already on the plane. She knew she looked stiff, was afraid that they would see the different shape of her body, would notice the weight of the vacuum cleaner and box.

"Seeing Hans tonight?" It was the woman who had introduced her to the security guard.

"What do you think?" she welcomed the diversion. "My bloody husband's home soon."

She went into the toilet and began to clean it, aware she was stooped over like a crab; the other women were cleaning the aisle, moving away from her. Christ, she suddenly thought, they'd already cleaned it, would see what she was doing, tell her not to bother. She ignored them and locked the door behind her.

"What are you doing, a crafty smoke?" she heard the voice through the door.

"No," said another of the women. "She's thinking of what Hans will get up to tonight."

"Bugger off," she replied, returning their humour. "Call of nature."

She unzipped the overalls, unstrapped the weapons and magazines and laid them across the wash basin, feeling the relief when she was able to move. Then she took out the screwdriver and undid the panels. Her hands, she noticed, had begun to shake slightly. No rush, she told herself, plenty of time. It took five minutes to tape the weapons, explosives and grenades inside the sections beneath the wash basin and behind the toilet, each weapon and its ammunition together in the agreed places, each item designated by the different colour tags on the bags. When she had finished she flushed the toilet, opened the door, and vacuumed the floor.

"Who did you have in there with you?" asked the woman with whom she had shared the original foursome. "Hans up to his tricks again?"

"It was too long for Hans," Gent Mueller replied. "He couldn't even last half that time." Once more with the bastard, she knew, only once more.

They knew she was joking and laughed with her.

AHSAD KAYEH and Salma Sayeh returned to the Steigenberger Hotel at thirty-five minutes past ten. She was carrying a bunch of roses which he had bought for her. Ulrich Silewski and Martin Hauser were drinking coffee in the lounge; the waitress from the café off Alfred-Brehm Platz was hidden in the manager's office.

"That's them," she said confidently when they had gone upstairs.

"You're positive," said Silewski. He knew there was no way anyone could mistake the two.

"I'm positive," said the waitress. "She's so beautiful, he's so handsome."

It was nineteen hours to the hijack.

THE CAB RANK outside the station was empty; Walid Haddad had to wait five minutes before a taxi came. He was tired, physically and mentally, could feel the nervousness beginning to eat at him. Like any other job, he tried to reassure himself, it was like any other job. And the people he had chosen were good, good in themselves, good in the roles he had allocated them. A cab appeared, he took it to the Marriott Hotel on the Ringstrasse and checked into the room he had reserved by telephone two days before. It was eight thirty. He went to the room, showered, took a light dinner in the hotel restaurant and went back to his room, satisfied with his own security. Nobody knew his movements, nobody knew the name he was using, not even the other members of the hijack team.

He booked an alarm call for eight, took two fifteen mil. capsules of dalmane and went to bed. The dose would make sure he slept but would not interfere with the combination of amytal and amphetamines he carried with him, as did each member of the hijack team, for use over the next five days.

The last image which passed across his mind before the medication took effect was that of the man and his son through the haze in the corner of the field in Esh Shikara.

It was eighteen hours to the hijack.

THE MEETING BEGAN at one in the morning, the blinds of the windows were drawn and the only light came from the lamp on Silewski's desk. Stacked beside the lamp were a pile of sandwiches and two flasks of coffee. There were three men present: Silewski, his immediate superior, and the counter-terrorism expert who had arrived by helicopter from the GSG-9 headquarters at Hangelaar, near Cologne, half an hour before. It was the first time Silewski had worked directly with anyone from Grenzschutzgruppen 9, though he had met representatives at conferences in both Bonn and Frankfurt. He poured them each a mug of coffee and took a sandwich: it was the first time he had eaten since breakfast the previous day.

"I know the background," said the man from Hangelaar. "Perhaps you could update me?" He was in his thirties, lean-faced.

Silewski nodded. "As you know, we're acting on suspicion, nothing definite." He felt he had to be careful, explain their actions; it was, he could not forget, the first time a report of his had gone to the head of state.

The man from GSG-9 knew how the policeman must feel. "Better to over-react before than to kick yourself after," he suggested.

Silewski welcomed the support. "The two we suspect are using the names Alameh and Akache. They are in a suite at the Steigenberger Hotel. They checked in on Friday and are due to leave tomorrow."

"Alameh checked in, Akache joined him?" queried the man from Hangelaar.

"Yes," said Silewski, the others waited for him to continue. "What makes them stand out, in addition to the conversations the waitress overheard, is that they've paid for everything in cash, the hotel, their airline tickets, a restaurant. We'll carry on checking in the morning to see if there's anything else about their movements that singles them out."

"Good. What about tonight?"

"They went to the suite at twenty to eleven. We don't know if they have weapons or explosives in the room, there wasn't time to check before they returned. We've got two surveillance teams on them, two more teams standing by for the morning. The rest of the boys are still trying to locate the West German, as well as the other suspects."

They all knew the enormity of the task.

"What about the room?" asked the man from GSG-9.

"The management are cooperating fully and have moved the people out of the room above, told them a cock and bull story about problems with the plumbing. We put in listening equipment half an hour ago."

"What's happening?"

"Nothing." Both Silewski and the man from Hangelaar knew it was significant. "They took a shower and went straight to bed."

"What did they do then?"

Silewski knew why he had asked. "They went straight to sleep."

His superior asked why it was significant. Silewski looked at him. "If you or I went to bed with that woman, we'd be screwing her all night."

He turned back to the man from Hangelaar. "I'm assuming they took sleeping tablets. I'll get the glasses from the bedside in the morning and have them checked."

His superior was still confused.

"If they're going to hijack a plane tomorrow," explained Silewski patiently, "they'll be awake for the next four or five days. They'll be carrying drugs with them to keep them going, but tonight they'll need all the sleep they can get."

The man from Hangelaar began to think the policeman was wasted in Frankfurt. "What do you want to do with them?" he asked.

"I'm not sure, I'd like your advice on that." He poured himself another coffee.

"My instinct is to leave them. We've got them covered; they can't move without us knowing. We know there's at least one more member of the team, but even three isn't a big enough unit to take out a 727. If we pick them up now we risk the chance of losing the German, plus any others there are."

"What about the German? What are we doing about him?"

Silewski picked up another sandwich. "I'm trying to cut corners," he said. "I have a list of all Germans on the same flight as Alameh and Akache and have asked for a check to be run on each of those names on the computer at Wiesbaden. I'm assuming that if there is a German on the team, he'll be using a false identity that won't be recorded on the ID computer. That way, we'll at least know the name he's using."

The man from Hangelaar nodded again. The policeman was good, very good. "What if he's being very careful, using a real identity, using a name that will be on the ID list?"

"That's where you could get help. If I supplied you with a list of names and addresses, could you get the local police to check them out?"

"I'll arrange it tonight. You're obviously assuming there's a fourth member of the team."

"Yes," agreed Silewski, "I think the three who have already showed are waiting for the leader.

"So do I," said the man from Hangelaar.

"Any news on your front?" asked Silewski's superior.

"Not so far," said the counter-terrorism expert. "We've telexed the names and descriptions to anti-terrorist units throughout Europe. The names are now known, which is predictable. We might get something back tomorrow morning." He looked at his watch and corrected himself. "Later this morning, but I doubt it."

"Anything else?"

"One thing." It was the question one of his squad had asked Silewski in the briefing that evening. "If they are planning a hijack," he said, "then why the hell choose a place on a day when they must know the security is going to be as tight as hell?"

The man from Hangelaar looked at him. "It's simple," he said. "You could call it the Dubai factor."

He explained what it was, how he had gleaned it from the masses of reports he studied daily. Silewski saw it, remembering the reaction when he had asked for more men, how the bureaucrats had told him how much overtime the state visit was already costing. How he had looked at the rota and seen that within ten minutes of the end of the state visit, practically every policeman in the city would be off duty.

"Transit passengers," the counter-terrorism expert asked suddenly. "Is there any chance the rest of the team could be coming in from somewhere else?"

It was a point Silewski's superior had not considered.

"I've already checked," said Silewski, putting down the sandwich he had just started and picking up his notebook. "There are only four transit passengers for the flight to Tel Aviv, coming in from Vienna."

"Any interest to us?"

"No," said Silewski.

"Why not?" asked his superior.

"They're a family, parents and two kids."

"Why the hell are they going to Israel at this time of year? I thought everybody went at Christmas or Easter?"

Silewski looked at him. "If you asked them," he said quietly, "I expect they would tell you they were going home. They're Jews, they came out of Russia yesterday. Apparently they've been waiting six years for permission to leave."

"Why aren't they flying direct from Vienna?"

It was a question Ulrich Silewski had also asked. "El Al are on strike at the moment, this connection is the quickest and easiest."

There was a silence in the room.

"What are they called?"

It was not a question Silewski had expected the man from Hangelaar to ask. He checked his notebook. "Zubko," he said, "Stanislav Zubko and his wife and their two children."

"Stanislav Zubko and his wife and children," repeated the man from Hangelaar. For the first time there was a trace of feeling in his voice. "Poor sods," he said, "poor little sods."

It was fourteen hours to the hijack.

5

YAKOV ZUBKO rose at five; for the first morning since they had arrived in Beita he did not have to worry about waking Alexandra and the children—the entire family had barely slept. In the next room he could hear the children talking about their cousins. He left the house at six and walked to the stones at the top of the hill called Bethesda. The morning was bright and clear. At fifteen minutes to seven he left the hill and walked to work.

THE FIRST MEETING of the day began shortly after seven thirty. Ulrich Silewski felt tired and dirty, he had slept badly on the camp bed crammed against the wall in his office and had been woken at intervals by the reports of the surveillance teams at the hotel. Some time, he knew, he should make time for a shower and a proper breakfast.

He took the one page summary of the computer print-outs that had reached his task force during the night, read it through, wiping the sleep from his eyes, and began the briefing. "We've made some progress," he announced, "but not enough. As of fifteen minutes ago, our two main suspects are still asleep. Of the other possibles, we have located three of them and have them under surveillance, the others are still unaccounted for."

"What about the West German?"

"Nothing so far. All the names on the passenger list have been verified by the ID computer at Wiesbaden. Either the man is very smart, and is using someone's real identity, or he's not on the flight list yet."

"What are your people doing about it?" Silewski's superior asked the counter-terrorism expert.

"We knew about the ID computer at five," said the man. "Since five thirty, local police have been checking the home addresses of people on the list. They've covered twenty-two passengers so far, all genuine."

"Does anyone on the flight list have a political record?"

"No, that was the first thing we checked."

"Transit passengers?"

"The only ones so far are the Jewish family," said Silewski. He checked the file. "Their flight plans have been confirmed."

His superior sat back. "You're convinced you're dealing with a real hijack threat?" Silewski knew what the man was thinking, knew he was calculating how he could account for the extra cost to the politicians who sat like vultures on the finance committees.

It was the man from Hangelaar who answered on Silewski's behalf. "Are you prepared to think otherwise?" He put the point bleakly, succinctly.

"No," conceded the man.

The meeting ended at eight forty. Silewski went outside to update his squad.

THE TELEPHONE CALL came at nine thirty, Yakov Zubko had waited for it since seven. "Yes," he said, knowing who it was.

"Today, Yakov Zubko, we are coming today." He heard the excitement in his brother's voice, the excitement in his own.

"When, what time?" It was strange, he would remember later, that the conversation had been so concerned with the details of flights and timetables, so devoid of emotion.

"Tonight. We fly from Vienna to Frankfurt, pick up Lufthansa Flight LH608 to Tel Aviv, and arrive at Ben Gurion late this evening."

"We will meet you," said Yakov Zubko. They discussed arrangements, he confirmed the details with the representative of the Jewish Agency and was told that the Agency staff who had dealt with him in Tel Aviv would meet him at the airport to welcome his brother. In the background he heard the asthmatic breathing of his brother's daughter, remembered what she had always said in Russia, that all she needed was the sun of Israel, then she would get better, then she would be able to breathe properly.

He talked to his brother for another three minutes, put the phone down and went to ask if he could take the rest of the day off work. The shop-floor was quiet; he saw they were all looking at him.

"My brother is coming today," he said, beginning to ask the supervisor about time off. The man silenced him.

"How are you going to get to Tel Aviv?" he asked.

Yakov Zubko had not thought. "By bus," he suggested.

The supervisor shook his head. "Arik and Joseph have cars. They will take you and bring you back."

Yakov Zubko wanted to thank the man, for the cars, for the understanding, but did not wish to impose. "One car would be enough," he said. "We could all go in one car."

The supervisor smiled. "One car is for you," he said. "The other is to bring Stanislav and his family home to Beita."

Yakov Zubko did not know what to say.

WALID HADDAD left the hotel at ten and took a cab to the airport; the security was tight, he could see it, feel it. One check,
he told himself, knowing that he would not see anything he did
not already know, reminding himself it was too late to change
anything. He thought of the others, Gent Mueller, the team,
Ahsad Kayeh and Salma Sayeh, his clothes and her looks, the
West German Gunter Pohl. Outside the terminals was a line of
police cars; he thought of the last time he had visited an airport other than on a recce, the last time he had driven to an
airport on an operation, remembering the coachload of children on the motorway from Heathrow, the face of the man in
the newspaper he had used to conceal the transmitter of the
bomb.

It was seven hours to the hijack.

AT TEN THIRTY the anti-terrorist teams at Hereford went on
amber alert, the first of the stages of readiness other than the
normal ten-minute stand-by. The mobilisation was routine,
based on reports telexed to the operations room at Hereford of
the alert in Frankfurt in line with the various agreements arrived at between most European countries.

Graham Enderson read the reports carefully, first the pré-
cis, then the full background report and request for information which the West German authorities had circulated during
the night, remembering what he had thought on the morning
Klars Christian Mannheim had been buried, that they were
building up to a hijack.

It was so logical. West Germany in a state of tension, one
hunger-striker dead, the girl called Christina about to be the
second to die, no bombings or killings to divert public sympathy from their cause. And the target city itself, high security
profile for the state visit; just the target the authorities would
not expect a terrorist organisation to pick, precisely the location and date he himself would have chosen.

The Dubai factor, he thought, remembering when he had
first seen it, how he had known then that he would have built
it into a hijack if he had been a terrorist.

One campaign, he had suspected all along, remembering
where it had started, on the motorway from Heathrow; the man

who had started it, who had risked it all to save the children on the coach, the same man who was about to finish it.

He picked up the reports again and concentrated on the details. Frankfurt police had traced two hijackers so far, and were looking for the others; they were planning to let them get to the airport, he assumed, to pick up the West German when he made contact with them. Plus the leader, the man who hadn't yet shown. The airport was the only place, he agreed with their tactics, risky if the hijackers were armed, but the only proper way, the only sure way of picking up the entire team. It was also, in its way, the safest place; at that point the hijackers would not be armed, at that point they would be carrying nothing to jeopardise their access to the plane. He wondered how the man from Heathrow was planning it, how he was getting his weapons on board, how he would organise his team during the hijack itself, wondered if the man would admit to the Heathrow job when they caught him that evening.

Something else, he thought, feeling uncomfortable. He sat back and tried to analyse what he was thinking: the initial lead, the toasts overheard in the restaurant, the descriptions, the girl very beautiful, the man handsome, well-dressed, the bouquet of flowers the night before. The suite, the tickets, all paid for in cash. He put the report back on the table and tried again to work out what he was thinking, why he was thinking that way.

The man at Heathrow had been very good, but only as a loner, not as the leader of a team, as a planner. There were bound to be mistakes, but in Frankfurt there had been too many. Not on his part, on the part of the man and woman in the Steigenberger. One mistake on the man's part, Enderson corrected himself, the biggest mistake of all, choosing the couple in the first place.

Even the Dubai factor, he thought. If he had seen it, then the man from Heathrow should have seen it, but if the man from Heathrow had seen it he should have realised that people like Enderson would also have seen it, and planned against it.

He knew what his thoughts were, aware that he should not analyse them in depth. Relief that the man from Heathrow would not succeed, admiration for the authorities in Frankfurt. And anger, in a strange way anger, that the man who had done such a good job at Heathrow should have done such a bad job in Frankfurt.

He even knew what the police in Frankfurt would find next, that the couple still asleep in the hotel had visited practically every airline office and travel agency in the city asking about Lufthansa flights out on the Monday. Not only that they had asked specifically about Lufthansa flights, but that they had asked about them to a degree that was almost obsessive.

Anger, he thought again, and disappointment.

THE SECOND MEETING of the day, excluding the one that had begun at midnight and ended shortly after three, began at eleven. Silewski felt better, partly because he had showered and shaved and was wearing a fresh shirt; mainly because he had established the name which the West German was using.

"Rolf Heinnemann," he announced. "Aged twenty-seven. Home address in Hamburg. Booked onto the flight yesterday morning, about the same time as the other two." The picture was coming together. "Economy seat. Paid cash like the others."

"How do you know?" asked the superior.

"The ID check," said Silewski. "Rolf Heinnemann is an architect living in Hamburg. The police traced him this morning and spoke to him at his office. He says he hasn't been near Frankfurt for months."

He could feel the excitement.

"Any idea where the man using his name is staying, what he's doing?"

"None at all." Silewski knew it didn't matter. "If he's West German, which he seems to be, he'll know better than to stay in a plush hotel like the Steigenberger. He'll have found himself a little *pension* somewhere, almost certainly under another name, and will surface only when and where he's been told."

"At the airport?"

Silewski nodded. "That's what it seems like, which dictates when we pick up the other two."

"Not necessarily." His superior was cautious.

"Necessarily," interjected the man from Hangelaar. "We want to stop the hijack, we want the Palestinians, but in a way we want the West German even more. If we pick up the man and the woman before they check in at the airport, we would have no guarantee that they hadn't arranged a meeting, a check, with the West German. And if they miss that, it might scare him off."

"We'd also lose any chance of getting the fourth member of the team," said Silewski quietly.

"You still think there's another one?" asked his superior.

"The leader," said the man from Hangelaar. "The one who planned it all, that's why he's staying low, keeping out of touch with the others. He won't even see them till he checks in, probably won't make contact until the moment of the hijack."

"So where do you intend to take them?"

"Just before they get on the plane," said the GSG-9 man. "In the departure lounge after the flight has closed. That way we know we have them all, that way we can cover the two we know, plus the West German once he checks in as Rolf Heinnemann, and we can establish the identity of the fourth. We should have a good idea at the check-in." He turned to Silewski. "Anything more about the couple?"

"Two things. The first is that they hired a car from the hotel yesterday; our boys have located it in the car park."

"And the second?"

"When they made their reservations, they made a number of enquiries about planes out of Frankfurt, separately of course, and at different travel agents, but the one thing they were both adamant about was that they wanted to fly Lufthansa."

His superior sat back, nodding. "Good," he said, "that's the confirmation I needed. Good."

"I suppose so," said Silewski. He wondered why he did not share his superior's confidence.

"Weapons and explosives?" asked the man from Hangelaar.

"No idea," confessed Silewski, dismissing the sudden doubt. "We've had no chance to check the room yet, but there was nothing in the car."

"Any more on the transit passengers?"

"No, the Jewish family are still the only ones." He knew what the man from Hangelaar was thinking, was aware they were risking the lives of all the passengers, wondered why he wanted to exclude the family called Zubko, why he even remembered their name. He looked at the counter-terrorism expert.

"There might be a way," he began.

"We can't," said the man from Hangelaar. "I know what you mean, but even getting passengers off a connecting flight would be a security risk."

Silewski knew he was right.

It was six hours to hijack.

WALID HADDAD returned to the hotel at eleven thirty, showered, took lunch in the restaurant on the ground floor and checked out, arranging to collect his suitcase later from the porter's desk.

Yakov Zubko and his family left the house in Beita at two thirty. The sun was hot and the children were wearing their best clothes. They travelled in the first of the two cars the supervisor had arranged; the second would join them at Ben Gurion later that evening. The journey was pleasant. He remembered the first time they had travelled the road, the Sunday they had first seen the house. It was so small, he remembered he had thought then, even smaller now, with the extra beds the neighbours had lent so that Stanislav Zubko and his family could spend their first days in Israel with them.

When they arrived at the airport, the woman from the Jewish Agency was waiting for them. "A good day, Yakov Zubko," she greeted him.

"A very good day," he told her.

Stanislav Zubko, his wife Mishka and their son and daughter left the hostel at three and were driven to the airport. Natasha's breathing was better, they had given her the last of the Ventolin and told her and her brother about the short flight to Frankfurt and the plane that would be waiting to take them to Israel. Tomorrow, the woman from the Jewish Agency told the children, tomorrow you will be playing in Beita.

Ahsad Kayeh and Salma Sayeh checked out of the Steigenberger Hotel at three fifteen; because of the house rule that rooms were to be vacated by mid-day, Kayek agreed to pay extra. He paid in cash. As they left the hotel and made their way to the hire car in the parking lot at the rear every step was recorded on video and reported immediately to Ulrich Silewski.

Stanislav Zubko and his family arrived at the airport at three thirty. The timing was precise and deliberate, enough time to check in and confirm the flight details, not enough time for the family to become anxious.

Walid Haddad collected his case at three forty-five and took a cab to the airport. None of his movements created the slightest suspicion.

Ahsad Kayeh and Salma Sayeh arrived at the airport at five minutes past four. During the drive from the hotel they had been tailed by a combination of five motor cars and two motor cycles, none of the vehicles staying with them for longer than three minutes for any one period. Ulrich Silewski was taking no chances. The car which was shadowing them when they reached the airport was a BMW 520. The driver reported that they had entered the area and driven into the long-term multi-storey carpark. He watched them through the barrier then pulled past, allowing the units at the airport to pick them up as they left.

The airport in Vienna was crowded, the Zubkos felt lost and frightened. It was what the woman from the Jewish Agency had expected, the reason she had arranged their timetable with such precision. She took them to the Lufthansa desk, aware of how they were clutching each other. In the control room in Frankfurt Ulrich Silewski listened to the reports and relayed them to the man from Hangelaar in place at the airport.

The woman from the Jewish Agency was talking to the Lufthansa representative, checking the connection in Frankfurt. Stanislav Zubko saw the concern on her face, then the relief.

"There's been a problem," she said, when she came back to them. "Only a slight problem. They've sorted it out for us."

Stanislav Zubko heard the words, thanking her silently for always saying "us". In the control room in Frankfurt Ulrich Silewski received the same message and spoke to the man from Hangelaar.

"You've heard about the Jewish family?"

"Yes, I've heard."

"Thank God," said Silewski.

The counter-terrorism expert had never believed in religion. "Thank God," he agreed silently.

In the terminal in Vienna Stanislav Zubko was trying to understand, trying to fight off his panic, trying to comfort his children.

"The plane to Frankfurt has been cancelled," the woman from the Jewish Agency was explaining, gathering them around her. "So you will not be able to catch the flight to Tel Aviv that you were supposed to."

She saw the look on the faces, the one look on all their faces.

"But there's no problem," she was telling them. "The airline had arranged for you to go on another plane. You'll get to Tel Aviv later, but you'll still get there tonight."

The concern was still in their eyes, the fear that they would not make it, that they would get lost, that the new connection would not work.

"What if we are late?"

She looked at the small boy who had the courage to ask what they all thought, smiled at him.

"It's all arranged," she told him. "The other plane will wait for you, there's nothing in the world that will make it leave without you."

She wondered how the Lufthansa agent had arranged it, had a special reason for thanking him for it.

Both her parents had died at Dachau.

"Come," she said, "we have to hurry."

In the temporary control room overlooking the departure terminal at Frankfurt airport, the man from Hangelaar directed his teams. Silewski had done his job, done it well, now responsibility had changed hands. Outside it was still sunny.

Walid Haddad blinked in the light as he stepped from the cab and paid the driver.

In the terminal the plain-clothes men from GSG-9 skimmed the crowd for the two Palestinians whose photographs they had memorised. Behind the check-in desk, dressed in Lufthansa uniform, another waited for the West German bearing the name of the Hamburg architect to present his ticket. In the queue at the check-in desk, posing as passengers, were more GSG-9 men, checking in as if they were catching the flight to Tel Aviv, passing through passport control, waiting in the departure lounge.

The Vienna check-in was easy, the woman from the Jewish Agency and a representative from Lufthansa hurried Stanislav Zubko and his family through to the departure lounge fifteen minutes before boarding. When the call came, the woman from the Jewish Agency went with them to the door of the aircraft, made sure they were safely on, and kissed each of them goodbye.

"Remember me to Yakov Zubko," she said.

In the control room in Frankfurt the man from Hamgelaar waited to close his net.

Lufthansa 267 took off from Vienna on schedule, at thirty minutes past five local time. When they had been three minutes in the air the stewardess told Stanislav Zubko and his family that they could undo their seat belts.

"The plane to Tel Aviv will wait for you," she assured them. "Captain Schumpter will make sure you catch it."

Stanislav Zubko thanked her and looked at his wife and children. So long, he thought, they had all waited so long, now they were almost there.

His daughter bent close to him and whispered to him. Her breathing was so shallow he could feel the pain in her lungs.

"Please, Daddy," she said. "I want to go to the toilet."

He smiled at her, held her hand and took her to the cubicle, standing in the doorway so that she would not be locked in. The stewardess saw the way he shepherded her as they left, hand upon her shoulder.

Stanislav Zubko smiled at her, and began to go back to his seat, turning sideways so that the man who had got up to use the toilet after them could pass.

The only thing he noticed about Walid Haddad was that he was still wearing an overcoat.

GRAHAM ENDERSON had been home forty minutes, talking to the children, helping his son repair a toy plane he had dropped that afternoon. He was sitting in the kitchen when he heard the sound of the news flash through the half-open door to the lounge; the voice of the newscaster was cold, almost piercing.

"We are just getting word that a Lufthansa jet with a hundred and twenty-eight passengers and eight crew has been hijacked. The plane was on a flight from Vienna to Munich when the gunmen took over. A report from our correspondent in Vienna."

He went into the lounge and stood in front of the set. There was a still photograph of the correspondent on the screen and the line from Vienna was crackling. "Lufthansa 267 left Vienna at five thirty this evening. Half an hour into the flight, air traffic control received the first warning that something was wrong."

The man from Heathrow, Enderson knew he was thinking, the bloody man from Heathrow, knew what he had done, how he had done it. He listened to the bulletin, knowing there was little the reporter could add then he picked up the telephone and dialled the security line.

"Enderson," he said. "Ops room."

He waited three seconds before he heard the voice of the duty operations officer. "Graham Enderson," he said. "Any more details of the Vienna hijack?"

"None so far."

"What about Frankfurt?"

"Off. The man and woman drove into the airport carpark and disappeared. The West German didn't show at all."

"I'm at home."

The man from Heathrow, he was thinking again, aware of the hint of admiration, the slightest relief, that the man from Heathrow had not made the mistakes in Frankfurt. He thought about the Frankfurt connection, saw what the man from Heathrow had done, how he set them all up.

Not one hijack team, two. One lying quietly and inconspicuously in Vienna, the other sent into Frankfurt as a decoy; he'd given them the back door out, of course, but it must have been close, bloody close. He went through the moves, the location of the rendezvous in the café off Alfred-Brehm Platz, the toasts the waitress had overheard, the two Palestinians, one conspicuous by his clothes, the other by her stunning beauty. So obvious, he remembered he had thought, too obvious. Everything paid in cash, too many enquiries about Lufthansa flights. And the West German, the name the police could check with the computer at Wiesbaden. Even the roses the woman had carried the night before the hijack. The man from Heathrow had chosen the Frankfurt team well.

The police in the city had done a good job. He felt sorry for them, felt again the respect for the man from Heathrow, knew what he had done, how he had done it, even down to the disappearance of the two Palestinians. One hire car, deliberately exposed, driven to the multi-storey, the tails afraid to stay too close, confident that the exits were covered, down the stairs, into the back of a second car, already waiting, and away.

Poor bastards, he thought. The poor bastards in Frankfurt.

The telephone rang. It was the man who had waited for him at the top of the steps to the Knightsbridge underground station. "I heard," Enderson said. "No more details yet." They talked about it, exchanged views on what would be happening in Germany.

The man from Heathrow had even used the Dubai factor, Enderson thought.

In December 1984 Princess Anne, second child of Queen Elizabeth the Second, had visited the United Arab Emirates, partly in connection with an equestrian event in which her husband was competing. On the final day of the visit Shi'ite Moslems had hijacked an airbus of Kuwaiti Airlines en route from Dubai to Karachi and diverted it to Teheran. Press attention had concentrated on the fact that the hijack had ended in Iran when guards, acting under Ayatollah Khomeini's orders and dressed as mechanics and doctors, had overpowered the hijackers. The key aspect of the hijack, however, was not where it had ended, but how and where it had begun. In a place and at a time when security was massive, but focussed elsewhere.

As the hijackers sat with their weapons concealed in the transit lounge in Dubai waiting for Kuwaiti flight KU221, protection was being concentrated on Princess Anne, less than thirty-five yards away, as she prepared to board British Caledonian flight 381 to London at the end of her visit.

Enderson knew the man from Heathrow had seen it as he had seen it, that the man from Heathrow had assumed the authorities would also see it and turned their knowledge against them, focussing their attention on Frankfurt and taking it away from Vienna.

"Grah," his wife asked the question they both knew was inevitable. "Will you be involved?"

He looked back at her reassuringly. "No," he said, meaning it. "It's a West German affair, GSG-9 will handle it."

FROM THE CAFÉ overlooking the airport Yakov Zubko could see the outline of the city and the lights to the east. They had been waiting an hour, did not mind how long they waited, when they heard the tannoy for the representative of the Jewish Agency seated with them, watching as she rose and took the call on the telephone at the side of the restaurant, waiting as she came back.

"There's been a slight problem," she began. "The plane from Vienna that your brother was due to catch was delayed, so he would have missed the connecting flight in Frankfurt."

She saw his face. "There's no problem, though. They've arranged for him to get a different flight, with a connection in Munich. They'll be an hour later, that's all."

Yakov Zubko smiled and thanked her, apologising to the man who had driven them from Beita, to the second man who had arrived with the car for Stanislav and his family, believing them when they told him it did not matter. The children were excited and tired.

"Don't worry," he told them, "they will all be here soon."

They had waited another forty minutes when the Agency woman was tannoyed for the second time. He watched as she took the call, saw her face, even in the distance he saw how it changed. Saw the way she listened, the way she put the phone down not knowing what to say, deciding how to say it. He was staring at her. She sat down at the table, put her hands in her face and began to cry. Then she looked up at him and saw his eyes, saw the way he was looking at her.

Yakov Zubko reached across the table and took her hand, thinking of the house in Beita, the food on the table, the beds made upstairs, thinking of the years they had all waited.

"Don't be afraid to tell me," he said gently.

IT WAS PAST MIDNIGHT when she heard them, the foxes on the Brecons. Jane Enderson knew what was going to happen, tried to shut out the noise, tried to burrow deeper into sleep, tried to wake up. She saw the face, fresh and innocent, heard the voice, clear and still.

And you, my father, there on the sad height,
Curse, bless, me now with your fierce tears, I pray.
Do not go gentle into that good night.
Rage, rage against the dying of the light.

The voice was fading over the hills, the dream beginning. She remembered what had happened the last time she had had the dream—the phone call to school asking if she knew where her husband was.

The tunnel was long, filled with smoke, the flames coming at him. He was moving down it, eyes sweeping left to right. Not his eyes, she was dreaming, as if he was behind his eyes, as if he was looking through their sockets. He was moving on, the death around him. She was not sure whether it was his death or the death of another. The hold-all in the wardrobe at the foot of the bed. The bleeper, she was praying for the bleeper, knew it would end the dream, would begin another day.

She heard the sound and began to wake up, pulling herself from the dream. Beside her Grah was getting up. She saw the sunlight through the window and looked at the time. It was six in the morning.

BOOK
FIVE

CHAPTER ONE

1

THE LIGHTS OF THE CITY blinked in the darkness. Jurgen Schumpter ignored them and concentrated on the instruments in front of him and the words of the air traffic controller.

"Lufthansa 267, change to Rome Control on one two four decimal two. Cleared flight level nine zero."

For the first time since the hijack, he realised, his hands had stopped shaking.

Jurgen Schumpter was forty-five years old, married with two children. The one thing he would remember, the one thing he would always remember, especially in the moment he knelt down to die, was that he should not have been on Lufthansa 267. He had been on stand-by when he received the call and only just made it to the airport on time, telling his wife he would be home that night. He remembered the moment of the hijack, that it was not as he had expected it would be, not like the training films had prepared him to expect. He looked again at the instruments. Fifteen minutes out, approaching Linz, about to pass from air traffic control at Vienna to air traffic control at Munich. The knock on the door, the senior stewardess. That part had been like the training film, the calm voice, the gunman behind her.

"Lufthansa 267 from Rome Control. Cleared six thousand feet, speed two one zero knots. Change to Director on one one nine decimal two."

The gunman had been different though no less frightening, more frightening in a way. Calmer, quieter than the training films had taught him to expect, more controlled, more in control. Security, they had always said, was tight, at least in the major European cities. In Europe there was no way of getting on a plane without the security screens picking up everything and everybody. Especially in places like Vienna, he assumed, remembering the OPEC incident ten years before. But the man behind the stewardess had been carrying a gun, not just a gun, a sub-machine gun. He did not know the details, all he knew was that there was no way the man could be standing behind him with a sub-machine gun. That was what had frightened him, almost as much as the shock of the hijack itself, that was what had made his hands begin to tremble.

"Lufthansa 267, this is Rome Director. Turn left on to one eight zero degrees, cleared two thousand five hundred feet, Q.N.H. one zero one eight."

He banked the aircraft gently to the left, felt it turn then straightened up.

"Landing in five minutes. Are your people strapped in?"

Funny, he thought, how his instincts, his training, should over-rule is fear, make him check with the hijacker that his team was safely in the seats, strapped in. Funny how he himself had half-turned, checked that the man with the sub-machine gun knew how to do up the seat belt.

No name, he thought, no identification, no linking the group to the name of a martyr like the training films suggested, no hysteria, no threatening of passengers. Just the face of the hijack itself, the fact of the weapons which had suddenly appeared.

"Cleared to lock on I.L.S. for runway one six left, speed one eighty knots."

He eased the controls forward, and began the final turn, the lights of the city disappearing below him. Two hours they had been in the air, two hours circling over Europe, turning from one radio beacon to another. He had known immediately that it was deliberate, known from the fact that the hijacker had told him the frequencies, the timings, told him when to turn, what new course to take, as if it had all been planned.

At first he had wondered why the hijacker had done it, why he was giving the authorities time to plan their reaction, alert their security forces, then he had realised that it was precisely to give them that time, to allow them to share the fear, to allow them to know that the hijackers knew what they were doing. To give them time, he thought, for the hijack to be reported, for its movements to be followed, for the news bulletins to speculate about its destinations, for the television and newspaper editors to alert their crews.

He understood why he was frightened.

"Lufthansa 267, call the outer marker, reduce to final approach speed."

Only once during those two hours had he left the controls,
when he had asked to go back to the cabins and check his passengers. Partly for himself, to familiarise himself with what was
happening, partly for the passengers, for them to know he was
still in charge of the aircraft. It had done little good, height-
ening rather than diminishing the fear they all felt. It had,
however, allowed him to see how many hijackers there were,
where they were, had reminded him of the training films, of the
need for him to tell the authorities as much as he could. Four
hijackers in all; he wondered how and when he could get the
information out, the leader and the man behind him, covering
him wherever he went, whatever he did. And the two others,
another man, one woman. In the middle of the aisle, dominat-
ing everything, everybody, the guns on their shoulders, the
grenades in their hands. He remembered the way the passengers had been shrunk in their seats, had known then why the
hijacker had allowed him into the cabins. He would be the one
who would talk to the authorities, his would be the voice which
would be recorded, played back, analysed; his would be the
voice which would convey to those listening the fear they were
all feeling.

The lights were in front of him, coming up at him fast.

He remembered again the passengers, the families, the one
family in particular, remembered their name. The Jewish family called Zubko. The father and daughter on one side of the
aisle, the mother and son on the other. It was he who had told
the stewardess to put them in first class, told her to give them
special attention, he had even checked personally that the connecting flight to Tel Aviv would wait for them.

"Lufthansa 267 is cleared to land on runway one six left,
out."

He remembered the way they had come aboard, the way the
mother had tended the children, knew even then what it reminded him of. The black and white photograph in the exhi-
bition room at Dachau. It had been sunny and warm when he
had gone to the camp but cold inside with not even the sound
of birds. When he left he had taken with him one memory
above all others, one image he would never forget. He even remembered the exhibit number, the page in the book he had
bought at the camp. Number four hundred, page one hundred
and ninety-two. Not the gas chambers or the furnaces, not the
barbed wire. The one photograph, the mother, the Jewess,

going into the camp, her arms round her children, the last child one step behind, socks round her ankles, shuffling them along, loving them, protecting them. Like a mother hen, he had thought at the time, like a good kind mother hen and her chicks.

Taking them, though she did not know it, to the gas chambers.

The way the woman called Mishka Zubko had taken her son and daughter onto his plane that evening.

The wheels of the 727 struck the ground, the tyres screeching. Automatically Schumpter eased the stick forward, pulling the reverse thrust levers, feeling the power of the deceleration, remembering too late the hijackers in the cabin, the grenades in their hands, the pins out.

"They put them in for landing," said Walid Haddad. "They'll take them out again when we stop."

Jurgen Schumpter felt the relief and began to thank the man, then realised what he was doing and stopped himself, concentrating on the lights of the runway and the instructions from ground control.

"Lufthansa 267, this is Ground. Proceed via taxiways Delta and India."

"Ask him which stand they're putting us." The hijacker's voice had lost none of its calm, none of its menace. Schumpter asked. The ground controller took twenty seconds to reply; when he answered, he did not give a position.

"We have a slight traffic problem at the moment, please do as I say."

The 727 was creeping forward.

"Ask him again which stand."

Schumpter realised that the hijacker had a map of the airport on his knees.

"Ground, this is Lufthansa 267. You didn't give us a stand."

There was a silence. He knew what the controller was doing, how he was asking instructions, would remember later how he had automatically trusted the man.

"Tell him we want November One." Walid Haddad leaned across and indicated the precise position on the map.

"Ground, this is Lufthansa 267."

"Go ahead, 267."

"Ground, I wish to park on November One, repeat November One." He realised what he had said, how he had said it and corrected himself. "Ground, I have been instructed to park on November One, repeat November One."

There was another silence. The 727 was still moving forward: to his right, he saw, the co-pilot was stiff with fear. "It's OK," he reassured the man. "We'll be OK."

"Lufthansa 267, this is Ground." Schumpter detected a change in the man's voice, could tell he was under pressure, would think about those who had put him under pressure as he knelt on the floor to die. "I'm sorry, Lufthansa 267, that won't be possible. As I said, we have problems in that area."

He knew the man was lying to him, was being told to lie to him.

"OK," said Walid Haddad. "Tell him Bravo Three."

"OK, Ground, if November One is out I have been told to park on Bravo Three."

No traffic problems there, he thought subconsciously, no traffic problems anywhere so late at night.

"Lufthansa 267, this is Ground, proceed to Bravo Three."

Schumpter felt the relief and looked across at the hijacker. Walid Haddad nodded. "Well done," he told the pilot.

"Thanks," said Schumpter, without realising he had said it. For the first time he wondered who had told his wife, how she had told the children.

GRAHAM ENDERSON woke at five thirty. He had showered, dressed and was drinking a cup of tea before the bleeper was tested at six. By six thirty he had driven to the barracks and made his way to the operations room in the centre of the complex.

"Anything new on the Lufthansa hijack?" he asked, pouring himself a coffee.

"Nothing since it landed in Rome. No demands yet, no indication who's responsible."

A stop-over, thought Enderson. Give everyone the chance to begin to worry, give the media a chance to get some good pictures. It was interesting how events like hijacks depended on the media, how without the media there probably wouldn't even be any hijacks.

"Who's handling it?"

"GSG-9. Two reps in Rome already, as well as the West German government officials and the Lufthansa people. Plane on stand-by in Frankfurt."

He stayed another fifteen minutes in the operations room, looking at the telexes and reports, then went to the anti-terrorist building. The teams who had been on stand-by overnight were watching the early morning television programmes for the pictures from Rome. As soon as he saw the first images, saw where the 727 was parked, Enderson knew there was something wrong.

The plane was where he would have put it if he had been the hijacker, not where he would have placed it if he had been in charge of airport security. He watched till the end of the reports, listening to the updates on the conditions of the West German hunger-strikers, then returned to the operations room.

"Any chance of finding out what happened in Rome this morning?"

"Why?" The intelligence officer was interested.

"The plane's in the wrong place." He explained what he meant.

"I'll check."

"Anything else?" he asked.

"A breakdown of the passenger list came in an hour ago."

"Anybody on the flight we should be worrying about?"

The intelligence officer shook his head. "Nobody who concerns us," he said. He gave Enderson the list. Of the one hundred and twenty-eight passengers, the majority were German, twelve were British, and twenty-three were American. Of the one hundred and twenty-eight passengers, four stood out.

The family called Zubko.

He read the details, the background on them and thought again about the man from Heathrow, wondered what he would do when he found out, what the authorities were doing to prevent him finding out.

"Poor sods," he thought. "Poor little sods."

THE SUNLIGHT REACHED the wing, and spread along it, bringing its warmth to them. Stanislav Zubko cradled the head of his daughter in his arms and listened to her breathing, hearing the rasping sound every time she filled her lungs.

"Look," he whispered. "Look at the sun, look at the patterns on the wings." He stroked her hair and, tried to keep her attention, prayed for her to sleep again.

"I want to go to the toilet, Daddy."

He pretended he did not hear and kept looking out the window, telling himself he must do nothing to attract the hijacker's attention. The nearest was only four feet from them, in the aisle, the gun on her shoulder, the grenade in her hand. The woman had stood like that all night, had made a point of showing them all that she had removed the pin of the grenade.

"Daddy, I want to go very badly, why can't I go?"

He told her to wait, his voice gentle, knowing she could not wait much longer, and looked at the grenade, remembering how he had prayed during the night that the hijackers would fall asleep and be overpowered, how he had prayed they would stay awake and not release their grips on the safety mechanisms of the grenades.

"Daddy, I need to go."

Just a little longer, he thought, hearing her breathing, just until somebody else has the courage to put up their hand. He knew the hijackers were Palestinians, three of them anyway, knew that the last thing he should do was put up his hand and single out his family as trouble-makers and Jews.

"Perhaps Natasha would like to hear the story of Deduska Moroz?" It was his son; he smiled at the boy, thanked him, looked at his daughter and saw her nod.

"Once upon a time," he began, "there was a little flower girl." It was the story he had told them when the first frosts of winter took hold in Moscow. "She was poor and the winter was hard. Each day she stood on the corner and sold her flowers, each day she stood on the corner and felt the cold and the pain because no one cared for her." He looked at the girl and saw he had her attention. Somebody else, please, he prayed, anybody else.

"Then Dedushka Moroz saw her, didn't he, Daddy," his son took over the story, "then Grandfather Frost took pity on her." He saw the way the girl was looking at him. "Then Dedushka Moroz wrapped his cloak around her and took away her suffering."

"Yes," said Stanislav Zubko. "Then Dedushka Moroz saw her and took pity on her, then Dedushka Moroz wrapped his cloak around her and took away her suffering."

"Daddy, I can't stop myself."

He knew what it would mean to her if she could not go to the toilet, if she had to soil her clothes. He looked at his wife, seeing that she was sharing his dilemma, his fear. His daughter began to cry, a soft, muffled sound, growing louder. The hijacker was staring at him. He knew what he must do, felt like his people throughout history, felt like the first of his people when they put up their hands in the concentration camps, sensed the hand go up, slowly, carefully, so as not to startle the hijackers, saw the woman with the grenade turn, the muzzle of the gun coming up.

"Yes." The hijacker spoke in English.

"Please, I need to go to the toilet."

"Get up." The hijacker's voice was harsh, without feeling. He saw the movement behind, knew who it was, knew it was the stewardess who had given the children the sweets when they had got on the plane the night before, the one who had assured them that the plane to Tel Aviv would wait for them.

"Step forward, leave your handbag on the seat."

The entire plane was watching. Behind the woman with the gun Stanislav Zubko saw the cockpit door open and the hijack leader step out with the pilot.

"What is it?" asked Walid Haddad.

"This woman, she has asked to use the toilet."

Jurgen Schumpter guessed why she was doing it: for the Jews, for the girl called Natasha who could not breathe properly.

There was silence. Stanislav Zubko knew he must have the courage, must raise his hand. "I'm sorry," he said. "My daughter would also like to go."

Walid Haddad looked down the plane. "Has anyone been to the toilet since last night?"

Not the Jews, prayed Schumpter, do nothing to draw their attention to the Jews.

"No," said the woman with the gun.

"All right," said Walid Haddad. "One at a time. Everyone stays in their seats before and after they have been."

"Please, Daddy, I need to go now."

They all heard the voice, heard the breathing.

Stanislav Zubko waited as the hijack leader stepped forward from the cockpit door and looked at them, at his daughter, at the stewardess. "As you did it for the girl," said Walid Haddad, "perhaps you would let her go first."

Stanislav Zubko held his daughter's hand. "Come," he said quietly, as if no one else existed, "you can go to the toilet." His wife watched as he went up the aisle, past the hijacker and into the cubicle.

"Thank you," Stanislav Zubko said as he passed the man.

It was the second time someone had thanked Walid Haddad.

JOHN KENSHAW-TAYLOR ROSE at six thirty, watched the breakfast time television reports, made himself a coffee, and went over the briefs that had been delivered during the night. One hundred and twenty-eight passengers plus eight crew, the reporter was saying, the majority of the passengers West German, twelve British, twenty-three American. And the family the reporter had not announced, the Jewish family called Zubko, the family just out of Russia. The name and details had been on one of the data sheets which had been delivered to the flat, he had seen immediately both the danger and the advantage of having such a family as part of the negotiations, had thought immediately it was a pity the authorities could not tell the press, conceded there was no way they could without endangering the four of them. He poured himself the coffee, remembering the conversation with Saeed Khaled in New York. The telephone rang, he picked it up, agreeing immediately to have breakfast with the Prime Minister at seven fifteen. Nothing he could do to prevent a hijack, he had told himself then, realising now that if he had not agreed the hijack would probably not have taken place. It did not concern him. He phoned his driver and arranged to be picked up at seven sharp. Jordan, he had said to Khaled as they stood by their cars outside the restaurant in New York, then he could become involved. Jordan, Saeed Khaled had agreed, then Kenshaw-Taylor could bring in the SAS.

AT SIX IN THE MORNING Eastern Standard Time Michael
Joseph Stephenson left his home in Westfield, New Jersey and
began the twenty-five mile drive to his office in the centre of
New York. The morning was bright and fresh and the traffic,
at this time of the morning, was light. He cleared the Holland
Tunnel and parked beneath the building in Federal Plaza.

Michael Joseph Stephenson was forty-two years old and had
been with the Federal Bureau of Investigation since 1963, firstly
on the street, then for two years at headquarters before he had
been promoted to field supervisor. After five years running
cases he had been promoted to supervise the anti-terrorist programme of the FBI's New York office.

On the day that Yakov Zubko and his family had left Moscow and begun their journey to the West, Michael Joseph Stephenson had authorised the first stage of an investigation into
a Provisional IRA plan to run arms and explosives from New
York to Northern Ireland.

He was at his desk on the twenty-sixth floor of the building
at seven fifteen precisely.

Fifteen minutes before that, Staff Sergeant Daniel Eduardo
Furtado had signed on duty in the seemingly innocent office
complex eight blocks from the FBI building. Daniel Eduardo
Furtado was thirty-six years old; he had joined the United
States army in 1967, serving with distinction in Vietnam and
related campaigns, primarily in special forces. In 1980 he had
volunteered for and been accepted in the anti-terrorist Delta
unit.

On the day that Yakov Zubko and his family had left Mos-
cow and begun their journey to the West, Daniel Eduardo
Furtado had completed a six-month attachment to the British
Special Air Service in Hereford.

Anna Maria Luskin woke two hours and ten minutes later.
She showered, took a light breakfast of fresh orange juice and
scrambled egg, and checked her diary for the day. The inside of
her thighs still ached from the way she had exercised them for
three hours the previous evening, though she did not object; her
bank balance was five hundred dollars the richer because of
those exertions. Anna Luskin was twenty-three years old; she
had worked in her chosen profession for the past three years.

On the day that Yakov Zubko and his family had left Moscow and begun their journey to the West, Anna Luskin had been introduced by a friend to the highly lucrative network of the United Nations circuit.

Like the two men before her, Anna Luskin paid little attention to the hijack which had taken place in Europe the night before, despite the presence of a number of Americans among the passengers: Michael Joseph Stephenson because he was arranging, as part of the IRA arms investigation, an undercover meeting in a motel room in New Orleans with a man wishing to buy a consignment of surface-to-air missiles for use by the IRA against British helicopters in Northern Ireland, Daniel Eduardo Furtado because he was involved in a security alert at JKF airport, Anna Luskin because she assumed it was linked to the politics of the Middle East, a subject in which she was not interested, and because she also assumed it would be over before the day had finished.

In addition to their lack of immediate interest in the fate of Lufthansa flight LH267, however, the three shared two other characteristics. The first, which was of little consequence, was that they were all Catholics. The second, which seemed equally inconsequential at the time, was that they were all first generation Americans.

3

STANISLAV ZUBKO could see the soldiers on the roof of the building fifty yards from the plane; if he pushed his head against the slight curve of the window he could also see the television cameras. They were almost close enough for him to speak to them, to ask them for help, he thought were so far away they might as well be on the other side of the world. The children were snuggling against him, Natasha on his lap, her breathing still rasping, his son on the seat beside him.

He looked at his daughter and thanked God that she was asleep, that she was free, however briefly, from the torment of the hijack and the torture of her illness. He wanted to stroke her hair but was afraid it would wake her. Across the aisle Mishka smiled encouragement at him.

"Daddy," said his son, "I'm hungry. I want something to eat." Stanislav Zubko felt the emptiness in his own stomach. It was more than fifteen hours since they had eaten the small meal before leaving for the airport.

"I know," he said tenderly. "We are all hungry. I expect we will eat soon." He tried not to look into his son's eyes.

Jurgen Schumpter felt the same hunger and thought of the chocolate he had bought in Vienna, then decided against it. The sun was streaming through the windows of the cockpit; to his left he could see the terminal buildings; in front, at an angle of forty-five degrees, was the crowd of people and vehicles he supposed were the press and television. Strange, he thought, how nothing was real unless it was on television, as if being on television made it real, no matter what it was. Even the hijack.

Four hijackers, he thought again, remembering the training films, the lectures. Information, he reminded himself, the authorities needed information on the hijackers, the number of hijackers.

It was ten hours, nearer eleven since they had landed in Rome, almost seven hours since there had been any communication between the control tower and the plane, as if each side was waiting for the other to make the first move. At least, he told himself, he would be the first to know what was happening. To his right and slightly behind him the hijacker was turning to the flight engineer, asking him about the radio, looking as the man began checking in his manuals. Schumpter wondered what the hijacker was doing, what he wanted, beginning to realise that the man's attention was totally on what the flight engineer was telling him, saw the opportunity for which he had been waiting.

"It's getting hot," he said. "Do you mind if I open a window?"

Walid Haddad glanced at him and nodded. It was eerie, thought Schumpter, how little the man spoke. Almost as if it was intentional, as if the hijacker knew that the silence was the most frightening thing of all. He turned away from Walid Haddad and reached for the handle, remembering the training films, the instructions about the details the men watching the plane would need to know, the ways he could tell them, knew they would have their cameras trained on the plane, the close-up lenses watching the doors, the windows, the cockpit.

He pulled the handle, glancing across and confirming that the hijacker was looking the other way and began to slide the window open. Thumb inside fingers outside, four fingers spread wide against the hardened perspex. He moved his hand up and down, up again, away from the window, fingers resting on the metal above it. Thumb still in, four fingers still spread wide. For Chrissake see it, he thought, somebody see it. See what I'm doing, what I'm telling you. Too long, he also thought, he had already taken far too long. He pulled his hand back inside and saw what the hijacker was doing.

Walid Haddad checked the frequency and began tuning in the cockpit radio; Jurgen Schumpter looked at him, realising it was something he himself had never used, something he had forgotten, heard the first words. In English. The BBC World Service, broadcast twenty-four hours a day, news bulletins every hour, on the hour.

In the Operations room two hundred yards away the *carabinieri* captain watched the rows of monitors, switching his attention from one to another. "Three," he said suddenly. "Give me a playback on three, the close-up of the cockpit."

The tape was wound back and played for him. He saw the quarterlight on the pilot's side open, and the hand come out, the fingers only, no thumb, the movement of the hand drawing attention to the fingers, to the number of fingers. Good man, he thought, good man, and picked up the telephone.

"Four hijackers," he told his commanding officer. "The pilot just indicated through the window, four hijackers."

"Anything else?"

Christ, he thought, what else do you expect? "No," he said. "Nothing else."

"Nothing at all?"

He knew the pressure his chief was already under, both from his own political masters and from the negotiators who had flown in from West Germany. "Nothing at all," he confirmed. "Bastards."

THE NEXT NEWS BULLETIN on the BBC World Service was at nine London time, ten local time. The hijack was the first item: Jurgen Schumpter heard the voice of the news reader and wondered how long it would remain that way, how long it would be before they were forgotten. Two reports, the news reader was saying, the first from the BBC man in Rome. Schumpter listened to the description of the scene at the airport, the outline of the political discussions already under way between the authorities in Rome and Bonn.

The second report was from Vienna, the background to the hijacking, an extended radio version of what Graham Enderson had seen on breakfast television in the anti-terrorist rooms at Hereford, and John Kenshaw-Taylor had seen in his flat in Pimlico; the details of the origin of the hijack, the breakdown of the passenger list.

Jurgen Schumpter knew what the reporter was going to say, even before he heard the words, the drama laid heavily into them. No, he pleaded, for God's sake no. He thought of the family, the way they had boarded his plane, the father in front, the mother shepherding her children like the mother in the photograph at Dachau. No, he pleaded again, for Chrissake no.

A hundred and twenty-eight passengers and eight crew members, the reporter was saying, detailing how many were West Germans, English, American. No, pleaded Schumpter, for the love of God no. One family in particular, the reporter was saying. You're killing them, Schumpter was thinking, you're signing their death warrants.

The family Zubko, the reporter was saying, Stanislav Zubko, his wife Mishka and their two children Anatol and Natasha.

Don't you know what you're doing, Schumpter was thinking, don't you know you're murdering them. He knew the authorities assumed there was no way that the hijackers would hear the information they released to the press, looked at Walid Haddad listening to it.

The Zubkos were Russian Jews, the reporter was saying, they had waited six years to leave Russia and had arrived in the West only two days before the hijack. The irony, the reporter was saying, the terrible irony, was they weren't even scheduled to be on the hijacked plane. He was going into the details, the first connection cancelled, the flight from Frankfurt to Tel Aviv which they would have missed, the way the authorities had rearranged their flight plans, held up a connecting flight in Munich so that they could get to Israel.

Bastards, Schumpter was aware he was thinking, the stupid bastards, was not aware of what else he was thinking, the fear so deep in his subconscious that he did not even know it existed, the fear of what else the authorities would tell the hijackers.

Walid Haddad left the co-pilot's seat and went back into the cabins. Jurgen Schumpter followed him, looking at the father, the two children, the mother opposite. The girl called Natasha was asleep. Not the Zubkos, he thought, anybody but the Zubkos. He saw the way the father looked at the hijacker and wondered what it had been like to wait, what it was like to wait now. Six years, he thought, before the East had let them go and now the West was trying to kill them. Walid Haddad stopped and looked at the father, at the children, then back at the father. Schumpter saw the look in the Jew's eyes, the way he protected his son, saw the way the Palestinian was carrying the sub-machine gun. The pilot did not look at the mother, could not look at her, sensed that she knew they were near the end, sensed that they all knew they were near the end.

The movement was sharp and sudden. Walid Haddad turned away, walked on down the aircraft and began to talk to the two hijackers guarding the passengers. Schumpter could not hear what they were saying, saw again the look on the faces of Stanislav and Mishka Zubko, the way they were staring ahead, waiting.

He turned to go back into the cockpit, remembering the moment he had followed the hijacker into the cabin, the moment the man had stopped and looked at the family. Remembering back to the moment the hijacker had allowed the girl to use the toilet after they had landed in Rome. It was almost as if, Schumpter thought for a moment, the hijacker had already known who they were, what they were. He dismissed the thought and returned to his seat.

THE BEDROOM was twenty feet long and eleven feet wide, the double bed taking up almost half the floor space, the connecting door to the room where the children had slept in the centre of the wall at the foot of the bed. Yakov Zubko had paced it, measured it out. As if, he thought, it was a prison cell, as if it was a place to which he and his family had been condemned for ever.

They had arrived late the night before, accompanied by the woman from the Jewish Agency; the men from Beita had driven home: the cars empty, Yakov Zubko had thought as he and Alexandra had been shown into the hotel room, the cars not filled with the sound of the children, talking to each other, not filled with their parents nodding their heads in happiness. Not even, he had thought, the sound of poor Natasha's breathing.

In the corner of the room stood a television set, he switched it on as Alexandra and the children came out of the bathroom and sat beside him. They had waited fifteen minutes when the news bulletin started, the pictures from Rome, the plane on the tarmac and the police on the rooftops above it. A Jewish family were amongst the hostages, the reporter was saying, a family from Russia, *refusniks*. Naming them, describing them. Yakov Zubko was numb, could hardly hear it, could not understand why it needed to be on television to make it true.

The bulletin ended, he allowed the children to watch the next programme, went into the adjoining room and sat on the bed, closing the door behind him. *Beshanah Hazu b'Yerushalaim*, his brother had said to him from Vienna. This year in Jerusalem. He thought about his brother and his brother's family, wondered if they would see Jerusalem this year, if they would ever see Jerusalem, knew already in his heart of hearts that they would not.

4

AT FIVE MINUTES past ten that morning, Eastern Standard Time, Michael Joseph Stephenson received the first information from one of his teams that the meeting with the Provisional IRA arms buyer who wished to purchase surface-to-air missiles was probable for the following evening. The only thing they did not know about the man, said the agent, possibly the most important thing they did not know about the man, was his identity. At fifteen minutes past ten Daniel Eduardo Furtado stood his men down from the alert at Kennedy and returned to base. At thirty minutes past ten Anna Luskin checked in at the health club she used daily.

None of them was aware of the chain of events which was about to link them to the Lufthansa hijack, or the awesome nature of the event which would end that connection.

At fifteen minutes to eleven, they heard about the Jewish family called Zubko on the hijacked plane, the Jewish family who had been *refusniks*, the Jewish family who had just come out of Russia: Stephenson was informed by his secretary, who was herself Jewish, Furtado read it on the telex printer into his team office, Anna Luskin saw it on the twenty-four hour news station on the television set in the lounge of the health club. They reacted to it in the same way they had reacted to the first news of the hijack, with nothing more than passing interest. That night, however, Michael Stephenson remembered the photographs his parents had shown him of their passage to America from the poverty of Ireland; that night Daniel Furtado remembered the stories his parents had told him of the way they had begged and borrowed the money to make the journey from Colombia to the United States. That night they both thought of the struggles of the Jewish family to leave Russia; that night the first seeds were sown of their interest, personal not professional, in the fate of the family on the hijacked Lufthansa aircraft.

For Anna Luskin, the seeds had been sown much earlier, almost as soon as she had heard the bulletin, almost as soon as she had left the lounge of the health club had gone into the sauna. She had been eight years old when her parents had taken her to Ellis Island and told her how, when they had been little older than eight themselves, each of their families had made the long journey from Poland, how they had stood with the queues at the immigration desks, saw some rejected, turned back, saw the joy and relief on the faces of their parents when they had been allowed to pass through, when they had been permitted to enter a new land.

It was a part of her life of which she was never ashamed, a part of her life, however, in which she took no great joy. She closed off the memories, shut out the thought of the Jewish family called Zubko, and relaxed.

"THERE ARE GOING to be problems."

"What do you mean?"

It was two hours since Enderson had asked the operations officer to enquire why the hijacked plane was in the specific parking bay it occupied in Rome, thirty minutes since the man had found out, five minutes since he had been able to inform Enderson in one of the cinema ranges in the killing house, the team rehearsing their entry techniques against a film of the interior of a Boeing 727, complete with dummies of passengers and hijackers.

"It's what you thought about the plane being parked in the wrong place," the operations officer said. "Apparently ground control had a run-in with the hijackers."

"What sort of run-in?"

"When the plane landed, control began to direct it to the stand reserved for such uses, but the pilot said he was under instructions and specified another stand. The controller was already under pressure, too many big-wigs, too many politicians sticking their noses in, and was told to deny them the request, to say they had traffic problems in that area."

"So late at night?"

"So late at night," confirmed the operations officer.

"So what happened?"

"The pilot came back immediately and specified another stand."

"What happened then?"

"The Italians had no option, they had to agree, which explains why the plane is parked where it is now."

Where he would have put it if he had been the hijacker, Enderson remembered he had thought, the last place he would have allowed if he had been in charge of airport security. "So why are there going to be problems?" he asked.

"Two reasons," said the operations officer. "The first is that the Italians are under heavy pressure from West Germany. There's already a team of negotiators from Bonn at the airport and GSG-9 are standing by to intervene. It seems they want a quick end to the hijack."

"Why?" asked Enderson.

The operations officer shrugged. "They're being very tight-lipped about the whole deal. The feeling is that it's to do with the hijackers' demands, which they haven't made yet. It seems certain that those demands will be substantial, and that they'll be connected to the hunger-strike."

"So how does that present a problem?"

"I don't know," said the operations officer. "I just get the feeling somebody isn't telling us the truth."

Enderson nodded. "What's the other reason?"

"The Italians themselves. It seems that because they were forced to concede on where the plane was to park, the negotiators have been ordered not to give in on anything else."

"Nothing at all?"

"Nothing at all."

Enderson shook his head. "Any other developments?"

The intelligence officer looked at his pad. "I was just coming to the last point. Apparently the pilot showed four fingers out the window, they think he was indicating the number of hijackers on the plane."

Enderson remembered the mass of reports that morning, including the disclosure that a Jewish family from Russia was on Lufthansa 267. "How positive are they?" he asked.

"Certain, the movement was deliberate. They've checked it out on the surveillance tapes. He did it twice."

Enderson thought of the position of the plane relative to the television cameras and press photographers. A hero, he thought, a stupid bloody hero. He wondered how long it would be before the pilot began to worry about what he had done.

"They're not releasing the information, I hope."

The operations officer looked at him. "You won't believe it," he said, "but they already have."

Enderson shook his head. "I don't envy him when the hijackers find out."

"You think they'll find out, even on a plane?"

He thought of the man from Heathrow. "Yes," he said, "especially on the plane."

THE GIRL'S BREATHING was haunting him. Jurgen Schumpter tried not to listen, could not help thinking about his own daughter, how he sometimes woke at night worrying what he would do if anything happened to her, hearing again the awful sound of Natasha's attempts to breathe, knowing how much she must be suffering.

"I think you should ask if there's a doctor on the plane," said Walid Haddad.

Schumpter switched on the public address system. "This is the captain," he began, knowing the passengers would be frightened by the suddenness of his voice.

"If there's a doctor on board could he please come to the cockpit." He realised he had not been authorised by the hijacker to ask anyone to come to the cockpit and looked at the man, feeling the relief when the hijacker nodded. "If there's a doctor on board," he repeated, "could he please come to the cockpit."

He put the microphone down and waited, guessing at the chances of there being a doctor amongst the passengers, and even if there was, what the chances were of the man having the courage to stand up and allow himself to be singled out. Outside the sun was directly over the aircraft; he felt the heat and knew it would get worse.

The figure appeared in the doorway.

"I'm a doctor."

Schumpter heard the voice, and turned in his seat. Strange, thought Walid Haddad, how the pilot had assumed the doctor would be a man, how he himself had known all along that if the doctor was a woman she would have no hesitation in standing up and being counted.

"The little girl," he said. "Find out what's the matter with her, what she needs." There was no humanity in his voice, Schumpter thought, no anger either, nothing at all, it frightened him. He watched as the doctor went back to the cabins and knelt by the girl and her parents, feeling her pulse and forehead, talking to the mother and father. After five minutes she came back to the cockpit, the hijacker at the door covering her movements.

"She has asthma," she said, "very badly indeed. She always suffers from it, but it comes on particularly badly when she is under stress."

Walid Haddad looked back down the plane, at the father holding his daughter, then back at the doctor. "Don't they have any medication for her?" he asked.

The doctor returned his stare. "They gave her the last tablets on the way to the airport yesterday." The pilot knew what she was going to say and willed her to stay silent. "They didn't expect to be still on the plane, nobody did." Schumpter waited for the hijacker's reaction, knew it would be angry.

"What can you do for her?" asked Walid Haddad.

The doctor looked straight at him again. "On the plane, nothing. I have to get her off."

Walid Haddad shook his head. "Nobody can leave the plane, absolutely nobody. For any reason."

The pilot saw the look in the doctor's eyes, sensing she was about to show the stress they were all under.

"Don't you understand?" she said. "The girl is ill, very ill. Unless I get her off the plane, there is nothing I can do for her." She looked at him again. "In those circumstances, I can't be held responsible for what might happen to her." Her voice had been raised, everyone had heard what she had said, how she had said it. Schumpter wondered again how the hijacker would react.

Walid Haddad looked at the woman. She was in her late fifties, unattractive; he knew that everyone had heard, that everyone was waiting for his answer. "I appreciate," he spoke quietly, "that you do not wish to leave the plane for your own sake, that your sole concern is for the child, but absolutely nobody can leave the plane."

Schumpter listened to the words, realising how much the hijacker frightened him, how much he frightened all of them, not realising how they were drawing closer to him.

"Thank you," said the doctor. It was the third time someone had thanked the hijacker.

"What drugs would help?"

"Intravenous hydrocortisone as a matter of urgency, then Becotide or Ventolin tablets or inhalers."

"Write them down," Walid Haddad told her. She did as he instructed and went back to her seat, past the hijacker at the cockpit door and the woman standing over the Zubko family.

Schumpter watched the way she walked, the way the other passengers looked at her, not understanding what was happening to them all, seeing the way she sat down and folded into tears. Walid Haddad gave him the list.

"Speak to ground control," he said. "Tell them you have been ordered to ask for two things. Food, and these drugs. Nothing more. You are to say nothing more."

The pilot looked at the list, and reached for the microphone.

"Ground, this is Lufthansa 267."

He heard the voice, a different voice, and wondered why they had changed controllers.

"Ground, I have been ordered to ask for food and drugs." He looked at the list and tried to pronounce the words properly.

"Lufthansa 267 from Ground, why do you want the drugs?"

He turned to the hijacker and saw the gun come up. Nothing more, the man had told him, he was to say nothing more.

"I repeat," he said, "I have been ordered to ask for food and the following drugs." He read the list again. "That is all I have been authorised to say."

He realised the cockpit door was open and they could all hear.

"Lufthansa 267 from Ground, stand-by."

Stand-by, Schumpter thought, not please stand-by, just the order. *"There are going to be problems," the operations officer had told Graham Enderson. "The West Germans are taking a hard line, the Italians won't make any concessions because of what happened this morning."*

"None at all?" Enderson had asked.

"None at all."

"Lufthansa 267 from Ground."

Schumpter waited to hear that they would soon eat, that the girl called Natasha would soon be able to breathe properly.

"Ground, this is Lufthansa 267." He realised he had revealed his relief to the hijacker and told himself it was something he should avoid in the future.

"Lufthansa 267, I am not, repeat not, authorised to give you any food or drugs."

Schumpter knew he had not heard the words properly. "I'm sorry, control, please repeat."

There was a harshness in the voice that he would remember. "I am not, repeat not, authorised to give you food or drugs."

The tension in him almost broke through. For Chrissake, he wanted to say, what the hell are you playing at? Who the hell do you think you are? He controlled himself, made himself remember the training films, reminded himself that the people who had just refused Natasha her drugs were on his side, that it was the man who had asked for those drugs who was his enemy.

"I hear you, Ground. Out."

He turned to the hijacker. "They said no." He heard his own voice, the anger in it.

"I know," said Walid Haddad. "You'd better get the doctor."

The woman was already standing in the cockpit doorway. "I heard," she said. "May I sit next to the girl?"

"Thank you," said Walid Haddad. For the second time Jurgen Schumpter sensed the hijacker was thinking about the Jewish family. "There are some soft drinks left," he said. "Can the stewardesses share them out?"

"I suggest," replied the man to his right, "that you keep them in reserve, we may have a long time to wait."

In the corner of the cockpit Schumpter heard the radio, the next news bulletin, the voices of the reporters in Rome and Vienna, repeating the details of the Zubko family. He remembered his disbelief the first time he had heard it on the radio, the first time the authorities had told the hijackers about the Jewish family, realised suddenly what else they were going to tell them. Not as directly as they had told them about Stanislav Zubko and his wife and children, perhaps not this bulletin, even the next, but they would tell them.

The authorities, he tried to stop himself thinking, his own bloody people. First they had betrayed the Zubkos to the hijackers, signed their death warrants, then they had refused little Natasha her drugs, now they were going to betray him. He knew what the hijackers would do to him, what they would do to the Jews; thought, for one awful moment that the authorities wanted the hijackers to do it, had contrived to make it impossible for them not to do it, to give themselves an excuse to storm the plane, and finish it quickly. He told himself to stop thinking about it and remembered again his wife and children.

THE ROVER MOVED efficiently through the Whitehall traffic, past the Cenotaph. The morning had gone well, decided John Kenshaw-Taylor, relaxing back into the rear seat and flicking through the briefs which the European and Middle East desks had prepared for him on the background and potential implications of the Lufthansa hijacking. Over breakfast at Downing Street the Prime Minister had agreed with his analysis of the hijack, the consequences of the involvement of twelve Britons amongst the hostages and the possibility of a British initiative in any political or military solution, and had suggested that she herself speak to the Chancellor and the President and promise them whatever support they might need. Telexes confirming both the West German and American appreciation of the offer of British support had reached Kenshaw-Taylor's office by eleven.

The Rover turned off Whitehall into Trafalgar Square.

An hour before the telex, the Foreign Minister had personally telephoned the Israeli ambassador in London and offered his sympathies to members of the Zubko family. If at any stage, he had suggested, the British government found themselves in a position to help, he would do all in his power to get the Zubkos to Israel. Not for political reasons, he had stressed, but for reasons of humanity.

"I am aware," he had continued, "that you like to take care of these things yourselves, but if the circumstances arose where this was impossible, even for your people," he had added, lending the intonation of conspiracy and admiration to his voice, "you can rely on my personal support."

The ambassador had said he understood and thanked him for his sympathies, both men phrasing the conversation in a way that had left many things agreed, many things unspoken. Fifty minutes later the ambassador had telephoned back to say that Tel Aviv had welcomed his words. For reasons of humanity.

The traffic in Trafalgar Square was congested: the official driver cut through it and turned into Pall Mall.

John Kenshaw-Taylor looked out of the window and thought of Stanislav Zubko and his family. He already had the Arab side; now the Zubkos might get him the Israelis. And if they did, he thought, Henry Armstrong would have no problems with the Jewish Lobby in Washington for the foreseeable future. "The man the President chooses will himself choose friends he knows can deliver," the President's next foreign affairs advisor had offered him in Washington.

The Rover stopped outside the Carlton Club, he told the driver to pick him up at one thirty and went inside. He was five minutes early; the sight of a British cabinet member waiting for him would make his guest feel even more important.

A hijack, Saeed Khaled had said in New York. He had been approached as an Arab mediator, would Kenshaw-Taylor consider being his European counterpart? One problem, he himself had seen: there was no certainty of British involvement, no reason for him to be called in. He remembered the moment the solution had come to him, the solution and the bonus.

The Jordanian ambassador arrived exactly on time. The Foreign Minister rose to greet him and escorted him to the table, making a point of telling the wine waiter he wanted one of the clarets he knew the man kept for special occasions.

The lunch lasted five minutes under one hour, the two men leaving at the time they had agreed. Both, after all, were busy men. They were interrupted only once, when Kenshaw-Taylor took a call from his office informing him that the hijackers had asked for food and drugs and that their request had been turned down. Later, in the car back to Whitehall, later still in the flat in Pimlico, he would reflect on how very well he had played it. The ambassador had been flattered to be asked his evaluation of the situation, he was also too experienced a diplomat not to sense, when Kenshaw-Taylor raised the possibility, however slim, of a British involvement in any solution of the Lufthansa hijack, that he was being made what his advisors would call an offer.

The lunch, Kenshaw-Taylor emphasised, was purely informal, an unofficial meeting of like minds given Jordan's importance in the future of peace negotiations in the Middle East. The ambassador agreed, remembering what he had been told about the Foreign Minister, that John Kenshaw-Taylor was the man for the future, that he was close to Henry Armstrong, and that Henry Armstrong was the man who would dictate United States foreign policy in the Middle East in the years to come.

John Kenshaw-Taylor understood what the man was thinking and allowed himself to enjoy it, noting with pleasure that it was the ambassador who raised the subject of the Special Air

Service and who told him, as if he did not already know, of King Hussein's British connections, both in general and with the regiment in particular, mentioning in passing that the king often visited Hereford, quietly and unnoticed, during his trips to Britain.

It was going well, he decided as he took sherry that evening, going bloody well. He wondered when Khaled would contact him. It would be through official channels, at least to start with, and it would also be soon. The evening outside the office overlooking Whitehall was lighter; he refilled his glass and drank a silent toast to the stroke of fate which had put Stanislav Zubko and his wife and children on Lufthansa 267.

8

THE AFTERNOON SUN had moved round, so that now it was shining into the hardened perspex on the side of the cockpit where Walid Haddad sat in the co-pilot's seat. It was strange, he thought, how he seemed to have measured the passage of time that day by the movements of the sun, rather than by his wristwatch, realising it was only a game he played with himself, a way of passing the waiting. He was used to waiting, had spent most of his life waiting.

It was twenty-four hours since he had left the hotel and taken the cab to the airport. He wondered where Gent Mueller was, what she was doing. She would have left the flat, and her job at the airport, bathed herself clean of her despised security guard. And the other unit, the decoy team, the three who had asked to call themselves the Commando of the Martyr Klars Christian Mannheim; he assumed they had got away safely, their job done, his only just beginning.

Across the cockpit Jurgen Schumpter looked tired, the stubble of growth on his face seeming to emphasise his weariness. Neither of them had slept since the hijack; at least, Walid Haddad knew, he had the benefit of the amytal and amphetamines he would use over the next days. He began to think about the pilot, what he should do when the radio announced it, how Schumpter would conduct himself when his time came.

It was hot in the cockpit. In the cabins behind, the smell was beginning to impose itself on the air, the passengers feeling tired and dirty. Not as hot as it would get later, not as hot as it would get in the sands of the places they would go in the days to come, but hot enough. The pilot was sweating; he had undone his tie and loosened his shirt. In the cabin behind he could hear the rasp of the girl's breathing.

"Do you want to open a door?" Walid Haddad asked.

Schumpter looked at him in surprise, partly because the hijacker rarely spoke, partly because it seemed a concession, mainly because he thought the hijacker would have considered it a security lapse, the first opportunity for the authorities to know a small part of what was happening inside the plane. Except, he thought, for his message to them that morning. He prayed they would keep it a secret, knew subconsciously that they would not.

"Yes," he replied. "It would be good for the passengers."

They stood up, the pilot first, and went to the door. Walid Haddad saw the other hijackers glance at him then at the pilot. They had put the pins back in the grenades and made themselves comfortable, made it clear, despite this, that they were still alert and in control.

Jurgen Schumpter swung the lever, and began to open the door, then saw the way the passengers were looking at him, wondering what he was doing.

"Tell them I'm letting some air in," he ordered a stewardess. Strange, he thought, how most of his communication over the past twenty-four hours had been with the hijacker, how he was already becoming isolated even from his own crew.

The air was warm but fresh. He imagined what would be happening in the operations room, the men leaning forward, looking at the rows of monitors, the cameras zooming in on the sudden movement. He stood still, breathing the air.

Walid Haddad nodded to the hijacker who had stood guard at the cockpit door, the man pulled a handkerchief over his face and stepped forward, joining the pilot in the doorway.

In the control room the watchers leaned closer to the screens, seeing the doorway, looking at the man framed in it.

"Schumpter, the pilot," said the Lufthansa representative. "He looks all right."

The second man appeared. They concentrated on him, seeing the handkerchief over his face, his neat clothes, the weapons he was carrying, the sub-machine gun hanging from his right hand, the grenade in his left, the spare magazines on his belt.

It was not only important for the weapons to be correct, Walid Haddad had decided in Damascus, it was equally important that they should be seen to be correct.

"Jesus Christ," the Lufthansa representative heard a gasp behind him. "Jesus Christ Almighty."

In the doorway Jurgen Schumpter heard the beginning of the BBC World News bulletin and returned to the cockpit, saw the way the hijacker was looking at him, hearing the voice of the reporter in Rome, the man less than two hundred yards from him. Four hijackers, the reporter was saying, the authorities believed there were four hijackers on the plane; they would not say how they had obtained their information, had asked the press who were present at the airport and who might be in a position to know how they knew, not to divulge anything. Lives were at stake, said the reporter.

Schumpter knew what they would have said about him when he signalled to them. Good man: they would have said, looking at the tapes, confirming his message. Then they had betrayed the Jews, denied Natasha her drugs. Now they had betrayed him. The thoughts that had been subconscious began to surface. They had not named him, but they had said enough, condemning him anyway. He thought of his wife and children and wondered who would tell them he was dead, what they would do without him. The hijacker was still looking at him; he realised the man had known all along, that he would have done nothing if the authorities had not exposed him.

He turned to the hijacker, feeling almost as if he had betrayed him. "I'm sorry," he said.

"Get up."

The gun was pointing at him.

"Go back down the plane."

There was something different about the voice. An anger, he thought, his mind and body in a vacuum, as if they no longer belonged to him. He felt afraid, alone, thinking again of his wife and children, could not think of anything else, knew he would never see them again. He had thought about death as a child, when his grandfather had died, had forgotten about it in the long hot summer that had followed; had thought about it as a teenager, as a young man, had known it was inevitable, that it would come to him as it came to everyone, had forgotten about it because it was a long way off; had thought about it when his father had died, found comfort in the fact that his father had had a good life, that he himself still had a good life in front of him. Now no more. He rose and turned to the doorway. Not anger in the hijacker's voice he thought, something else, something worse than anger. Finality, he decided, like the voice of a judge passing the death sentence.

He walked out of the cockpit and into the body of the plane, the hijacker behind him, the gun against his back. The passengers and crew were looking at him, he saw the horror on their faces, the awful comprehension of what was about to happen.

They passed the first class seats and the Jewish family, till they reached the point a third of the way into the economy section where they were in full view of the passengers.

"Stop," said Walid Haddad.

Jurgen Schumpter stopped, trying to hide his shaking, trying to stand upright.

"Turn round."

Jurgen Schumpter turned to face him.

"Kneel down."

Jurgen Schumpter knelt down, knew it was the end. Looked up at the hijacker, at the gun, the end of the barrel close to him. Steady, he thought, the gun was so steady, wondered what constituted the man that he could hold the weapon so steadily when he was about to kill someone.

"Tell them," said Walid Haddad.

He tried to look away from the gun, from the hijacker, but could not.

"They know," he said. "They know how many hijackers there are." He no longer felt the confusion or the anger, just the emptiness. In the awful quiet he heard the girl's breathing.

"How do they know?" Walid Haddad asked him.

I'm sorry, he wanted to say, I was only doing my job, what I was expected to do, what they taught me to do in the lectures, in the training films. I was only doing my job, and they let me down. Betrayed me, made my wife a widow.

"I told them," he said. "This morning, when I opened the cockpit window I held up four fingers. Twice," he needed to tell them the entire truth. "I did it twice so they would be certain."

He realised he was holding his hands behind his back, as if they were bound, then heard the sharp, almost hollow, sound and saw the faces of his wife and children for the last time.

"Get up," said Walid Haddad.

He heard the words, did not understand them, could not understand what was happening.

"Captain Schumpter is a brave man," said Walid Haddad, "he did what he was trained to do."

The gun was still on the pilot.

"Unfortunately, what he did was a very silly thing." Schumpter thought he saw the first movement of the butt and braced himself for it. Not a killing, he thought, just a beating, bloody and brutal, was suddenly more frightened of the pain of the beating than the release of the execution.

"This time," he heard the hijacker's voice, "I will spare him, next time he will not give me that option."

Jurgen Schumpter felt the relief, knowing he would not be able to maintain his dignity much longer, wanting to thank the man, remembering the training film would say he should not. He heard the voice again and saw that the hijacker was turning round so that for part of his next words he was facing every one of the passengers and crew.

"I do not want to harm any of you," said Walid Haddad. "I hold no personal grudge against any of you. No matter what your country or nationality. No matter what your religion." His eyes swept past the Zubkos, deliberately not staying on them. "But if there comes a time when I have to die, when we all have to die, then we will all die."

Schumpter knew that what had happened on the plane in the last few minutes, the circumstances of his execution and his last minute reprieve from it, strengthened rather than weakened what the hijacker had said.

Walid Haddad turned to him. "Captain Schumpter, we all know the authorities have refused us food, as well as drugs for the girl. I suggest you distribute what food and drink is left."

Schumpter nodded to the stewardess and went back to the cockpit. It was empty. He sat in his seat, glad to be alone, aware that the hijacker had allowed him the moment, that the man had not made him thank him for not killing him. Then he dropped his head and cried with relief.

THE MAN FROM HEATHROW, Enderson thought, it had to be the man from Heathrow. He shut the thought from his mind and concentrated on the plans and model on the table in the main room of the anti-terrorist headquarters. It was not their hijack, not at the moment. But the plane might take off from Rome, and head for Britain, then it would become their hijack, then they would have to deal with it. They went through the model and specifications again, the points of entry, the diversions they would use.

In the cinema of the killing house that morning they had run the film of the interior of the Boeing 727, introduced the dummies of the hijackers, practised entering the plane. In the operations room that afternoon Enderson had pored over the details from Rome, the number of hijackers, the figures in the doorway, the pilot and the man who had scared the hell out of all of them. He had queried what the drugs were for and confirmed that the people in Rome had made another mistake, that they should have checked before the blanket refusal, should have worked out that the drugs were for a passenger, that there was no way they could have been for one of the hijackers. The Stockholm syndrome, he was thinking, the empathy between gunmen and their victims, the gradual feeling that they were on the same side, that the authorities were opposed not just to the gunmen, but even to the hostages.

One thing puzzling him, he knew, one thing which had been puzzling him all day. Most planes had a blind spot at the rear, by which the assault teams could approach the aircraft. But the 727, in addition to the main passenger door on the port side behind the cockpit, also had a door beneath the tail. By opening this and letting down the steps the hijacker could cover the rear approach. Yet he had not done so.

On the television set in the corner of the room he saw the beginning of the news bulletin. One of the team leaned forward and started the cassette recorder. Dramatic developments in Rome, the announcer was saying, first pictures of the hijackers themselves. The sequence of images began, the main door opening, the men coming into vision, the pilot, obviously the pilot, and the man behind. He saw the weapons in the man's hand, knew why the monitoring team in Rome had been taken aback, heard the reaction of his own unit, wondered how the man from Heathrow had done it.

It was no mistake, he was sure, that the plane had been parked where the television cameras had full view of it, no accident that the gunman had appeared in the doorway with the pilot, that the man had revealed the magnitude of his weaponry. No mistake either that the rear door had not been opened, that the man from Heathrow had not covered the line of approach from the back. There had been no security risk to the hijacker, no reason to open the rear door, every reason not to open it, every reason not to take away the impact of the other door opening, the first image of the gunman with the submachine gun and the grenades.

It was just like the job on the motorway from Heathrow, he thought, just like the set-up in Frankfurt. Even the request for food and drugs, planned to perfection. And the authorities had fallen for it, thought they were refusing the hijackers, did not know they were denying the passengers.

He wondered why the hijacker had allowed the pilot to signal the number of gunmen on board, how he had used it.

The man from Heathrow, he thought again, the bloody man from Heathrow.

THE MAN IN THE PHOTOGRAPH, Walid Haddad thought, the man in the newspaper he had used on the drive from Heathrow. He knew what he was about to do, what he would do later, how it would involve the man in the photograph, wondered how the man in the photograph would react.

The night had closed around them, cutting them off. In the semi-circle outside the cockpit window Jurgen Schumpter could see the arc of television lights, trained on him, almost dazzling him. He felt cold and detached, had not stopped thinking about his wife and children since he had knelt on the floor of the plane.

"I'm going to check the passengers."

Walid Haddad nodded. Schumpter went out of the cockpit, the hijacker guarding the door followed him. He pretended the man did not exist and walked down the aisle. Walid Haddad watched him go, seeing the way he delayed over the Zubko family, the girl and boy asleep beside their father and mother.

Stanislav Zubko looked at his wife and children and tried to smile at them. It was dark outside, a strange darkness, the black of the night mixed with the glare of the lights that played on the aircraft. He thought of Yakov Zubko and wondered where he was, what he was doing. They should have been in the house in Beita now, seated round the table in the kitchen, looking at the photograph the American family from Norfolk had agreed to send for them.

He could hear the children, asleep upstairs, his poor Natasha breathing easily, could smell the air, taste the food of welcome. The water on the table from the well in the middle of the village, the oranges from the grove opposite the field at the foot of the hill called Bethesda.

He felt hungry and thirsty; the single glass of water and the handful of biscuits they had been given early had helped, but not much. Besides he and Mishka had allowed the children to drink their share, and saved their biscuits for when the children needed them.

The pilot passed him again. He watched as the man disappeared into the cockpit, heard the hijacker's voice and saw the pilot shut the door. The first time that he had closed the door.

"It is time," said Walid Haddad. "Get ground control."

Schumpter did not know what he meant, did as he had been ordered.

"Ground, this is Lufthansa 267."

In the operations room the observers sat up. The first communication with the plane since they had rejected the demands for food, since they had realised their mistake in refusing the medication.

"Lufthansa 267, this is Ground."

Schumpter took a breath. "I have the leader of the hijack team for you," he said, passing the microphone across the cockpit, sensing the change in the control room.

"This is the leader of the hijack team," Walid Haddad repeated the pilot's words. No title, thought the men in the control tower, no reference to the names of martyrs and heroes as in previous hijackings and killings. It unnerved them.

"I have one demand," said Walid Haddad, "and one condition."

He knew that he was being recorded, that they would play back the tape, again and again, try to analyse his accent, his

nationality, get the psychologists to try to tell them his state of
mind, knew it did not matter.

No rhetoric, the negotiators thought again, no names, no
reference to any groups. They felt the same fear they had experienced when they had seen the figure of the gunman in the
doorway.

He told them the demand.

Jurgen Schumpter stared at him in disbelief. Is that all, he
thought, are we all going through this for such a simple request? He told himself that the authorities would agree, that he
and the passengers and crew would be off the plane by midnight, then made himself admit that the authorities would not,
could not.

The voice from the control tower did not comment. "And if
the West Germans do not agree?"

"I will blow up the plane and everyone on it."

Jurgen Schumpter knew he meant it, wanted to tell the man
in the control tower that the hijacker meant it.

The controller stalled. "I cannot give you an answer immediately. I will have to pass your demand to the West Germans.
Only they can reply."

"I understand," said Walid Haddad. In the darkness in front
of them one of the television lights went out then flicked back
on again.

"How long do they have?" asked the controller. "What is
your deadline?"

Schumpter knew the man had made a mistake, that he should
not have asked.

"I will not tell you that," said Walid Haddad. "All I will tell
you is this: there will be one deadline, and only one deadline. I
will give you plenty of time before it, but once the deadline is
reached, I will blow up the plane and everyone on it."

He gave the microphone back to the pilot. The controller
began to ask something but Schumpter cut him short.

"He has finished talking to you," he told the man, seeing the
faces of his wife and children. "Please pass his request to the
West Germans immediately." The Germans were already there,
he knew, in the control room, listening to the demand as the
hijacker made it. He put down the microphone and turned to
the man in the co-pilot's seat.

"Is that all you want?" he asked incredulously. "Is that
really all you want?"

"Yes," said Walid Haddad. "That is all I want."

10

THE CHILDREN were almost too tired to sleep. Stanislav Zubko felt it in their limbs, the way they moved, the way they could not settle. His son Anatol was sucking his thumb as Stanislav had done when he was a boy.

"Tell us about Yakov Zubko, Daddy," said the boy. "Tell us about the way the boys and girls play by the well."

Stanislav smiled at his son, reached across the aisle for the photograph and showed it to him. They had looked at it so often, he had told the story so often; in the flat in Moscow, on the train to Vienna, in the flat when they had been waiting for the plane that would take them home, but now was the first time he had shown the photograph or told the story on the plane. Mishka moved across from the other seat and sat beside him, Natasha on her lap.

In the next seat the doctor who had asked for the drugs listened. Three seats away the stewardess who had raised her hand to go to the toilet listened. In the cockpit Walid Haddad listened.

"Once upon a time," Stanislav Zubko began, "there were two families who lived in a far-off land. They loved each other very much, the fathers were brothers and the children played together. But they did not belong where they were, the one thing they wished was to go where they belonged. One day, one of the families went to another land."

"The land where they belonged," said Natasha.

"Yes," said Stanislav Zubko. "The land where they belonged."

"*Beshanah Habaah b'Yerushalaim.*" Anatol had heard his parents say the words so often.

"Yes," said his father. "*Beshanah Habaah b'Yerushalaim.*"

Walid Haddad remembered the old man in the room in the refugee camp of Ain Helweh, the way the eyes, blind with cataracts, had looked at him, the way the hands, weak with sickness and age, had held his.

"The family went to a place where the sun shone," said Stanislav Zubko, "where there were trees with oranges, where there was a well. The father picked oranges from the trees for his son and daughter. The boy, who was older than the girl, went to school and played with his new friends by the well."

They were looking at the photograph of the two families outside the station in Moscow.

"Is that the day the first family left?" asked Anatol.

"Yes," said Stanislav Zubko. "That is the day the first family left."

"Is that us with them?" asked his daughter.

"Yes," her father told her, "that is us with them."

"One day did we go as well?" asked his son.

In the seat close to them the doctor could not bear to hear.

"Yes," said Stanislav Zubko, "one day the second family were also told they could go to the village. They went on a long train ride, a very long train ride, then they went in a plane."

"And did we get to the village, Daddy, did we play again with our friends, did Anatol play with his cousin by the well? Did Natasha breathe without crying?"

"Yes, my son," said Stanislav Zubko, "we got to the village, the children played again with their friends. You played with your cousin by the well, and Natasha could breathe without it hurting her."

In the haze of heat across the field, Walid Haddad saw the man and the boy.

"Can I tell them about the demand?" asked Jurgen Schumpter.

"Yes," he said.

The pilot got up and walked back into the cabin.

"The hijackers have just made their demand of the West German government," he said simply. There was no need to wait for silence, no need to pause.

"They have made one demand, and this has been passed to Bonn."

He told them the demand.

Stanislav Zubko did not understand, looked around, sensing the release of the tension, the feeling that they would soon be free, that their ordeal would soon be over.

"There is one thing."

Jurgen Schumpter's voice was sombre. The atmosphere changed abruptly.

"The hijackers have also told the authorities that if their demands are not met, there will be one deadline, and only one deadline." He had questioned whether to tell his passengers, and had decided that they both had a right to know and he should be the one to tell them.

"They have told the authorities that they will give them adequate time before the deadline, but that once that deadline passes, they will blow up the plane and everyone on it."

Stanislav Zubko wanted to understand. Understood enough. A single voice in the plane asked a single question.

"Is that all they have demanded?"

It was a man seated in the front of the economy section. He was in his mid-forties, overweight, sweating.

"Yes," said Jurgen Schumpter. "That is all."

He waited. There were no more questions. He turned and went back to the cockpit.

The children were fast asleep, Stanislav Zubko tried to comprehend what was happening; to his right the doctor who had tended Natasha was talking to Mishka; his wife was asking what had happened, what was going on, why everyone was suddenly happier, the doctor telling her about the hunger-strike in West Germany, about the hijacker's demand.

The woman knew Mishka was frightened.

"Don't worry," she said. "It will be all right. We will soon be free."

Stanislav watched.

"You think so?" asked his wife. "You really think so?"

I don't know, the doctor wanted to say, remembering the way the authorities had exposed the Jewish family, the way they had betrayed the pilot, the way they had refused drugs for little Natasha. I don't know what's happening, don't know anything any more. In this plane, in my own country, in the world.

"Yes," she said, "I really think so."

Stanislav Zubko watched as his wife patted the doctor on the arm, unsure who was comforting whom.

THE NEWS FLASH came at ten minutes to nine. Graham Enderson knew what it was before he saw the grim face of the presenter and heard the hard edge in her voice.

"We are receiving reports," she was saying, "that the hijackers of the Lufthansa jet with a hundred and thirty six passengers and crew on board have issued a demand to the government of West Germany." He knew what she was going to say, remembered the moment he had seen it, the day they had buried Klars Christian Mannheim, the way he had known everybody would even remember the girl's name, the way he had remembered it himself. The teenager called Christina.

"The hijackers have demanded that the West Germans meet the demands of the hunger-striker Christina Melhardt. Sources in Bonn said tonight that Christina, who is due to be released from prison in just under three weeks, has an estimated fourteen days to live." A photograph of the hunger-striker appeared on the screen; the woman in it was no older than a girl, her hair was short and her large eyes had the ring of innocence. "The hijackers have said that unless their demand is met they will blow up the plane," continued the presenter, "though they have not issued a deadline."

Of course there would be no deadline, Enderson thought, not until the very end, not until the hijacker knew he had to carry it through. He remembered what the ops officer had said about the West Germans, that they wanted a quick resolution to the hijack, that they were not telling the entire truth.

The man from Heathrow, he knew for certain.

MICHAEL STEPHENSON and Daniel Furtado heard the news of the demand as they were preparing to finish work. Anna Luskin heard it as she was preparing to begin.

Her client that evening was a French civil servant. She had just left the bath and was towelling herself, watching the television through the door of the lounge, when she heard the item and saw the pictures of the Lufthansa Boeing in Rome, the single photograph of the hunger-striker called Christina Melhardt. The girl was so young, she thought, so much younger even than herself. She finished towelling and began to dress. The Frenchman was a regular client, he did not pay as much as some of the others, not nearly as much as the Arabs, but neither his demands nor his energy were excessive. They would dine first, then return to the hotel in which he stayed during his monthly trips to the United Nations.

She finished dressing and put on the perfume he had given her on their last appointment. That was how she chose to view the relationships with the men who paid for her services, appointments rather than dates. Although she did not necessarily enjoy what it required her to do, she did not, in general, doubt the profession she had chosen. The only thing she regretted, the only memory which still pulled her from her sleep, was the bastard who had marked her, physically and psychologically, five weeks before.

She switched off the television and left the flat. The Jewish family on the hijacked plane, the thought began to eat into her mind, the Jewish family called Zubko.

11

JURGEN SCHUMPTER was back in the Black Forest, the plane was moving down the runway, he was playing with the children, trying to keep awake, easing back the controls, smelling the camp-fire, feeling the plane lift off, trapped in the recesses between sleep and half-sleep, caught in the nightmare a man has after he has driven a long way and fought to keep awake, the nightmare, the fear, that he is still driving. The hijacker was shaking his arm. He woke, blinking in the glow of the cockpit lights.

Two hours, he saw, since they had made the demand, one hour since the West Germans had rejected it.

"What is it?" he asked, unsure for the briefest of moments where he was.

"Tell them we wish to refuel," said Walid Haddad.

Twenty minutes into another day, the pilot was thinking, trying to pull the strands of thoughts together, remembering that the authorities had already refused the hijacker's requests for food and drugs, rejected his single demand, assuming they would refuse them again.

"Why?" he asked without thinking.

"You refuelled last in Frankfurt two nights ago," said Walid Haddad. "A 727 burns three point eight tons of fuel per hour, you have been in the air almost seven hours. There's little fuel left."

The hijacker knew everything, the pilot thought, absolutely everything. He switched on the microphone. "Lufthansa 267 to Ground."

The response was immediate. "Lufthansa 267, this is Ground."

"This is Lufthansa 267, we wish to refuel." He was already checking the gauges, working out how much they could take, knew again the request would be turned down.

"Lufthansa 267 from Ground. How much fuel do you want?"

"Twenty-four tons." He was certain that they would refuse him.

"Ten minutes," said control. "Stand by for refuelling in ten minutes."

Fifty-five minutes later, at one twenty, the refuelling was complete; the hijacker who had been supervising the operation shut the main door and returned to the cabin.

"Tell them we are taking off," said Walid Haddad.

Schumpter had almost expected it. "Lufthansa 267 to Ground. Permission to take off."

He felt the hijacker's movement, short and fast, hand over the microphone.

"I didn't say ask for permission, I said to tell them."

Jurgen Schumpter saw the look in the man's eyes. "Lufthansa 267 to Ground," he forced himself to speak differently. "We are leaving. Instructions for take-off, please."

The controller's response was immediate, for the second time that night it took him by surprise. "Lufthansa 267, you are cleared for take-off, proceed to runway two five by taxiways Romeo and Bravo."

They didn't care that he was going, he suddenly thought, the bastards didn't even want to know where he was going.

"What's our destination?" he asked. Walid Haddad told him. Jurgen Schumpter checked the distance, the fuel it would take. Enough fuel, some left over. He wondered how it would be in the cabins, how hot it would be, how long the toilets would hold before they became blocked up, how the girl with asthma would react. The lights of the runway were passing beneath them.

"Why?" he asked. "Why there?"

Walid Haddad did not reply, did not know himself. He was back on the motorway near Heathrow, the coach with the children jamming on its brakes as he pulled in front of it, the hire car accelerating away, level with the Granada, the PLO man in the rear seat, past it, seeing it disappear in his rear view mirror, the last check that the road was clear, the newspaper on the front passenger seat, the transmitter inside. The photograph on the front page of the paper, the three words of the headline, the man in the photograph.

The wheels lifted off the runway, he felt the plane climbing then heard the thump of the undercarriage as it locked into place.

"The only thing they gave us was the fuel," Jurgen Schumpter said suddenly, "and that was to get rid of us."

"Did you expect anything else?" asked Walid Haddad.

"No," conceded the pilot. "I don't suppose I did."

12

THE GIRL'S VOICE was brittle, as thin as ice; there was a still-ness about the pallor of the face that seemed to come from be-yond the grave. Jane Enderson heard her, saw her, across the valleys, the night closing round her, taking her away till she could no longer see her, till she could only hear the voice.

And you, my father, there on the sad height,
Curse, bless, me now with your fierce tears, I pray.
Do not go gentle into that good night.
Rage, rage against the dying of the light.

Even the voice was fading, drifting to the west, passing over her as the night was passing over her. She knew what would fol-low, tried to wake, saw the first images of the dream beginning to seep into her mind, occupying it, filling it. The tunnel was long, filled with smoke, the flames coming at him. He was moving down it, eyes sweeping left to right. Not his eyes, as if he was seeing through the sockets of his eyes. His breathing was deep and rasping, as if it was not his breathing. The voice guiding him, protecting him. Committing him. The death around him, his or somebody else's, she was not sure, the death from the hold-all in the wardrobe at the foot of the bed. A West German affair, she heard Grah's voice, GSG-9 were handling, no way he could become involved.

She wondered again what the poem meant, realised suddenly what the dream was, knew for the first time that her husband was going down the long slim body of Lufthansa 267.

She longed for the bleeper, for it to pull her out of her sleep, to take him away from the death. He was ignoring her, not even remembering she existed, moving on, deeper into the plane, the flames and screams coming at him. She heard it as she heard it at six every morning, felt the relief coming on her, saw the images fade away, heard her husband get out of bed, knew what would happen, waiting for him to bring her the tea and kiss her good-bye, take the hold-all from the wardrobe at the foot of the bed. She began to relax, eyes half-closing, relieved that she would not have the dream again that morning.

The realisation jerked her out of her sleep. She was sitting up, looking round. It was dark, too dark. Too dark to be six in the morning, too dark for the hour they always tested the bleeper. She was feeling for the light, switching it on, running down the stairs. The kitchen was empty, she was going from room to room, even the children's rooms. No, she was praying, for God's sake, no. Still running, knowing he was not there, checking the garage anyway, his car gone. Remembering the dream, remembering the hold-all in the wardrobe at the foot of the bed. No, she was almost shouting inside herself, for God's sake, no. She was at the top of the stairs, in the bedroom, looking at the clock, looking in the wardrobe at the foot of the bed.

It was one in the morning.

The hold-all was gone.

CHAPTER TWO

1

IT WAS HOT, getting hotter, even at six in the morning. He could imagine what it would be like later, when the sun rose above them, when the heat began beating down upon the thin metal of the 727. Walid Haddad looked out of the cockpit window, the shadow giving way across the tarmac, at the outline of the airport building against the blue of the morning sky.

The Queen Alia International Airport, Amman.

Not so far, he thought, from the spot where he had crossed into the West Bank, the place in the wire where the needles had almost stolen the earth of Esh Shikara from him.

Jordan, he thought, why in Allah's name Jordan?

It was the first thing he had thought when they had told him, the spectre that had been at the back of his mind, refusing to leave, even when he had been planning the other stages, working out the details of the weapons, setting up the false trail in Frankfurt. In the pilot's seat Jurgen Schumpter was dozing, his head jerking up and down as if he was either trying to wake or was fighting against a nightmare.

Why had Abu Nabil chosen Jordan?

The sun crept up the plane, across the wings. Like yesterday in Rome, he thought, time standing still, repeating itself.

Six o'clock. So long since he had last eaten, so long since any of them had eaten. If he asked for food, he knew, they would give it to him, but he had not asked.

It was the first thing in the entire hijack that he had not planned, except for Stanislav Zubko and his family, the fact that he had not asked for food but did not know why.

Jordan, the thought would not leave him, why Jordan?

He pulled himself up from the co-pilot's seat, feeling stiff, motioned for the hijacker at the door to remain there and went back into the cabins. The stewardesses were taking the blankets from those passengers who had asked for them during the night, replacing them in the luggage racks above the seats. In the centre of the cabins the other two hijackers were watching them.

At the door of the toilet he could detect the first faint odour from inside, knew that before the day was out the toilets would be blocked; already he could smell the sweat of the bodies. He turned into the kitchen area, poured himself a quarter beaker of water, took two tablets from the tin he carried in his pocket and washed them down, then turned back into the cabins and talked to the hijackers on duty there. He had been with them five minutes when he heard the words, the beginning of the story that Stanislav Zubko had told his children the night before.

The Zubko family was looking at the photograph again, the father was holding it, the son hunched against him, the daughter on her mother's lap, listening to the story, hearing how Anatol and Natasha would soon be playing with their cousins by the well of Beita, how their cousins would show them where to pick the oranges. How, Walid Haddad knew, the son of Yakov Zubko would tell them he had once met a stranger who had been born in the room where the boy now slept, how the stranger could remember the first day he had been able to touch the beam over the stairs leading to the room.

How Alexandra would tell them of the day the copy of the photograph they were now looking at had arrived, how she had placed it on the mantelpiece so that they could always see it, how Yakov Zubko would tell them how he had shown it to the stranger who had saved his son's life. How Yakov Zubko would not tell them how he, in turn, had saved the stranger's life.

The girl was still fighting for breath. In her face was a faint tinge of blue. It had not been there thirty minutes before.

Walid Haddad turned away and walked back to the cockpit. Even there he could hear the girl. The Zubkos, he thought, the bloody family Zubko.

THE VC10 LEFT British air space at four twenty-two, cleared to thirty-three thousand feet; there was nothing in its call sign or flight requests to indicate to the air traffic controllers who would guide its movements over the next few hours either its origin or the purpose of its flight. Radio silence was strict. In 1977 an Israeli journalist specialising in radio interception had picked up messages from the Lufthansa Boeing 707 carrying West German GSG-9 commandoes on their way to the assault on a hijacked charter jet at Mogadishu; three years later the same journalist had picked up messages from the White House as the remnants of the United States attempt to recover its people from the US embassy in Tehran had struggled to extricate themselves from the funeral pyre of burning planes and helicopters at Tabas.

At six twenty-nine the VC10 passed over the south coast of Greece and turned east over the Mediterranean.

Five minutes later the pilot left the cockpit, went back to the cabin and updated the man seated in the first row on the left. Graham Enderson nodded, thinking of the rehearsals at Pontrilas, the sessions in the killing house at Hereford, the hours he and the teams had pored over the maps and models. Stand-by, the routine was already drumming through his mind, stand-by, stand-by. First diversion in. Stand-by, stand-by. Second diversion in. Go, go, go, go, go.

The sun was coming in the window opposite him, the new sun from the east. Five and a half hours since the bleeper had gone off, he remembered how he had heard it, felt his hand move to switch it off, seen it was black, too black for six in the morning, too black to be the routine check call. He had left the house within a minute, and was at the barracks within eight.

He had been second to arrive. The teams on stand-by were already loading the boxes of equipment into the backs of the Range Rovers. At one twenty the commanding officer and squadron commander had given a three-minute briefing, by one thirty-five the anti-terrorist teams were on the road, closely followed by the vehicles carrying the support teams, the armourers and signallers. By one thirty-five, the crew of the VC10 were being pulled out of their beds, and receiving their own briefing on flight paths and security measures. At four in the

morning the plane had lifted off from the RAF base at Brize
Norton, climbing gently above the early morning grey of the
Oxfordshire countryside, and turned south.

The sky to the east had lost its darkness. Soon, Enderson
thought, Jane would know where he was going, what he was
going to do. He could imagine her, sitting in the kitchen, waiting for the first news bulletin on the television; the latest details of the hijack. Then she would know.

It was the last time, he realised subconsciously, that he would
think of Jane and the children, the last time he could afford to
think of them, until it was over. He checked his watch again
and began going through the details of the Boeing 727. Nine
entry points, team in position, two diversions. He was on the
ladder, the man who had waited for him at the top of the steps
at Knightsbridge at his side, the other two men tight behind
them. Stand-by, stand-by. He could hear the first diversion
going in. Stand-by, stand-by. Knew the second diversion was
going in, heard the stuns. He was opening the door, entering the
plane. Go, go, go, go, go.

Something wrong. It was not a suspicion, more a premoni-
tion. Not just what the ops officer had suggested about the
West Germans, something else.

The VC10 changed course to one three zero; Jordan, he
thought, why the hell Jordan?

JANE ENDERSON woke at five minutes past six; she was not
certain whether she woke or simply got out of bed, for four
hours and fifty-five minutes, ever since the bleeper had woken
her, ever since she had realised that Grah had left the house, she
had lain on the bed, unsure whether she was asleep or awake.

The house was quiet, the door of the wardrobe at the foot of
the bed was open. She went downstairs, taking care not to wake
the children, made herself a cup of tea, and sat in front of the
television set. The room was empty, almost cold, the hands of
the clock on the wall scarcely moving. It seemed an eternity
before she switched the television on and heard the opening of
the breakfast programme, the familiar voice of the presenter
reading the first news bulletin.

She only half registered the words of the report, only half saw
the pictures, heard again the voice of the girl in the classroom,

remembered again the dream, saw the Lufthansa jet in the sun, the terribly hot sun, of the airport in Jordan.

Her daughter appeared in the kitchen doorway. She was wearing a dressing gown and holding a teddy bear Grah had bought her on the day she had been born.

"Mum," she asked. "Where's Dad?"

3

JOHN KENSHAW-TAYLOR was awake by five. By five fifteen he had showered and dressed, made coffee, and placed a check call to the duty officer at the Foreign Office. There was little he could do but he enjoyed the feeling anyway. He ground some more coffee beans and made himself a fresh pot.

Five and half hours since they had first heard, five hours since the message, via the Jordanian ambassador in London to the Foreign Office, routed to him as a matter of urgency (the ambassador had, in fact, already informed him personally), formally requesting the assistance of Her Britannic Majesty's Government in dealing with the threat, potential or actual, caused by the presence of the hijacked Lufthansa 727 at the Queen Alia International Airport outside Amman. Four and a half hours since the car to Downing Street, four hours since the Jordanians had agreed to the despatching of an anti-terrorist team from Britain. Just over an hour since he had been informed that the plane carrying the team had left.

He sat back, tasting the coffee, thinking of where and how it had begun: the suite at London Hilton, the table in the Palestinian restaurant in New York. Jordan, he had said as they waited to get into their cars, the hijack should end in Jordan. Then he could get involved, then he could bring in the SAS.

His car arrived at six forty precisely. He kept it waiting for two minutes. Any less would have diminished his importance, any more would have reduced the urgency of his mission.

The streets were quiet; there was a bodyguard in the car as well as the driver.

The Rover slid out of Bridge Road and into Millbank; to his right the Thames was at half-tide, the mud banks showing. How he had envied those, he thought, who had sat on the COBRA committee during the Princes Gate siege, those who had sat in the inner sanctum of the war committee during the Falklands campaign, consoled himself with the fact that he had been too young, too short a time in the House, had hardly been a junior minister. Now he was at the centre. The Rover moved past Westminster itself and into Whitehall.

Too soon to talk to even the selected press, he thought. There would be time when he had pulled it off, when he had received the message of congratulations from the man in the United States, when the Prime Minister had taken her moment of glory, when she allowed him his.

The Rover turned left into Downing Street.

THE VC10 LANDED in Amman five hours and thirty minutes after it had taken off from the airstrip in the west of England. As they circled, Graham Enderson had seen the criss-cross runways of the Queen Alia International Airport on the starboard side, dropping behind them as they descended to the Amman Marka airfield on the other side of the city.

The airfield was busy. Even after the plane had stopped and the doors opened no one moved, partly for reasons of diplomacy, mainly for reasons of security. Almost immediately a blue Mercedes left the block of offices at the side of the airfield, approached the plane and stopped beneath it. Two men got out of the rear doors and ran up the steps which had been placed in position. Graham Enderson knew from the briefing in Hereford who they were: the British Defence Attaché, and the Jordanian Defence Minister, himself a member of the royal family, who would be in charge of both military and political considerations whilst the hijacked jet was on Jordanian soil.

The introductions were brief and to the point; when they were over the Jordanian nodded to the Defence Attaché that he should update the teams from Britain.

"Lufthansa 267 came in early this morning, another plane with representatives of the West German government, someone from the airline, and a couple of chaps called Siegler and Fuchs followed just after."

Uri Seigler and Hans Fuchs were members of the West German GSG-9 anti-terrorist unit. Enderson knew them both. "The rest of their team?" he asked.

"Frankfurt, under wraps," the attaché replied. "There's a bit of a diplomatic tussle on here at the moment, the West

Germans say it's their plane and they want their people to deal
with it, the Jordanians point out that the plane is in their ter-
ritory and it is they who decide what happens."

"Anything from the plane itself yet?"

"Nothing at all. They're sitting tight, haven't said a word,
other than during landing. The doors are still shut."

Enderson imagined what the conditions were like in the plane
and remembered the dispute when it had landed in Rome.
"Any trouble when they came in?"

"None at all. They went exactly where ground control put
them."

Why the hell Jordan, Enderson thought again. Through the
door he saw the covered lorries pull up.

"Transport," said the attaché, "the press and television
people are already at the airport, we've contained them in a
reasonable area, nobody knows you're here."

They stepped from the plane into the sunshine. The wall of
heat was almost overpowering. Enderson wondered again what
it was like in the Boeing, how long it would be before the air
conditioning failed and the sanitation became blocked.

The teams began loading their equipment into the lorries.
"Who's the negotiator?" he asked.

"The Defence Minister is in charge, but the Jordanians have
accepted a West German negotiator. He's already at the airport."

"By himself?" asked Enderson. It was accepted practice that
the negotiator played no part in the political and military discussion concerning the hijack, even to the extent of being denied information. Just as the voice of the hijacker would be
examined, so it was assumed that the hijackers would monitor
the voice of the negotiator, not only listening to what he was
saying, but trying to decide what he was not telling them.

"By himself," confirmed the Defence Attaché.

Thirty minutes after the VC10 had landed, the convoy of
trucks left the military airfield, skirted the city, and turned into
the Queen Alia International Airport, the vehicles lost in the
lines of military traffic which seemed to be pouring in and out
of the area. The Central Command room had already been established in the main airport buildings, the surveillance equipment was already being installed. No rear steps down, Enderson
noted. He confirmed that the first team of snipers were moving into position and arranged for the assault teams to be based

in a holding area near the airport, then requested a helicopter for an aerial reconnaissance of the hijacked plane.

THE SUN ROSE over the Jordan. Yakov Zubko watched the land change colour, the shadows filling out, as the day increased its warmth. It seemed so long since the woman from the Jewish Agency had taken the message at the airport and turned back to him, afraid to look at him. They had spent that night in the hotel the Agency had provided, then he and Alexandra had come home to Beita.

The three figures came up the hill behind him, moving so quietly that he did not hear them. The trees at the foot of the hill called Bethesda began to grow green. Alexandra and the children reached the outcrop of stones and sat beside him, not speaking. In the clear blue of the morning he saw the silver of a plane, high in the sky, travelling east, its vapour leaving a thin line of white above them.

The family Zubko sat still and waited.

JOHN KENSHAW-TAYLOR left Downing Street at eight, walked to the Foreign Office and was at his desk fifteen minutes before the first of his staff appeared. By ten thirty he had cleared his administration, cancelled two appointments that afternoon, and rearranged his schedule to meet the Prime Minister's brief. At eleven precisely the team he had hand-picked gathered for their first meeting; he updated them on the hijack, and informed them that the Prime Minister had handed responsibility for any British participation to his department.

"What manner of participation do you anticipate, Minister?" He felt the atmosphere in the room, the sense of involvement, of being on the inside, the knowledge that the new man was at the centre of things, that he was bringing the Foreign Office back to where it had always belonged. He waited, relishing the moment.

"Everything discussed here is confidential." He knew he had their full attention.

"We are already involved," he paused, savouring the reaction, enjoying the moment. "We are already involved in two ways. Firstly, we are in contact with various governments over a peaceful solution to the matter."

He let them wait a little longer. Secondly, he heard someone ask, not quite under his breath.

"At one o'clock this morning, after consultation between this office and Downing Street, a detachment of the SAS was sent to Jordan." He heard the gasp round the room. "I sincerely hope they will not be necessary. I am confident that if they are, they will not fail us."

The meeting ended at eleven thirty, at twelve he received the phone call he had been expecting. He waited while his secretary informed him the Prime Minister wished to speak to him, and was told that the British government had been approached by a Middle East oil state who were proposing an Arab negotiator for the hijack. Given the relationship between the oil state and the United Kingdom, as well as London's traditional influence in Jordan, it was suggested that Britain, rather than any other Western power, should provide a European negotiator. Specifically, said the Prime Minister, the Arabs had asked for John Kenshaw-Taylor. She had agreed immediately, she said, he would receive a call from the man the Arabs were proposing at twelve thirty.

Saeed Khaled was put through to him exactly on time. The conversation, which lasted ten minutes, was formal and diplomatic. There was nothing in it to suggest, even remotely, that the two men had already discussed the subject. When it was over Kenshaw-Taylor summoned his team and updated them on the development.

At one o'clock he contacted the Jordanian ambassador; the man had already been notified of the Arab proposal and confirmed to the Foreign Minister that his government would fully endorse the nomination should the need arise.

At one thirty he telephoned the West German ambassador and informed him of the suggestion. When the calls were complete he took a lunch of smoked salmon and mineral water and settled down to wait.

Two hours earlier, at six in the morning Eastern Standard Time, Michael Stephenson received a telephone call from one of his undercover agents informing him that the previous night's meeting with the anonymous Provisional IRA man had just ended. The prospective buyer had not suspected the men posing as arms dealers, nor had he realised that the entire negotiation had been recorded on video. The next meeting which they had arranged for two weeks' time, the agent suggested, would be the last before payment was made and they could close the operation. They had also, the man reported, secured a lead to the buyer's identity; he had given them a name and a bar in New York where a message could be left for him. The name was Chopper, the agent was unsure whether it was a code or a nickname.

At six fifteen Daniel Furtado prepared to leave home for the weapons test he and his Delta team would conduct over the next two days.

The last thing both Stephenson and Furtado did before they left their respective houses was to check the latest details of the Lufthansa hijack on the twenty-four hour cable news network to which both subscribed. The first thing they did when they arrived at work was to check the telex updates from Amman.

At six thirty Anna Luskin returned to her flat after her appointment with the French diplomat, made herself coffee, and switched on the television. She did not normally watch television in the morning, especially after returning from work. Today, however, she switched on the set and turned to the news channel.

Lufthansa 267, the newscaster was saying, was now in Jordan, having refuelled and left Rome late the previous night. She looked at the pictures, the plane isolated on the concrete, the sun beating down on it. The station had an exclusive interview, the newscaster was saying, with an American couple from Norfolk, Virginia, who knew the Jewish family on the plane. She watched the interview, listening to the couple describe how they had met Stanislav and Mishka Zubko in Moscow, how they had a son called Anatol and a daughter called Natasha who suffered badly from asthma. How they had sent a letter and a photograph which Stanislav Zubko had given them for his brother in Israel. The couple had kept a copy of it which they allowed to be shown.

In the breakfast room of her house in the suburbs of Chicago the woman saw the photograph, the two families standing together outside the station in Moscow and recognised the man, remembering the holiday in Russia, the moment in the hotel when he had looked at her, the moment he had drawn the star of David on the wall, the moment he had told that all he wanted to do was to take his family home to Israel.

In the lounge of her flat in New York Anna Luskin heard the words, the explanation that the photograph had been taken the afternoon that the brother of Stanislav Zubko had left with his family. She looked at the faces of the children, remembering when she had been their age, slightly more than their age, when she had been eight years old. Remembering again the day her parents had taken her to Ellis Island, the day they had told her how they had starved and suffered with their parents in the bowels of the boat that had brought them from Poland, how they had waited with their parents in the unending lines of people to see if they would be allowed to enter America.

For the first time in her life Anna Luskin realised the magnitude of what her parents and their parents before them had done, the enormity of what the family called Zubko were trying to do. For the first time she began to think seriously about the Lufthansa hijack.

For the first time she began to think there was something about it which she should remember.

5

WALID HADDAD heard the sound of the helicopter, hovering over them. Why Jordan, he thought again. No real reason for it not to be Jordan, ample reason why it should be; Jordan, the beginning of the split, the bloody days of Black September. Fifteen years on, the country occupying a key position in the discussions about the future, one of the hopes for a land where the Palestinians could finally come home.

He listened to the helicopter and remembered the drive from Heathrow, the race down the motorway, the way he had jammed the hire car across the coachload of children, the mo-

ment he had unfolded the newspaper to detonate the bomb, the
photograph in the paper. He realised why it was Jordan. The
country was one of the few places where the British could become involved in a hijack, one of the handful of places where
they could send the man in the photograph.

The helicopter was still above him.

Graham Enderson looked down at the plane, remembering
the diagrams and models of the 727 they had pored over at
Hereford, the blind spots, working out where he would position the assault teams, the lines of approach they would take to
the aircraft.

"That's enough," he told the pilot. "Let's get back."

Why Jordan, he thought again. No reason for it not to be
Jordan, ample reason why it should be.

The pilot swung the helicopter behind the airport building
and brought it gently to the ground; Enderson thanked the man
and hurried inside to the Central Command. The Defence
Minister was waiting for him.

"Is there anything you want?" he asked.

"A 727, somewhere quiet, for my men to practise on, and a
helicopter at their disposal with a combat pilot, one who is used
to working with your own special forces people. Plenty of
movement round the airport, particularly where it can be seen
from the Lufthansa jet, and at least one helicopter, sometimes
two, over the hijacked plane every ten minutes."

"I'll arrange it," said the Minister, not needing to ask why.
"Anything else?"

"One more thing. Most planes have a blind spot, you can
approach them directly from the back without being seen, but
the 727 has rear steps which can be operated from the inside. If
we're going to fit any monitoring onto the plane, now's the time
to do it, before the hijacker lets down the steps and sits somebody at the top." He wondered why the man from Heathrow
had not done so already, suspected what the Jordanian would
say, sensed the political pressure the man was already under.

"I'll make a decision after the conference," said the Defence Minister, turning back to the room which the Jordanian
and West German delegates were using.

Enderson watched the door shut and realised what he had
been thinking all along: Jordan was one of the handful of
places where the British could still become involved in a hijack. Most countries now had their own anti-terrorist teams,

many of them trained by the British, Jordan included. But because of the country's links with Britain, because of Hussein's special links with the regiment, it remained one of the handful of places where the SAS could be asked to help.

Jordan, he realised he had known all along, was one of the few places in the world where he could be set against the man from Heathrow.

WALID HADDAD heard the helicopter pull away. It was ironic, he began to think, that he had almost brought Stanislav Zubko and his wife and children to the place they called home, the land, he was thinking, that he also called home. He wondered whether they knew, whether they had looked down as the Boeing had dropped out of the sky. In the cabin behind he heard the terrible sound of the girl breathing.

Jurgen Schumpter knew what the hijacker was thinking. Time to change the pace, he thought, time to show the authorities that the hijackers were serious, to shock them out of their complacency. In the cabin behind he heard the sound of the girl struggling to breathe and realised what the hijacker intended to do.

Not the Jewish family, he thought, not the little girl called Natasha.

Walid Haddad rose from the co-pilot's seat and went back to the cabins, sensing the sudden fear, the realisation that he was about to do something.

Stanislav Zubko was bent over the photograph with his children. Stanislav Zubko, thought Walid Haddad, was always bent over the photograph with his children. They were talking together, quietly, the girl coughing, not seeing the man standing over them. He stopped and listened to them. Even in the past hour, he thought, the blue in the girl's face had darkened.

"This is my uncle, Yakov Zubko," the boy was saying to him. He realised that the boy was not aware to whom he was talking, that the whole plane was waiting for his reaction, that they all knew what was about to happen.

Not the Jewish family, prayed the doctor.

"This is my aunt, Alexandra Zubko, on the day they left Moscow. Soon, my father says, we will see them in Beita."

Not the Jewish family, prayed the stewardess, please not the Jewish family.

"This is my cousin…" the boy's voice faded as he looked up and saw who was standing over him.

Not the Jewish family, Jurgen Schumpter prayed again. Anybody, even himself, but not the Jewish family.

One hour, thought Walid Haddad, he would do it in one hour. He turned back to the cockpit and tried to think of a justification.

6

ENDERSON STOOD AGAINST the wall, looking at the images of the 727 on the banks of monitors. The operations officer was completing his checks, his communications with the snipers; Enderson did not speak or interrupt, as the man in the control room would not interfere with his teams when the time came for him to be ordered in.

The first green lights flickered on the panel in front of the major, the voices of the snipers as they registered their positions. One to control, contact. Two to control, contact. Soon, he thought they would be his eyes, soon they would begin to tell him at least some of the things he needed to know, soon they would be seeing into the plane with their Swift telescopes, would switch to the image intensifiers when it grew dark.

Stand-by, he did not even realise he was thinking; he was at the top of the steps, the men beside him, behind him, stand-by, stand-by, the sound of the second diversion. Go, go, go, go, go.

"Your people OK?" the ops officer swung in his chair.

Enderson nodded. "Just the wait," he said. "Just the wait," agreed the other man.

They were both used to waiting. In the holes in the ground in Northern Ireland, in the trenches behind the Argentinian lines in the Falklands.

"Anything happening?" he asked.

"Conference. The West Germans and Jordanians are trying to decide what to do."

Part of the game, Enderson thought, unfortunate for the people on the plane, for those with relatives on the plane, but inevitable. Each side trying to wear down the other, create the doubts, the mistakes. Neither side prepared to concede, to show a weakness. No more requests for food and water, for drugs, no offers of food and water, even drugs. He wondered again what was happening on the plane.

The door into the control room opened, he saw the West Germans and the Jordanians. Something about the Germans, the specialist in the operations room at Hereford had said, something they're not telling.

The chief delegate stood in front of them. "No concessions," he said. "My government will make no concessions to the hijackers."

"What about food and water, fuel if they ask for it, drugs, sanitation?"

"We will meet their requests if and when they ask for them. Provided, of course, they show some good will."

"What about the monitoring equipment?" asked Enderson.

The delegates looked at him. "No monitoring equipment at this stage," said the Defence Minister. "Nothing that would interfere with the status quo."

7

JURGEN SCHUMPTER knew that someone was about to die. Not because he or she had done anything but because the authorities had done nothing.

"Get ground control," said Walid Haddad.

Not the Jewish family, Schumpter thought. In the cabin behind he heard the girl struggling to breathe and picked up the microphone, feeling the sweat on his hands. Not me, he thought, it can't be me, they need me to fly the plane. He remembered there was a co-pilot and felt ashamed of his fear.

"Ground, this is Lufthansa 267." It was the first contact since they had landed.

"Hello, Lufthansa 267. This is Klaus Rudegar. I am the West German negotiator."

"Tell them to bring a set of steps to the door in five minutes," said Walid Haddad. "The driver only, nobody else."

"This is Lufthansa 267." Schumpter was unsure what to say, how to phrase the request. Remembering the training films, the voice instructed him, try to tell them something about the hijackers each time you speak to them. Screw the training film, another cautioned, remember what they did to you in Rome, how they betrayed you, how they almost killed you.

"A set of steps to the door in five minutes, the driver only, no tricks please."

The listeners heard the way he spoke, picking up the desperation in the single word at the end of the message.

"Stand-by." Enderson heard the voice of the operations officer alerting the snipers, telling them something was happening. Just like the training exercises, he thought, just like the mornings and nights they had practised in the snow at Pontrilas. "Request from pilot for steps to door in five minutes. No response from negotiators yet."

Stand-by, he was thinking, stand-by, stand-by. First diversion in. Stand-by, stand-by. Second diversion in. Go, go, go, go, go.

"The Defence Minister" said the operations officer. "Urgent."

In the cockpit of the 727 Jurgen Schumpter remembered the refusals in Rome, the way the authorities had betrayed the family from Russia, the way they had betrayed him, and knew again what the hijacker was going to do. Not the Jewish family, he prayed, please not the Jewish family.

Enderson heard the tightness in the pilot's voice and recognised the contradiction in which the hijacker had placed the authorities, that they could neither agree to nor reject the request without querying it, but that even to make that query would constitute a concession in itself. "This is the negotiator, can you tell us why you need the steps?"

Jurgen Schumpter felt the pain in his stomach. Tell them why you have asked for the steps, he wanted to ask the hijacker; for God's sake give him his bloody steps, he wanted to shout at the negotiators. He could see the dilemma, see what was about to happen: if they gave him the steps, somebody would die, if they did not give him the steps somebody would die.

"Tell them again," said Walid Haddad.

Not ask them, thought the pilot, tell them. The same as in Rome.

"This is Lufthansa 267, Captain Schumpter speaking. I have been instructed to repeat the message." The listeners picked up the suggestion of coercion in the words, the strain the pilot was under.

"A set of steps to the door in five minutes. We want a set of steps to the door in five minutes." The repetition, the reference to "we", was accidental, he was not aware he had said it. The listeners heard, would hear again and again as they played and replayed the tape. No second request for tricks, they also noted, understood that the threat was greater without the words, that it was the pilot, not the hijacker, who was threatening them.

Enderson saw what the man from Heathrow was doing and wondered what would happen next.

"This is the negotiator to Lufthansa 267. The steps will be at the door in five minutes."

Jurgen Schumpter felt the relief and the new fear. No tricks, he prayed. Nobody posing as the driver. The hijacker would know, the hijacker knew everything. In the Central Command the door opened and the senior West German delegate and the Defence Minister came into the room.

"Does one of your people want to handle the steps, get a closer look at the plane?"

"No," Enderson had anticipated the suggestion. "They'd spot us a mile off, know immediately it wasn't the right driver." He saw the look of disappointment in their faces, could tell they needed some reason for optimism. "Besides," he said. "We can see all we need in the monitors."

"Good," said the delegate, the mask coming over his face again.

"One thing." The operations officer addressed the Jordanian, not taking his eyes off the monitors. "It's unlikely, but what if my men get clear targets?"

The two men looked at him then at Enderson. "Your men aren't ready." There was a hint of escapism in the voice.

The operations officer was still looking at the monitors. "The snipers have been in position thirty-five minutes. As I say, it's unlikely they will, but what if they get clear views of all the hijackers?"

"I'll tell you when the steps go in," said the Minister.

ANNA LUSKIN LOOKED at the faces of the people in the photograph. She had seen it on the news bulletin, then she had left the flat to buy a newspaper. Not just any newspaper—an afternoon edition with the photograph of the family in it.

She studied it again, the two families outside the station in Moscow, the men holding back their emotions, the women having the strength not to conceal theirs, the children confused and frightened. The coffee she had made for herself had gone cold. She remembered again the other child, eight years old, standing in the empty buildings on Ellis Island, the parents telling her of when they had stood there, then looked back at the photograph, could not stop looking at the photograph, repeating their names, Yakov Zubko and his wife Alexandra and their two children in Israel, Stanislav and Mishka, their son Anatol and their daughter Natasha, in the plane in Jordan.

Something she knew about the hijack, the thought refused to leave her, something about the fact that the Zubko family were in Jordan.

STANISLAV ZUBKO watched as the vehicle towing the steps emerged from the terminal and came towards them. He had not stopped being afraid since the first moment of the hijack, but the fear he felt now was different, partly because he did not understand what was happening, partly because he thought that the other passengers did.

The heat in the plane was crushing him, the boy in his arms was limp, like a rag doll. On her mother's lap Natasha was crying with the fear that came when she could barely breathe. He tried to comfort her and saw that the other passengers were looking at him.

THE MAIN PASSENGER DOOR, thought Enderson, why not the rear steps? He looked at the monitors and remembered where the television cameras and press photographers were positioned.

The Defence Minister was behind him, the senior West German delegate by his side, both studying the banks of monitors. "Only when they have killed a hostage," the politician said, assuming that he knew what Enderson was thinking. "Your men can only become involved when they kill a hostage."

The man from Heathrow, thought Enderson, the bloody man from Heathrow.

THE VEHICLE backed towards the plane and pushed the steps towards the door.

Jurgen Schumpter saw that the driver was a Jordanian and felt the slight shudder as the steps made contact with the body of the plane. In the cabin behind him one of the hijackers moved to cover the operation. Not the Zubkos, Schumpter thought for the last time, not the family who had left Russia only four days before. The vehicle pulled away leaving the steps in position.

"Get the doctor," Walid Haddad told the gunman in the doorway of the cockpit.

Schumpter felt the relief in his body, for himself, for the Zubkos, felt the sorrow for the doctor. He wanted to look across, ask the hijacker why he had chosen the woman, tell him she had done nothing to deserve it, that the only thing she had done was to help the child. Instead he remained in his seat, saying nothing, doing nothing, admitting that later he would be ashamed of himself, knowing only that he wanted to see his wife and children again.

In the rows of monitors Enderson watched the plane and the steps. He leaned forward and spoke to the operations officer.

"Can we get closer on five, see what's happening inside? Might be useful later."

The man nodded to the technician on his right. "Five," he said. "Tight as you can."

The technician eased the zoom control till the doorway of the aircraft occupied almost the whole screen. "I can't get any closer," he apologised, "and I can't get a better definition on anything inside."

Enderson stood back. "It was worth a try," he thanked the man.

The steps had been in position for ten minutes.

The doctor saw the gunman come out of the cockpit and felt the sorrow, the great sorrow, for the family called Zubko, the anger with the authorities that they had not agreed to the single simple request of the hijackers, that all they had done was deny the daughter her drugs and betray her parents, try to kill the pilot. The gunman was closer, she did not look at him, could not bear to look at the Jews. On the mother's lap she heard the girl fighting to breathe. Damn them all, she almost cried out loud, damn the bloody authorities who have imposed this on us, damn the people who have refused to allow us to walk free.

The gunman stopped and looked at the Zubkos then turned and motioned to her to get up.

She knew what it meant, felt the panic, the sudden loneliness. The relief for the Jews, the realisation that she was about to die in their place. The gunman was saying something, she did not hear, did not hear anything, and walked in front of him to the cockpit. It was hot, she felt faint, saw the pilot's face as he avoided her stare, looked at the hijacker sitting in the co-pilot's seat.

"The girl and the mother," began Walid Haddad.

The words were crashing through her head. She was confused, hearing what the hijacker was saying, not understanding him. She felt the second wave of shock, knew that she had accepted that it was *she* who was going to die, could not accept that, after all, it was the Jewish family, the mother and daughter, who were to be sacrificed.

She looked at the pilot then turned back to the hijacker. Walid Haddad knew she had not understood him. He repeated the words, slowly and quietly, till he saw the understanding in her face.

"I want you to go with them," he said, "take them fifty metres from the plane, then I will tell the control tower to collect them." He knew that he was making a mistake, that it would be a security risk, reminded himself that the pilot had already told the authorities how many hijackers there were, that the mother would never be able to tell them anything else.

The doctor wanted to thank him, ask him why he was doing it but could think of only one question. "What about the others, what about the father and his son?"

Walid Haddad looked at her. "The girl is sick," he said. "There is no point in prolonging her suffering. If she goes, then her mother must take her."

"But why not the father and the son?" The questioning was persistent, she saw the way he was looking at her.

"If you must," said Walid Haddad, "you can ask the father."

She turned and went back into the cabin, feeling the passengers staring at her, the eyes of the family called Zubko on her. She reached their seats and knelt beside them, taking Mishka's hand.

"The hijacker does not want Natasha to suffer any more," she said gently, caringly. "He wants her to leave the plane, he wants you to go with her."

She looked at the mother. "I am to take you fifty metres from the plane, then the hijacker will tell the authorities to come for you."

She knew what the woman would say.

"What about my husband, what about my son?"

She tried to think how many times she had told someone he or she was going to die, that he or she had only a month, a week, to live. Wondered why she had always told the truth, if the day would come when she would be asked a question of life and death and not tell the truth.

"The hijacker said I was to ask your husband."

She got up and went back to the cockpit, leaving them by themselves.

"Five minutes," she heard the hijacker's voice, "then you must take the mother and child."

Once, only once, did she look at the Jewish family. When she did the father was talking to his wife, strongly, lovingly: with one hand he was holding the shoulder of his son, with the other he played with the hair of his daughter. She knew the woman was saying she would not leave her husband, that the man was insisting.

"It is time," said Walid Haddad. "Ask the father."

The doctor left the cockpit and walked back to the Jewish family, as if they were the only passengers on the plane, as if nobody else mattered. The husband and wife were talking to each other, she knew what they were saying, knew she did not have to ask. Stanislav Zubko, kissed his wife, his daughter, remembering the morning she had been born, the first time he had held her. Mishka Zubko kissed her son, her husband, remembering the first time she had met him, the day they had married, the evening she had told him that she was bearing his child.

"I will be waiting for you, Stanislav Zubko," she said. "I will always be waiting for you."

She turned from him, knowing that if she delayed any longer she would not go, walked up the aisle, past the woman hijacker and stopped in front of Walid Haddad. The girl was by her side, the breath scarcely seeping into her lungs, the blue in her face even deeper.

"Thank you," Mishka Zubko said.

He saw the girl was frightened and confused, saw the way she was looking at him and the gun he was carrying. He took it off and gave it to the hijacker who guarded him, then bent close to the girl, knowing she wanted to ask him something but was too afraid, wondering how he knew what she wanted, how she knew he would have the answer.

"Soon," he told her, "you and your brother will play with your cousins by the well. Nikki has a ball, I'm sure he will let you play with it."

What colour is the ball, he knew the girl wanted to ask, watching the smile grow in her eyes, even though she was still too afraid to speak.

"Blue and white," he whispered to her. "Nikki's ball is blue and white."

He straightened up, took back his gun and nodded to the doctor.

She stepped out the door into the sunlight.

In the operations room they saw the single figure, not knowing who it was, then the other two, the woman the small girl.

Enderson remembered the request for the drugs in Rome, realising suddenly who they were for, seeing what the hijacker was doing. He looked at the television cameras and press photographers, sensing what was about to happen, knowing that long after the world had forgotten the hijack it would remember what would take place in the next few minutes.

"Come," said the doctor. "It is time."

IN THE OPERATIONS ROOM two of the green lights blinked to red. Tell me, one, the operations officer was saying. Gunman at top of stairs, left side. Two, said the major. Same target, the second sniper was saying. Ident clothing for later, the major was telling him. Male, long brown hair, yellow windcheater, white shirt. Assign one and two, the major was telling them.

The three figures took their first steps.

Possible second gunman inside, behind hostages. It was the voice of a third sniper.

Not sufficient for contact, he was saying, voice calm, controlled. Moving away. Lost him. The first two lights were still on red, the three figures were halfway down the steps. The sniper lights returned to green. The figures reached the bottom. The Jewish family, Enderson thought, the mother and her daughter. He wondered who the third person was, knew she would be the key, the one in control of herself, the one who would be able to tell him what was going on inside the plane.

The doctor held the mother's hand, blinking in the fierceness of the sun. "Come," she said, trying to smile, sharing the mother's concern for her daughter, her reluctance to leave her husband and son, knew the woman was about to turn, to walk back into the plane.

Slowly, Enderson urged them.

They began to walk forward, the women holding hands, the mother clutching the hand of her daughter. The heat from the concrete was shimmering up at them, almost distorting them.

Twenty metres from the steps.

Slowly, he thought, nice and slowly. He looked back at the plane, at the monitors, nothing, no more contacts, no more red lights.

Thirty metres, almost forty.

The heat beating down on them.

Fifty metres.

The doctor stopped and turned to the mother.

"Keep walking," she said. "Go towards the truck by the corner of the building. Walk slowly, don't hurry. They will be waiting for you, they will look after you. They will have medicine for Natasha."

She remembered what the hijacker had said, what he had not said, realised that he had given the decision to her, that she could walk to freedom with the mother and he would not kill her.

"Go carefully," she said. "They'll be waiting for you."

She let go of the mother's hand and kissed her, kissed the child. Mishka Zubko bent down and picked up her daughter.

On the monitors, Graham Enderson saw the mother and child moving forward, the other woman standing still, looking at them. On the plane Stanislav Zubko took the photographs from his pocket and held his son tight.

"Once upon a time," he began, "there were two families who lived in a far-off land."

The child was heavy in her arms. A hundred metres, Mishka Zubko she told herself, and Natasha will be free. The heat was blazing down on her. She felt tired, dizzy, felt the lack of food and water, began walking towards the corner, her head beginning to swim. Slowly, the doctor had told her to walk slowly. Natasha was heavy in her arms. They are waiting for you, Mishka Zubko, she reminded herself, they have medicine for Natasha. She concentrated on the lorry at the corner of the building, moving, shimmering in the heat, the sweat running down her face, into her eyes. Seventy steps, Mishka Zubko, she told herself, seventy steps and Natasha will be safe. She knew they were watching, knew they were all watching. Don't look round, Mishka Zubko, she was speaking aloud, don't look back. Fifty steps, still so far away. The child heavy in her arms, so heavy in her arms she could hardly bear the pain. Don't look for your husband, Mishka Zubko, don't look for your son. The sweat was stinging her eyes, she could hardly see. Keep walking, Mishka Zubko, don't think of anything other than your daughter. The clothes were hot and heavy round her, she thought of the single suitcase they had brought with them, the moment they had crossed the border into the West. Don't think of your husband, Mishka Zubko, don't even think of your son. Thirty steps. Mishka Zubko, only thirty steps now.

On the runway the doctor watched her, willing her on. In the cockpit of the 727 Jurgen Schumpter watched her, remembering again the photograph at Dachau. Don't look back, Mishka Zubko, he urged her, they all urged her, for God's sake, don't look back.

The child was so heavy in her arms. She was crying, could not see anything, did not know how much further she had to go. Then she was feeling the coolness of the shadows, the arms around her, supporting her, taking Natasha from her.

The doctor saw her disappear behind the lorry and knew she was safe, was unsure suddenly what she herself should do. She saw the television cameras looking at her, how close they were, saw the lorry on the corner, even closer.

Enderson watched her, knowing the choice she faced. His only contact, he thought, the only person who could tell him what was happening on the plane. He knew what she was about to do, cursed her for it, admired her for it. She began to turn, hesitating, then took her first steps back to the plane. The man from Heathrow, he thought, the bloody man from Heathrow.

A hundred metres, almost a hundred and fifty. She was closer to the buildings than to the plane, had not realised how far she had come with the mother. She was walking slowly, automatically, knowing she could still turn back, go to the corner, find safety; understanding why she would not, seeing why the father had stayed, why he had kept his son with him. She wondered how the hijacker had known, what the hijacker had said as he bent over Natasha in the seconds before they had left the plane. She reached the steps.

On the monitors Enderson saw her pause, hands on the rail. The television cameras were on her. He knew what the pictures would do, what the pictures of the mother carrying her child to safety would do, thought for a moment of the face of the girl on her deathbed in Germany.

The door of the operations room opened; the delegates came in and stood looking at the monitors, watching as the figure climbed up the steps to the plane.

"Food and water," said the West German, "when they ask I think we can give it to them."

"They won't," Enderson said.

The delegate looked at him. "Why not?" he asked disparagingly.

Enderson held up his hand, concentrating on the monitors as the doctor reached the top of the steps and began to go inside the plane, seeing the two figures coming towards her, the snipers' lights flashing to red. He knew they were hijackers, was aware not only of the way they were reaching for the woman but the way she was reaching for them. The lights turned to green.

He stood back and looked at the delegate. "He won't ask for food or water, or anything else," he began, "because if he did, it would mean that the two passengers had been released as part of the negotiations, that you were giving him something in return."

"But the hijackers need food and water."

"He needs food and water," Enderson agreed, "but what he has just done is worth more than anything you could ever give him." He realised that the others were talking about the hijackers as a whole, that he was only talking about the man from Heathrow. "He has you exactly where he wants you," he pressed the point, knowing they did not want to hear it. "Can you imagine the impact in West Germany when those pictures are shown?" Not just West Germany, they did not want to admit, knew that the single unending image of the woman carrying her child to freedom had done more for the hijackers' cause than the years of fighting and killing which had preceded it.

Enderson wondered, for the briefest of moments, whether there was another reason, was certain there could not be. The delegate was beginning to protest, to exert his authority. Enderson knew he had already said too much and should stay silent.

"Think back to Rome," he confronted the man. "The moment he asked for the drugs, the moment you refused. Now he has given the girl her life and asked for nothing in return." He knew he was angry. "You may as well give in now."

"Why?"

"Because he's won. No matter what you do, no matter how it ends, he's won."

"What if he kills someone?" There was a desperation in the question.

"He won't."

"Why not?"

Enderson knew the man from Heathrow never intended to. He looked at the politician. "He doesn't have to any more, does he?"

The doctor stepped out of the heat and into the plane. A stewardess stepped forward and handed her one of the few remaining cans of mineral water. She took it, feeling her resolve dissipate, seeing the way both the hijackers and the passengers were looking at her, standing up, clapping.

The sound drifted across the runway and was picked up by the monitors, by the television and radio crews.

The man from Heathrow, Enderson thought again, the bloody man from Heathrow.

8

MICHAEL JOSEPH STEPHENSON left his office in the FBI building on Federal Plaza at six fifteen and was home by seven thirty; Daniel Furtado left his unit at six twenty and was home by seven forty-five; the last thing each did before they left their respective offices, the first thing each did when they reached their respective homes, was to check on the Lufthansa hijack. Anna Luskin did not need to check, she had been watching the news channel since mid-afternoon, the re-play after re-play of the moment in the hijack when the figures had appeared at the top of the steps, the long, seemingly unending walk to freedom, the mother bearing her daughter in her arms. The child, the report said, for whom the hijackers had asked for drugs in Rome; the request, it added, that the authorities had refused.

She sat in front of the set waiting for the moment when the three figures stopped, the moment the mother picked up her child and walked on alone, forgetting how long she had been sitting there, how many times she had watched it. The woman was moving forward, she could see how tired she was, felt how heavy the child was in her arms, saw she was weakening. Keep walking, Mishka Zubko, she told her, for God's sake keep walking. She knew the woman wanted to look back, at the plane, at her husband and son, knew that if she did, if she hesitated even once, she would turn back. Keep walking, Mishka Zubko, she urged her, keep walking for Natasha, keep walking for Anatol. She was remembering the children waiting with their parents in the long lines on Ellis Island, the spirits of the children who had suffered so terribly to come to America. Keep walking, Mishka Zubko, she was urging the woman, keep walking so that one day you can tell your daughter about her father and her brother, tell her how brave they were, how they were men among men. She was seeing the ghosts of the children on Ellis Island again, the haunting eyes of those who had travelled across the world and who had been turned away from the land of freedom. Keep walking, Mishka Zubko, for God's sake keep walking. The blood was on her hands where her nails were digging into her palms. She could feel the heat, the sweat trickling down her face, stinging her eyes, blinding her. Almost there, Mishka Zubko, she told her, almost to safety. Don't look back, Mishka Zubko, even now, even so close, whatever you do don't look back. She saw the hands coming out, helping the woman, taking the child from her, knew at last that she was safe. Saw the next picture, the woman who had brought them across the runway, turning, going back to the plane, the hands coming out to greet her. Heard the sound of the clapping and the cheering as the woman went inside.

She thought about the demand the hijackers had made. It was not much, she thought, hardly anything at all. She herself supported the notion that the presence of nuclear missiles in Europe had prevented the world destroying itself in war, believed, when she thought about it, in the notion of deterrent, worried about the Russians. It was not much though, she thought again about the demand, hardly anything. Not the release of bombers and terrorists, of people who had killed and maimed, just the life of a girl who had protested about dying in a nuclear holocaust.

She knew for certain that she knew something about the hijack, could not imagine what it was or why she should know it.

9

THE SHADOW CREPT ALONG the wing, away from the body of the plane. Stanislav Zubko watched, as he had watched the sun spread along the wing so many hours before. He thought of what Mishka had done, the courage it had taken, aware that hers had been the difficult decision, his the easiest. He remembered how he had wanted to leave the plane with her, give his son to her so that Anatol might also be saved, remembered how he knew he could not, how he had understood that there was one thing more precious even than life itself, that if he had left the plane, even if he had allowed his son to leave the plane, he would have given it to the hijacker. More than that, much more than that, the world would have seen him give in, the world would have seen his people give in to their enemies. And the one thing his people had never done, the one thing his people could never do, was to give in to their enemies. He wanted to hold his son to him and tell him how much he loved him, but did not dare wake him.

10

IN HIS THIRD FLOOR OFFICE overlooking Horse Guards Parade John Kenshaw-Taylor sat back and waited for the news bulletins; he had seen the tapes already, sent to him by the BBC and ITN, studied the pictures of the mother as she carried her child to freedom.

The release had been totally unexpected. And no demands, no requests for food or water, no requests for the toilets to be emptied. For the first time he wondered what was going on in-side the plane, could not understand the cheering he had heard, the cheering they had all heard, as the woman who had es-corted the mother and child to safety went back inside.

The bulletin was running the picture, the woman was pick-ing up the child, beginning to walk; he reflected again on the impact the one sequence was producing. An hour before he had talked to the West German Foreign Minister, just before the man went into his third crisis meeting that day, and been in-formed of the pressure in the country; half an hour ago he had received the report he had commissioned on the international reaction to the incident. The mother's walk, it said, had lasted little more than thirty seconds, not quite a minute, but it had totally changed the world's interest in and perception of the hijack. Not just of the hijack but of the Palestinian terrorist who had given the little Jewish girl from Russia her life and asked for nothing in return.

He rose, crossed the room, and poured himself a drink. Thank God for the Jewish family, he thought, thank God for the fate which had put them on the hijacked plane. The eve-ning sun was coming through the window, he sipped the drink and told himself to be careful, not to become too optimistic. He could not help thinking, however, that it was all going rather well.

THE STREET OUTSIDE was dusty and quiet. At this time of day it was always dusty and quiet.

Yakov Zubko sat with his wife and children in the small room of their neighbour's house, staring at the television picture. Mishka was bending down, picking Natasha up, beginning to walk with her. He saw how she was struggling under the weight, felt the sweat stinging her eyes, watched as she reached the corner, wondered about his brother Stanislav and his son Ana-tol, if they also had been given the chance of freedom, knew what Stanislav would have done if he had been offered. Stan-islav, he thought, who had taught him how to play the re-corder, who had rehearsed his Bar Mitzvah with him. He knew that Natasha had gone because she was so ill, that Mishka had had no option but to take her. If the girl had been well the family would have stayed together, on the plane, even if they had been offered freedom. Of that he was certain.

He rose, partly because the item was over, partly because he did not want the neighbours to see him weep and went outside. In the square down the road a couple were sitting on the wall of the well.

"Yakov Zubko?" He did not recognise the man. "Yes," he said, "I am Yakov Zubko."

"We are proud of what Stanislav and Anatol did today," the man said simply. "We are proud of what Mishka and Natasha did."

Yakov Zubko turned down the street, past the orange grove and the field, and climbed to the top of the hill called Bethesda. The sun was pulling down in the west. He thought of the table in the kitchen, the extra places still laid, the beds crammed into the two rooms upstairs. Behind him his wife and children came up the hill and sat beside him, not speaking.

Only when it was dark did the family Zubko cease their vigil and return to their house.

11

THE BED WAS HARD. She sat on the edge, pulling the handkerchief through her fingers, hearing the sounds of their questions, not hearing the words, not hearing the sentences. One of them was offering her tea, another coffee. She stared ahead, knowing that she had had to leave the plane, that she should have stayed, that Stanislav had done the right thing. How many hijackers on the plane, they were asking her again, what sort of guns do they have, where do they stand? The noise was a blur, all she could hear was the last thing Stanislav Zubko had said to her, the last thing she had said to him, to her son. They were offering her a cold drink, suggesting she take a bath.

It was so long since the doctor had been called to the cockpit, so long since the woman had come back to them. She had known then that they had not long to live, had known then that they had been singled out to die.

They were asking her again: how many, what guns, where do they stand, do they sleep? The same words, the same questions, time after time, as if it was an interrogation. As if she was the hijacker. How many are there, what guns do they have, what do they do all the time? She was stepping out of the plane again into the sun, into the sudden glare and heat. How many hijackers, how many guns? She was down the steps, walking across the tarmac, leaving the doctor behind. Natasha heavy in her arms. Keep walking, Mishka Zubko, keep walking. The sweat was stinging her eyes, blinding her. How many hijackers, what are they like? She wanted to look back, how she wanted to look back, to be back on the plane with Stanislav and Anatol. Do they ever sleep, how do they rest, do they take drugs? Keep walking, Mishka Zubko, keep walking for your child, for the sacrifice your husband and son have just made. How many hijackers, men or women, what sort of guns? The child was even heavier in her arms, she could no longer see through the tears. Keep walking, Miska Zubko, keep walking so that Natasha can live, so that one day she will know what a great man her father was, what a noble man her brother.

It was so long since the hands had come out for her, taking Natasha from her, so long since they had brought her to the hotel, let her into the bedroom, given her back her daughter. So long since they began to ask her the questions, so long since she had stopped hearing them.

They were getting up, leaving her alone.

Mishka Zubko watched the door shut and held her daughter to her.

12

ALMOST DARK ENOUGH, thought Enderson, almost dark enough to approach the plane, to hide beneath its body and attach the sensors, almost dark enough to be able to hear what was happening inside.

Almost dark enough, thought Jurgen Schumpter, almost dark enough to see the first star. The lights in the building to their left were coming on, in the east the sky was purple, turning black.

"Why?" he suddenly asked the question that had been troubling him since mid afternoon. "Why did you release them?"

Walid Haddad knew there was more to the question than the pilot dared ask. "Why release the innocents, is that what you

mean, why allow them their lives when it is always the innocents who are the victims?''

''Yes,'' said Schumpter. ''Why not let them die as the innocents always die?''

Walid Haddad remembered the photographs: the photograph Yakov Zubko had shown him in the house at the top of
the street in Esh Shikara, the photograph Abu Nabil kept on the
desk of his solitary flat in Damascus, the photograph of the
man tending the boy in Belfast. He wondered if the man in the
photograph would have understood, whether the man in the
photograph would work it out. ''Four hours,'' he said, not re-
plying. ''We will have food and water in four hours.''

Schumpter realised that the conversation was ended, that the
hijack was about to enter a new phase. ''You're going to ask
them?'' he suggested, trying to keep the hope out of his voice.

''No,'' said Walid Haddad. ''I'm not going to ask them.''

''But they won't give us anything unless you ask.''

''No.''

A second star had appeared.

''So how do we get the food and water?''

Walid Haddad looked at him. ''You took on twenty-four
tons of fuel in Rome.'' It all seemed so long ago, thought Jurgen Schumpter. ''Yes,'' he said, ''we took on twenty-four tons
in Rome.''

''So you should have thirteen tons left.''

The hijacker knew everything, the pilot thought, absolutely
everything. He checked the gauge, six and a half tons in the
starboard tank, six and a half in the port. ''Yes.''

''How far will that get us?''

They worked well as a team, Schumpter tried to stop himself thinking, doing the calculation. ''Seventeen hundred miles,
almost eighteen hundred.''

''Good,'' said Walid Haddad.

''How far are we going?''

''About as far as the fuel will take us.''

Jurgen Schumpter thought of the passengers, of the woman
and children, the boy sitting on his father's lap. ''And they will
give us food and water?''

''They will give us anything I ask for.''

''When?''

Walid Haddad looked out the window; almost dark enough
for the man in the photograph to be able to approach the plane,

he thought. Almost dark enough for him to attach the sensors.

"Five minutes," he said. "Tell control we are leaving in five minutes."

THE TELEX updating London reached John Kenshaw-Taylor's office six minutes after Jurgen Schumpter had informed ground control that he was taking off. Within four minutes Kenshaw-Taylor had spoken personally to the Jordanian ambassador, reaffirming his offer of assistance to the Amman government, and repeated the same message to the West German Foreign Minister in Bonn. He received acceptance from each fourteen minutes after Lufthansa 267 had trundled down the runway of the Queen Alia International Airport and lifted into a deepening sky.

GRAHAM ENDERSON stood on the runway for a full three minutes after the lights of the 727 had disappeared and the sound of its engines was lost in the sounds of the night, thinking of the man from Heathrow, of the mother carrying her child to freedom, checking that his lines of approach had been correct, noting the light, seeing that it would have been dark enough. Then he turned and went back to the airport buildings.

The night air was cool and refreshing, in the area below the operations room the sniper teams were unloading their equipment, in the room itself the technicians were dismantling the banks of monitors.

"How much fuel did they take on in Rome?" Enderson asked the Lufthansa engineer who accompanied the negotiating team.

"Twenty-four tons."

"Given the flight between Rome and Amman, how much do they have left?"

The engineer wondered why Enderson was interested and worked it out. "With what was left from the refuelling before Rome, about thirteen tons."

"How far can they get with that?"

The engineer already knew. "Seventeen hundred miles, almost eighteen."

Enderson crossed to the map table at the side of the room and drew a radius of eighteen hundred miles from Amman.

"They're still on the same course?" he asked the air traffic controller.

"The last indication was that they were still on the same course."

Enderson pencilled the line on the map, noting the point where it cut the arc, the location at which the Boeing would run out of fuel. There were three countries in the area covered, by adjusting the flight path slightly he was able to add another two. He looked at the map and knew where the man from Heathrow was going, why he was going there. Tight, he thought, it would be very tight.

"Could they make it to Addis?"

He saw one of the West Germans look at him, disbelief in his face. The Lufthansa engineer was preoccupied with his calculations.

"Impossible," said the delegate. "It's impossible he should go there, there's absolutely no reason."

"There's every reason," suggested Enderson.

"Tell me."

"It's the one place he won't be attacked if he lands, the one place he's guaranteed they won't storm the plane for local glory. It's also the one place he's guaranteed food and water and whatever else he wants."

"Why?" asked the politician.

Enderson looked at him. "If you check with your intelligence people," he said calmly, "You'll find that a Soviet military mission is due to land in Addis at eight o'clock the morning after next." It was one of the many details the intelligence officer at Hereford had collated in the hours after the Vienna hijack, one of the factors the anti-terrorist teams had taken into consideration when they analysed which airports would be open to the plane and which closed. "The Ethiopians will do anything to get the plane out before the Russians arrive."

"How do you know about the Soviet mission?"

More to the point, thought Enderson, how did the man from Heathrow know?

There was a knock on the door, one of the signallers came in. "Message from home, boss," he said, handing him a sheet of paper.

The Lufthansa engineer had finished his calculations. "They might do it," he began, the hesitation in his voice, "but it would be very close."

"How close? What if they don't manage it, don't get permission to land?" It had happened before, they all knew, the tankers blocking the runways, the lights switched off, the air traffic controllers under orders not to give flight information.

"They will have it." The engineer looked at them. "According to my calculations, their fuel should run out on their first approach."

The delegate turned his attention back to Enderson. "And where will they go after they leave Addis the morning after next?" There was a hint of sarcasm in his voice.

Enderson looked at the instructions on the sheet of paper he had just been handed, the order for his units to remain in Jordan.

"Back here," he said simply.

Fifteen minutes later the plane carrying the West German negotiating team and the airline representatives, as well as the two members of the GSG-9 assault group left Jordan in pursuit of Lufthansa 267. Seven minutes later air traffic control was notified that an aircraft carrying seven units of GSG-9 had left Frankfurt and would be overflying the Mediterranean in forty minutes.

The controller took the message and looked at Enderson. "They don't believe you," he said.

"No," said Enderson, "they don't."

JANE ENDERSON saw the news flash at twenty minutes to twelve. Four times that evening she had watched the pictures from Jordan, four times she had willed Mishka Zubko to keep walking, four times she had stared with admiration and disbelief as the woman she did not know was a doctor turned back to the plane. All evening she had wondered what was happening, waiting for the news that the SAS had been sent to Jordan. All evening it had remained unreported.

She made a hot chocolate and went up the stairs. On the right, at the top, she could hear the children breathing. She opened their doors and looked inside wondering, not for the first time that evening, what the Jewish mother must now be thinking, wondering, not for the last time that night, where Grah was, what he was doing, whether he would come home again.

The door of the wardrobe at the foot of the bed was open. She looked inside, involuntarily, almost expecting to see the hold-all on the floor, remembering the news flash, the information that Lufthansa 267 had left Jordan and was flying south. Airports in the Middle East had been sealed off, the presenter had said, runways packed with fuel trucks and fire engines to prevent it landing. There were reports that the plane was running out of fuel.

She got into bed. At least, she thought, it had left Jordan, at least there was no longer a reason for Grah to be involved. She ignored the drink and switched off the light. No poem, she prayed, no girl looking at her from across the valleys, no dream taking her husband down into hell.

13

SHE HEARD THE NOISE and felt the slight shudder in the walls, knowing what it was without needing to get up, imagining the lights as the plane vanished into the halo of dark which was settling above the desert. She held the girl close to her, trying to shield herself from the guilt, hearing the second noise as the West German negotiators turned south.

Then, and only then, was Mishka Zubko sure that her husband and son had gone. Then, and only then, did she know for certain that she would never see them again.

The room was cold, she was shivering, shaking; she ignored it, felt too hot, wanted to walk, stay still, did not know what to do, did not know what she wanted to do, knew only where she wanted to be. On the plane with her family, with all her family. *"Beshanah Habaah b'Yerushalaim,"* they had said. "Next year in Jerusalem." For the first time she wondered what it would be like there without her husband.

The knock on the door was gentle, as if the person at the door did not want to intrude into her secrets, as if the person knew she wanted someone to talk to, someone to tell. Not the interrogators, something inside her said, not the men who only wanted to know about the plane, someone who wanted to know what she needed to tell them. The door opened and a man came in. She did not know who he was, only that he was not one of those who had questioned her earlier.

Enderson saw her looking at him, the child looking at him. He pushed the door shut with his foot, put the three bottles of Coca-Cola on the table at the side of the bed, and sat down in the chair on the left of the woman, away from the girl.

Nothing, she knew, she had said nothing. As if, the psychologist had said, she had a block; as if she considered herself the guilty party, as if she blamed herself for deserting her husband and son. More, as if she was not only protecting herself, as if she was protecting someone else, as if she did not know she was protecting them.

The Stockholm syndrome, the psychologist had suggested, hostage identification with the hijackers, transfer of loyalty from the authorities, the people who were trying to save them, to the hijackers.

Enderson knew the theory, had heard it developing in the tapes from Rome, the brief exchanges in Amman, the change in the voice and the attitude of the pilot as the hijack progressed, had seen it each time the authorities had made a mistake. More than that, he thought, much more than that, remembered the moment the doctor had stepped back into the aircraft, the cheering that had drifted across the concrete of the airport.

He reached forward, picked up the bottle closest to him, took one sip through the straw, and put it back on the table. The woman had hardly noticed him, the child was sucking her thumb, staring at her mother. He looked at her and smiled, then looked at Mishka.

"Children," he said, shaking his head.

It was the last thing in the world she expected, the last way in the world she expected it to be said. A laugh in the voice, not an ordinary laugh, the laugh of a parent. She knew what the man meant, understood that he was a father, that his son and daughter sucked their thumbs as Anatol and Natasha sucked theirs. She smiled, the smallest of smiles, before she had even been aware she had reacted. Then she tried to shut herself off again, to seal herself into her guilt.

"Two," the stranger said, not needing to hear her question. "I have two children. A boy aged nine, a girl aged seven." He was not a stranger, she felt already, he never had been a stranger. She saw him feeling in his pocket, searching for something and watched as he pulled out a sweet, wrapped in paper, and put it on the table. Not a stranger, a parent like herself, a father like Stanislav.

The barrier almost clanged shut again.

"How is she now?" He was smiling at the girl, reaching out, playing with her hair as a father plays with the hair of his own daughter, the girl looking at him.

"Better," Mishka heard herself say. "Much better."

It was the first thing she had said since she had said goodbye to her husband and son five hours before. She wondered what he would say next, remembered how the others had known everything about her.

"What's her name?" asked Enderson.

It was like a conversation in the park between parents, she did not even realise they were speaking Russian.

"Natasha," she said, turning, looking at her daughter, smiling at her. "She's named after her great grandmother. Anatol is named after his grandfather."

They both heard her words, knew she had broken the barrier, named the son she had left on the plane. He wondered whether she would close in on herself again, knew he had to talk to her, keep her talking to him, remembered the language classes, slipping easily into the Russian, remembering the last time he had spoken it. Not like the last time, he thought, not at all like the last time.

"She's a good girl," he said, smiling, nodding.

"They've both been good," said Mishka.

He knew what he had to say, what she needed to hear.

"You have no reason to feel guilty, Mishka Zubko," he said. "No reason at all."

She heard the words, did not want to be reminded of what she felt, heard the way he said them. It was what her husband would have said, the way her husband would have said it. She looked at the man for the first time.

"What your husband did was right," Enderson told her. "What you did was also right." He was talking to her as her father would have talked to her, as her brother-in-law would have talked to her. "Sometimes the hardest decisions we have to make are to do with our families and children." She heard the voice of Stanislav Zubko, the voice of Yakov Zubko. "Your husband was a very brave man to stay on the plane. You were a very brave woman to leave it." She was staring at him, listening to him.

"Sometimes," he said, "the act which seems the least brave is the bravest of all."

He sat back and allowed her time to herself. She wanted to tell him, talk to him but did not know what to say or where to begin.

"How long did you wait?" he asked at last. It was the question she did not expect, the question she wanted to hear, wanted to answer. The point at which she would start her absolution.

"Six years," she began, going back, remembering. "We first applied in 1979."

He listened to her, knowing she would tell him in her own time, knowing she would tell him everything.

She told him about Russia, about the flat at the top of the stairs, the flat like that of Yakov Zubko and his family, how they had seen Yakov and Alexandra and the children off the day they had left, how they had continued to wait, told him of the photograph that had been taken that day, the photograph they had sent to Israel via the American family from Norfolk.

He listened to her, not interrupting, remembered later, much later, the first time she stopped and took a sip from the bottle in front of her. Remembered later, much later, the way she unwrapped the paper and gave the sweet to her daughter. Four things he asked her in that time, only four things.

"When did you last eat, Mishka Zubko?" he asked.

"Yesterday," she told him. "Yesterday after the pilot."

He wanted to ask her what she meant, knew he could not, knew she would tell him when she was ready.

"What would you like, Mishka Zubko?" he asked. "Some sandwiches perhaps, some chicken sandwiches?"

"Yes," she said. "Some chicken sandwiches."

What about the pilot, he wanted to know, what the hell was going on inside the plane?

"And what do you want to drink, some tea, some coffee?"

Coffee, she said, she would like some coffee.

"What about Natasha?" he asked, finding another sweet in his pocket, unwrapping it for her, giving it to her.

The girl understood, pushed the empty bottle towards him, looked at him. "Another Coca-Cola?" he asked. The girl nodded, the mother smiling.

He phoned for the sandwiches and drinks.

What about the pilot, he wanted to know, what about the hijackers?

She told him about the day the letter arrived, the insignia of the OVIR office in the top left corner, the way she had been afraid to open it, their feelings when they knew they were going home.

The sandwiches and drinks arrived.

A secret, her subconscious began to realise, a secret she must not tell him. She knew she could tell the rest, wanted to tell him the rest, to tell him everything. Except the secret. Slowly, effortlessly, so that she did not know, her subconscious pulled the barrier round the secret, concealing it, creating a gap between it and the rest of her knowledge, prising the gap wider, till it was so wide she had never known the secret existed in the first place.

She told him about the days before the drive to the station in Moscow, the constant fear that the authorities would change their minds and not release them, would release only some of them, would make the others stay.

Closer, he thought, she was getting closer.

She told him of the evening they boarded the train, the moment they passed into the West, the woman from the Jewish Agency stepping forward to greet them, the telephone call to Yakov Zubko in Beita, the way he had arranged to meet them at Ben Gurion. The clouds were beginning to gather, they both knew it, felt her resolve weakening.

Don't stop now, Mishka Zubko, he urged her as the world had urged her on the runway that afternoon, whatever you do, however much you are hurt, don't stop now. For the sake of your husband, your son, for the sake of everyone on the plane.

She told him of the wait at Vienna airport, the change of flights.

The moment of the hijack.

The landing at Rome.

The way little Natasha had struggled to breathe, the way the doctor helped her, the way the hijacker had asked for drugs for her, the way the authorities had refused.

It was tumbling out fast, almost too fast; he let her pour the coffee and offer him a sandwich.

The way the hijacker knew the authorities had been told there were four gunmen on the plane.

The way the authorities had betrayed them, the way they had told the hijacker there was a Jewish family on board, the way the authorities had condemned them to death.

The moment the hijacker had made the pilot kneel in front of the passengers and explain what he had done, explain how the authorities had betrayed him. The way they had celebrated with the last food and drink after the hijacker had called the pilot a brave man, and spared his life.

Something she was not going to tell him, he thought, something she herself was not aware she knew.

The moment the doctor had been summoned to the cockpit, the moment they thought they were going to die, her last moments with her husband and son, the long walk away from them.

He offered her more sandwiches and coffee and made her eat, gently but firmly, taking her back to the beginning, edging her closer to the details he needed to know, guiding her through her memories till she began to tell him. The details of the hijackers, the weapons, how they had got them, where they stood, what they did, what they wore, what they looked like.

Sometimes she drifted back, to her husband and son, to the photograph that had been taken at the station in Moscow, how Stanislav had told the children the story of the two families from a far-off land who would live together in the village called Beita, how Stanislav had told the story so many times, she laughed with the memory, the tears beginning to fill her eyes, that everyone on the plane knew it by heart, even the hijacker.

It was strange, he thought, how she always referred to the hijacker, to the one man. Not the three men and one woman. Only the one.

She had almost finished. He knew he had enough, more than he could ever have expected. Everything except the one thing she was not aware she knew. He did not know how to draw it from her, sensing that she had finished talking for the night, and rose to leave.

"Will you come back in the morning?" she asked.

"Yes," he said, "I'll come back in the morning." He told them both to sleep, and kissed Natasha good night, smiling one more time at Mishka.

Her subconscious knew the secret was safe, that it had protected it well.

He was crossing the room. Tomorrow, he was thinking, perhaps she would know tomorrow, perhaps she would tell him then.

He heard the voice of the girl.

The first words the girl had spoken since she had told her father she needed to go to the toilet three days before.

He turned and saw the shock on the woman's face, realising what it was that she had not been able to tell him, confirmed that she was protecting somebody. He looked at the girl then back at the mother.

"What did Natasha say?" he asked gently.

The mother looked at him, knowing that she could not tell him, that she was going to tell him anyway, and began the trespass into her soul.

"She said he knows Yakov Zubko."

"Who knows Yakov Zubko?"

She was remembering: the way her husband had shown the children the photograph, the way he had told them the story of Yakov Zubko and his family in the village called Beita, the way they played in the square round the well.

She remembered what her husband had said, what he had not said, remembered the moment she stood in front of the hijacker, the moment before she stepped into the sunlight, the moment the hijacker had taken off his gun and comforted her daughter.

"Soon," Walid Haddad had said to her, "you and your brother will play with your cousins by the well. Nikki has a ball, I'm sure he will let you play with it."

What colour is the ball, he had known the girl wanted to ask, had known she was still too afraid to speak.

"Blue and white," he had whispered to her. "Nikki's ball is blue and white."

Two things, Mishka Zubko remembered, breaking through the last wall of her subconscious, two things that the children knew after the telephone calls to Yakov Zubko when they were in Vienna, two things so small, so insignificant, that Stanislav had omitted them when he had told the story on the plane.

That the son of Yakov Zubko had a ball and that the colour of that ball was blue and white.

"Who knows Yakov Zubko?" he asked again.

She looked at him and told him the secret.

"The hijacker," she said. "The hijacker knows Yakov Zubko."

CHAPTER THREE

1

THE MORNING WAS CLEAR, the early mist had lifted off the Dead Sea, the day had not grown old enough for the heat haze to rise from the lowlands. Yakov Zubko sat on the rock and thought about his brother. Yesterday he had seemed so close, not so many miles away; in a strange way it had been a comfort that Stanislav and his family were at least near to home, now he was far away again. He had heard it on the radio the night before, had waited all night in the chair in the kitchen till the first news bulletin of the day, the confirmation that the plane had landed in Addis. A long way, he had thought, a very long way, across the deserts of Egypt, into the sands of Africa.

So many years they had waited, he also thought, now they were divided, now his brother and the son of his brother were going to die.

He heard the footsteps behind him, thought it would be Alexandra and the children and turned to welcome them.

The man sat down. "Yakov Zubko?" he asked.

Yakov Zubko remembered the other stranger who had come to the village. "Yes," he said, "I am Yakov Zubko."

They sat without talking, from the east came the sound of oxen.

"Mishka and the child are well," the newcomer said at last. "They will soon be home."

"You have seen them?" Yakov Zubko did not turn his head. It came as no surprise that the man brought news of the hijack.

"Last night," said Graham Enderson.

The oxen had reached the *wadi* at the foot of the hill. Yakov Zubko watched them. "Why have you come?" he asked.

"I have come about the stranger." He wondered if Yakov Zubko would know what he meant, what he was talking about. Below them the oxen had stopped to drink. He waited for a response, wondered how he could explain himself.

"You have come about the stranger and my son."

The words took Enderson off guard. "Yes," he said, "I have come about the stranger and your son."

It was almost, he thought, as if the man who had brought his family out of Russia had been waiting for him, almost as if he had known he was coming.

"How will it help my brother and his son?"

Enderson knew he had to tell Yakov Zubko the truth.

"Because he is the man holding your brother and his son hostage."

The oxen had finished drinking and were moving on.

"Does he know?"

It was as if Yakov Zubko was not surprised.

"He didn't when he hijacked the plane, he does now."

"What do you mean?"

"He ordered Mishka to take Natasha from the plane, he gave your brother and his son the chance to go with them."

Yakov Zubko was nodding. He was no longer on the hill called Bethesda, he was back in the factory, switching off the machine, picking up his coat. Walking home, the sun on his back. Hearing the scream, the long unending terrible scream from Alexandra's soul. He was running, dropping his coat, hearing the thud, knowing it was over, knowing the dream had ended. He was at the top of the hill, seeing his wife, seeing that she was holding their son to him, seeing that he was alive and well. There's the man, the neighbours were saying, there's the man you have to thank.

"The man saved my son's life," he explained, still nodding his head. "I also saved his."

The first haze of the day was beginning to rise from the lowland to the east.

The man from Heathrow, Enderson thought, the bloody man from Heathrow.

"Tell me about him," he said.

JOHN KENSHAW-TAYLOR received his first briefing at seven. By seven thirty he had been driven to Downing Street and was updating the Prime Minister over toast and coffee. He informed her that the Boeing 727 had been given food and water. They were about to begin negotiations on fuel, as well as emptying the toilets.

"Will they give in to him?" The Prime Minister had a busy schedule, she kept her questions sharp and to the point.

"Yes," he said. "They want the aircraft to leave and the only way they can do that is to give them fuel."

"Why didn't the hijackers ask for these things in Jordan?"

"I'm not sure. Politics probably. He didn't want the Jordanians to refuse him."

"Will it end in Addis?"

Jordan, he had said as they stood by the cars in New York, then he could get involved, then he could bring in the SAS.

"Definitely not. Addis is part of the Soviet sphere of influence, it would be against the Soviets' interests to be seen to be involved so directly with a hijack."

"So what do you think will happen?"

Kenshaw-Taylor was enjoying the briefing. He had always got on well with the Prime Minister.

"The Ethiopians will do a deal. They will give the hijackers what they want in terms of food and fuel, as long as the plane is out of Addis by seven o'clock tomorrow morning." He knew the Prime Minister would ask why. "A Russian military delegation is due to arrive at eight, they will want the plane well gone by then."

"And where will it go from there?"

Jordan, Saeed Khaled had agreed in New York, then Kenshaw-Taylor could become involved, then he could bring in the SAS.

"Jordan," he said decisively, "nobody else will allow them to land."

"And the Jordanians are waiting for them?"

He changed the reference slightly. "The Jordanians will let them land."

The Prime Minister took his point. "And our people are still there?"

"Yes, our people are still there."

They both knew the Prime Minister's car was waiting.

"When will it end?"

"Tomorrow," he said. "Tomorrow when the plane is back in Jordan."

YAKOV ZUBKO left the hill and walked back to the house. He did not dare look at the field at the bottom or at the orange grove on the side of the road. In the square round the well a group of boys were playing. He remembered the morning again, the sound of the body against the jeep, then walked up the street and into the house, thinking of the way he had broken bread with the stranger, the way the man had laughed and joked with his son. The kitchen was quiet, he went up the stairs and stood in his son's bedroom, looking at the bed in the corner, seeing the Palestinian there, hearing the words of the Palestinian.

He felt unclean, wished he had never been born, that they had never set him free, wished they had never let him leave Russia.

2

THE MORNING in New York was warm. Michael Joseph Stephenson left home early and was in his office in Federal Plaza by seven. Daniel Furtado was on duty forty-five minutes before, at six fifteen. By the time Stephenson had poured his first coffee of the morning Furtado was locked into an eight-hour weapons exercise. The last thing both men had checked before they left their homes that morning, the first thing both had checked when they had arrived at their places of work, was the Lufthansa hijack.

Anna Luskin woke at seven. She had hardly slept, not because she had been otherwise employed until four, not even because she could not shake off the memory of the woman with the child in her arms, but because, at twelve thirty that morning, as she stepped from the cab outside her client's hotel, she had remembered what it was that she knew about the hijacking of Lufthansa 267.

She percolated some coffee, made herself fresh orange juice, and wondered what she should do. For the past six hours and thirty minutes she had not stopped wondering what she should do.

At five minutes past eight Michael Joseph Stephenson received a call from the undercover agent working on the Provisional IRA assignment requesting an urgent meeting and suggesting there had been a breakthrough in the identity of the previously anonymous Irishman who wished to buy surface-to-air missiles for use in Northern Ireland. The meeting was arranged for nine thirty.

At eleven minutes past eight, Anna Luskin made her decision; at twelve minutes past eight she phoned the FBI. At eight nineteen one of his agents informed Stephenson that he had just received a telephone call from a contact who worked the United Nations circuit. The woman, he said, wanted to discuss something with him. It was too important, he said she had told him, to disclose over the telephone, and had suggested they meet for breakfast immediately.

At twenty-five minutes past nine, five minutes early, Stephenson began the meeting with the team of agents working on the IRA arms purchase assignment. At the previous meeting with the hitherto anonymous purchaser, the undercover agent précis-ed, the man had given them the name Chopper and a bar where messages could be left for him. After two days of checking, the agent said, he had discovered that the nickname was that of an Irishman excluded from the United Kingdom in December 1976 under the Prevention of Terrorism Act because of his alleged roles in the Provisional IRA bombing campaigns in the mid-seventies. Specifically, he said, the man had used the name in an IRA operation smuggling weapons from the United States to Ireland via the British port of Southampton as early as 1970. The nickname, he said, came from the man's reputation as a defender in a local football team. He was now resident in New York.

At fifteen minutes to ten Stephenson authorised an application for a wire-tap on the suspect's residence and the team left, two minutes later he was joined by the agent who had informed him of the telephone call from a contact at the United Nations. He motioned to the man to sit down, and fetched them both a coffee.

"OK," he said, his mind on the wording of the IRA wire-tap application. "What is it?"

The agent settled in the chair. "About six weeks ago, three hookers were hired by some Arabs to attend a celebration dinner. My contact was one of them. The girls are all high class, expensive. My contact drives a Merc."

"I'm surprised you can afford it on your salary," said Stephenson. The court application for the wire-tap would go through that afternoon, he was thinking, the wire-tap could begin that evening.

"I wish I could," said the agent, sipping his coffee. "The hookers were there to supply some ornament at the dinner. It was at an Arab restaurant, apparently a pretty exclusive one." He put the cup down. "And, of course, they were to provide some entertainment after."

Stephenson knew he was beginning to wonder what was so different.

"There were seven men at the dinner, all but one of them Arabs."

"Who were they?"

"The host was Sheikh Saeed Khaled, two of the others were introduced to the non-Arab as his advisors, the rest were his bodyguards. The girls were meant for the minders, it seems. After dinner, the other two went with them, but my contact was told to stay. She ended up with the other man, the only one who was not an Arab."

Stephenson tried to make himself forget about the wire-tap and concentrate on what the agent was telling him. Saeed Khaled, he was remembering the intelligence reports on the Lufthansa hijacking, the sheikh already nominated as an intermediary if the situation required.

"My contact had the impression that Khaled and his guest had just worked out some sort of deal, which was the reason for the celebration, and were just setting up another."

"Why?"

"Twice during the evening the girls were asked to leave the table, on one of those occasions Khaled and his guest were alone at the table for about fifteen minutes. She thinks it was set up then, she also thinks that one of the men who were introduced as advisors was also part of the deal."

"What was set up?"

"You're not going to believe this," the agent warned him.

"Try me anyway."

The agent looked at him. "The hijack," he said. "The Lufthansa hijack."

A scam, Stephenson knew immediately, they were being set up for a scam.

"As the group was leaving the restaurant," the agent continued, "the guest said something to Khaled and Khaled said something back. My contact was close enough to hear."

"What did they say that confirms your contact's hypothesis that they had just set up the Lufthansa hijack?" He thought again about the IRA wire-tap, hearing the cynicism in his own voice.

The agent told him what the woman had overheard.

Stephenson thought about the images on the television screen, the pictures from Amman of the mother and her daughter. "Tell me again," he said.

The agent looked at him. "If it ended in Jordan, he could become involved, if it ended in Jordan he could bring in the SAS. Khaled then agreed."

A scam, he thought, it had to be a scam. "The plane is German, it was hijacked from Vienna, it *was* in Jordan, but now it's left. The SAS are British, there's no reason for them to be involved."

The agent remained silent.

"Is there any record of the involvement of the SAS?"

"No."

There wouldn't be any such report anyway. Stephenson felt the thought begin to eat its way into his brain, wondered why it was there, wondered, suddenly and unexpectedly, why he was beginning to believe the agent, beginning to believe the man's contact. "Does she have any idea who the guest was?"

"That's why it could be important."

"Who was it?"

"The British Foreign Minister."

For the second time that morning Stephenson remembered the intelligence reports on the hijack, the suggestion of the organisation responsible, the name of the European politician who had been asked to liaise with Saeed Khaled should there be an attempt at a political intervention on an international level.

"How does she know who he is?" A scam, he told himself, it could still be a scam.

"She works the UN circuit, makes it her job to know who's who. Besides, his face was all over the papers at the time, something to do with a settlement of the oil crisis and the value of the British pound."

"How do we stand it up?" He was already working out the implications, deciding who he would inform, the order in which he would inform them, the questions they would ask him.

"I've arranged to see her again at ten thirty. I think it would be an idea if you were there."

Stephenson sipped his coffee. By ten thirty they could have begun to check on the contact, begun to discover whether she had any political motivations, any connections. "Why is she telling you?" he asked.

"Partly because of the American involvement, partly because of the pictures on the news, the woman and her daughter on the runway."

"And the other reason?" he knew it would be personal.

"Partly because of what he did to her that night. Apparently he's a real bastard."

One flaw, thought Stephenson, there was one flaw that invalidated everything. "OK," he agreed. "We'll see her at ten thirty. What's her name?"

"Luskin, Anna Maria Luskin."

3

GRAHAM ENDERSON crossed the Jordan again at the Allenby Bridge, passing through the check-point and spending ten minutes lounging against a wall while his documents were checked and his hire car examined. His passport gave no indication either of his real identity or his profession. At eleven thirty, as the sun was nearing its zenith, he passed through Shunat Nimrin, his car sending a spray of white dust over the ditches by the roadside; an hour later he had left Na'ur behind and was closing on Amman.

4

THE WOMAN WAS WAITING for them. She was nervous, playing with the spoon of her coffee cup. Stephenson and the agent sat down.

"More coffee?"

Anna Luskin nodded. Stephenson let the agent order then waited to be introduced. The coffee was served immediately; he sat back, watching the woman as the waiter stood over the table. She was in her mid-twenties, he estimated, with sharp features and a pleasant smile. Her dress was from one of the French boutiques on Fifth Avenue and she looked as if she had just stepped out of a health clinic. He supposed that it was a necessary requirement, understood she was waiting till the waiter left them.

"Before I say anything," she began, "I want you to agree to one thing." She had been through it already with the agent. "There are to be no comebacks, no way anyone can know I've been talking to you."

It was the way she had to organise her business, he thought, price and conditions up front.

"There's one problem with that," he suggested, knowing she had already identified it, knowing he had to confirm their credentials by playing straight with her. "The man you're going to tell us about will know."

"It depends how you use the information." He heard the edge in her voice and knew she would tell them anyway.

"No comebacks," he agreed. "No way it can be traced back to you." He stirred his coffee. "I imagine," he said, "that some of the things you may want to talk about are painful." He saw the way she was looking down. "Tell us what you can."

She told them everything.

The arrangements for the evening, the men present at the dinner, the snatches of conversation she had picked up, the words on the pavement as they got into the cars. The horror of the events in the hotel after. There was enough detail, he was beginning to think in relief, for them to begin to check, enough points to cross-reference before they had to decide whether or not she was telling the truth. The more Stephenson listened to her, the more he realised he was believing her. When she had finished he asked her three questions.

"What were the exact words you heard outside the restaurant?" She repeated them verbatim, assuring him she was not mistaken. He knew there was no mistake, knew also that unless the record check he had requested turned up something on her, there was no reason for there to be a scam.

The second question and answer were equally simple.

"How sure are you that the man is who you say he is."

"I've seen his photograph, I'll never forget his face."

He knew again she was telling the truth and passed to the third question.

"Why are you telling us? Is it because of what he did to you, is it because you want revenge?"

She looked at him, knew she should not tell him about the day she had stood with her parents on Ellis Island, the day she had seen the ghosts of the children who had been turned away. "Partly because of what he did to me," she said. "Mainly because of what he did to Mishka Zubko and her family, what he made her go through."

Forty-eight hours ago, he thought, and nobody had heard of Mishka Zubko, nobody cared a damn about her. Now the whole world knew who she was, that she had a daughter called Natasha and a husband and son who were still on the hijacked Lufthansa plane.

"Why?" he pressed her. "Why do you say it's because of what he did to Mishka Zubko?"

"Because he knew there was going to be a hijack." There was an anger in her voice. "Because without his agreement to whatever was proposed to him that night there would not have been a hijack." Because without his agreement to whatever was proposed to him that night, Stephenson was sure she was thinking but would not say, Mishka Zubko and her husband and children would be safely in the village called Beita.

"There are some photographs I'd like you to look at," he said. "I wonder if you would mind coming back with us."

She said she did not mind.

The cab to Federal Plaza took fifteen minutes. Stephenson checked from the foyer that the room he had booked was clear and escorted her in the lift to the twenty-sixth floor and into the office he had set aside. She was nervous, he asked if she wanted coffee, telephoned his secretary for some, and began to take her through the photographs.

The twenty-third photograph she was shown was that of Sheikh Saeed Khaled, the thirty-ninth of John Kenshaw-Taylor. She picked both out immediately, showing no surprise that they had been shown at random in an assortment of more than fifty faces she might not have been expected to know, accepting that they would check on her.

There was a knock on the door. The agent opened it, shielding her from outside, took the coffee, and locked the door behind him.

The images began flickering across the screen again, different faces, different people. Stephenson knew them, had lived with them, knew there was no way the woman could know any of them, watched anyway for a reaction. The Cubans, the Venezuelans, the Irishmen. The men, the otherwise faceless men, from Libya and the Middle East. The Palestinians.

"Go back," she said.

He flicked back.

"Farther."

The images flickered back across the screen.

"That's one of them," she said. "That's one of the men at the dinner."

He knew who the man was, could not believe what she was telling him, knew he had to test her, try to catch her out.

The picture was of a young man lifted from a photograph of a family standing in an orange grove, the children in the arms of their parents. The man in it kept and treasured it because it was the only photograph he had of his wife and sons; others kept and valued it because it was the only photograph of him known to exist.

"One of the bodyguards?" Stephenson asked. "One of the men who went with the other girls?" The enormity of her allegation was sinking into him.

"No." There was no hesitation in the answer. "He was too serious, too important for that." He knew what else she was going to say. "He was the one I said seemed to be part of what was being arranged that night, even though the Englishman didn't know it. He was that important."

Stephenson showed her the picture again and asked her if she was positive.

"He looks older now," she said, concentrating on the face. "Much older, fifteen, twenty years older, perhaps more, but it's the same man."

He was certain she was telling the truth, remembered what he had thought earlier, the one flaw that invalidated her entire story. "I want to show you a final set of photographs," he said, thinking about it, knowing he had to test her one last time. "There are some people in it you should recognise." He knew there were not, began flicking through the images again. She did not stop him once.

THE OFFICE WAS half empty.

Michael Joseph Stephenson sat back in his chair, working out the time differences, considering what he should do. Twelve noon Eastern Standard Time, five in the afternoon in London, eight in the evening where the 727 presently stood. The confirmation had started coming in, the details of the restaurant, the cars, the hotels. Partly because of what he had done to her, she had said, mainly because of what he had done to Mishka Zubko, what he had done to her daughter and her family.

Still the flaw, he thought, still the flaw that invalidated it all, yet he believed her despite it.

He checked the last update on the Boeing, confirming that the aircraft was still in Addis, then re-read the reports he and the agent had already submitted, looking again at the personal details of the woman. Her name and age, known associates, parental and educational background. He had done everything he could do, knew there was nothing more he should do.

The telephone rang. He picked it up, and heard the confirmation that the wire-tap on the IRA arms buyer had been approved, thinking again of the hostages, of the single image that had scarred itself on the consciousness of the woman, the mother carrying her child to freedom, reflecting again on the one single detail that had stood out in the personal background of Anna Luskin. That she, like him, was a first-generation American.

Nothing more he could do, he had already decided, one more thing he would do.

The call took ten seconds to connect, the voice that answered identified neither the number nor the organisation. Stephenson asked for Daniel Furtado and was told that the sergeant was engaged.

"How long will he be?" he asked.

"Two hours, probably nearer three."

Losing time, he thought, they were already losing time.

"Get him out," he said, "Priority."

"Who wants him?"

"No name," said Stephenson.

Daniel Furtado was at the phone two minutes later.

"Dan, this is Mike from the AT unit at the Bureau." The other man recognised him at once. "I need to speak to you right away."

"We're in the middle of something, can't it wait?"

"It's about Lufthansa 267."

The man from the Delta unit was looking at his watch. "Mine's a Jack Daniels," said Furtado, "Twenty minutes."

EDDIE'S BAR is ten minutes' walk from Federal Plaza, at the end of the street on which it is situated is a demolition area. Stephenson arrived five minutes early and ordered two Jack Daniels: in Addis, he was thinking, it would already be dark. Furtado arrived two minutes later.

The bar was crowded, they moved to a corner table.

"What is it?" The Delta Unit man came straight to the point.

"The Lufthansa hijack. Are any of your people involved?"

They accepted the meeting was confidential without needing to say so.

"No," said Furtado. "We're monitoring it, obviously, but it's nothing to do with us, too many political considerations."

"Who *is* dealing with it?"

"The West Germans primarily. They have a team of negotiators following the 727 wherever it goes, GSG-9 are on standby in Frankfurt, they've been airborne twice but have been refused landing permission in both Amman and Addis."

"What about the SAS?" He knew Furtado would not have looked surprised even if he had been.

"They went into Jordan early yesterday and are still there."

Every time he asked a question, Stephenson thought, it confirmed Anna Luskin's story, every time he received an answer it led him one step closer to believing the impossible. "Does anybody know the SAS have been sent in?"

"No," said Furtado. "Why?"

One flaw, he thought, that invalidated what she had told them, invalidated it or made it irrelevant. "It could be," he said carefully, "that they're being set up, that they're all being set up."

He began the story, starting with the OPEC meeting, the dinner party, the two politicians present whom Anna Luskin had named and the other man she had singled out from the photographs, ending with the words she had overheard on the pavement and the violence which had followed.

"You're sure?" Furtado asked when Stephenson had finished.

"As sure as I can be. She's told the same story each time, picked out the right people, including Abu Nabil. She even knew the SAS would be involved." One thing was still troubling him, one point in which the hijack did not match her story.

"The only problem," he approached the subject carefully, "is her reference to Jordan. We know the plane has been in Jordan, but the words she says she overheard pointed to the hijack ending in Jordan. We now know that's wrong."

"Why do you say that?" asked Furtado.

"Because the plane has left Amman for Addis."

"It will be back," said Furtado quietly.

Stephenson put down his glass. "What do you mean?"

Confidential, they had both known from the beginning.

"According to our intelligence, a Soviet military mission is due at Addis at eight tomorrow morning. It's our assumption that the hijackers will leave before then and return to Jordan."

"Why Jordan?"

"Until now," said Furtado, "I would have said that it was one of the few places, if not the only place, in the Middle East where they can still land. Most other airports are sealed off."

"And now?"

"Now I think it's because they're being set up, they're all being set up."

They had been talking for twenty minutes.

"Why are you telling me?"

"It's all in a report, even at this moment the report's going through the right channels. It'll get passed to the right people who will make the right decision." He looked at the ice in the bottom of the glass.

"But?" Furtado knew what he was going to say.

"But by then it will be too late."

"So what are you telling me?" Furtado asked again.

Mishka Zubko, Stephenson thought, walking across the goddam runway, her child in her arms, the whole world, the entire bloody world, willing her to keep going.

Himself included.

"I thought you might know somebody who would appreciate a phone call," he suggested.

Daniel Furtado remembered the two images, the first of the woman and her child, the second of the couple, lost and afraid, who had risked everything so that he himself could be born in the land of freedom.

"I do," he said.

6

THE AIR IN THE PLANE was cool, the air conditioning had been working since they had been refuelled six hours before. It was unreal, thought Jurgen Schumpter, almost as unreal as the hijack, merely a temporary interlude in the awfulness from which they had come, the awfulness to which he assumed they would soon return.

He had checked the passengers, been allowed to talk and joke with them, to sit in the open doorway and breathe the air of the desert. It had been strange, he thought, how they had all shared the release from the pressure, the crew and the passengers, even the hijackers. Just as they had begun to share the pressure itself.

On no occasion, he realised, even when he had sat alone and unguarded in the doorway, had he contemplated escape.

In the row of seats ten feet away, Stanislav Zubko played with his son, was glad that the boy had been able to eat and drink, thought about Mishka and Natasha, could not stop thinking about Mishka and Natasha, wondered if there was anyone in the entire world, outside the immediate circle of family and friends, who knew about them, who cared what happened to them.

Jurgen Schumpter looked at the father and son, pulled himself up, and went back into the cockpit. Walid Haddad was sitting in the pilot's seat, gazing out the window; he looked round, saw who was standing behind him, and offered Jurgen Schumpter his own place. Strange, thought the pilot, how certain formalities were maintained between them, certain positions respected. He shook his head and sat in the co-pilot's seat.

"How much longer will we stay here?" he knew he could ask.

"Twelve hours," said Walid Haddad. "Then we will leave. That is the agreement."

"Where do we go then?"

The hijacker did not answer.

Jordan, Schumpter thought, they were going back to Jordan, then the hijacker would issue his single deadline, then it would be all over.

7

JOHN KENSHAW-TAYLOR received the telephone call from Saeed Khaled at ten minutes to six, it was the third time they had spoken that day. They had both been busy, lobbying the various governments involved, playing themselves into a position in which, when all else failed, they would be the only people to whom the others could turn. In the past thirty-six hours, they were aware, the politicking across Europe and the Middle East, the negotiations with Washington, had been intense. In the past thirty-six hours, they were also aware, it had all come to nothing.

Their conversation was friendly but formal. As was the case in each of their telephone exchanges, there was no reference to New York, not even the slightest suggestion of a conspiracy.

They discussed the almost impossible position in which the Bonn government found itself, the seeming intransigence of both sides, the way round the deadlock. The following morning, they stated for the record, they both assumed the hijacked plane would leave Addis and, given the lack of alternatives, return to Jordan. By the end of the conversation they had examined, also for the record, the actual demand of the hijacker, and discussed the details of its application to the situation in West Germany. The only problem, they both agreed, again for the record, was that they were running out of time. Reports from Bonn, both official and unofficial, suggested that Christina Melhardt, the girl who would be next to die, the girl around whom the Lufthansa hijackers had centred their single demand, was weakening fast.

The conversation lasted twenty minutes. When it was over John Kenshaw-Taylor stood by the window and toasted himself with a glass of malt.

THE TWO MEN who entered Westminster at seven minutes past eight that evening were well-dressed and inconspicuous. The suits they wore were the uniform of the City businessman, the briefcase the older man carried bore no insignia, the Rover which delivered them to St Stephens entrance carried no markings.

The brigadier had been Director of Operations, SAS, for almost two years, the colonel who accompanied him, and who had arrived by helicopter from Hereford twenty minutes earlier, had commanded the regiment for a little over one, having himself served with distinction first as a captain, then as a major in charge of a squadron.

The corridors were busy; they made their way to the Prime Minister's room, passing the system of security checks, and were shown in. Three minutes later they were joined by the Prime Minister. It had been the brigadier who had suggested that the meeting take place at the House, visitors there being less conspicuous than at Downing Street, particularly in a time of crisis. He had asked for five minutes, emphasising the urgency of the request, and been given ten.

Ever since the dramatic end to the Iranian Embassy siege in central London, the Prime Minister had retained what others would call a soft spot for the regiment; one of her favourite photographs showed her standing in front of, and dwarfed by, two men in full assault gear.

She bustled into the room and shook them both by the hand. "Now," she said. "What's all this about?"

The brigadier had not explained why he wished to speak to her; he had worked out, however, both what he had to say and the most effective way of saying it.

"The Lufthansa hijacking," he came straight to the point. "There may be a complication which could have serious military consequences for the men I have in Jordan, and equally serious political repercussions for Her Majesty's Government in the future."

The Prime Minister noted the way he had removed her from the equation, recognising it for what it was, an indication of the seriousness of the matter he was about to raise.

"You'd better tell me," she said.

The brigadier indicated that the commanding officer of the regiment should begin. "Late this afternoon," the colonel began, "one of my sergeants received a telephone call from his equivalent in the United States Delta force." The Prime Minister was familiar with the unit. "The man trained with us for six months last year. He said he had been approached by a colleague in the anti-terrorist division of the Federal Bureau of Investigation about an allegation the FBI man had just received from a high-class prostitute who works at the United Nations."

A confidence trick, the Prime Minister was already thinking, it was a confidence trick. Either that or the beginnings of a political manoeuvre, which she assumed had also been the initial response of the two men now with her. She wondered why the brigadier had suggested they meet in her rooms at Westminster rather than in Downing Street, why he had also suggested the meeting should not be logged.

"The allegation," continued the colonel, "is two-fold. Firstly, that following a meeting with various political figures, a member of this government not only used the services of the woman in question with the knowledge that other people knew what he was doing, but treated her in a particularly sadistic and brutal manner."

She knew it was only the background to the second allegation. "And secondly?"

"That the same member of this government knew in advance that the Lufthansa hijacking was probable, if not imminent, and made certain suggestions about the locations involved and the participation of the SAS. The allegation is that the hijacking would probably not have taken place unless he had been party to certain agreements." The Prime Minister's stare did not waver. "The agreements," said the colonel, "were allegedly made at the meeting after which he used the services of the woman."

"What specifically is the alleged connection between the member of my government and the Lufthansa hijack?"

The colonel told her the conversation the woman had overheard at the cars outside the restaurant in New York.

The Prime Minister was tapping the edge of her chair. "How reliable is this information?"

"It seems to be standing up. The FBI have apparently confirmed many of the details already: the hotel room, the restaurant, the cars. What seems to have convinced them, however, is not only that the woman has identified your minister from a random set of photographs, but the identity of the other men she identified.''

''Who else did she identify?''

The brigadier knew they were close to the heart of the matter. ''That's what makes the hijack connection seem plausible. The first person she identified was Sheikh Saeed Khaled.''

The man nominated as Middle East negotiator in the hijack, thought the Prime Minister. The man who had apparently suggested John Kenshaw-Taylor as the European negotiator.

''Who else?''

''One other. His name is Abu Nabil. There is only one photograph of him in existence, it has never been published. The woman picked it out from almost seventy others. She was sure about him, said he was older than in the photograph, which is true, and refused to pick out anybody else even though she was under considerable pressure to do so.''

Still a trick, the Prime Minister was thinking, it could still be a trick.

''Who is Abu Nabil?'' She knew already.

''He leads a Palestinian splinter group with strong backing from Syria and the Soviet Union. Directly or indirectly his group have been behind most of the acts of terrorism in Europe and the Middle East over the past few years. There are strong indications that it is Abu Nabil who planned the Lufthansa hijack, and that he is behind the bombings and killings in Europe since Christmas.''

''Including the Heathrow assassination?''

''Yes, including the Heathrow assassination.''

There was a silence.

''Which member of my government is alleged to be involved?''

He sensed that she had guessed already. ''Your Foreign Minister.''

She did not hesitate, reached for a telephone and spoke to her private secretary. ''I'm sorry,'' she said without explanation. ''I'll be engaged for the next hour. Could you rearrange my timetable accordingly.'' She put the phone down and looked back at the brigadier.

''Tell me the details again,'' she said.

For the next thirty minutes they went through the information supplied by the FBI in New York; already the Prime Minister was working out the connections, the configurations of names and events: Kenshaw-Taylor's suggestion so many months ago that he should speak to Khaled, she remembered the day, could establish the date, have his timetable checked. If it was found that his meeting with Khaled had already taken place, she began to think... The oil negotiations in New York, the fact that the Foreign Minister had been there at all, the speed with which the private engagement had been offered, accepted. She was beginning to feel uncomfortable, beginning to work out the alternatives, thought of the violence he was supposed to have wrought upon the woman in New York, of his wife and children in England. It would check out, she was beginning to think, it would all check out, thought of the conversations since the hijack, the fact that Kenshaw-Taylor seemed to be in touch with the Jordanian ambassador even before the Lufthansa jet had left Rome, the fact that it had been Kenshaw-Taylor who had suggested offering the assistance of the Special Air Service. The fact that, only hours before, the Foreign Minister was adamant that the 727 would return to Jordan.

She knew what the Americans would do, despite the so-called special relationship, knew they would not tell her, that they would keep it to themselves, investigate it, build up the file, incriminate the Foreign Minister further. Until they needed him. She saw the damage to the party, knew it was more than that, more than even the security of the state. Knew it was the lives of the people on the plane.

"So what can we do?" she asked.

The brigadier looked at her. "There is only one thing we can do," he said. "Let him carry on."

She waited.

"There's a Palestinian saying," he began. "Not so much a saying as a feeling, a wisdom." He had spent his early years in the region, knew its way, loved its people. "If a man took a Palestinian outside at night and showed him the moon, then took him outside again the next morning and showed him the sun, he would wonder why the man was telling him that the moon rose at night and the sun shone during the day."

The Prime Minister was looking perplexed.

"In such a wisdom," he went on, "a Palestinian would say that nothing is as it seems. If the world tells a man he has won and tells you that you have lost, then he has lost and you have won."

He saw she was beginning to understand and thought about the Foreign Minister, the men from his regiment whom the bastard had been prepared to sacrifice for his own personal gain.

"The Foreign Minister thinks he is about to win. In a way he is. So far there have been no real negotiations about the hijacked plane, or about the West Germans' refusal to meet the demand. If, as you say the Foreign Minister suggests and our intelligence indicates, the plane will be back in Jordan by tomorrow, then it seems likely that he and Khaled will be called upon to intervene. And, if as is being alleged, they have already worked out a solution, then the hijack will end peacefully."

"And he will have won," said the Prime Minister.

"He will think he has won," suggested the brigadier quietly.

"Nothing is as it seems," the Prime Minister mused, half aloud. They both knew what she was going to say next.

"Will you tell your men in Jordan?"

The colonel waited for the brigadier to reply.

"Some will have to know for operational reasons."

The Prime Minister knew he was correct, knew also that there was another reason. "And because of who you are," she suggested.

"Yes," said the colonel, "because of who we are."

Sixty-five minutes after they had arrived the two men left Westminster as quietly and unnoticed as they had arrived. Ten minutes later the Prime Minister telephoned John Kenshaw-Taylor personally and spoke to him for fifteen minutes, listening with even more than her usual interest when he informed her that he and Sheikh Saeed Khaled had identified the beginnings of a possible solution to the hijack should Lufthansa 267 return to their sphere of influence.

BOOK
SIX

CHAPTER ONE

1

THE OLD MEN SAW the way the sun rose, red and angry, as if on fire, the layers of cloud drifting across it, dissecting it like knives. In the villages outside the city they shook their grandchildren from their sleep and took them outside, showing them the sign, remembering the day their grandfathers had taken them from the tents and shown them the sun rising as it rose this day, remembering what had happened that day, telling their grandchildren that one day they themselves would speak to the children of their children of the way the sun had risen, of the wrath, the terrible wrath, which followed.

AT FIVE THAT MORNING Yakov Zubko rose and went to the hill called Bethesda. At six Enderson rose and went to the room in the building near the airport where his men had waited; slowly and deliberately, he looked along the photographs they had put on the wall, looking at the faces, remembering who they were. The pilot, Schumpter, the air crew, the passengers whose photographs they had been able to obtain, the image of the doctor lifted from the video tape of the day she had walked from the plane with Mishka Zubko, the likenesses of Stanislav Zubko and his son Anatol. He knew them already, as each member of his team knew them, wondered only about the circumstances under which he would first see them.

In the cockpit of the 727 Walid Haddad checked his watch and thought of what was planned for the day, the timings, what the politicians were supposed to do, how and when it was supposed to end. In the seat opposite him Jurgen Schumpter was dozing fitfully, fighting back the nightmares that never left him. In the cabins behind the passengers saw the sun rise. In the second seat from the front Stanislav Zubko held his son close to him and wondered for the first time whether he should have sent the boy from the plane with his mother.

"Tell them we are taking off," said Walid Haddad.

It was seven in the morning, Addis time, on the last day of the hijack. Schumpter heard the words, was unsure whether or not he had slept, felt the tiredness in him. "Where are we going?" he asked without thinking, knowing that the hijacker would tell him, that it was too late not to tell him, knowing anyway.

"Jordan," said Walid Haddad. "We're going back to Jordan."

In the operations room in Amman, Enderson heard the voice of the air traffic controller as he received the message. "He's leaving Addis," the man was saying, "requesting clearance to overfly Asmara and Jeddah. If that's the case, he'll be here in three and a half hours."

In her apartment in New York Anna Luskin heard the news on the twenty-four hour television news station, the pictures beamed by satellite fifteen minutes later, of the blue and white Lufthansa Boeing climbing off the runway and banking into the sky.

In his flat in London, John Kenshaw-Taylor was informed immediately, told the duty officer at the Foreign Office to bring in his emergency team and ordered his car. He was in his office twenty-three minutes later, the team already assembling, disregarding the fact that it was not yet five in the morning London time.

"Extra telephones," he ordered, "engineers on stand-by in case we have any trouble with the lines. Cancel all appointments for the next twenty-four hours; check with the West German and Jordanian ambassadors where they'll be all day, contact numbers for Prime Minister, West German Chancellor and Foreign Secretary. Open line to Khaled and negotiators in Amman."

For a moment he forgot that he knew how it was supposed to end.

In Bonn the political editor of *Die Welt* made a check call to the cabinet office and was told that the condition of the hunger-striker Christina Melhardt was stable.

YAKOV ZUBKO did not know how long he had been sitting on the rocks. Four days, he could not help thinking, four days that his brother and his family should have been with them, four days that the beds had been made and the table laid. In the sky to the east he thought he saw a plane, wings glinting in the sun, then he lost it in the brightness, and could not find it again. In the 727 Stanislav Zubko looked out the window, and saw the land to the left, knew what land it was. On his lap Anatol was half asleep; he woke the boy gently, pointed out the window, and showed him Israel.

IN THE CENTRAL COMMAND in Amman Enderson heard the feed-through from air traffic control, identified the voice of the Lufthansa pilot. He went outside and watched as the plane came in, the sunlight gleaming on its paintwork, the Boeing seeming to hang in the heat haze above the ground, almost distorted, then dropping slowly, the dust rising in clouds as the wheels made contact. Stand-by, he did not even know he was thinking, stand-by, stand-by. First diversion in, stand-by, stand-by, second diversion in, go, go, go, go, go. Down, he was shouting, heads down; he was identifying the passengers, hoping they were keeping their heads down. More photographs, he thought, he wished he had more photographs.

Jurgen Schumpter eased the controls, and heard the voice on the radio.

"Lufthansa 267, this is ground control. Proceed via taxiways Bravo and Alpha to stand two and await further communications."

He looked at the hijacker, saw the man nod and did as he had been instructed. In the cabin behind, Stanislav Zubko looked out of the window and saw the airport buildings rolling past, recognised them from two days before, realised they were back in Jordan. In the seat opposite the doctor knew they were near the end.

The plane eased to a halt. Almost immediately one of the hijackers let down the rear steps and took up position at the top of them.

In the Central Command Enderson saw the steps beneath the tail of the plane fold down and knew it was the last day. The man from Heathrow, he thought, it had to be the man from Heathrow.

Something different, thought Walid Haddad, saw what it was: the whitewashed screens, the trees in front of them, where two days ago he had been able to see the television cameras, where they had been able to see him.

The man in the photograph, he thought, it had to be the man in the photograph.

By the time the Lufthansa jet carrying the West German negotiators and their advisors landed and taxied to its position on the other side of the terminal building, the snipers were in position and the banks of monitors had been reconnected in the operations room. Thirty minutes later the two charter aircraft carrying the world's press landed.

Jurgen Schumpter looked at his watch. Gone nine, almost ten. It was frightening how three days before in Rome, two days before in Jordan, even yesterday in Addis, the minute hand, even the second hand, of his watch barely seemed to move. Now even the hour hand was moving so quickly. It was as he remembered the summers when he was a boy, he suddenly thought, the long summers that never seemed to end. Now, he was thinking, it was like growing old, seeing the summers pass so quickly, knowing there were few summers left.

In front of him the helicopter rose from behind the buildings and turned towards the 727.

The West Germans and Jordanians were already locked in the suite they had set aside as a conference room; in the room at the side of air traffic control the negotiator was already waiting. Enderson saw the buildings disappear below him then the 727 come into view as the helicopter turned across the runway. On all sides of the plane he could see the trucks and jeeps already in position; he told the man to stay over the plane, analysing the lines, working out the approaches he would use, knowing he could not use them until after last light, then turned back to the buildings. It was getting hot. By the time he was inside the Central Command, the delegates were filing out from the conference room; he could see by their expressions that they had made little progress, even amongst themselves.

Five minutes later Enderson left the airport, returned to the holding area where the assault teams were waiting and updated them.

In the cockpit of the 727 Jurgen Schumpter heard the helicopter returning, then the whine of its engines as it hovered above the cockpit.

On the hill called Bethesda Yakov Zubko heard the noise behind him and waited as his wife and children climbed the last few feet and sat beside him.

"They are back in Jordan," said Alexandra.

At ten thirty London time John Kenshaw-Taylor received his first telephone call of the day from Saeed Khaled. There were no developments in Jordan, he was told. There had been no communications with the hijackers and no agreement amongst the politicians about what could be done.

"I think," suggested Khaled, confirming what they had placed on record the night before, "it is time we took an initiative."

For the next ten minutes they discussed formally what each would do; within five minutes of the end of the conversation Kenshaw-Taylor had made two telephone calls, one to the West German ambassador in London, the other to the Jordanian ambassador, and updated the Prime Minister.

2

THE SUN HAD ALREADY moved on, past the height of midday, and was beginning to beat on the starboard side of the Boeing, so that Stanislav Zubko could see its shadow on the ground outside. Gone one, Jurgen Schumpter thought, well gone one. Almost two, thought the doctor, almost two in the afternoon. Above him the pilot could hear the helicopters, hovering, changing position, disorientating him, disorientating all of them. Inside the faintest draught of air flowed from the open rear steps.

"Get ground control," said Walid Haddad.

Schumpter knew what it was and felt the fear, remembering the only other time the hijacker had spoken direct to the authorities, at the end of the first day in Rome. The day he had made his single demand, the day he had said he would issue one, and only one, deadline.

The cockpit was open. He knew the passengers in the front areas would hear and pass it to the others and asked whether he should close the door.

"They will have to know some time," said Walid Haddad. "They may as well know now."

The pilot picked up the microphone.

"Ground, this is Lufthansa 267."

In the control tower they heard the voice, in the operations room they heard the voice. In their earpieces, the snipers round the plane were informed of the first contact with those inside.

"Lufthansa 267, this is the West German negotiator."

They all suspected what it was, what it was going to be.

"This is Lufthansa 267. The leader of the hijackers wishes to speak to you."

They knew for certain.

Walid Haddad took the microphone. Later, as they waited, as the afternoon drew quickly on, they would study his words, his voice, search for weakness, for strength, for clues to his physical and mental condition. Would find nothing.

"In Rome," he spoke quietly and calmly, "I said that unless my demand was met, I would issue a deadline. That time has now come."

The timetable, they had insisted to him before he left Damascus, everything depended on him adhering rigidly to the timetable: when to issue the demand in Rome, when to leave Rome for Jordan, when to depart from Jordan and when to return. He had even been told the hour he should issue the deadline, the exact time in the evening when it should expire.

"Unless the demand is met by eight o'clock this evening, I will blow up the plane and everyone on it."

A political solution, he was sure. Just as they had worked out a military tactic, so they had also worked out a political strategy, needing the exact wording of the original demand as well as the precise timing of the deadline to give the politicians the opportunity to come to their agreements. It was not the time he would have chosen for the deadline, it was too late, too long after the light had gone, it would give the man in the photograph time to get to the plane, to get inside, but it was the time he had been given. He reminded himself there was a reason, even though he did not know it, and told himself again that the politicians would not fail him.

In the cabin behind Stanislav Zubko held his son, could not understand all the words, understood enough.

"What are they saying, Father?" the boy asked. "What are they talking about?"

Two in the afternoon, Schumpter began to think, it was already two in the afternoon, had not realised how much time had passed, how little was left. Six hours, thought the doctor, only six hours remaining, knew they would be both the longest and shortest of her life.

"Nothing, my son," Stanislav Zubko stroked the child's hair, comforting him. "Nothing that concerns us."

One deadline, thought the doctor, there would only be one deadline: no extensions to it. No more summers after this one, thought the pilot, no more summers ever.

In the operations room Enderson looked at the politicians and thought of the gunman sitting at the top of the rear steps. No approaches, he knew, no way of getting close to the plane, of attaching the monitors and finding out what was happening until after light. The deadline, he was aware he was thinking, there was something wrong with the deadline. He wondered why the hijacker had timed it to expire after dark, after the moment he could get near the plane, get onto the plane.

The Defence Minister came across the room. "Only when they have killed a hostage," he said.

Enderson looked at him. "By then," he replied, "it will be too late. By then they'll all be dead."

3

THE SANDWICHES and coffee were brought to Kenshaw-Taylor's department at eleven, his team eating at their desks in the outer office. In the rest of the building, he allowed himself to reflect, in similar buildings in Europe, they were waiting. For him to produce something, for him to pull it all out of the bag. He drank his coffee leaning against one of the desks, sleeves rolled to just below the elbow, listening to the updates and assessments, enjoying himself. At eleven thirty-five the man who had replaced him at Energy telephoned, wished him luck. At eleven fifty the Prime Minister's office came through, explained they would be updating the Head of State at twelve, and asked if there were any developments. He said there had been none, adding that he was not letting it stand in his way.

The priority call from Amman came in at twelve precisely.

Kenshaw-Taylor took it on the scrambler, listening to the British *chargé d'affaires* at Queen Alia International Airport. The door between his office and the outer area where his team was looking at him was open; he held the telephone between his head and shoulder, signalled to his team that they should come in, and listened to the attaché in Jordan then put the phone down.

"They've just issued a deadline," he said tersely. "Six hours. Eight this evening Jordan time, six in London."

He was issuing orders, instructing someone to contact Downing Street. Not much time, someone was saying, the Germans still in their crisis meeting, another aide was informing him. The Jordanian ambassador still at the embassy, a third was briefing him. A good team, he thought, the best team the British Foreign Office had assembled for years. Everything they needed at their disposal, whatever it was, however much it cost, and they all knew it.

Almost simultaneously he saw the interruptions to the scheduled programmes on the televisions in the corners of his office, the faces of the newscasters, the words almost identical. In Jordan, the BBC and ITN bulletins were saying, the hijackers had issued their deadline, it was only six hours away. In West Germany, said both channels, the government was still not prepared to give in to the hijackers' demands; in Bonn, they both added, the condition of the hunger-striker Christina Melhardt was reported to be stable.

"Update on the West German ambassador and the Prime Minister." He issued more instructions. "And another update on the condition of Melhardt." He turned to his secretary. "Our ambassador in Bonn," he told her.

The call took less than thirty seconds to connect. The West German inner cabinet, the ambassador said, was still locked in its emergency meeting, now that a deadline had been announced it was expected that that meeting would continue. Well-placed contacts within the government, he added, suggested that despite press reports to the contrary, Christina Melhardt had less than thirty-six hours to live.

"What's it like in Germany at the moment?" Kenshaw-Taylor asked.

"Like waiting for the Bomb," said the ambassador grimly.

At eighteen minutes past twelve Kenshaw-Taylor received the call from Downing Street; the Prime Minister said she had just spoken to the West German Chancellor, and that anything the British could do would never be forgotten. Five minutes later he took a second call from Downing Street; she had just received a call, the Prime Minister told him, from the President of the United States promising his personal backing for any initiative the British took, his support for any pressure they might feel able to apply.

At twenty-eight minutes to one he received his second call within the hour from the British Defence Attaché at Queen Alia International Airport. The negotiations were at a standstill, the man told him, the atmosphere tense.

"Our people?" asked Kenshaw-Taylor.

"Ready."

"Thank you," Kenshaw-Taylor told his man in Amman. Not long now, he knew, not long at all.

The call from Saeed Khaled came at eleven minutes to one; he shut the door to his outer office and spoke for a little less than three minutes. When he emerged his team could see that something was happening.

"The West German ambassador," he told his secretary. "Immediately." He turned to another member. "Police escort from the embassy to here as priority." His secretary was already through to the embassy, was telling him the ambassador was locked in a meeting with his staff.

"Interrupt him," said Kenshaw-Taylor.

Twenty seconds later the ambassador came on the line.

John Kenshaw-Taylor apologised for disturbing him. "I think," he took care to make his voice measured, "that you and I should talk immediately. Not the sort of thing we can discuss on the telephone. I wonder if you would mind coming over?"

"When?" asked the ambassador.

"There's a police escort waiting," said Kenshaw-Taylor.

On the first of the main lunchtime news programmes, the presenter was updating the information on the Lufthansa hijack, the imposition of the deadline, the number of passengers still on the plane, the crisis meetings in Bonn, the condition of the hunger-striker Christina Melhardt.

"The Jordanian ambassador," Kenshaw-Taylor instructed. "Fifteen minutes after the West German."

Reports from Amman, the newscaster was saying, pictures of the jet taking off from Addis, landing in Amman, more pictures of the streets in Bonn. Even on the television screen he could feel the tension.

"Confirm where the PM will be at one forty," he instructed.

Activity in Whitehall, the newscaster was saying, a report from their man at the Foreign Office. The reporter was standing outside the main door, describing the emergency team assembled by Kenshaw-Taylor, the fact that it was standing by, the suggestion that top-level discussions in Amman had still got nowhere. He signed off the report and handed back to the studio.

In Jordan, Kenshaw-Taylor thought, it would be mid-afternoon. At the airport, they would be feeling the fear. In the Chancellor's offices in Bonn, they would be living through organised panic. He sat back in his chair, clearing his mind, and considered how he should phrase his words to the West German.

His secretary knocked on the door and told him that the ambassador had arrived and was on his way up.

"Coffee for two," he told her.

On the television in the corner he heard the newscaster say that there were developments at Whitehall, that they were going live to the Foreign Office. He saw the reporter, then the pictures, recorded on tape less than a minute before, the glare of the headlights, then the flashing lights, the police outriders slewing their machines across the road, stopping the traffic, the men from the Diplomatic Protection Group shielding the ambassador as he hurried from his Mercedes into the building.

His secretary knocked on the door and showed in the ambassador.

It was four hours and forty minutes to the deadline.

"Thank you for coming so quickly." Kenshaw-Taylor offered the man a seat and waited as the secretary poured them each a coffee. Time running out, the ambassador knew, knew there was a reason why he had been summoned. He remembered Kenshaw-Taylor's reputation, how he had solved the oil crisis in New York, how he was spoken of as the man of the future.

"Still nothing?" asked the Foreign Minister.

"Still nothing," confirmed the ambassador.

"What does your government think the hijackers will do when the deadline expires?"

The ambassador looked at him. "They think the hijackers will blow up the plane."

"But you still feel you cannot concede?"

"We still feel we cannot concede."

Kenshaw-Taylor walked to his desk and picked up a file. The ambassador remembered again his reputation and knew that he was about to make an offer, that it was the beginning of the breakthrough they had all thought was impossible. Enough time, he began working it out, his people on stand-by at the embassy, the direct line to Bonn, just enough time.

"It's only a possibility," said Kenshaw-Taylor slowly, "and your government might not feel able to accept it, but I think there's a chance of a way out."

Let it work, thought the ambassador, for God's sake let it work, let there be a way. He did not betray his feelings. Waited.

The Foreign Minister selected a sheet of paper from the folder, consulted it, then looked up.

"The hijackers' demand," he said, "asks that your government meet the demands of the hunger-striker Christina Melhardt."

"Yes." The ambassador wondered what the minister was leading to.

Kenshaw-Taylor sat on the edge of the desk and laid the sheet of paper beside him.

"You feel, quite correctly, that you cannot give in to her demands because they represent merely the demands of the rest of the hunger-strikers, that if you gave in to her you would also be giving in to convicted terrorists and killers."

"That is precisely our dilemma."

Kenshaw-Taylor shuffled the paper slightly.

"But if we were careful," he said, "if we were very careful, there might be another way of looking at the hijackers' demand."

Time running out, the ambassador knew again, waited again.

"If we stick absolutely to the hijackers' demand, it requires only that the demands of the girl Christina Melhardt be met, not the others. It requires only that you save *her* life, no one else's."

Not much time, the ambassador was thinking, just enough time. If they moved quickly, if the Foreign Minister was right.

"What do you mean?" he asked.

"What if we separated the two, removed the demands of the girl from those of the others? Would your government feel able to meet her demands if they applied only to her?"

The ambassador remembered the phrasing of her demands, the demands of the other hunger-strikers.

"It's possible," he replied, "just possible."

More than possible, Kenshaw-Taylor was certain, something they would jump at.

"The girl hasn't been convicted of any terrorist offences," continued the ambassador. "As long as we could restrict it to her, it's just possible we could meet her demands." He knew it was not only possible, it was the only way out.

"What about the hijackers, would they agree to this separation?"

Kenshaw-Taylor looked again at the sheet of paper, remembering what he and Khaled had worked out, what they had agreed. "It's what their demand says, they have always been very specific about it. They refer only to the demands and the life of the hunger-striker Christina Melhardt, they have never referred to the demands or the lives of any other hunger-striker."

"Could you persuade them?" asked the ambassador.

"I could try," said John Kenshaw-Taylor.

The ambassador began to rise. Something more, his instinct told him, something else he would need if he was to persuade Bonn that he had found the way out.

"There is one thing," said Kenshaw-Taylor. He had planned it, worked it out, ever since the meeting in New York, ever since he had known about the hijack. Thought about it the night before, thought about it that morning, organised the order of his solution so that the offer the West German could not refuse would come last.

"What is that?" asked the ambassador.

Kenshaw-Taylor looked at him. "It is not only important for you to save the people on the plane, it is also important for you to be seen to do all you can to save the lives of the people on the plane."

The ambassador began to understand what he was saying, what he could not say. The man of the future, he had been told, John Kenshaw-Taylor was the man of the future. He began to walk towards the door, seeing again what Kenshaw-Taylor was saying, what Kenshaw-Taylor was offering him.

If you don't accept this solution, Kenshaw-Taylor was telling him, if you don't take this way out, and if the hijackers blow up the plane and everybody on it, then the world will hold your government responsible. If you accept this solution, and the hijackers also agree, then the world will praise you for having the wisdom to save the people on the plane without giving in to international terrorism.

He was almost at the door.

But the most important thing, Kenshaw-Taylor was telling him, was that it did not matter whether the people on the plane lived or died. What mattered was that by accepting the solution the Bonn government had done all in its power to save them. Or appeared to have done so.

And if the hijackers did not accept the compromise and the people on the plane died, then it would be the fault of the hijackers and not the responsibility of the West Germans.

He turned to face Kenshaw-Taylor, "It might work," he said, "it might just work."

One minute later Kenshaw-Taylor had updated the Prime Minister. Five minutes later he had outlined the situation to the Jordanian ambassador. Ten minutes later he had spoken to Saeed Khaled.

At two minutes past two he received an urgent call from the British ambassador in Bonn saying there were reports that the Chancellor's crisis cabinet was discussing a solution to the hijack based on proposals coming out of London. At nine minutes past two Saeed Khaled came through to report, for the record, that at first sight the British proposals appeared acceptable to the political masters of those holding the Lufthansa jet. Kenshaw-Taylor communicated this immediately to the West German ambassador and to the Prime Minister. Eight minutes later he received a call on the scrambler from the Defense Attaché in Amman saying that the West German negotiating team were locked in what the man described as a make or break session with the Jordanians at the airport, but that the suggestion of a solution, originating in London, was in the wind.

John Kenshaw-Taylor left his inner office and joined his team for coffee and sandwiches, sitting in his shirt-sleeves on the edge of his secretary's desk, and updated them. The first whispers of success, he knew, were already seeping along the corridors of Whitehall.

It was three hours and forty-one minutes to the deadline.

4

THE SUN WAS BEGINNING to dip; on the hill called Bethesda Yakov Zubko waited with his family. In the cockpit of the 727 Jurgen Schumpter heard the noise of the helicopters overhead and watched as the shadows began to lengthen on the port side. It was terrifying, the thought would not leave him, how he had become accustomed to thinking of the hijack in the number of days it had lasted, how he was now counting the hours and minutes that were left. To his right Walid Haddad sat still and remembered the politicians. Almost through, he knew, his time was almost through. In the cabins behind he heard the father talking to his son, telling him of the family who came from a far-off land.

"Will my mother be waiting?" he heard the boy ask. "Will my mother and sister be waiting?"

In the sky above them Jurgen Schumpter heard the silence as the helicopter pulled away.

"Yes," Walid Haddad heard the father tell the boy, "your mother and sister will always be waiting."

Above them another helicopter hovered into position.

5

ENDERSON FELT the first down draught of the blades on them, the sound of the engines almost deafening them. They were moving carefully, placing the ladders in position, tops against the door, climbing in twos, one man at his side, two behind, leaning forward, leaning tight against him. His hand was on the door handle of the 727. Stand-by, stand-by. In his earpiece he heard the confirmation that the other units were in position. Stand-by, stand-by.

The helicopter was moving, the sand swirling round them, the machine disappearing from the sky above them. Stand-by, stand-by. He heard the sound of the diversion and felt the 727 rock gently as it went in, the men behind him leaning tighter against him. Stand-by, stand-by. He heard the second diversion go in, felt the impact of the stun grenades inside the plane. Go, go, go, go, go.

In five minutes the exercise was over, within ten minutes the assault teams had left the Boeing, parked and protected in the corner of the military airfield where they had first landed, and returned to their rooms that had been established as their holding position, pulling off their body armour and checking their weapons before they began to relax. It was just like the first walk-through in the snows of Pontrilas, Enderson thought, just like the run-throughs they had practised in the heat of Jordan two days ago, when the Lufthansa jet first sat on the runway three miles away. Except, he thought, that two days ago there had been no deadline, two days ago there had not been just three hours and thirty minutes before the deadline expired.

The telephone rang. The man who had waited for him at the top of the steps to the underground station at Knightsbridge picked it up, listened for five seconds, then handed it to him. It was the operations officer from the airport. Enderson talked to the man for another twenty seconds then replaced the telephone.

"Airport," he said, then saw the look on the faces of the assault teams. "Nothing to do with us," he said. "Administration."

He wiped the sweat from his face, and wondered what was happening, checked that his weapons and equipment were in order, then was driven to the airport in a closed jeep. The colonel and operations officer were waiting for him in the Central Command. With them was a sergeant from the squadron from whom Enderson's men had taken over the anti-terrorist duty at Hereford. "Hello, Mike," he greeted the man. "Didn't expect to see you here." Something wrong, he knew, something very wrong.

For fifteen minutes the sergeant briefed them on what the American Daniel Furtado had told him from New York, what he had told the commanding officer, what the colonel and the brigadier had told the Prime Minister.

Enderson knew he should have felt the anger, the reaction against the fact that he was being set up, that they were all being set up. Instead, he was cutting out the anger and emotion from his response, working out how the knowledge would give him an advantage over the man from Heathrow. Knew that was why he was being told. Something about the deadline, he remembered his reaction at the time, how he had seen immediately

that it was too late in the day, too long after last light, how he
had known that the man from Heathrow would have set it before the light had gone, before the assault teams could approach the plane with any degree of success, before they could
approach the plane at all.

"Anything else happening?" he asked.

"No idea," said the operations officer. "The delegates have
been locked up for almost an hour. The Attaché came through
twenty minutes ago looking very hot under the collar and put
through a call to London on the scrambler."

The door opened and the Defence Minister entered and
looked at the monitors. Enderson saw that he was smiling.

"It looks," the Jordanian said, "as if we may not need your
people after all."

They all knew what he meant, why he meant it.

"There is a strong possibility," continued the Minister, "of
a peaceful solution to the hijack. The men controlling the hijackers have agreed, the West Germans are in session at the
moment, there's no reason why they should not agree."

"Where did the solution start?" asked Enderson.

"London. Your own Foreign Minister, John Kenshaw-
Taylor."

Why Jordan? he remembered thinking earlier. Now he knew.
He turned away in disgust and poured himself a coffee.

6

NO RESPONSE, Jurgen Schumpter thought, three and a half
hours to the deadline and still no response from the authorities; he wondered what they were doing, what game they were
playing, what right they had to make him sit here and sweat it
out, make him count away the hours and minutes to his death
without even raising a finger to help him.

In the cabin behind, Stanislav Zubko held his son and wondered how he would react if the end came, how he could protect him when it came; since he had asked about his mother and
sister the boy had grown quiet, almost introspective.

In the seat opposite, the doctor thought about the demand
the hijacker had made. So simple, she thought, so straightforward. It was not as simple, she knew, not as straightforward;

there were other hunger-strikers who had been found guilty of
bombings and killings and who had made the same demand as
the girl called Christina. On the other hand, she began to think,
it was not as complicated as the authorities pretended. She began to see the solution, to become convinced of it.

Just the hunger-striker called Christina, she thought, that
was all the hijacker had asked, had never even mentioned the
others, just give them the life of Christina as he had given them
the lives of Mishka and Natasha.

She looked at her watch and wished she had not. Four in the
afternoon, she had calculated, saw now that it was almost five.

In the co-pilot's seat Walid Haddad listened to the noise of
the helicopter above them and thought of the politicians, knew
they were working it out, suspected that was why he had been
ordered to stage the hijack in the first place, so that the politicians could work it out. They were leaving it very close, he
thought. To the deadline, to the moment it would all end. He
knew what was going to happen, reminded himself of the order of events and told himself it would be all right. He looked
at his watch and wondered for the first time during the hijack
if he could trust the politicians. Gone five, he saw, almost five
thirty.

Two hours and thirty minutes to the deadline.

It was not the hijackers' fault, thought Jurgen Schumpter.
The hijackers had done all they could, had asked for food and
water, saved Natasha, made their single request so simple it was
impossible for the authorities to reject. It was the authorities
who had refused them, refused them everything, refused them
food and water, refused to talk to them, refused little Natasha
her drugs, even refused to talk about the girl on hunger strike
in Germany whose life the hijackers had asked to save. It was
not the hijackers who would kill them at eight o'clock, he realised, it was the authorities.

In her apartment in New York Anna Luskin heard the telephone ring and ignored it: no clients today, she thought, no
clients until it was over, until the husband and son of the
woman who had carried her daughter across the runway were
safe. She looked at the television set, the update every thirty
minutes, the pictures from Amman, the pictures of the church
in Norfolk where the American family who had met Mishka
Zubko and her family in Moscow worshipped regularly, the
congregation now gathered in prayer. A weekday afternoon yet

the church was filled to overflowing with people from all denominations praying for the delivery of a Jew and his son, for the delivery of a woman who was no more than a child on her deathbed in a German prison. Praying for the delivery of the Palestinian gunman who had had the humanity to release Mishka Zubko and her child.

In the school in Hereford Jane Enderson left her class, went to the staff-room, switched on the radio and sat in the corner by herself. The other teachers were still in their classes. Someone came in and asked her casually why she wasn't in class; she told them she was feeling unwell and carried on listening to the radio, thinking of the discussions in the news programmes, the speculation about what the authorities were doing, the suggestion that the British had come up with a solution that would save the girl in West Germany and end the hijack. She had seen the pictures on the lunchtime news, the West German ambassador arriving at the Foreign Office, the police escort, the way his convoy had screamed away up Whitehall fifteen minutes later. She knew there was just a chance, knew what would happen if they did not take it, did not make it succeed. Her mind was at the airport in Amman, wondering where exactly Grah was, what he was doing. She heard the news flash, the interruption to the afternoon programme, knew they were almost there.

Anna Luskin was in the kitchen when she heard the words and ran back into the lounge. More signs of a breakthrough, the newscaster was saying, in London the West German ambassador had left his embassy and was on his way back to the British Foreign Office; armed police had sealed off his route and stopped traffic. Save them, please God, she prayed, would realise later it was the first time she had prayed since she had left home, please save them. Save them all. Save the passengers, save the girl in Germany, save the hijackers. Above all save Stanislav Zubko and his son Anatol so that Mishka and Natasha may see them again.

On the hill called Bethesda Yakov Zubko and his family heard the sound and turned, saw the neighbour hurrying up the hill, knew instinctively what the man was going to tell them, knew that it was over. Knew that Stanislav and his son were dead.

"There's a breakthrough," said the man, not pausing to gather breath. "In London. They think the English have found a way out, the West Germans are on their way to finalise it now.'' His message was as confused as their minds. They knew what he meant and began to smile.

7

CLOSE, thought John Kenshaw-Taylor, he was so close.

He waited for the ambassador to be shown up the stairs. So long, he thought, he had planned it, worked at it, for so long, now it was about to come to fruition. He remembered the first meeting at the London Hilton, the way he had engineered Saeed Khaled into the compromise, the way he had massaged him into delivering on the OPEC oil prices, the way Khaled, in turn, had approached him about the hijack.

Close, he thought again, so very close.

His secretary showed the West German in. Kenshaw-Taylor rose from his desk and greeted the man, knew it was the moment he had waited for, knew it was the turning point in his career. He had already planned what he would do that evening, how he would make a brief appearance at the House of Commons, anticipated the way he would be greeted. The ambassador was shaking his hand, sitting down. Giving nothing away, Kenshaw-Taylor thought. He would not have expected otherwise; the man was a professional like himself. His secretary left the room and closed the door behind her. He returned to his desk and asked if the visitor wanted coffee. The ambassador shook his head.

''You have heard from Bonn,'' Kenshaw-Taylor knew it was his responsibility to open the discussion.

''Yes,'' said the ambassador, ''I have heard from Bonn.''
Kenshaw-Taylor waited for the moment.

''My government thanks you for your suggestion of a solution to the Lufthansa hijacking, but regrets it is unable to accept it.''

He heard the words, not believing them, wondered what the man was playing at, what Bonn was playing at.

''May I ask why not?'' He kept his voice polite, calm.

''Even if we separated the demands of the hunger-striker called Christina Melhardt from the others, and even if the hijackers were prepared to accept this, my government is not in a position to meet her demands.''

Kenshaw-Taylor picked up the subtle difference in terminology, saw that the ambassador was looking at the desk, not directly at him as he would have expected.

''Why not?'' It was the time to be blunt.

The ambassador looked at him.

''Because the hunger-striker called Christina Melhardt died three days ago.''

8

THIRTY MINUTES, thought Enderson, since the Defence Minister had told him they were near a solution and informed him that his units would not be needed then gone back into the conference room, nearer forty. Politicians, he had thought during that time, one politician above all. John Kenshaw-Taylor. He set them up, set them all up, the passengers and crew, himself and his men, just so that he could arrange the political deal the delegates were concluding behind the closed doors of the conference room. It did not matter that the man had known all along that the hijack would end peacefully, that the solution had been agreed before the hijack had even begun. He had never trusted politicians, would trust them even less in the future.

''They want you in the conference room, you and the operations officer.''

The politicians on both sides were as bad as each other, he thought. The men who had ordered the man from Heathrow to hijack the plane, the men who had arranged for the SAS to be sent against him. He followed the operations officer into the conference room; there were six men round the table, the ashtrays in the middle were filled to overflowing and the plastic coffee cups were cracked. The Defence Minister was grey with anger.

''How long will it take your teams to get ready?'' asked the chief West German delegate.

They were supposed to have found a solution, thought Enderson. ''They're ready,'' he said. ''Why?''

''No questions. When could they go in?''

"Last light. They could be on the plane seventeen minutes after that."

"Why wait till then, why not now?" It was the West German again.

"The hijacker has total vision of the ground round the plane, from the cockpit and from the man sitting at the top of the rear steps. We couldn't get anywhere near it at the moment without being seen."

"But what if you had to go now?"

Suicide, he knew, it would be suicide, for everyone. He knew it was pointless telling them that it was not like a building, not like the Iranian Embassy in London where there was cover and protection. He looked round the table, thought for thirty seconds then gave them the percentage chances: from the probability of getting some of the passengers off with no loss of his men, to the chances of getting them off with a certain loss of his men, to the chances of getting them all off with the loss of all his men, himself included.

"What are the chances of no one surviving?" asked the politician.

"It depends whether they have time to lay the explosives," said Enderson.

They looked at him in astonishment. "Who said they had explosives?" someone asked.

"They have automatic weapons, grenades, spare ammunition, drugs. The whole thing is meticulously planned, even down to the cover in Frankfurt, they're bound to have put explosives in the toilet when they hid the weapons there."

"So if they do have explosives and time to lay them?"

"If they have time to lay them, there would be a high probability the plane would go up with everyone on it."

"What probability?"

He told them the percentages.

"And if you went in after last light?"

He gave them the percentages. Something wrong, he remembered the intelligence officer at Hereford had said on the first morning of the hijack, something the West Germans weren't telling anybody.

"What's happened," he asked, "what happened to the solution?"

"We can't meet it," said the chief delegate.

He knew what it was, knew the intelligence officer had been correct. "Why not?"

"The girl's dead."

"When did she die?"

He knew the politician was not going to answer.

"Three days ago," said the Jordanian. Enderson sensed he had only just been told.

"The first morning in Rome?" he asked.

"Yes," the politician conceded. "The first morning in Rome."

"Before the man on the plane had even made his demand?"

"Yes."

There was silence in the room. Enderson got up from the table and moved towards the door. There was a look of concern on the faces of the delegates.

"The teams," he said.

He walked back into the operations room and telephoned the assault teams on the secure line. "Now," he said simply. "Final briefing at airport in ten minutes then into the start points. We go at last light."

"What's happened?" the man who had given him the gun at Knightsbridge asked.

"The hunger-striker's dead."

"What are they going to tell the hijackers?"

"I imagine they're going to tell them they've given in to their demands and hope to Christ they can stall them long enough for us to get on board."

He went back to the conference room, the cigarette smoke was hanging low over the table; he sat down between the Defence Minister and the Lufthansa representative and waited.

"This is what we do," said the chief delegate without preamble. "We tell the hijackers we have agreed to their demand, we do not tell them that the girl is dead. It is possible, though unlikely, that they will release the hostages, subject to discussions over safe conduct for themselves, at this point. It is also unlikely, given what they think is the girl's condition, that they will ask for her to be released from prison immediately." He lit himself another cigarette.

The man from Heathrow, Enderson was thinking, sitting on the plane, waiting for the politicians to pull him out, set up by his own side as Enderson and his men had been set up by theirs.

Everyone sure there would be no problem, now everyone trying to kill them all.

"I imagine," the West German was saying, "that the hijackers will ask for an assurance from a third party, the girl's lawyers or an organisation like Amnesty International or the Red Cross, that the terms have been met." He turned to face Enderson. "If that is the case, we should be able to stall them long enough for you to act."

"How will you manage that?" It was not his business but it affected the man on the plane, to that extent it was his legitimate concern.

The politician took delight in showing that he had worked it out. "In the hijack that ended at Mogadishu in 1977," he said, "those in control stalled for time by telling the hijackers they had agreed to their demands for the release of terrorists held in Germany and informed them the prisoners were on their way in a chartered aircraft to Mogadishu, then worked out the flight paths and timings of the aircraft and fed these to the hijackers. I propose to do the same thing in the present case."

He stubbed out the cigarette, enjoying his position. "Not the flight times, of course, but the apparent progress of whoever the hijacker chooses to confirm our part of the agreement. The journey from his or her office to the prison, the length of time they spend at the prison, the time back to the office, the time it will then take them to communicate with Amman, the time it will take us to pass their confirmation to the hijackers."

The man from Heathrow, Enderson thought, the politician's plans did not allow for the man from Heathrow.

The delegate turned to him again and asked for his timetable.

"Last light is at nineteen ten." He had stood on the runway the night before, noting the times, seeing how the shadows fell across the routes his men would take to the plane. "We will be in our start positions before then. It will take us eleven minutes to get to the plane, five minutes to set up monitors to confirm what is going on inside and make any changes to our plans, one minute after that to execute those plans. We can be inside at nineteen twenty-seven."

Thirty-three minutes to the deadline, they were all thinking.

"Good," the politician called the meeting to order, checking his watch. "Let's work out our own timetable." He began to list the times. "I have to clear it with Bonn—that will take fifteen minutes—then talk to the hijackers, make our offer, hear their conditions. Assuming they ask for verification, it will take another fifteen minutes to contact whoever they ask for, plus half an hour to get to the prison, fifteen minutes inside, and another half hour to get back. Plus a final fifteen for them to arrange their verification procedures.''

They each made the calculation, each realised that the confirmation would arrive twelve minutes before Enderson's teams would be in the plane.

The chief delegate looked at the pad in front of him and came to his decision. ''We put the timetable back fifteen minutes,'' he said simply. ''That way the teams will be in the plane three minutes before the hijackers expect confirmation.''

Enderson thought again about the man from Heathrow and wondered what he was planning, what the man was calculating the authorities were planning, remembering Frankfurt, the way the man from Heathrow had used the Dubai factor against them, wondering what he would do on the runway in Amman in the last precious minutes as the assault teams closed in on him. Knew what he himself would do, wondered if the man from Heathrow would do the same.

9

THE LIGHT had the awesome clarity of late afternoon in the last minutes before the dusk begins to gather. The doctor looked out the window and saw how much the sun had fallen, thought how much longer there was before they would die. She had seen death so many times, she thought, other people's deaths. On the seat opposite, Stanislav Zubko held his son on his lap and looked at the shadow of the plane as it lengthened on the runway. In the cockpit Jurgen Schumpter thought of the walks he had made with his wife and children in the Black Forest, of their favourite time of the year for the walks, wondered what the hijacker was thinking, how he could carry out his own execution.

Walid Haddad left the co-pilot's seat, checked with the man guarding the door and the hijackers in the cabin and at the top of the rear steps, and went back to the cockpit. So many times he had waited, he thought, from the first time, when he was eight years old, waiting for the patrol to come down the road, the Kalashnikov too heavy for his thin shoulders, to the last time, on the motorway from Heathrow. He was accustomed to waiting, was particularly accustomed to waiting for death, but never before his own. The sun slipped past the window and out of view. The politicians, he thought, what the hell were the politicians doing?

"Lufthansa 267. Come in please Lufthansa 267."

Jurgen Schumpter knew what it was, what the authorities were going to say. Knew he was going to live. In the enclosed area at the rear of the airport buildings the assault teams slipped into the jeeps and began their journey to the start points.

"This is Lufthansa 267," replied Schumpter. He sensed suddenly that he was wrong, that they were not going to negotiate, that after all he was going to die.

"Lufthansa 267, may we speak to the hijackers, please."

The negotiator heard the sound, the words, as the microphone was passed to the man in the co-pilot's seat. In the sky to the west, the sun was fierce red, the clouds cutting across it as they had done that morning.

"This is the leader of the hijackers."

Two hours, thought the doctor, two hours and they would be free or dead.

"This is Klaus Rudegar, the representative of the West German government. I am authorised by the Chancellor to say that we have agreed to your demand."

Jurgen Schumpter let his shoulders drop, and felt the relief pour through him, the gladness for them all, the Jewish father and his son, the doctor, the passengers. The hijacker opposite him.

"Could you repeat that?" asked Walid Haddad.

"I am authorised by the Chancellor to say that, in return for the safe release of the passengers and crew, my government is prepared to meet your demand, the demands of the hunger-striker Christina Melhardt."

Above them they could hear the noise of the helicopter.

"I will need confirmation."

The first assault team arrived at their start point.

"I understand that. What do you propose?"

They had already worked it out, Jurgen Schumpter saw, both sides had already worked it out.

Walid Haddad named an Arab ambassador in West Germany. "He should accompany the girl's lawyer to the prison and confirm her acceptance and the fact that you have agreed to her demands, he should then relay this to his embassy in Amman, and the ambassador in Amman should confirm this to me that all is in order."

Time, Schumpter thought, it would take time. For one awful second, he was afraid that the authorities had left it deliberately late, had given the hijacker almost no time at all before his deadline to confirm their acceptance of his demand, that they were stalling for time so that they could storm the plane. Then he knew that he was wrong, that the authorities were telling the truth.

"It will take time," said the negotiator. "Will you extend the deadline to accommodate this?"

Schumpter heard the concern in the man's voice and admonished himself for ever thinking that it would be the authorities who would be responsible for their deaths.

"The embassy is twenty-two minutes by car from the prison," Walid Haddad said. "There is time for the ambassador to reach the prison and contact his embassy in Amman from the prison. There will be no extension to the deadline."

"What if the ambassador prefers to return to his embassy?"

"In that case, let us agree that the ambassador in Amman comes to the airport immediately and waits with you for the confirmation."

"But what if the ambassador cannot provide confirmation before the deadline?"

"Then I will blow the plane up."

"But what if the ambassador in Bonn is not at the embassy?"

You're wasting time, thought Schumpter, you're wasting bloody time.

"I think you will find he is waiting," said Walid Haddad.

He switched off his mouth-set.

"You've won," Schumpter said suddenly, knowing again that he was going to live, that they were all going to live.

"Not necessarily." The words were bleak and unwelcome.

"But the authorities have agreed to your demand," protested Schumpter. "The negotiator has just agreed."

Walid Haddad shook his head. "No he hasn't," he said slowly.

Schumpter did not know what the hijacker meant. "What are you talking about?" he asked, aware that his voice was showing the strain.

"The negotiator said that he was authorised by the Chancellor to say that his government had agreed to our demand." He was looking straight into the pilot's eyes. The politicians, he was thinking, the bloody politicians. "At no point did he actually say that they had agreed."

Jurgen Schumpter felt the tightness grip him and told himself that the hijacker was playing at semantics.

"But they agreed to contact the ambassador in Bonn," he protested. "They agreed to a timetable."

Walid Haddad looked at him again. "In 1977," he said at last, "a Lufthansa jet was hijacked en route from Majorca to Frankfurt. After four days it landed at a place called Mogadishu. Just before the last deadline, the West Germans told the hijackers they agreed to meet their demands, the release of the Baader-Meinhoff prisoners from Stammheim. In the hours before their deadline, the West Germans told the hijackers the prisoners were on their way to Mogadishu, they even worked out the flight path and the times of the aircraft along it, and kept the hijackers informed of the plane's supposed progress." He had not stopped staring at Jurgen Schumpter. "As you will recall," he said bluntly, "it was a hoax, they were simply stalling to give GSG-9 the time to storm the plane."

The man from Heathrow, Graham Enderson would have thought, the bloody man from Heathrow.

"But the negotiator is telling the truth," Jurgen Schumpter was arguing as much with himself as he was with the hijacker. "You can hear it in his voice, tell it by the way he speaks."

"The negotiator is saying what he thinks is the truth," said Walid Haddad. "Even his own people are telling him only what they want him to know, what they want him to tell us. They know we will be listening to his voice just as they are listening to ours." He looked across at the pilot. "You're right when you say he is telling the truth, because he is telling us what he himself believes. It's what they do, what they always do."

Jurgen Schumpter felt the cloud settling on him. "You're not suggesting that's what they're doing now?" There was a plea in his voice.

The politicians, thought Walid Haddad, the politicians on both sides.

"Who knows," he half smiled, "who knows what any of them are doing?"

10

IT WAS BEGINNING to rain. Jane Enderson remembered the morning before Christmas, the water pouring in sheets from the skies, the man in the coat on the pavement opposite the staff-room. No more bulletins, no more news from Amman.

She left school, listening to the car radio, and picked up the children, first their daughter, then their son. "Mum," said the boy as he pulled off his wet anorak, "when will Dad be home?"

She heard the voice, not her son's voice, the voice of the girl, so distant, so far away over the hills, heard the words of the poet.

And you, my father, there on the sad height,
Curse, bless, me now with your fierce tears I pray.
Do not go gentle into that good night.
Rage, rage against the dying of the light.

There was an interruption in the programme. She heard the first words of the news flash, told the children to be quiet, almost screamed at the children to be quiet. The words were registering, the news from Amman, the relief sinking in.

"Soon," she told her son. "Dad will be home soon."

It was two hours to the deadline.

11

THE SUN WAS LOW in the west, to the east the horizon was smudged with the first purple of dusk. Yakov Zubko sat still, Alexandra by his side, their son and daughter at their feet, and waited. Not long now, he thought, not much longer now. The shadow from the rock had reached the olive trees, was creeping over them, lengthening. Not much longer at all. He felt the sadness growing in him then heard the steps behind them.

"They're safe, Yakov Zubko, they're safe."

It was the supervisor from the factory, the man who had taken the first call from Vienna and arranged the cars for them to pick up his brother at Ben Gurion.

"It's just been announced, the West Germans have agreed to the hijackers' demands. The passengers will be released when the Arab ambassadors in Bonn have confirmed it."

In her apartment in New York, Anna Luskin heard the news and wiped her eyes. In the church in Norfolk, the congregation knew their prayers had been heard and thanked God for his deliverance. On the hill called Bethesda the shadow passed over the olive tree and spread across the stony ground beyond.

"They're safe, Yakov Zubko," the supervisor said again. "They're all safe."

The family Zubko rose and ended its vigil.

It was one hour and fifty minutes to the deadline.

12

"TELL ME AGAIN, Daddy, tell me the story of Dedushka Moroz, tell me the story of Grandfather Frost."

Stanislav Zubko heard his son's voice, so low, so distant, as if he was far away. It was the first time the boy had asked for the story since the morning in Rome, the first time since they had all thought they were going to die.

"Once upon a time," he began, "there was a little flower girl. She was poor and the winter was hard. Each day she stood on the corner and sold her flowers, each day she felt the cold and the pain because no one cared for her."

The boy was looking at his father, seeing his father's eyes, not able to understand why his father could not continue.

"And then Dedushka Moroz saw her, didn't he, Daddy?" the boy took over the story. "Then Grandfather Frost took pity on her." He saw the way his father was nodding. "Then Dedushka Moroz wrapped his cloak around her and took away her suffering."

"Yes, my son," said Stanislav Zubko. "Then Dedushka Moroz wrapped his cloak around her and took away her suffering."

It was one hour and twenty minutes to the deadline.

13

THE PURPLE WAS SPREADING across the sky, the heat of the sun long gone from the concrete of the runway, the land to the east beginning to merge into the sky where the night was coming upon them. Seventy-five minutes to the deadline, thought Jurgen Schumpter, seventy-five minutes to live or die. In front of him the first lights were beginning to appear. Seventy minutes, thought Stanislav Zubko, seventy minutes and he would know whether he would see his beloved Mishka again. Sixty-five minutes, thought Walid Haddad, for the politicians to fail him, sixty-five minutes for him to steel himself for what he would have to do if they failed him. Sixty minutes, thought Jurgen Schumpter, sixty minutes and they would all know.

"Lufthansa 267, this is ground."

He responded immediately.

"Come in, ground."

"Lufthansa 267, the West Germans for you."

Jurgen Schumpter waited for the negotiator, feared the worst, listened to the words.

"This is Klaus Rudegar. I have just been informed that the ambassador has arrived at the prison with the lawyer of the hunger-striker Christina Melhardt. It is expected that they will see her immediately and leave the prison in ten minutes."

Jurgen Schumpter knew he was going to live. Knew totally and positively for the first time that he was going to live.

"How long before we receive the confirmation?" he asked.

Strange, they would realise later, how the pilot had taken over what they assumed was the hijacker's role, was asking the questions they had expected the hijacker to ask.

"Thirty minutes," said the negotiator. "You can expect confirmation in thirty minutes."

"And the ambassador in Amman, where is he?"

"I have been informed that he has left the embassy and is on his way to the airport. He should be here soon." There was no hesitation in the reply.

Thirty minutes, thought Jurgen Schumpter, then we will be free. Thirty minutes, thought the doctor, then we will live. Thirty minutes, thought Stanislav Zubko, whispered to his son, then we will go home.

Ten minutes, thought Graham Enderson, ten minutes and it would be last light, ten minutes and they would move forward. In the gloom that was gathering above the plane he could see the helicopter, hear the whine of its engines. Stand-by, he was thinking, not aware he was doing so, stand-by, stand-by.

Pilot in his left seat, hijacker in right. Second hijacker in cockpit door, third in cabin, fourth, since that morning, at top of rear steps. Stand-by, stand-by. He checked the streamlight on the sub-machine gun, felt the spare magazines on his belt, tested the radio in his gas-mask. Stand-by, he was still thinking, stand-by, stand-by.

"Are we really going home?" Stanislav Zubko heard his son ask.

"Yes," he whispered to the boy. "In thirty minutes we are going home."

"Tell me again the story of Dedushka Moroz," asked the boy. "Tell me again the story of Grandfather Frost."

"Once upon a time," began Stanislav Zubko again, gently, quietly, "there was a little flower girl."

The sky was dark, almost dark enough. Twenty-five minutes, thought Jurgen Schumpter, twenty-five minutes and they would know. No traffic jams, he prayed, no accidents on the way from the prison to the embassy in Bonn, no punctures on the road from the embassy in Amman to the airport. He told himself to calm down, think rationally, reminded himself that there would be police escorts, that the ambassador was probably already at the airport, waiting to pass on the confirmation to them.

Stand-by, thought Enderson, stand-by, stand-by.

"It's getting cold, Daddy," said the boy. "Is it time for us to go home?"

"Yes," said Stanislav Zubko. "It is almost time for us to go home."

The last of the light had gone. The start points where the assault teams had waited were empty.

In the street in Beita Yakov Zubko stood in the doorway of his house and looked towards the square. In her apartment in New York Anna Luskin sat and waited. In the house in Hereford Jane Enderson made the children their tea and remembered the voice of the girl across the hills, the words of the poet. In the hotel room by the airport Mishka Zubko held her daughter to her and prayed.

"This is the West German negotiator. I understand that the ambassador is almost at the embassy in Bonn. Repeat, the ambassador is almost at the embassy in Bonn. I expect the confirmation in ten minutes. Repeat, I expect the confirmation in ten minutes."

Ten minutes, thought Jurgen Schumpter, and I will know whether I will see my wife and children again. Ten minutes, thought the doctor, and we will know if we are free. Ten minutes, Stanislav Zubko told his son, and we will know whether we can go home.

Seven minutes, thought Enderson, and they would be on the plane. The outline of the 727 was less than a hundred yards away, grim against the sky. They were closing in, the units moving quickly, quietly, unseen in the sudden dark. Nine minutes, thought the pilot. Six minutes thought Enderson. Tight, it had suddenly got so very tight.

They were almost under the plane, the wings and wheels looming up at them. He heard the message in his earpiece, the sniper seeing into the cockpit with his image intensifier. Pilot in left seat, hijacker in right co-pilot seat. The politicians, thought Walid Haddad, the bloody politicians. Under the body. Close now, so close now, the men with the ladders creeping forward, the first sensors being attached to the underbody of the plane. The man from Heathrow, he thought, remembering the switch in Frankfurt.

Jurgen Schumpter heard Walid Haddad's words, registered the instructions, could not believe them. Reacted automatically.

Enderson heard the noise, the change in the hum of the engines, felt the wheels beside him begin to move, closing in on him where he knelt, towering suddenly above him. He was moving quickly alerting the men in front, pulling himself out of the way. The wheels brushing past him, turning, the aircraft moving, trundling forward and sideways, the body then the tail moving over him and his teams, the stars suddenly appearing above them in the night sky, the plane moving away from them, pulling down the runway, the rear steps clanging shut. The man from Heathrow, he was thinking, the bloody man from Heathrow.

"Lufthansa 267, this is the negotiator. What's happening? Can you tell me what's happening?"

The lights were coming up at them. Schumpter looked at the hijacker, knew there would be no reply. Right, Walid Haddad was telling him, right onto the taxiway. Schumpter was turning, the red and green lights flickering up at him, passing beneath the nose of the 727. The voice of the ground-controller coming at him. Left, the hijacker was saying, left at the next taxiway. What's happening, the boy was asking his father, are we going home? The father was smiling, not answering. In the seat opposite the doctor was telling herself that nothing was wrong. Enderson was watching the plane, thinking it through, no point moving until he knew where it had stopped. Right, Walid Haddad was saying, right onto the runway, the 727 turning sharply. The negotiator was still asking what was happening. Just like the man from Heathrow, Enderson thought, just like the trick at Frankfurt. Just as he himself would have done, just as he had done in the exercises. The last precaution, the last trick on the assault teams. Change the position of the plane on the runway. Just when the authorities thought they had you, just when the sensors were connected and the assault teams were in position. Give yourself the last protection.

"Stop here," said Walid Haddad.

It was fourteen minutes to the deadline.

Walid Haddad left the cockpit and spoke to the hijacker in the doorway, then went down the aisle and spoke in turn to each of the two hijackers in the middle of the cabin. Jurgen Schumpter waited, ignoring the voice of the controller, not seeing what was happening behind him. Knowing anyway. Slowly, calmly, the hijackers undid the plastic bags they had removed from the toilet and began laying the thin white cord along the plane.

Five hundred yards, thought Enderson, moving back, skirting through the shadows so that he would not be seen, working out the new lines of approach. No rear steps down, he was thinking, no problem there any more. Aware what it meant, what the hijacker was doing. He heard the voices of the snipers in his earpiece and knew they were moving. Enough time, he thought, just enough time.

Eleven minutes to the deadline.

Tell us what's happening, thought Jurgen Schumpter, for God's sake tell us what's happening. Someone, anyone. The authorities, the hijackers. Tell us where the ambassador in Bonn is, tell us he's at the embassy, on the phone. Tell us the ambassador in Amman is at the airport, waiting for the call, receiving it.

It was strange, he suddenly found himself thinking, that the authorities hadn't asked the hijackers to extend the deadline again, strange that they hadn't put the ambassador in Amman on, asked him to speak to the hijackers, tell them everything was under control.

"Two hundred yards," Enderson whispered in his microphone. "Two hundred yards and closing."

Above the plane the helicopter was hovering into position.

Ten minutes to the deadline.

"Ask them if the ambassador is at the airport," Walid Haddad told the pilot.

The fuselage was against the stars, a hundred and fifty yards away, a hundred, the assault ladders and equipment getting heavy.

"Lufthansa 267 to ground, can the negotiator tell us if the ambassador is at the airport?"

Nine minutes to the deadline.

"This is the West German negotiator, I'll check." There was a silence. "Yes," the voice came back, "the ambassador has just arrived and is on his way up."

Eight minutes to the deadline.

No request for a delay, thought Schumpter, no hesitation in the response. He knew the man was telling the truth even as he saw the explosives being laid.

Seven minutes to deadline.

The first sniper confirmed he was in position. "Pilot in left seat, hijacker in right co-pilot seat."

"What news from Germany, control? What is happening in Germany?" Schumpter heard the sound of the helicopter over the plane again.

"The ambassador is almost at the embassy, confirmation in five minutes, repeat five minutes."

Six minutes to the deadline.

The tail was above them, no rear steps down now, no gun-man looking for them. They were moving beneath the plane, beneath the wings, the stars disappearing. Past the wheels, the units splitting, the sensors being attached, the first sounds from inside the aircraft.

"Tell them to put the ambassador on," said Walid Haddad.

Thank God, thought Schumpter, thank God the hijacker was going to speak to the ambassador. He knew the ambassador would confirm everything, that the hijacker would listen to him, and postpone the deadline, would agree to wait for the confirmation.

"Lufthansa 267 to ground, can you confirm that the ambassador is at the airport?" He did not realise it was the second time he had asked, did not realise he had forgotten the noise of the helicopter above them.

"Yes, 267," said the negotiator again. "I can confirm that the ambassador is at the airport."

Jurgen Schumpter felt the relief, knew they would not have brought the ambassador to the airport unless his counterpart in Germany had been to the prison and confirmed the agreement.

"Tell them to put the ambassador on to us," said Walid Haddad again.

Schumpter realised suddenly that the authorities could put anybody on to them, that anybody could speak to them and say he was the ambassador. He looked at the hijacker and saw that it was all arranged, that there was a way that the hijacker would check that the man who would speak to them was the ambassador. "There's a code, isn't there?" he said. "So you know that the man you're speaking to is the ambassador, so you know that what he's telling you is the truth?"

"Yes," said Walid Haddad, "there is a code."

Schumpter asked for the ambassador to speak to them.

Five minutes to the deadline.

"Lufthansa 267, this is the negotiator. I'm sorry, there was a misunderstanding, the ambassador has not yet arrived. Repeat the ambassador has not yet arrived. We have confirmation that he has left the embassy, but he has not yet arrived at the airport."

Jurgen Schumpter heard the change in the voice and knew the negotiator was lying, that the man was suddenly afraid, that the negotiator was suddenly aware of the truth. He tried to keep his voice calm, keep the anger from it.

"You said he was with you, twice you said he was with you." The anger took over. "What the hell are you playing at, what the hell are you doing to us?"

Enderson heard the voice of the sniper. "Hijacker getting up, leaving seat."

Four minutes to the deadline.

Around him the assault teams were leaning the ladders into position, the sides of the Boeing almost ghostly above them, laying the foam-covered ends carefully against the thin metal. He was listening to the sensors, hearing what was happening in the plane, knowing it was not enough, that they were not telling him where the hijackers were or what they were doing.

There was never any agreement, Schumpter saw, never any messages to Bonn, any ambassador at the prison or the airport. Saw also that there should have been, that was what the hijacker had been waiting for, had expected. He was looking at the man, felt suddenly that he had been betrayed by his own side as much as the pilot and passengers had been by theirs. He wanted to tell them but could not, knew only what was about to happen, that they were all going to die. My wife, he thought, reaching for the microphone, I want you to tell my wife something, then he realised what he was doing, what he was thinking, and stopped himself. The helicopter, he heard the noise again, the bloody helicopter.

Three minutes to the deadline.

The negotiator was speaking to them, pleading with them, knowing there would be no answer from the cockpit. Jurgen Schumpter sat in his seat and waited. In the cabins the hijackers began connecting the detonators, ignoring the way the passengers were staring at them, avoiding their looks. So far, thought Walid Haddad, he had come so far, done so much. He wondered what had gone wrong, why the politicians had failed him. Knew it was too late to ask the questions, knew there was only one more thing he had to do before the end, the last thing he would ever do.

No time to listen any more, Enderson decided, no time for the sensors to tell him what was happening in the plane. No time at all. The teams were at the bottom of the ladders. He pulled the gas-mask on; stand-by, he did not even realise he was thinking, stand-by, stand-by. First diversion in, the routine was pounding through his head, stand-by, stand-by. Second diversion in. Go, go, go, go, go. He pulled the sub-machine gun from the clip round his neck, put it on to burst fire, and climbed the ladder, one man to his left, two behind. Stand-by, stand-by.

Two minutes to the deadline.

Strange, thought Walid Haddad, how they were all waiting, nobody complaining, nobody screaming or fighting back. He saw the doctor standing up, coming forward to the cockpit, saw the guard at the door of the cockpit stop her, told the man she could come in. Stand-by, the words had a rhythm of their own, stand-by, stand-by. She asked if she could speak to the negotiator, to the people in the control tower. Walid Haddad nodded. The helicopter moving away slightly, thought Schumpter, the noise still beating down on them. Not leaving them, he thought, just changing position. Stand-by, stand-by. The voice of the sniper in his ear-piece. "Female entering cockpit, taking microphone." His hand was on the door, he was leaning hard against it, the man at his side leaning forward, the two men behind them tight against them. Stand-by, stand-by.

One minute to the deadline.

They all heard the voice of the doctor, in the cockpit, in the cabins, in the operations room.

"We know that this is the end, we know we must die. It will be very hard for us but we will die as bravely as possible." They remembered the moment she had stood on the runway, the moment she could have saved her own life, the moment she had turned back to the plane. "We are all too young to die, even the oldest of us. We hope that it will be quick, that we suffer no pain." Stanislav Zubko held his son to him. Not the boy, he prayed, please God may there be a way my son will not feel the pain. "But perhaps it is better to die than to live in a world in which human life counts for so little, in a world in which something like this is possible. In which it is more important to let one girl die than it is to save the lives of one hundred and thirty-four people."

The poem, Jane Enderson thought, the poem from across the hills. She knew what time it was, what was about to happen, knew they had all been lying. Stand-by, stand-by. The men behind leaning forward, pressing him against the plane. Last light fifty minutes before. Stand-by, stand-by. The helicopter moving, stand-by, stand-by.

Thirty seconds to the deadline.

The doctor was standing up, going back to her seat.

"The story of Dedushka Moroz." They all heard the boy's voice. "When Grandfather Frost wraps his cloak round the little flower girl and takes away her pain and suffering, does that mean she dies?"

Stanislav Zubko looked up and saw the hijacker standing over him, held his son close to him.

"Don't worry," said Walid Haddad. "The boy will not suffer, I will shoot him first."

"Thank you," said Stanislav Zubko.

Twenty seconds to the deadline.

Stand-by, stand-by. First diversion almost ready, stand-by, stand-by. His hand was on the door, the men behind him tight against him. He wondered who would live, who would die. Which of his team would not come back. Stand-by, stand-by. Wondered if he himself would come back.

Ten seconds to the deadline.

Stand-by, stand-by.

She heard the words, the voice of the girl, not the words of the poem, the words of the poet, anguished, angry. Knew what he had meant the words to mean for himself, what he had meant them to mean for her. Knew again what time it was in Amman, knew that in Amman the sun had gone down, knew what was about to happen. Heard the lines for the last time, not all the lines, just the last two. Knew what he was about to do, what she was urging him, almost screaming at him, to do. Knew it was the only way he would live, the only way she would see him again.

Do not go gentle into that good night.
Rage, rage against the dying of the light.

THE HELICOPTER was no longer above the plane, the noise was unending, deafening. It was hanging in the sky over the tip of the starboard wing, coming down at them. Schumpter could see it, he was looking back, could see they were all looking back. Looking to the starboard wing, the helicopter hovering over it, almost touching it. Stand-by, stand-by. Enderson's body was rocking with the words, the men behind him, stand-by, stand-by. Stanislav Zubko was holding his son, looking across the plane, afraid, more afraid than he had ever been in his life.

Looking back, looking to the starboard side. Stand-by, stand-by. It was eight o'clock exactly.

Radio silence, total radio silence, the assault going in. Stand-by, stand-by. Enderson felt the plane rock, knew what it was, stand-by, stand-by. The men were coming out of the helicopter, running along the wing, towards the plane, coming at them. Schumpter was confused, looking back, looking to the starboard side. Stand-by, stand-by, first diversion going in, stand-by, stand-by. The doctor heard the sound, saw the flash behind them, coming from the door at the rear. Second diversion in. Go, go, go, go, go. Stanislav Zubko heard the explosions, knew the hijackers were blowing up the plane, he knew that he had begun to die.

He held his son tight against him, trying to protect him, knew they were walking through the valley of the shadow of death. His head was reeling, hurting from the noise, he was disorientated, his senses spinning. The men running along the wing of the plane on the right, the noise from behind, from the left. The plane was spinning, the hijacker beside him. No pain yet, he was thinking, no pain at all. Perhaps he was already dead, perhaps he and his beloved son had already passed through the valley. He was looking up, looking around, looking to see his father waiting to welcome him, his father before. Saw the flames, the smoke, the figures coming toward him, shouting at him. Black. Strange eyes. No eyes. Not from the starboard, his mind was confused, going in circles, not where he had seen the men on the wing of the plane. Not from behind either, not from where he had heard the noise, seen the flash. In front of him, coming at him. Shouting at him. Down, Stanislav Zubko, get down. In Russian, he thought, even after the grave someone was shouting at him in Russian. Black, he saw them again, all black, the fire spitting from them.

Stand-by, stand-by, Enderson was rocking with the words, hands on door, stand-by, stand, the man beside him, the men tight behind him. Stand-by, stand-by. The helicopter going in. He felt the movement as the first men landed on the starboard wing and began running towards the plane. First diversion in, he was thinking automatically, stand-by, stand-by. Knew what the team at the rear would be doing, knew they would be opening the door, the other team still halfway along the wing, throwing in the stun grenades. Stand-by, stand-by. He heard the second diversion going in, the sound of the grenades, his hand automatically opening the door, the shout coming out of his throat, the men behind pushing him up and in. Go, go, go, go, go. He was in the plane, turning right, the man to his left turning with him, the second two turning left, covering the cockpit. Down, heads down. The first hijacker in the doorway of the cockpit, bemused, looking down the plane at the points where the diversions had gone in. He was pressing the trigger. Three-round burst system. Twice.

The hijacker's torso disintegrating, the blood filling the air. He was turning right, allowing the men behind to turn left, one man tossing a stun grenade into the cockpit, stepping back from the doorway. Down, he was shouting, they were all shouting, get down. In English and in German.

"Grah, this is Dave," he heard the voice in his earpiece. "Hijacker at cockpit door is cleared."

Jurgen Schumpter was turning, still shocked, his head still spinning, seeing the man in the doorway. Down, the man was saying, get down, Jurgen, get down on the floor. He was reacting, hearing the German, not questioning who the man was, what he was, how he knew his name. Stay, the man was telling him, turning from the cockpit, going out the door. The pilot was crouching, squeezing in front of the seat, knew that he had heard a voice, that it was not a man who had told him what to do, remembered only the figure in black which looked as if it had come from another world.

"Grah, this is Steve, no hijacker in cockpit, repeat, there was no hijacker in the cockpit."

Enderson heard the voice and saw the smoke, the first of the flames. Sweep left to right, he was thinking, sweep left to right. Maintaining his arc of fire, each of them maintaining his arc of fire. The men from the first diversion were coming into the plane through the emergency window over the wing, those from the second diversion entering at the rear. Down, he was still shouting, voice muffled by the gas-mask, heads down. The smoke was filling the cabins. He was stepping forward, down the tunnel. "In front of you, Grah, in the middle." He heard the voice of the team leader at the rear and saw the two hijackers in the middle of the cabin, the man and the woman. Exactly where Mishka Zubko had said they would be, he thought. Looking the other way, looking at the points of diversion. He saw the guns they were holding, confirmed they were hijackers. Three-round bursts, his or someone from the team entering over the wing, he was not sure. The hijackers still looking the other way, looking away from him, disorientated by the diversions. The man falling, gun dropping. The woman half turning, seeing him, the grenade in her hand. Three-round burst. The look on their faces, the shock as the bullets hit them, the red spreading from them, their bodies folding. The team who had entered over the wing moving forward, confirming they were dead, the team from the rear door moving forward. The flames and smoke still coming at him.

He was moving on, sweep left to right. First class, room below the head rests, he thought, room for a hijacker. Room for anybody. The flames and smoke coming at him. Three down, one to go. If Mishka was right, he thought, if the pilot was right. The smoke coming at him, swirling round the eyepieces of the gas-mask, the streamlights on the weapons piercing the gloom. Thirty-two round mag, counting down, eighteen rounds gone, fourteen left. He was seeing the movement, the Heckler coming up. The head appearing over the top of the seat. Finger tightening on trigger. Zubko, Stanislav Zubko. Finger still closing on trigger. The father, the man in the photograph from Moscow. Down Stanislav Zubko, he was saying, get down. In Russian. Sweeping left to right. Down, he was still telling him, get down.

Walid Haddad was standing up, clearing the seat, gun coming up, his head clearing from the effects of the stun grenade. Seeing the man coming towards him. Knew it was the man in the photograph. Enderson was seeing him, seeing the gun coming up at him. Knew it was the man from Heathrow. By the boy, he was thinking, finger closing, he was right by the boy.

They both saw it.

The grenade rolling from the hand of the dead hijacker. The pin out. Rolling towards them, towards all of them. Three seconds they were both thinking, fingers still closing on triggers. Two seconds. One second. They knew they were both going to die. Knew the boy was going to die. Were both moving. Different directions. Same objective. The man from Heathrow moving away from the boy, thought Enderson, moving towards the grenade. The man in the photograph moving away from the grenade, thought Walid Haddad, moving towards the boy. The man from Heathrow on the grenade, thought Enderson, protecting the boy, saving him, saving all of them.

Walid Haddad was dropping, pushing the boy away, the floor coming up at him. No longer in the plane, in the refugee camp of Ain Helweh. Remembering the night they had put his father in the ground, the night he had delivered to his father the soil of Esh Shikara, the night he had left his father for the last time and passed himself into the darkness. The night he had known that the one thing he could give his people was his life, not just his life, but the manner of its passing.

The grenade was exploding, splintering, the shears of metal bursting open. He was feeling the pain as they cut through him, his flesh and bones absorbing them, taking them, stopping them. The force of the explosion was throwing him up, he could feel the edges of the steel, was coming to rest, turning his head, looking at the boy, seeing the man in the photograph covering the boy with his own body, protecting him from the grenade. He was looking at him, saying something to him, telling him he knew who he was, knowing the man knew who he was, knowing the man knew about the coachload of children on the motorway from Heathrow, knowing the man knew about the son of Yakov Zubko by the well in Esh Shikara. Telling him something else. It was growing dark, the night falling round him, the night they had laid his father in the soil. He was seeing the places for the last time, was back in the places for the last time, the well, the orange grove at the foot of the hill, the father and son in the corner of the field. He was back in the house, back in the small bedroom at the rear, could not touch the beam across the stairs. No more pain, no more images, not even the darkness.

Nothing.

"Out," Enderson was shouting. "Move them out."

They were picking the passengers from their seats and throwing them down the aisle, towards the doors, into the night, down the chutes, the support teams moving in, pushing the passengers to the ground, hands behind backs, legs open, checking them for identification. Confirming there were no hijackers amongst them, clearing the explosives.

The doctor was being picked up, pushed out the plane. Someone at the bottom recognised her, telling her she was safe, telling her she had done a good job. Jurgen Schumpter was being pulled out of the cockpit, through the door, feeling the sudden cold of the night air. Was on the ground outside, looking for the doctor, looking for the father and his son. Seeing

them. Seeing the boy was in his father's arms. Where he had
been, the pilot could not help thinking, where he had always
been. Stanislav Zubko was looking at his son, cradling him to
him.

"Are we going home now?" the boy was asking him.
"Yes," Stanislav Zubko said. "We are going home now."

14

THE PLANE WAS QUIET, empty.

Graham Enderson took off his mask and walked down the
aisle. Over the handbags, the coats, discarded in the moment
the passengers had left the plane, through the remnants of the
four days of the hijack, past the awesome destruction which
had ended it. He stepped over the bodies of the man and
woman in the centre of the aisle and came to the body by the
seat where the father and his son had sat. Slowly, carefully, he
turned the man over and saw the damage the grenade had done
to him, saw the look on his face. Remembered the moment he
had seen the grenade, the moment they had both seen the grenade, remembered what the man had done. How he had saved
the boy, as he had given the girl her life, as he had saved the
other boy in Beita. The smoke was clearing from the plane. He
thought about the day on the motorway from Heathrow, the
coachload of children, thought about the way the man had
looked at him, said something to him. Remembered what he
himself had said two days before, in the moments after the hijacker had released Mishka Zubko, in the minutes after the
world had seen the mother carry her daughter across the runway.

"You may as well give in now," he had told the politicians.
"Why?" they had asked.
"Because he's won," he had replied, "no matter what you
do, no matter how it ends, he's won."

He let the body fall back onto the floor and stood up, thinking of the other boy, in the street in Belfast six days before
Christmas, the photograph in the newspaper, the headline
above it.

Knew that the man from Heathrow had seen it.
Knew what the man from Heathrow had said to him.
Peace on Earth, he thought, peace on bloody Earth.

Epilogue

THE BOYS WERE NINE, almost ten.

They sat on the rocks beside the man, watching the sun set in the West, the sweep of darkness spreading from the Jordan in the East.

"That was the story of the little boy who was born in Bethlehem?" said the first of the boys.

"Yes," said the man, "that was the story of the little boy who was born in Bethlehem." He knew there would be questions, many questions.

"There is one thing I do not understand," said the second. "The next day, the day after the hijack ended, all the world talked of how the authorities had stormed the plane and killed all the hijackers, how they had rescued all the passengers. How the authorities had won."

The man nodded, waited.

"But the day after that," continued the boy, "they all knew the truth. The day after that all the newspapers and television programmes told the story of how the hijacker had given his life for the life of the little boy, how he had died to save them all."

The man nodded again, waited again.

"But how did they know?" asked the boy. "Who told them the truth?"

"I wonder," said the man, "I wonder who told them the truth."

The sun was almost gone.

"Was I the little boy he died to save?" the first boy asked suddenly.

The man looked at his nephew. "Yes," he said, "you were the little boy he died to save."

He knew what the second boy would ask, knew that one day he was bound to ask it.

"Was I the little boy who was born in Bethlehem," the boy asked, "could I be the little boy who dies to save us all?"

So young, the man remembered the stranger had said, the boy was so young, still had so many years to live, so many reasons for which to die.

"Yes, my son," said Yakov Zubko, "you were the little boy who was born in Bethlehem." No Peace on Earth, he thought, no peace at all. He wondered where it would end, who would end it. "Who knows if you will be the little boy who dies to save us all." He turned away so they would not see the tear on his face.